This Perfect Day

Ira Levin was born in New York City in 1929 and is a graduate of the Horace Mann School and New York University. His first novel, *A Kiss Before Dying*, was published in 1952 and has been in print ever since. *Rosemary's Baby* followed, and was made into a film, starring Mia Farrow and John Cassavetes. His other novels include *The Boys from Brazil* and *The Stepford Wives*, both published by Pan. He has also written several very successful plays, short stories and song lyrics. He lives in New York and has three sons.

Ira Levin
This Perfect Day

Pan Books London, Sydney and Auckland

First published in Great Britain 1970 by Michael Joseph Ltd
This edition published 1971 by Pan Books Ltd,
Cavaye Place, London SW10 9PG
9 8
© Ira Levin 1970
ISBN 0 330 02657 7
Printed in Great Britain by
Richard Clay (The Chaucer Press) Ltd, Bungay, Suffolk

Christ, Marx, Wood, and Wei
   Led us to this perfect day.
Marx, Wood, Wei, and Christ;
   All but Wei were sacrificed.
Wood, Wei, Christ, and Marx
   Gave us lovely schools and parks.
Wei, Christ, Marx, and Wood
   Made us humble, made us good.

> – child's rhyme for
>   bouncing a ball

CONTENTS

PART ONE

GROWING UP

ONE

A city's blank white concrete slabs, the giant ones ringed by the less giant, gave space in their midst to a broad pink-floored plaza, a playground in which some two hundred young children played and exercised under the care of a dozen supervisors in white coveralls. Most of the children, bare, tan, and black-haired, were crawling through red and yellow cylinders, swinging on swings, or doing group calisthenics; but in a shadowed corner where a hopscotch grid was inlaid, five of them sat in a close, quiet circle, four of them listening and one speaking.

'They catch animals and eat them and wear their skins,' the speaker, a boy of about eight, said. 'And they – they do a thing called "fighting". That means they hurt each other, on purpose, with their hands or with rocks and things. They don't love and help each other at all.'

The listeners sat wide-eyed. A girl younger than the boy said, 'But you *can't* take off your bracelet. It's impossible.' She pulled at her own bracelet with one finger, to show how safely-strong the links were.

'You can if you've the right tools,' the boy said. 'It's taken off on your linkday, isn't it?'

'Only for a second.'

'But it's taken off, isn't it?'

'Where do they live?' another girl asked.

'On mountaintops,' the boy said. 'In deep caves. In all kinds of places where we can't find them.'

The first girl said, 'They must be sick.'

'Of course they are,' the boy said, laughing. 'That's what "incurable" *means*, sick. That's why they're *called* incurables, because they're very, very sick.'

The youngest child, a boy of about six, said, 'Don't they get their treatments?'

The older boy looked at him scornfully. 'Without their bracelets?' he said. 'Living in caves?'

'But how do they *get* sick?' the six-year-old asked. 'They

get their treatments *until* they run away, don't they?'

'Treatments,' the older boy said, 'don't always work.'

The six-year-old stared at him. 'They do,' he said.

'No they don't.'

'My goodness,' a supervisor said, coming to the group with volley balls tucked one under each arm, 'aren't you sitting too close together? What are you playing, Who's Got the Rabbit?'

The children quickly hitched away from one another, separating into a larger circle – except the six-year-old boy, who stayed where he was, not moving at all. The supervisor looked at him curiously.

A two-note chime sounded on loudspeakers. 'Shower and dress,' the supervisor said, and the children hopped to their feet and raced away.

'Shower and dress!' the supervisor called to a group of children playing passball nearby.

The six-year-old boy stood up, looking troubled and unhappy. The supervisor crouched before him and looked into his face with concern. 'What's wrong?' she asked.

The boy, whose right eye was green instead of brown, looked at her and blinked.

The supervisor let drop her volley balls, turned the boy's wrist to look at his bracelet, and took him gently by the shoulders. 'What is it, Li?' she asked. 'Did you lose the game? Losing's the same as winning; you know that, don't you?'

The boy nodded.

'What's important is having fun and getting exercise, right?'

The boy nodded again and tried to smile.

'Well, that's better,' the supervisor said. 'That's a little better. Now you don't look like such a sad old sad-monkey.'

The boy smiled.

'Shower and dress,' the supervisor said with relief. She turned the boy around and gave him a pat on his bottom. 'Go on,' she said, 'skedaddle.'

The boy, who was sometimes called Chip but more often Li – his nameber was Li RM35M4419 – said scarcely a word while eating, but his sister Peace kept up a continuous

12

jabbering and neither of his parents noticed his silence. It wasn't until all four had seated themselves in the TV chairs that his mother took a good look at him and said, 'Are you feeling all right, Chip?'

'Yes, I feel fine,' he said.

His mother turned to his father and said, 'He hasn't said a word all evening.'

Chip said, 'I feel fine.'

'Then why are you so quiet?' his mother asked.

'Shh,' his father said. The screen had flicked on and was finding its right colours.

When the first hour was over and the children were getting ready for bed, Chip's mother went into the bathroom and watched him finish cleaning his teeth and pull his mouthpiece from the tube. 'What is it?' she said. 'Did somebody say something about your eye?'

'No,' he said, reddening.

'Rinse it,' she said.

'I did.'

'Rinse it.'

He rinsed his mouthpiece, and, stretching, hung it in its place on the rack. 'Jesus was talking,' he said. 'Jesus DV. During play.'

'About what? Your eye?'

'No, not my *eye*. Nobody says anything about my *eye*.'

'Then what?'

He shrugged. 'Members who – get sick and – leave the Family. Run away and take off their bracelets.'

His mother stared at him nervously. 'Incurables,' she said.

He nodded, her manner and her knowing the name making him more uneasy. 'It's true?' he said.

'No,' she said. 'No, it isn't. No. I'm going to call Bob. He'll explain it to you.' She turned and hurried from the room slipping past Peace, who was coming in closing her pyjamas.

In the living-room Chip's father said, 'Two more minutes. Are they in bed?'

Chip's mother said, 'One of the children told Chip about the incurables.'

'Hate,' his father said.

'I'm calling Bob,' his mother said, going to the phone.

'It's after eight.'

'He'll come,' she said. She touched her bracelet to the phone's plate and read out the nameber red-printed on a card tucked under the screen rim: 'Bob NE20G3018'. She waited, rubbing the heels of her palms tightly together. 'I knew something was bothering him,' she said. 'He didn't say a single word all evening.'

Chip's father got up from his chair. 'I'll go talk to him,' he said, going.

'Let Bob do it!' Chip's mother called. 'Get Peace into bed; she's still in the bathroom!'

Bob came twenty minutes later.

'He's in his room,' Chip's mother said.

'You two watch the programme,' Bob said. 'Go on, sit down and watch.' He smiled at them. 'There's nothing to worry about,' he said. 'Really. It happens every day.'

'Still?' Chip's father said.

'Of course,' Bob said. 'And it'll happen a hundred years from now. Kids are kids.'

He was the youngest adviser they had ever had – twenty-one, and barely a year out of the Academy. There was nothing diffident or unsure about him though; on the contrary, he was more relaxed and confident than advisers of fifty or fifty-five. They were pleased with him.

He went to Chip's room and looked in. Chip was in bed, lying on an elbow with his head in his hand, a comic book spread open before him.

'Hi, Li,' Bob said.

Chip said, 'Hi, Bob.'

Bob went in and sat down on the side of the bed. He put his telecomp on the floor between his feet, felt Chip's forehead and ruffled his hair. 'Whatcha readin'?' he said.

'*Wood's Struggle*,' Chip said, showing Bob the cover of the comic book. He let it drop closed on the bed and, with his forefinger, began tracing the wide yellow W of 'Wood's'.

Bob said, 'I hear somebody's been giving you some cloth about incurables.'

'Is that what it is?' Chip asked, not looking from his moving finger.

'That's what it is, Li,' Bob said. 'It used to be true, a long,

14

long time ago, but not any more; now it's just cloth.'

Chip was silent, retracing the W.

'We didn't always know as much about medicine and chemistry as we do today,' Bob said, watching him, 'and until fifty years or so after the Unification, members used to get sick sometimes, a very few of them, and feel that they *weren't* members. Some of them ran away and lived by themselves in places the Family wasn't using, barren islands and mountain peaks and so forth.'

'And they took off their bracelets?'

'I suppose they did,' Bob said. 'Bracelets wouldn't have been much use to them in places like that, would they, with no scanners to put them to?'

'Jesus said they did something called "fighting".'

Bob looked away and then back again. ' "Acting aggressively" is a nicer way of putting it,' he said. 'Yes, they did that.'

Chip looked up at him. 'But they're dead now?' he said.

'Yes, all dead,' Bob said. 'Every last one of them.' He smoothed Chip's hair. 'It was a long, long time ago,' he said. 'Nobody gets that way today.'

Chip said, 'We know more about medicine and chemistry today. Treatments *work*.'

'Right you are,' Bob said. 'And don't forget there were five separate computers in those days. Once one of those sick members had left his home continent, he was completely unconnected.'

'My grandfather helped build UniComp.'

'I know he did, Li. So next time anyone tells you about the incurables, you remember two things: one, treatments are much more effective today than they were a long time ago; and two, we've got UniComp looking out for us everywhere on Earth. Okay?'

'Okay,' Chip said, and smiled.

'Let's see what it says about *you*,' Bob said, picking up his telecomp and opening it on his knees.

Chip sat up and moved close, pushing his pyjama sleeve clear of his bracelet. 'Do you think I'll get an extra treatment?' he asked.

'If you need one,' Bob said. 'Do you want to turn it on?'

'Me?' Chip said. 'May I?'

'Sure,' Bob said.

Chip put his thumb and forefinger cautiously to the tele-comp's on-off switch. He clicked it over, and small lights came on – blue, amber, amber. He smiled at them.

Bob, watching him, smiled and said, 'Touch'.

Chip touched his bracelet to the scanner plate, and the blue light beside it turned red.

Bob tapped the input keys. Chip watched his quickly moving fingers. Bob kept tapping and then pressed the answer button; a line of green symbols glowed on the screen, and then a second line beneath the first. Bob studied the symbols. Chip watched him.

Bob looked at Chip from the corners of his eyes, smiling. 'Tomorrow at 12.25,' he said.

'Good!' Chip said. 'Thank you!'

'Thank Uni,' Bob said, switching off the telecomp and closing its cover. 'Who told you about the incurables?' he asked. 'Jesus who?'

'DV33-something,' Chip said. 'He lives on the twenty-fourth floor.'

Bob snapped the telecomp's catches. 'He's probably as worried as you were,' he said.

'Can he have an extra treatment too?'

'If he needs one; I'll alert his adviser. Now to *sleep*, brother; you've got school tomorrow.' Bob took Chip's comic book and put it on the night table.

Chip lay down and snuggled smilingly into his pillow, and Bob stood up, tapped off the lamp, ruffled Chip's hair again, and bent and kissed the back of his head.

'See you Friday,' Chip said.

'Right,' Bob said. 'Goodnight.'

''Night, Bob.'

Chip's parents stood up anxiously when Bob came into the living-room.

'He's fine,' Bob said. 'Practically asleep already. He's getting an extra treatment during his lunch hour tomorrow, probably a bit of tranquillizer.'

'Oh, what a relief,' Chip's mother said, and his father said, 'Thanks, Bob'.

'Thank Uni,' Bob said. He went to the phone. 'I want to

16

get some help to the other boy,' he said, 'the one who told him' – and touched his bracelet to the phone's plate.

The next day, after lunch, Chip rode the escalators down from his school to the medicentre three floors below. His bracelet, touched to the scanner at the medicentre's entrance, produced a winking green *yes* on the indicator; and another winking green *yes* at the door of the therapy section; and another winking green *yes* at the door of the treatment room.

Four of the fifteen units were being serviced, so the line was fairly long. Soon enough, though, he was mounting children's steps and thrusting his arm, with the sleeve pushed high, through a rubber-rimmed opening. He held his arm grownuply still while the scanner inside found and fastened on his bracelet and the infusion disc nuzzled warm and smooth against his upper arm's softness. Motors burred inside the unit, liquids trickled. The blue light overhead turned red and the infusion disc tickled-buzzed-stung his arm; and then the light turned blue again.

Later that day, in the playground, Jesus DV, the boy who had told him about the incurables, sought Chip out and thanked him for helping him.

'Thank Uni,' Chip said. 'I got an extra treatment; did you?'

'Yes,' Jesus said. 'So did the other kids and Bob UT. He's the one who told *me*.'

'It scared me a little,' Chip said, 'thinking about members getting sick and running away.'

'Me too a little,' Jesus said. 'But it doesn't happen any more; it was a long, long time ago.'

'Treatments are better now than they used to be,' Chip said.

Jesus said, 'And we've got UniComp watching out for us everywhere on Earth.'

'Right you are,' Chip said.

A supervisor came and shooed them into a passball circle, an enormous one of fifty or sixty boys and girls spaced out at fingertip distance, taking up more than a quarter of the busy playground.

17

TWO

Chip's grandfather was the one who had given him the name Chip. He had given all of them extra names that were different from their real ones: Chip's mother, who was his daughter, he called 'Suzu' instead of Anna; Chip's father was 'Mike' not Jesus (and thought the idea foolish); and Peace was 'Willow', which she refused to have anything at all to do with. 'No! Don't call me that! I'm Peace! I'm Peace KD37T5002!'

Papa Jan was odd. Odd-*looking*, naturally; all grandparents had their marked peculiarities – a few centimetres too much or too little of height, skin that was too light or too dark, big ears, a bent nose. Papa Jan was both taller and darker than normal, his eyes were big and bulging, and there were two reddish patches in his greying hair. But he wasn't only odd-*looking*, he was odd-*talking*; that was the real oddness about him. He was always saying things vigorously and with enthusiasm and yet giving Chip the feeling that he didn't mean them at all, that he meant in fact their exact opposites. On that subject of names, for instance: 'Marvellous! Wonderful!' he said. 'Four names for boys, four names for girls! What could be more friction-free, more everyone-the-same? Everybody would name boys after Christ, Marx, Wood, or Wei anyway, wouldn't they?'

'Yes,' Chip said.

'Of course!' Papa Jan said. 'And if Uni gives out four names for boys it has to give out four names for girls too, right? Obviously! Listen.' He stopped Chip and, crouching down, spoke face to face with him, his bulging eyes dancing as if he was about to laugh. It was a holiday and they were on their way to the parade, Unification Day or Wei's Birthday or whatever; Chip was seven. 'Listen, Li RM35M26J44-9988WXYZ,' Papa said. 'Listen, I'm going to tell you something fantastic, incredible. In my day – are you listening? – in my day there were *over twenty different names for boys alone!* Would you believe it? Love of Family, it's the truth. There was "Jan", and "John", and "Amu", and "Lev".

18

"Higa" and "Mike!" "Tonio!" And in my father's time there were even more, maybe forty of fifty! Isn't that ridiculous? All those different names when members themselves are exactly the same and interchangeable? Isn't that the silliest thing you ever heard of?'

And Chip nodded, confused, feeling that Papa Jan meant the opposite, that somehow it *wasn't* silly and ridiculous to have forty or fifty different names for boys alone.

'Look at them!' Papa Jan said, taking Chip's hand and walking on with him – through Unity Park to the Wei's Birthday parade. 'Exactly the same! Isn't it marvellous? Hair the same, eyes the same, skin the same, shape the same; boys, girls, all the same. Like peas in a pod. Isn't it fine? Isn't it top speed?'

Chip, flushing (not his green eye, not the same as *anybody's*), said, 'What does "peezinapod" mean?'

'I don't know,' Papa Jan said. 'Things members used to eat before totalcakes. Sharya used to say it.'

He was a construction supervisor in EUR55131, twenty kilometres from '55128, where Chip and his family lived. On Sundays and holidays he rode over and visited them. His wife, Sharya, had drowned in a sightseeing-boat disaster in 135, the same year Chip was born; he hadn't remarried.

Chip's other grandparents, his father's mother and father, lived in MEX10405, and the only time he saw them was when they phoned on birthdays. They were odd, but not nearly as odd as Papa Jan.

School was pleasant and play was pleasant. The Pre-U Museum was pleasant although some of the exhibits were a bit scary – the 'spears' and 'guns', for instance, and the 'prison cell' with its striped-suited 'convict' sitting on the cot and clutching his head in motionless month-after-month woe. Chip always looked at him – he would slip away from the rest of the class if he had to – and having looked, he always walked quickly away.

Ice-cream and toys and comic books were pleasant too. Once when Chip put his bracelet and a toy's sticker to a supply-centre scanner, its indicator red-winked *no* and he had to put the toy, a construction set, in the turnback bin. He couldn't understand why Uni had refused him; it was the right day and the toy was in the right category. 'There *must* be a reason, dear,' the member behind him said. 'You go call your adviser and find out.'

He did, and it turned out that the toy was only being withheld for a few days, not denied completely; he had been teasing a scanner somewhere, putting his bracelet to it again and again, and he was being taught not to. That winking red *no* was the first in his life for a claim that mattered to him, not just for starting into the wrong classroom or coming to the medicentre on the wrong day; it hurt him and saddened him.

Birthdays were pleasant, and Christmas and Marxmas and Unification Day and Wood's and Wei's Birthdays. Even more pleasant, because they came less frequently, were his linkdays. The new link would be shinier than the others, and would stay shiny for days and days and days; and then one day he would remember and look and there would be only old links, all of them the same and indistinguishable. Like peezinapod.

In the spring of 145, when Chip was ten, he and his parents and Peace were granted the trip to EURoooo1 to see Uni-Comp. It was over an hour's ride from carport to carport and the longest trip Chip remembered making, although according to his parents he had flown from Mex to Eur when he was one and a half, and from EUR20140 to '55128 a few months later. They made the UniComp trip on a Sunday in April, riding with a couple in their fifties (someone's odd-looking grandparents, both of them lighter than normal, she with her hair unevenly clipped) and another family, the boy and girl of which were a year older than Chip and Peace. The other father drove the car from the EURoooo1 turnoff to the carport near UniComp. Chip watched with interest as the man worked the car's lever and buttons. It felt funny to be riding slowly on wheels again after shooting along on air.

They took snapshots outside UniComp's white marble dome – whiter and more beautiful than it was in pictures or on TV, as the snow-tipped mountains beyond it were more stately, the Lake of Universal Brotherhood more blue and far-reaching – and then they joined the line at the entrance, touched the admission scanner, and went into the blue-white curving lobby. A smiling member in pale blue showed them towards the elevator line. They joined it, and Papa Jan came up to them, grinning with delight at their astonishment.

'What are you doing here?' Chip's father asked as Papa Jan kissed Chip's mother. They had told him they had been granted the trip and he had said nothing at all about claiming it himself.

Papa Jan kissed Chip's father. 'Oh, I just decided to surprise you, that's all,' he said. 'I wanted to tell my friend here' – he laid a large hand across Chip's shoulder – 'a little more about Uni than the earpiece will. Hello, Chip.' He bent and kissed Chip's cheek, and Chip, surprised to be the reason for Papa Jan's being there, kissed him in return and said, 'Hello, Papa Jan'.

'Hello, Peace KD37T5002,' Papa Jan said gravely, and kissed Peace. She kissed him and said hello.

'When did you claim the trip?' Chip's father asked.

'A few days after you did,' Papa Jan said, keeping his hand on Chip's shoulder. The line moved up a few metres and they all moved with it.

Chip's mother said, 'But you were here only five or six years ago, weren't you?'

'Uni knows who put it together,' Papa Jan said, smiling. 'We get special favours.'

'That's not so,' Chip's father said. 'No one gets special favours.'

'Well, here I am, anyway,' Papa Jan said, and turned his smile down towards Chip. 'Right?'

'Right,' Chip said, and smiled back up at him.

Papa Jan had helped build UniComp when he was a young man. It had been his first assignment.

The elevator held about thirty members, and instead of music it had a man's voice – 'Good day, brothers and sisters; welcome to the site of UniComp' – a warm, friendly voice that Chip recognized from TV. 'As you can tell, we've started to move,' it said, 'and now we're descending at a speed of twenty-two metres per second. It will take us just over three and a half minutes to reach Uni's five-kilometre depth. This shaft down which we're travelling ...' The voice gave statistics about the size of UniComp's housing and the thickness of its walls, and told of its safety from all natural and man-made disturbances. Chip had heard this information before, in school and on TV, but hearing it now, while entering that housing and passing through those walls, while on the very verge of *seeing* UniComp, made it seem new and exciting. He listened attentively, watching the speaker disc over the elevator door. Papa Jan's hand still held his shoulder, as if to restrain him. 'We're slowing now,' the voice said. 'Enjoy your visit, won't you?' – and the elevator sank to a cushiony stop and the door divided and slid to both sides.

There was another lobby, smaller than the one at ground level, another smiling member in pale blue, and another line, this one extending two by two to double doors that opened on a dimly lit hallway.

'Here we are!' Chip called, and Papa Jan said to him, 'We don't all have to be together.' They had become separated from Chip's parents and Peace, who were farther ahead in the line and looking back at them questioningly – Chip's parents; Peace was too short to be seen. The member in front of Chip turned and offered to let them move up, but Papa Jan said, 'No, this is all right. Thank you, brother'. He waved a hand at Chip's parents and smiled, and Chip did the same. Chip's parents smiled back, then turned around and moved forward.

Papa Jan looked about, his bulging eyes bright, his mouth keeping its smile. His nostrils flared and fell with his breathing. 'So,' he said, 'you're finally going to see UniComp. Excited?'

'Yes, very,' Chip said.

They followed the line forward.

'I don't blame you,' Papa Jan said. 'Wonderful! Once-in-a-lifetime experience, to see the machine that's going to classify you and give you your assignments, that's going to decide where you'll live and whether or not you'll marry the girl you want to marry; and if you do, whether or not you'll have children and what they'll be named if you have them – of course you're excited; who wouldn't be?'

Chip looked at Papa Jan, disturbed.

Papa Jan, still smiling, clapped him on the back as they passed in their turn into the hallway. 'Go look!' he said. 'Look at the displays, look at Uni, look at everything! It's all here for you look at it!'

There was a rack of earpieces, the same as in a museum; Chip took one and put it in. Papa Jan's strange manner made him nervous, and he was sorry not to be up ahead with his parents and Peace. Papa Jan put in an earpiece too. 'I wonder what interesting new fact I'm going to hear!' he said, and laughed to himself. Chip turned away from him.

His nervousness and feeling of disturbance fell away as he faced a wall that glittered and skittered with a thousand sparkling minilights. The voice of the elevator spoke in his ears, telling him, while the lights showed him, how Uni-Comp received from its round-the-world relay belt the micro-wave impulses of all the uncountable scanners and telecomps and telecontrolled devices; how it evaluated the impulses and sent back its answering impulses to the relay belt and the sources of inquiry.

Yes, he was excited. Was anything quicker, more clever, more everywhere than Uni?

The next span of wall showed how the memory banks worked; a beam of light flicked over a crisscrossed metal square, making parts of it glow and leaving parts of it dark. The voice spoke of electron beams and superconductive grids, of charged and uncharged areas becoming the yes-or-no carriers of different bits of information. When a question was put to UniComp, the voice said, it scanned the relevant bits ...

He didn't understand it, but that made it *more* wonderful, that Uni could know all there was to know so magically, so *un*-understandably!

And the next span was glass not wall, and there it was UniComp: a twin row of different-coloured metal bulks, like treatment units only lower and smaller, some of them pink, some brown, some orange; and among them in the large, rosily lit room, ten or a dozen members in pale blue coveralls, smiling and chatting with one another as they read meters and dials on the thirty-or-so units and marked what they read on handsome pale blue plastic clipboards. There was a gold cross and sickle on the far wall, and a clock that said 11.08

Sun 12 Apr 145 Y.U. Music crept into Chip's ear and grew louder: 'Outward, Outward', played by an enormous orchestra, so movingly, so majestically, that tears of pride and happiness came into his eyes.

He could have stayed there for hours, watching those busy cheerful members and those impressively gleaming memory banks, listening to 'Outward, Outward' and then 'One Mighty Family'; but the music thinned away (as 11.10 became 11.11) and the voice, gently, aware of his feelings, reminded him of other members waiting and asked him to move on please to the next display farther down the hallway. Reluctantly he turned himself from UniComp's glass wall, with other members who were wiping at the corners of their eyes and smiling and nodding. He smiled at them, and they at him.

Papa Jan caught his arm and drew him across the hallway to a scanner-posted door. 'Well, did you like it?' he asked.

Chip nodded.

'That's not Uni,' Papa Jan said.

Chip looked at him.

Papa Jan pulled the earpiece out of Chip's ear. 'That's not UniComp!' he said in a fierce whisper. 'Those aren't real, those pink and orange boxes in there! Those are *toys*, for the Family to come look at and feel cozy and warm with!' His eyes bulged close to Chip's; specks of his spit hit Chip's nose and cheeks. 'It's down below!' he said. 'There are three levels under this one, and that's where it is! Do you want to see it? Do you want to see the *real* UniComp?'

Chip could only stare at him.

'Do you, Chip?' Papa Jan said. 'Do you want to see it? I can show it to you!'

Chip nodded.

Papa Jan let go of his arm and stood up straight. He looked around and smiled. 'All right,' he said, 'let's go this way,' and taking Chip's shoulder he steered him back the way they had come, past the glass wall thronged with members looking in, and the flicking light-beam of the memory banks, and the skittering wall of minilights, and – 'Excuse us, please' – through the line of incoming members and down to another part of the hallway that was darker and empty, where a monster telecomp lolled broken away from its wall

24

display and two blue stretchers lay side by side with pillows and folded blankets on them.

There was a door in the corner with a scanner beside it, but as they got near it Papa Jan pushed down Chip's arm.

'The scanner,' Chip said.

'No,' Papa Jan said.

'Isn't this where we're—'

'Yes.'

Chip looked at Papa Jan, and Papa Jan pushed him past the scanner, pulled open the door, thrust him inside, and came in after him, dragging the door shut against its hissing slow-closer.

Chip stared at him, quivering.

'It's all right,' Papa Jan said sharply; and then, not sharply, kindly, he took Chip's head in both his hands and said, 'It's all right, Chip. Nothing will happen to you. I've done it lots of times.'

'We didn't *ask*,' Chip said, still quivering.

'It's all *right*,' Papa Jan said. 'Look: who does UniComp belong to?'

'Belong to?'

'Whose is it? Whose computer?'

'It's – it's the whole Family's.'

'And you're a member of the Family, aren't you?'

'Yes ...'

'Well then, it's partly your computer, isn't it? It belongs to *you*, not the other way around; *you* don't belong to *it*.'

'No, we're supposed to *ask* for things!' Chip said.

'Chip, please, trust me,' Papa Jan said. 'We're not going to take anything, we're not even going to touch anything. We're only going to look. That's the reason I came here today, to show you the real UniComp. You want to see it, don't you?'

Chip, after a moment, said, 'Yes'.

'Then don't worry; it's all right.' Papa Jan looked reassuringly into his eyes, and then let go of his head and took his hand.

They were on a landing, with stairs going down. They went down four or five of them – into coolness – and Papa Jan stopped, and stopped Chip. 'Stay right here,' he said. 'I'll be back in two seconds. Don't move.'

Chip watched anxiously as Papa Jan went back up to the landing, opened the door to look, and then went quickly out. The door swung back towards closing.

Chip began to quiver again. He had passed a scanner without touching it, and now he was alone on a chilly silent stairway and Uni didn't know where he was!

The door opened again and Papa Jan came back in with blue blankets over his arm. 'It's very cold,' he said.

They walked together, wrapped in blankets, down the just-wide-enough aisle between two steel walls that stretched ahead of them convergingly to a faraway cross-wall and reared up above their heads to within half a metre of a glowing white ceiling – not walls, really, but rows of mammoth steel blocks set each against the next and hazed with cold, numbered on their fronts in eye-level black stencil-figures: H46, H48 on this side of the aisle; H49, H51 on that. The aisle was one of twenty or more; narrow parallel crevasses between back-to-back rows of steel blocks, the rows broken evenly by the intersecting crevasses of four slightly wider cross-aisles.

They came up the aisle, their breath clouding from their nostrils, blurs of near-shadow staying beneath their feet. The sounds they made – the paplon rustle of their coveralls, the slapping of their sandals – were the only sounds there were, edged with echoes.

'Well?' Papa Jan said, looking at Chip.

Chip hugged his blanket more tightly around him. 'It's not as nice as upstairs,' he said.

'No,' Papa Jan said. 'No pretty young members with pens and clipboards down here. No warm lights and friendly pink machines. It's empty down here from one year to the next. Empty and cold and lifeless. Ugly.'

They stood at the intersection of two aisles, crevasses of steel stretching away in one direction and another, in a third direction and a fourth. Papa Jan shook his head and scowled. 'It's wrong,' he said. 'I don't know why or how, but it's wrong. Dead plans of dead members. Dead ideas, dead decisions.'

'Why is it so cold?' Chip asked, watching his breath.

'Because it's dead,' Papa Jan said, then shook his head. 'No,

26

I don't know,' he said. 'They don't work if they're not freezing cold; I don't know; all I knew was getting the things where they were supposed to be without smashing them.'

They walked side by side along another aisle: R20, R22, R24. 'How many are there?' Chip asked.

'Twelve hundred and forty on this level, twelve hundred and forty on the level below. And that's only for *now*; there's twice as much space cut out and waiting behind that east wall, for when the Family gets bigger. Other shafts, another ventilating system already in place ...'

They went down to the next lower level. It was the same as the one above except that there were steel pillars at two of the intersections and red figures on the memory banks instead of black ones. They walked past J65, J63, J61. 'The biggest excavation there ever was,' Papa Jan said. 'The biggest job there ever was, making one computer to obsolete the old five. There was news about it every night when I was your age. I figured out that it wouldn't be too late to help when I was twenty, provided I got the right classification. So I asked for it.'

'You asked for it?'

'That's what I said,' Papa Jan said, smiling and nodding. 'It wasn't unheard of in those days. I asked my adviser to ask Uni – well, it wasn't Uni, it was EuroComp – anyway I asked her to ask, and she did, and Christ, Marx, Wood, and Wei, I got it – 042C; construction worker, third class. First assignment, here.' He looked about, still smiling, his eyes vivid. 'They were going to lower these hulks down the shafts one at a time,' he said, and laughed. 'I sat up all one night and figured out that the job could be done eight months earlier if we tunnelled in from the other side of Mount Love' – he thumbed over his shoulder – 'and rolled them in on wheels. EuroComp hadn't thought of that simple idea. Or maybe it was in no big rush to have its memory siphoned away!' He laughed again.

He stopped laughing; and Chip, watching him, noticed for the first time that his hair was all grey now. The reddish patches that he'd had a few years earlier were completely gone.

'And here they are,' he said, 'all in their places, rolled

down my tunnel and working eight months longer than they would have been otherwise.' He looked at the banks he was passing as if he disliked them.

Chip said, 'Don't you – like UniComp?'

Papa Jan was silent for a moment. 'No, I don't,' he said, and cleared his throat. 'You can't argue with it, you can't explain things to it ...'

'But it knows *everything*,' Chip said. 'What's there to explain or argue about?'

They separated to pass a square steel pillar and came together again. 'I don't know,' Papa Jan said. 'I don't know.' He walked along, his head lowered, frowning, his blanket wrapped around him. 'Listen,' he said, 'is there any classification that *you* want more than any other? Any assignment that *you're* especially hoping for?'

Chip looked uncertainly at Papa Jan and shrugged. 'No,' he said. 'I want the classification I'll get, the one I'm right for. And the assignments I'll get, the ones that the Family needs me to do. There's only one assignment anyway, helping to spread the—'

' "Helping to spread the Family through the universe," ' Papa Jan said. 'I know. Through the unified UniComp universe. Come on,' he said, 'let's go back up above. I can't take this brother-fighting cold much longer.'

Embarrassed, Chip said, 'Isn't there another level? You said there—'

'We can't,' Papa Jan said. 'There are scanners there, and members around who'd see us not touching them and rush to "help" us. There's nothing special to see there anyway; the receiving and transmitting equipment and the refrigerating plants.'

They went to the stairs. Chip felt let down. Papa Jan was disappointed with him for some reason; and worse, he wasn't well, wanting to argue with Uni and not touching scanners and using bad language. 'You ought to tell your adviser,' he said as they started up the stairs. 'About wanting to argue with Uni.'

'I don't want to argue with Uni,' Papa Jan said. 'I just want to be able to argue *if* I want to argue.'

Chip couldn't follow that at all. 'You ought to tell him anyway,' he said. 'Maybe you'll get an extra treatment.'

'Probably I would,' Papa Jan said; and after a moment, 'All right, I'll tell him.'

'Uni knows everything about everything,' Chip said.

They went up the second flight of stairs, and on the landing outside the display hallway, stopped and folded the blankets. Papa Jan finished first. He watched Chip finish folding his.

'There,' Chip said, patting the blue bundle against his chest.

'Do you know why I gave you the name "Chip"?' Papa Jan asked him.

'No,' Chip said.

'There's an old saying, "a chip off the old block". It means that a child is like his parents or his grandparents.'

'Oh.'

'I didn't mean you were like your father or even like me,' Papa Jan said. 'I meant you were like *my* grandfather. Because of your eye. He had a green eye too.'

Chip shifted, wanting Papa Jan to be done talking so they could go outside where they belonged.

'I know you don't like to talk about it,' Papa Jan said, 'but it's nothing to be ashamed of. Being a little different from everyone else isn't such a terrible thing. Members used to be so different from each other, you can't imagine. Your great-great-grandfather was a very brave and capable man. His name was Hanno Rybeck – names and numbers were separate then – and he was a cosmonaut who helped build the first Mars colony. So don't be ashamed that you've got his eye. They fight around with the genes today, excuse my language, but maybe they missed a few of yours; maybe you've got more than a green eye, maybe you've got some of my grandfather's bravery and ability too.' He started to open the door but turned to look at Chip again. 'Try wanting something, Chip,' he said. 'Try a day or two before your next treatment. That's when it's easiest; to want things, to worry about things ...'

When they came out of the elevator into the ground-level lobby, Chip's parents and Peace were waiting for them. 'Where have you been?' Chip's father asked, and Peace, holding a miniature orange memory bank (not really), said, 'We've been waiting so long!'

'We were looking at Uni,' Papa Jan said.

Chip's father said, 'All this time?'

'That's right.'

'You were supposed to move on and let other members have their turn.'

'You were, Mike,' Papa Jan said, smiling. 'My earpiece said "Jan old friend, it's good to see you! You and your grandson can stay and look as long as you like!"'

Chip's father turned away, not smiling.

They went to the canteen, claimed cakes and cokes – except Papa Jan, who wasn't hungry – and took them out to the picnic area behind the dome. Papa Jan pointed out Mount Love to Chip and told him more about the drilling of the tunnel, which Chip's father was surprised to hear about – a tunnel to bring in thirty-six not-so-big memory banks. Papa Jan told him that there were more banks on a lower level, but he didn't say how many or how big they were, or how cold and lifeless. Chip didn't either. It gave him an odd feeling, knowing there was something that he and Papa Jan knew and weren't telling the others; it made the two of them *different* from the others, and the same as each other, at least a little ...

When they had eaten, they walked to the carport and got on the claim line. Papa Jan stayed with them until they were near the scanners; then he left, explaining that he would wait and go home with two friends from Riverbend who were visiting Uni later in the day. 'Riverbend' was his name for '55131, where he lived.

The next time Chip saw Bob NE, his adviser, he told him about Papa Jan; that he didn't like Uni and wanted to argue with it and explain things to it.

Bob, smiling, said, 'That happens sometimes with members your grandfather's age, Li. It's nothing to worry about.'

'But can't you tell Uni?' Chip said. 'Maybe he can have an extra treatment, or a stronger one.'

'Li,' Bob said, leaning forward across his desk, 'the different chemicals we get in our treatments are very precious and hard to make. If older members got as much as they sometimes need, there might not be enough for the younger members, who are really more important to the Family. And to make enough chemicals to satisfy everyone,

30

we might have to neglect the more important jobs. Uni knows what has to be done, how much of everything there is, and how much of everything everyone needs. Your grandfather isn't really unhappy, I promise you. He's just a bit crotchety, and we will be too when we're in our fifties.'

'He uses that word,' Chip said; 'F-blank-blank-blank-T.'

'Old members sometimes do that too,' Bob said. 'They don't really mean anything by it. Words aren't in themselves "dirty"; it's the actions that the so-called dirty words represent that are offensive. Members like your grandfather use only the words, not the actions. It's not very nice, but it's no real sickness. How about you? Any friction? Let's leave your grandfather to his own adviser for a while.'

'No, no friction,' Chip said, thinking about having passed a scanner without touching it and having been where Uni hadn't said he could go and now suddenly not wanting to tell Bob about it. 'No friction at all,' he said. 'Everything is top speed.'

'Okay,' Bob said. 'Touch. I'll see you next Friday, right?'

A week or so later Papa Jan was transferred to USA60607. Chip and his parents and Peace drove to the airport at EUR55130 to see him off.

In the waiting-room while Chip's parents and Peace watched through glass the members boarding the plane, Papa Jan drew Chip aside and stood looking at him, smiling fondly. 'Chip green-eye,' he said – Chip frowned and tried to undo the frown – 'you asked for an extra treatment for me, didn't you?'

'Yes,' Chip said. 'How did you know?'

'Oh, I guessed, that's all,' Papa Jan said. 'Take good care of yourself, Chip. Remember who you're a chip off of, and remember what I said about trying to want something.'

'I will,' Chip said.

'The last ones are going,' Chip's father said.

Papa Jan kissed them all goodbye and joined the members going out. Chip went to the glass and watched; and saw Papa Jan walking through the growing dark towards the plane, an unusually tall member, his take-along kit swinging at the end of a gangling arm. At the escalator he turned and waved – Chip waved back, hoping Papa Jan could see him –

then turned again and put his kit-hand wrist to the scanner. Answering green sparked through dusk and distance, and he stepped on to the escalator and was taken smoothly upwards.

In the car going back Chip sat silently, thinking that he would miss Papa Jan and his Sunday-and-holiday visits. It was strange, because he was such an odd and different old member. Yet that was exactly why he *would* miss him, Chip suddenly realized; because he was odd and different, and nobody else would fill his place.

'What's the matter, Chip?' his mother asked.

'I'm going to miss Papa Jan,' he said.

'So am I,' she said, 'but we'll see him on the phone once in a while.'

'It's a good thing he's going,' Chip's father said.

'I want him not to go,' Chip said. 'I want him to be transferred back here.'

'He's not very likely to be,' his father said, 'and it's a good thing. He was a bad influence on you.'

'Mike,' Chip's mother said.

'Don't *you* start that cloth,' Chip's father said. 'My name is Jesus, and his is Li.'

'And mine is Peace,' Peace said.

THREE

Chip remembered what Papa Jan had told him, and in the weeks and months that followed, thought often about wanting something, wanting to *do* something, as Papa Jan at ten had wanted to help build Uni. He lay awake for an hour or so every few nights, considering all the different assignments there were, all the different classifications he knew of – construction supervisor like Papa Jan, lab technician like his father, plasmaphysicist like his mother, photographer like a friend's father; doctor, adviser, dentist, cosmonaut, actor, musician. They all seemed pretty much the same, but before he could really want one he had to pick one. It was a strange thought to think about – to pick, to choose, to decide. It made him feel small, yet it made him feel big too, both at the same time.

One night he thought it might be interesting to plan big buildings, like the little ones he had built with a construction set he had had a long time before (winking red *no* from Uni). That was the night before a treatment, which Papa Jan had said was a good time for wanting things. The next night big-building planner didn't seem any different from any other classification. In fact, the whole idea of wanting one particular classification seemed silly and pre-U that night, and he went straight to sleep.

The night before his next treatment he thought about planning buildings again – buildings of all different shapes, not just the three usual ones – and he wondered why the interestingness of the idea had disappeared the month before. Treatments were to prevent diseases and to relax members who were tense and to keep women from having too many babies and men from having hair on their faces; why should they make an interesting idea seem not interesting? But that was what they did, one month, and the next month, and the next.

Thinking such thoughts might be a form of selfishness, he suspected; but if it was, it was such a minor form – involving only an hour or two of sleep time, never of school or TV time – that he didn't bother to mention it to Bob NE, just as he wouldn't have mentioned a moment's nervousness or an occasional dream. Each week when Bob asked if everything was okay, he said yes it was: top speed, no friction. He took care not to 'think wanting' too often or too long, so that he always got all the sleep he needed, and mornings, while washing, he checked his face in the mirror to make sure he still looked right. He did – except of course for his eye.

In 146 Chip and his family, along with most of the members in their building, were transferred to AFR71680. The building they were housed in was a brand-new one, with green carpet instead of grey in the hallways, larger TV screens, and furniture that was upholstered though non-adjustable.

There was much to get used to in '71680. The climate was somewhat warmer, and the coveralls lighter in weight and colour; the monorail was old and slow and had frequent breakdowns; and the totalcakes were wrapped in greenish foil and tasted salty and not quite right.

Chip's and his family's new adviser was Mary CZ14L8584. She was a year older than Chip's mother, though she looked a few years younger.

Once Chip had grown accustomed to life in '71680 - school, at least, was no different - he resumed his pastime of 'thinking wanting'. He saw now that there were considerable differences between classifications, and began to wonder which one Uni would give him when the time came. Uni, with its two levels of cold steel blocks, its empty echoing hardnesses ... He wished Papa Jan had taken him down to the bottom level, where members were. It would be pleasanter to think of being classified by Uni and some members instead of by Uni alone; if he were to be given a classification he didn't like, and members were involved, maybe it would be possible to explain to them ...

Papa Jan called twice a year; he claimed more, he said, but that was all he was granted. He looked older, smiled tiredly. A section of USA60607 was being rebuilt and he was in charge. Chip would have liked to tell him that he was trying to want something, but he couldn't with the others standing in front of the screen with him. Once, when a call was nearly over, he said, 'I'm trying,' and Papa Jan smiled like his old self and said, 'That's the boy!'

When the call was over, Chip's father said, 'What are you trying?'

'Nothing,' Chip said.

'You must have meant *something*,' his father said.

Chip shrugged.

Mary CZ asked him too, the next time Chip saw her. 'What did you mean when you told your grandfather you were trying?' she said.

'Nothing,' Chip said.

'Li,' Mary said, and looked at him reproachfully. 'You said you were trying. Trying what?'

'Trying not to miss him,' he said. 'When he was transferred to Usa I told him I would miss him, and he said I should try not to, that members were all the same and any way he would call whenever he could.'

'Oh,' Mary said, and went on looking at Chip, now uncertainly. 'Why didn't you say so in the first place?' she asked.

34

Chip shrugged.

'And *do* you miss him?'

'Just a little,' Chip said. 'I'm trying not to.'

Sex began, and that was even better to think about than wanting something. Though he'd been taught that orgasms were extremely pleasurable, he had had no idea whatsoever of the all-but-unbearable deliciousness of the gathering sensations, the ecstasy of the coming, and the drained and boneless satisfaction of the moments afterwards. Nobody had had any idea, none of his classmates; they talked about nothing else and would gladly have devoted themselves to nothing else as well. Chip could hardly think about mathematics and electronics and astronomy, let alone the differences between classifications.

After a few months, though, everyone calmed down, and accustomed to the new pleasure, gave it its proper Saturday-night place in the week's pattern.

One Saturday evening when Chip was fourteen, he bicycled with a group of his friends to a fine white beach a few kilometres north of AFR71680. There they swam – jumped and pushed and splashed in waves made pink-foamed by the foundering sun – and built a fire on the sand and sat around it on blankets and ate their cakes and cokes and crisp sweet pieces of a bashed-open coconut. A boy played songs on a recorder, not very well, and then, the fire crumbling to embers, the group separated into five couples, each on its own blanket.

The girl Chip was with was Anna VF, and after their orgasm – the best one Chip had ever had, or so it seemed – he was filled with a feeling of tenderness towards her, and wished there were something he could give her as a conveyor of it, like the beautiful shell that Karl GG had given Yin AP, or Li OS's recorder-song, softly cooing now for whichever girl he was lying with. Chip had nothing for Anna, no shell, no song; nothing at all, except, maybe, his thoughts.

'Would you like something interesting to think about?' he asked, lying on his back with his arm about her.

'Mm,' she said, and squirmed closer against his side. Her head was on his shoulder, her arm across his chest.

He kissed her forehead. 'Think of all the different classifications there are—' he said.

'Mm?'

'And try to decide which one you would pick if you had to pick one.'

'To pick one?' she said.

'That's right.'

'What do you mean?'

'To pick one. To *have*. To *be in*. Which classification would you like best? Doctor, engineer, adviser ...'

She propped her head up on her hand and squinted at him. 'What do you mean?' she said.

He gave a little sigh and said, 'We're going to be classified, right?'

'Right.'

'Suppose we *weren't* going to be. Suppose we had to classify ourselves.'

'That's silly,' she said, finger-drawing on his chest.

'It's interesting to think about.'

'Let's fuck again,' she said.

'Wait a minute,' he said. 'Just think about all the different classifications. Suppose it were up to us to—'

'I don't want to,' she said, stopping drawing. 'That's silly. And sick. We *get* classified; there's nothing to think about. Uni knows what we're—'

'Oh, fight Uni,' Chip said. 'Just pretend for a minute that we're living in—'

Anna flipped away from him and lay on her stomach, stiff and unmoving, the back of her head to him.

'I'm sorry,' he said.

'*I'm* sorry,' she said. 'For you. You're sick.'

'No I'm not,' he said.

She was silent.

He sat up and looked despairingly at her rigid back. 'It just slipped out,' he said. 'I'm sorry.'

She stayed silent.

'It's just a *word*, Anna,' he said.

'You're sick,' she said.

'Oh, hate,' he said.

'You see what I mean?'

'Anna,' he said, 'look. Forget it. Forget the whole thing, all

36

right? Just forget it.' He tickled between her thighs, but she locked them, barring his hand.

'Ah, Anna,' he said. 'Ah, come on. I said I was sorry, didn't I? Come on, let's fuck again. I'll suck you first if you want.'

After a while she relaxed her thighs and let him tickle her.

Then she turned over and sat up and looked at him. 'Are you sick, Li?' she asked.

'No,' he said, and managed to laugh. 'Of course I'm not,' he said.

'I never heard of such a thing,' she said. ' "Classify ourselves." How could we do it? How could we possibly know enough?'

'It's just something I think about once in a while,' he said. 'Not very often. In fact, hardly ever.'

'It's such a – a funny idea,' she said. 'It sounds – I don't know – pre-U.'

'I won't think about it any more,' he said, and raised his right hand, the bracelet slipping back. 'Love of Family,' he said. 'Come on, lie down and I'll suck you.'

She lay back on the blanket, looking worried.

The next morning at five to ten Mary CZ called Chip and asked him to come see her.

'When?' he asked.

'Now,' she said.

'All right,' he said. 'I'll be right down.'

His mother said, 'What does she want to see you on a Sunday for?'

'I don't know,' Chip said.

But he knew. Anna VF had called her adviser.

He rode the escalators down, down, down, wondering how much Anna had told, and what he should say; and wanting suddenly to cry and tell Mary that he was sick and selfish and a liar. The members on the upgoing escalators were relaxed, smiling, content, in harmony with the cheerful music of the speakers; no one but he was guilty and unhappy.

The advisory offices were strangely still. Members and advisers conferred in a few of the cubicles, but most of them were empty, the desks in order, the chairs waiting. In one cubicle a green-coveralled member leaned over the phone working a screwdriver at it.

Mary was standing on her chair, laying a strip of Christmas bunting along the top of *Wei Addressing the Chemotherapists*. More bunting was on the desk, a roll of red and a roll of green, and Mary's open telecomp with a container of tea beside it. 'Li?' she said, not turning. 'That was quick. Sit down.'

Chip sat down. Lines of green symbols glowed on the telecomp's screen. The answer button was held down by a souvenir paperweight from RUS81655.

'Stay,' Mary said to the bunting and, watching it, backed down off her chair. It stayed.

She swung her chair around and smiled at Chip as she drew it into her and sat. She looked at the telecomp's screen, and while she looked, picked up the container of tea and sipped from it. She put it down and looked at Chip and smiled.

'A member says you need help,' she said. 'The girl you fucked last night, Anna' – she glanced at the screen – 'VF35H6143.'

Chip nodded. 'I said a dirty word,' he said.

'Two,' Mary said, 'but that's hardly important. At least not relatively. What *is* important are some of the other things you said, things about deciding which classification you would pick if we didn't have UniComp to do the job.'

Chip looked away from Mary, at the rolls of red and green Christmas bunting.

'Is that something you think about often, Li?' Mary asked.

'Just sometimes,' Chip said. 'In the free hour or at night; never in school or during TV.'

'Night-time counts too,' Mary said. 'That's when you're supposed to be sleeping.'

Chip looked at her and said nothing.

'When did it start?' she asked.

'I don't know,' he said, 'a few years ago. In Eur.'

'Your grandfather,' she said.

He nodded.

She looked at the screen, and looked at Chip again, ruefully. 'Didn't it ever dawn on you,' she said, 'that "deciding"

38

and "picking" are manifestations of selfishness? Acts of selfishness?'

'I thought, maybe,' Chip said, looking at the edge of the desktop, rubbing a fingertip along it.

'Oh, Li,' Mary said. 'What am I here for? What are *advisers* here for? To help us, isn't that so?'

He nodded.

'Why didn't you tell me? Or your adviser in Eur? Why did you wait, and lose sleep, and worry this Anna?'

Chip shrugged, watching his fingertip rubbing the desktop, the nail dark. 'It was – interesting, sort of,' he said.

' "Interesting, sort of," ' Mary said. 'It might also have been interesting, sort of, to think about the kind of pre-U chaos we'd have if we actually *did* pick our own classifications. Did you think about that?'

'No,' Chip said.

'Well, do. Think about a hundred million members deciding to be TV actors and not a single one deciding to work in a crematorium.'

Chip looked up at her. 'Am I very sick?' he asked.

'No,' Mary said, 'but you might have ended up that way if not for Anna's helpfulness.' She took the paperweight from the telecomp's answer button and the green symbols disappeared from the screen. 'Touch,' she said.

Chip touched his bracelet to the scanner plate, and Mary began tapping the input keys. 'You've been given hundreds of tests since your first day of school,' she said, 'and UniComp's been fed the results of every last one of them.' Her fingers darted over the dozen black keys. 'You've had hundreds of adviser meetings,' she said, 'and UniComp knows about those too. It knows what jobs have to be done and who there is to do them. It knows *everything*. Now who's going to make the better, more efficient classification, you or Uni-Comp?'

'UniComp, Mary,' Chip said. 'I know that. I didn't really want to do it myself; I was just – just thinking *what if*, that's all.'

Mary finished tapping and pressed the answer button. Green symbols appeared on the screen. Mary said, 'Go to the treatment room.'

Chip jumped to his feet. 'Thank you,' he said.

'Thank Uni,' Mary said, switching off the telecomp. She closed its cover and snapped the catches.

Chip hesitated. 'I'll be all right?' he asked.

'Perfect,' Mary said. She smiled reassuringly.

'I'm sorry I made you come in on a Sunday,' Chip said.

'Don't be,' Mary said. 'For once in my life I'm going to have my Christmas decorations up before December twenty-fourth.'

Chip went out of the advisory offices and into the treatment room. Only one unit was working, but there were only three members in line. When his turn came, he plunged his arm as deep as he could into the rubber-rimmed opening, and gratefully felt the scanner's contact and the infusion disc's warm nuzzle. He wanted the tickle-buzz-sting to last a long time, curing him completely and for ever, but it was even shorter than usual, and he worried that there might have been a break in communication between the unit and Uni or a shortage of chemicals inside the unit itself. On a quiet Sunday morning mightn't it be carelessly serviced?

He stopped worrying, though, and riding up the escalators he felt a lot better about everything – himself, Uni, the Family, the world, the universe.

The first thing he did when he got into the apartment was call Anna VF and thank her.

At fifteen he was classified 663D – genetic taxonomist, fourth class – and he was transferred to RUS41500 and the Academy of the Genetic Sciences. He learned elementary genetics and lab techniques and modulation and transplant theory; he skated and played soccer and went to the Pre-U Museum and the Museum of the Family's Achievements; he had a girlfriend named Anna from Jap and then another named Peace from Aus. On Thursday, October 18th, 151, he and everyone else in the Academy sat up until four in the morning watching the launching of the *Altaira*, then slept and loafed through a half-day holiday.

One night his parents called unexpectedly. 'We have bad news,' his mother said. 'Papa Jan died this morning.'

A sadness gripped him and must have shown on his face.

'He was sixty-two, Chip,' his mother said. 'He had his life.'

'Nobody lives for ever,' Chip's father said.

'Yes,' Chip said. 'I'd forgot how old he was. How are you? Has Peace been classified yet?'

When they were done talking he went out for a walk, even though it was a rainy night and almost ten. He went into the park. Everyone was coming out. 'Six minutes,' a member said, smiling at him.

He didn't care. He wanted to be rained on, to be drenched. He didn't know why but he wanted to.

He sat on a bench and waited. The park was empty; everyone else was gone. He thought of Papa Jan saying things that were the opposite of what he meant, and then saying what he really meant down in the inside of Uni, with a blue blanket wrapped around him.

On the back of the bench across the walk someone had red-chalked a jagged *FIGHT UNI*. Someone else – or maybe the same sick member, ashamed – had crossed it out with white. The rain began, and started washing it away; white chalk, red chalk, smearing pinkly down the benchback.

Chip turned his face to the sky and held it steady under the rain, trying to feel as if he was so sad he was crying.

FOUR

Early in his third and final year at the Academy, Chip took part in a complicated exchange of dormitory cubicles worked out to put everyone involved closer to his or her girlfriend or boyfriend. In his new location he was two cubicles away from one Yin DW; and across the aisle from him was a shorter-than-normal member named Karl WL, who frequently carried a green-covered sketch pad and who, though he replied to comments readily enough, rarely started a conversation on his own.

This Karl WL had a look of unusual concentration in his eyes, as if he were close on the track of answers to difficult questions. Once Chip noticed him slip out of the lounge after the beginning of the first TV hour and not slip in again till before the end of the second; and one night in the dorm,

41

after the lights had gone out, he saw a dim glow filtering through the blanket of Karl's bed.

One Saturday night – early Sunday morning, really – as Chip was coming back quietly from Yin DW's cubicle to his own, he saw Karl sitting in his. He was on the side of the bed in pyjamas, holding his pad tilted towards a flashlight on the corner of the desk and working at it with brisk chopping hand movements. The flashlight's lens was masked in some way so that only a small beam of light shone out.

Chip went closer and said, 'No girl this week?'

Karl started, and closed the pad. A stick of charcoal was in his hand.

'I'm sorry I surprised you,' Chip said.

'That's all right,' Karl said, his face only faint glints at chin and cheekbones. 'I finished early. Peace KG. Aren't you staying all night with Yin?'

'She's snoring,' Chip said.

Karl made an amused sound. 'I'm turning in now,' he said. 'What are you doing?'

'Just some gene diagrams,' Karl said. He turned back the cover of the pad and showed the top page. Chip went close and bent and looked – at cross sections of genes in the B3 locus, carefully drawn and shaded, done with a pen. 'I was trying some with charcoal,' Karl said, 'but it's no good.' He closed the pad and put the charcoal on the desk and switched off the flashlight. 'Sleep well,' he said.

'Thanks,' Chip said. 'You too.'

He went into his own cubicle and groped his way into bed, wondering whether Karl had in fact been drawing gene diagrams, for which charcoal hardly even seemed worth a trial. Probably he should speak to his adviser, Li YB, about Karl's secretiveness and occasional unmemberlike behaviour, but he decided to wait awhile, until he was sure that Karl needed help and that he wouldn't be wasting Li YB's time and Karl's and his own. There was no point in being an alarmist.

Wei's birthday came a few weeks later, and after the parade Chip and a dozen or so other students railed out to the Amusement Gardens for the afternoon. They rowed boats for a while and then strolled through the zoo. While they were gathered at a water fountain, Chip saw Karl WL sitting on the railing in front of the horse compound, holding his pad on his knees and drawing. Chip excused himself from the group and went over.

Karl saw him coming and smiled at him, closing his pad. 'Wasn't that a great parade?' he said.

'It was really top speed,' Chip said. 'Are you drawing the horses?'

'Trying to.'

'May I see?'

Karl looked him in the eye for a moment and then said, 'Sure, why not?' He riffled the bottom of the pad and, opening it partway through, turned back the upper section and let Chip look at a rearing stallion that crammed the page, charcoaled darkly and vigorously. Muscles bulked under its gleaming hide; its eye was wild and rolling; its forelegs quivered. The drawing surprised Chip with its vitality and power. He had never seen a picture of a horse that came anywhere near it. He sought words, and could only come up with, 'This is – great, Karl! Top Speed!'

'It's not accurate,' Karl said.

'It is!'

'No it isn't,' Karl said. 'If it were accurate I'd be at the Academy of Art.'

Chip looked at the real horses in the compound and at Karl's drawing again; at the horses again, and saw the greater thickness of their legs, the lesser width of their chests.

'You're right,' he said, looking at the drawing again. 'It's not accurate. But it's – it's somehow *better* than accurate.'

'Thanks,' Karl said. 'That's what I'd like it to be. I'm not finished yet.'

Looking at him, Chip said, 'Have you done others?'

Karl turned down the preceding page and showed him a seated lion, proud and watchful. In the lower right-hand corner of the page there was an A with a circle around it. 'Marvellous!' Chip said. Karl turned down other pages; there were two deer, a monkey, a soaring eagle, two dogs sniffing each other, a crouching leopard.

Chip laughed. 'You've got the whole fighting zoo!' he said.

'No I haven't,' Karl said.

All the drawings had the A with the circle around it in the corner. 'What's that for?' Chip asked.

'Artists used to sign their pictures. To show whose work it was.'

'I know,' Chip said, 'but why an A?'

'Oh,' Karl said, and turned the pages back one by one. 'It stands for Ashi,' he said. 'That's what my sister calls me.' He came to the horse, added a line of charcoal to its stomach, and looked at the horses in the compound with his look of concentration, which now had an object and a reason.

'I have an extra name too,' Chip said. 'Chip. My grandfather gave it to me.'

'Chip?'

'It means "chip off the old block". I'm supposed to be like my grandfather's grandfather.' Chip watched Karl sharpen the lines of the horse's rear legs, and then moved from his side. 'I'd better get back to the group I'm with,' he said. 'Those are top speed. It's a shame you weren't classified an artist.'

Karl looked at him. 'I wasn't, though,' he said, 'so I only draw on Sundays and holidays and during the free hour. I never let it interfere with my work or whatever else I'm supposed to be doing.'

'Right,' Chip said. 'See you at the dorm.'

That evening, after TV, Chip came back to his cubicle and found on his desk the drawing of the horse. Karl, in his cubicle, said, 'Do you want it?'

'Yes,' Chip said. 'Thanks. It's great!' The drawing had even more vitality and power than before. An A-in-a-circle was in a corner of it.

Chip tabbed the drawing to the bulletin board behind the desk, and as he finished, Yin DW came in, bringing back a copy of *Universe* she had borrowed. 'Where'd you get that?' she asked.

'Karl WL did it,' Chip said.

'That's very nice, Karl,' Yin said. 'You draw well.'

Karl, getting into pyjamas, said. 'Thanks. I'm glad you like it.'

To Chip, Yin whispered, 'It's all out of proportion. Keep it there, though. It was kind of you to put it up.'

* * *

Once in a while, during the free hour, Chip and Karl went to the Pre-U together. Karl made sketches of the mastodon and the bison, the cavemen in their animal hides, the soldiers and sailors in their countless different uniforms. Chip wandered among the early automobiles and dictypes, the safes and handcuffs and TV 'sets'. He studied the models and pictures of the old buildings: the spired and buttressed churches, the turreted castles, the large and small houses with their windows and lock-fitted doors. Windows, he thought, must have had their good points. It would be pleasant, would make one feel bigger, to look out at the world from one's room or working place; and at night, from outside, a house with rows of lighted windows must have been attractive, even beautiful.

One afternoon Karl came into Chip's cubicle and stood beside the desk with his hands fisted at his sides. Chip, looking up at him, thought he had been stricken by a fever or worse; his face was flushed and his eyes were narrowed in a strange stare. But no, it was anger that held him, anger such as Chip had never seen before, anger so intense that, trying to speak, Karl seemed unable to work his lips.

Anxiously Chip said, 'What is it?'

'Li,' Karl said. 'Listen. Will you do me a favour?'

'Sure! Of course!'

Karl leaned close to him and whispered, 'Claim a pad for me, will you? I just claimed one and was denied. Five fighting hundred of them, a pile this high, and I had to turn it back in!'

Chip stared at him.

'Claim one, will you?' Karl said. 'Anyone can try a little sketching in his spare time, right? Go on down, okay?'

Painfully Chip said, 'Karl—'

Karl looked at him, his anger retreated, and he stood up straight. 'No,' he said. 'No, I – I just lost my temper, that's all. I'm sorry. I'm sorry, brother. Forget it.' He clapped Chip's shoulder. 'I'm okay now,' he said. 'I'll claim again in a week or so. Been doing too much drawing anyway, I suppose. Uni knows best.' He went off down the aisle towards the bathroom.

Chip turned back to the desk and leaned on his elbows and held his head, shaking.

That was Tuesday. Chip's weekly adviser meetings were on Woodsday mornings at 10.40, and this time he would tell Li YB about Karl's sickness. There was no longer any question of being an alarmist; there was faulted responsibility, in fact, in having waited as long as he had. He ought to have said something at the first clear sign, Karl's slipping out of TC (to draw, of course), or even when he had noticed the unusual look in Karl's eyes. Why in hate had he waited? He could hear Li YB gently reproaching him: 'You haven't been a very good brother's keeper, Li'.

Early on Woodsday morning, though, he decided to pick up some coveralls and the new *Geneticist*. He went down to the supply centre and walked through the aisles. He took a *Geneticist* and a pack of coveralls and walked some more and came to the art-supplies section. He saw the pile of green-covered sketch pads; there weren't five hundred of them, but there were seventy or eighty and no one seemed in a rush to claim them.

He walked away, thinking that he must be going out of his mind. Yet if Karl were to promise not to draw when he wasn't supposed to ...

He walked back again – '*Anyone can try a little sketching in his spare time, right?*' – and took a pad and a packet of charcoal. He went to the shortest check-out line, his heart pounding in his chest, his arms trembling. He drew a deep-as-possible breath; another, and another.

He put his bracelet to the scanner, and the stickers of the coveralls, the *Geneticist*, the pad, and the charcoal. Everything was *yes*. He gave way to the next member.

He went back up to the dorm. Karl's cubicle was empty, the bed unmade. He went into his own cubicle and put the coveralls on the shelf and the *Geneticist* on the desk. On the top page of the pad he wrote, his hand still trembling, *Free time only. I want your promise.* Then he put the pad and the charcoal on his bed and sat at the desk and looked at the *Geneticist*.

Karl came, and went into his cubicle and began making his bed. 'Are those yours?' Chip asked.

Karl looked at the pad and charcoal on Chip's bed. Chip said, 'They're not mine.'

'Oh, yes. Thanks,' Karl said, and came over and took them.

46

'Thanks a lot,' he said.

'You ought to put your nameber on the first page,' Chip said, 'if you're going to leave it all over like that.'

Karl went into his cubicle, opened the pad, and looked at the first page. He looked at Chip, nodded, raised his right hand, and mouthed, 'Love of Family'.

They rode down to the classrooms together. 'What did you have to waste a page for?' Karl said.

Chip smiled.

'I'm not joking,' Karl said. 'Didn't you ever hear of writing a note on a piece of scrap paper?'

'Christ, Marx, Wood, and Wei,' Chip said.

In December of that year, 152, came the appalling news of the Grey Death, sweeping through all the Mars colonies except one and completely wiping them out in nine short days. In the Academy of the Genetic Sciences, as in all the Family's establishments, there was helpless silence, then mourning, and then a massive determination to help the Family overcome the staggering setback it had suffered. Everyone worked harder and longer. Free time was halved; there were classes on Sundays and only a half-day Christmas holiday. Genetics alone could breed new strengths in the coming generations; everyone was in a hurry to finish his training and get on to his first real assignment. On every wall were the white-on-black posters: MARS AGAIN!

The new spirit lasted several months. Not until Marxmas was there a full day's holiday, and then no one quite knew what to do with it. Chip and Karl and their girlfriends rowed out to one of the islands in the Amusement Gardens lake and sunbathed on a large flat rock. Karl drew his girlfriend's picture. It was the first time, as far as Chip knew, that he had drawn a living human being.

In June, Chip claimed another pad for Karl.

Their training ended, five weeks early, and they received their assignments: Chip to a viral genetics research laboratory in USA90058; Karl to the Institute of Enzymology in JAP50319.

On the evening before they were to leave the Academy they packed their take-along kits. Karl pulled green-covered pads from his desk drawers – a dozen from one drawer, half

47

a dozen from another, more pads from other drawers; he threw them into a pile on his bed. 'You're never going to get those all into your kit,' Chip said.

'I'm not planning to,' Karl said. 'They're done; I don't need them.' He sat on the bed and leafed through one of the pads, tore out one drawing and another.

'May I have some?' Chip asked.

'Sure,' Karl said, and tossed a pad over to him.

It was mostly Pre-U Museum sketches. Chip took out one of a man in chain mail holding a crossbow to his shoulder, and another of an ape scratching himself.

Karl gathered most of the pads and went off down the aisle towards the chute. Chip put the pad on Karl's bed and picked up another one.

In it were a nude man and woman standing in parkland outside a blank-slabbed city. They were taller than normal, beautiful and strangely dignified. The woman was quite different from the man, not only genitally but also in her longer hair, protrusive breasts, and overall softer convexity. It was a great drawing, but something about it disturbed Chip, he didn't know what.

He turned to other pages, other men and women; the pictures grew surer and stronger, done with fewer and bolder lines. They were the best drawings Karl had ever made, but in each there was that disturbing something, a lack, an imbalance that Chip was at a loss to define.

It hit him with a chill.

They had no bracelets.

He looked through to check, his stomach knotting sick-tight. No bracelets. No bracelets on any of them. And there was no chance of the drawings being unfinished; in the corner of each of them was an A with a circle around it.

He put down the pad and went and sat on his bed; watched as Karl came back and gathered the rest of the pads and, with a smile, carried them off.

There was a dance in the lounge but it was brief and subdued because of Mars. Later Chip went with his girl-friend into her cubicle. 'What's the matter?' she asked.

'Nothing,' he said.

Karl asked him too, in the morning while they were fold-ing their blankets. 'What's the matter, Li?'

'Nothing.'

'Sorry to be leaving?'

'A little.'

'Me too. Here, give me your sheets and I'll chute them.'

'What's his nameber?' Li YB asked.

'Karl WL35S7497,' Chip said.

Li YB jotted it down. 'And what specifically seems to be the trouble?' he asked.

Chip wiped his palms on his thighs. 'He's drawn some pictures of members,' he said.

'Acting aggressively?'

'No, no,' Chip said. 'Just standing and sitting, fucking, playing with children.'

'Well?'

Chip looked at the desktop. 'They don't have bracelets,' he said.

Li YB didn't speak. Chip looked at him; he was looking at Chip. After a moment Li YB said, 'Several pictures?'

'A whole padful.'

'And no bracelets at all.'

'None.'

Li YB breathed in, and then pushed out the breath between his teeth in a series of rapid hisses. He looked at his note pad. 'KWL35S7497,' he said.

Chip nodded.

He tore up the picture of the man with the crossbow, which was aggressive, and tore up the one of the ape too. He took the pieces to the chute and dropped them down.

He put the last few things into his take-along kit – his clippers and mouthpiece and a framed snapshot of his parents and Papa Jan – and pressed it closed.

Karl's girlfriend came by with her kit slung on her shoulder. 'Where's Karl?' she asked.

'At the medicentre.'

'Oh,' she said. 'Tell him I said goodbye, will you?'

'Sure.'

They kissed cheeks. 'Goodbye,' she said.

'Goodbye.'

She went away down the aisle. Some other students, no

longer students, went past. They smiled at Chip and said goodbye to him.

He looked around the barren cubicle. The picture of the horse was still on the bulletin board. He went to it and looked at it; saw again the rearing stallion, so alive and wild. Why hadn't Karl stayed with the animals in the zoo? Why had he begun to draw living humans?

A feeling formed in Chip, formed and grew; a feeling that he had been wrong to tell Li YB about Karl's drawings, although he knew of course that he had been right. How could it be wrong to help a sick brother? Not to tell would have been wrong, to keep quiet as he had done before, letting Karl go on drawing members without bracelets and getting sicker and sicker. Eventually he might even have been drawing members acting aggressively. Fighting.

Of course he had been right.

Yet the feeling that he had been wrong stayed and kept growing, grew into guilt, irrationally.

Someone came near, and he whirled, thinking it was Karl coming to thank him. It wasn't; it was someone passing the cubicle, leaving.

But that was what was going to happen: Karl was going to come back from the medicentre and say, 'Thanks for helping me, Li. I was really sick but I'm a whole lot better now,' and *he* was going to say, 'Don't thank *me*, brother; thank Uni,' and Karl was going to say, 'No, no,' and insist and shake his hand.

Suddenly he wanted not to be there, not to get Karl's thanks for having helped him; he grabbed his kit and hurried to the aisle – stopping short, uncertainly, and hurried back. He took the picture of the horse from the board, opened his kit on the desk, pushed the drawing in among the pages of a notebook, closed the kit, and went.

He jogged down the downgoing escalators, excusing himself past other members, afraid that Karl might come after him; jogged all the way down to the lowest level, where the rail station was, and got on the long airport line. He stood with his head held still, not looking back.

Finally he came to the scanner. He faced it for a moment, and touched it with his bracelet. *Yes*, it green-winked.

He hurried through the gate.

PART TWO

COMING ALIVE

ONE

Between July of 153 and Marx of 162, Chip had four assignments: two at research laboratories in Usa; a brief one at the Institute of Genetic Engineering in Ind, where he attended a series of lectures on recent advances in mutation induction; and a five-year assignment at a chemo-synthetics plant in Chi. He was upgraded twice in his classification and by 162 was a genetic taxonomist, second class.

During those years he was outwardly a normal and contented member of the Family. He did his work well, took part in house athletic and recreational programmes, had weekly sexual activity, made monthly phone calls and bi-yearly visits to his parents, was in place and on time for TV and treatments and adviser meetings. He had no discomfort to report, either physical or mental.

Inwardly, however, he was far from normal. The feeling of guilt with which he had left the Academy had led him to withhold himself from his next adviser, for he wanted to retain that feeling, which, though unpleasant, was the strongest feeling he had ever had and an enlargement, strangely, of his sense of being; and withholding himself from his adviser – reporting no discomfort, playing the part of a relaxed, contented member – had led over the years to a withholding of himself from everyone around him, a general attitude of guarded watchfulness. Everything came to seem questionable to him: totalcakes, coveralls, the sameness of members' rooms and thoughts, and especially the work he was doing, whose end, he saw, would only be to solidify the universal sameness. There were no alternatives, of course, no imaginable alternatives to anything, but still he withheld himself, and questioned. Only in the first few days after treatments was he really the member he pretended to be.

One thing alone in the world was indisputably right: Karl's drawing of the horse. He framed it – not in a supply-centre frame but in one he made himself, out of wood strips ripped from the back of a drawer and scraped smooth – and hung it in his rooms in Usa, his room in Ind, his room in Chi. It was a lot better to look at than *Wei Addressing the Chemotherapists* or *Marx Writing* or *Christ Expelling the Money Changers*.

In Chi he thought of getting married, but he was told that he wasn't to reproduce and so there didn't seem much point in it.

In mid-Marx of 162 shortly before his twenty-seventh birthday, he was transferred back to the Institute of Genetic Engineering in IND26110 and assigned to a newly established Genic Subclassification Centre. New microscopes had found distinctions between genes that until then had appeared identical, and he was one of forty 663B's and C's put to defining subclassifications. His room was four buildings away from the Centre, giving him a short walk twice a day, and he soon found a girlfriend whose room was on the floor below his. His adviser was a year younger than he, Bob RO. Life apparently was going to continue as before.

One night in April, though, as he made ready to clean his teeth before going to bed, he found a small white something lodged in his mouthpiece. Perplexed, he picked it out. It was a triple bend of tightly rolled paper. He put down the mouthpiece and unrolled a thin rectangle filled with typing. *You seem to be a fairly unusual member*, it said. *Wondering about which classification you would choose, for instance. Would you like to meet some other unusual members? Think about it. You are only partly alive. We can help you more than you can imagine.*

The note surprised him with its knowledge of his past and disturbed him with its secrecy and its 'You are only partly alive'. What did it mean – that strange statement and the whole strange message? And who had put it in his mouthpiece, of all places? But there was no better place, it struck him, for making certain that he and he alone should find it. Who then, not so foolishly, had put it there? Anyone at all could have come into the room earlier in the evening or during the day. At least two other members had done so; there had been notes on his desk from Peace SK, his girlfriend, and from the secretary of the house photography club.

He cleaned his teeth and got into bed and reread the note. Its writer or one of the other 'unusual members' must have had access to UniComp's memory of his boyhood self-classification thoughts, and that seemed to be enough to make the group think he might be sympathetic to them. Was he? They were abnormal; that was certain. Yet what was *he*? Wasn't he abnormal too? *We can help you more than you can imagine.* What did *that* mean? Help him how? Help him do what? And what if he decided he wanted to meet them; what was he supposed to do? Wait, apparently, for another note, for a contact of some kind. *Think about it*, the note said.

The last chime sounded, and he rolled the piece of paper back up and tucked it down into the spine of his night-table *Wei's Living Wisdom*. He tapped off the light and lay and thought about it. It was disturbing, but it was different too, and interesting. *Would you like to meet some other unusual members?*

He didn't say anything about it to Bob RO. He looked for another note in his mouthpiece each time he came back to his room, but didn't find one. Walking to and from work, taking a seat in the lounge for TV, standing on line in the dining-hall or the supply centre, he searched the eyes of the members around him, alert for a meaningful remark or perhaps only a look and a head movement inviting him to follow. None came.

Four days went by and he began to think that the note had been a sick member's joke, or worse, a test of some kind. Had Bob RO himself written it, to see if he would mention it? No, that was ridiculous; he was *really* getting sick.

He had been interested – excited even, and hopeful, though he hadn't known of what – but now, as more days went by with no note, no contact, he became disappointed and irritable.

And then, a week after the first note, it was there: the same triple bend of rolled paper in the mouthpiece. He picked it out, excitement and hope coming back instantaneously. He unrolled the paper and read it: *If you want to meet us and hear how we can help you, be between buildings J16 and J18 on Lower Christ Plaza tomorrow night at 11.15. Do not touch any scanners on the way. If members are in sight of*

55

one you have to pass, take another route. I'll wait until 11.30.
Beneath was typed, as a signature, *Snowflake.*

Few members were on the walkways, and those hurrying
to their beds with their eyes set straight ahead of them. He
had to change his course only once, walked faster, and
reached Lower Christ Plaza exactly at 11.15. He crossed the
moonlit white expanse, with its turned-off fountain mirror-
ing the moon and found J16 and the dark channel that
divided it from J18.

No one was there – but then, metres back in shadow, he
saw white coveralls marked with what looked like a medicentre red cross. He went into the darkness and approached
the member, who stood by J16's wall and stayed silent.

'Snowflake?' he said.

'Yes.' The voice was a woman's. 'Did you touch any
scanners?'

'No.'

'Funny feeling, isn't it?' She was wearing a pale mask of
some kind, thin and close-fitting.

'I've done it before,' he said.

'Good for you.'

'Only once, and somebody pushed me,' he said. She seemed
older than he, how much he couldn't tell.

'We're going to a place that's a five-minute walk from
here,' she said. 'It's where we get together regularly, six of
us, four women and two men – a terrible ratio that I'm counting on you to improve. We're going to make a certain suggestion to you; if you decide to follow it you might
eventually become one of us; if you don't, you won't, and
tonight will be our last contact. In that case, though, we
can't have you knowing what we look like or where we
meet.' Her hand came out of her pocket with whiteness in
it. 'I'll have to bandage your eyes,' she said. 'That's why
I'm wearing these medicentre cuvs, so it'll look all right for
me to be leading you.'

'At this hour?'

'We've done it before and had no trouble,' she said. 'You
don't mind?'

He shrugged. 'I guess not,' he said.

'Hold these over your eyes.' She gave him two wads of

cotton. He closed his eyes and put the wads in place, holding them with a finger each. She began winding bandage around his head and over the wads; he withdrew his fingers, bent his head to help her. She kept winding bandage, around and around, up on to his forehead, down on to his cheeks.

'Are you sure you're really not medicentre?' he said.

She chuckled and said, 'Positive.' She pressed the end of the bandage, sticking it tight; pressed all over it and over his eyes, then took his arm. She turned him – towards the plaza, he knew – and started him walking.

'Don't forget your mask,' he said.

She stopped short. 'Thanks for reminding me,' she said. Her hand left his arm, and after a moment, came back. They walked on.

Their footsteps changed, became muted by space, and a breeze cooled his face below the bandage; they were in the plaza. 'Snowflake's' hand on his arm drew him in a diagonal leftward course, away from the direction of the Institute.

'When we get where we're going,' she said, 'I'm going to put a piece of tape over your bracelet; over mine too. We avoid knowing one another's namebers as much as possible. I know yours – I'm the one who spotted you – but the others don't; all they know is that I'm bringing a promising member. Later on, one or two of them may have to know it.'

'Do you check the history of everyone who's assigned here?'

'No. Why?'

'Isn't that how you "spotted" me, by finding out that I used to think about classifying myself?'

'Three steps down here,' she said. 'No, that was only confirmation. And two and three. What I spotted was a look you have, the look of a member who isn't one-hundred-percent in the bosom of the Family. You'll learn to recognize it too, if you join us. I found out who you were, and then I went to your room and saw that picture on the wall.'

'The horse?'

'No, *Marx Writing*,' she said. 'Of course the horse. You draw the way no normal member would even think of drawing. I checked your history *then*, after I'd seen the picture.'

They had left the plaza and were on one of the walkways west of it – K or L, he wasn't sure which.

'You've made a mistake,' he said. 'Someone else drew that picture.'

'You drew it,' she said; 'you've claimed charcoal and sketch pads.'

'For the member who drew it. A friend of mine at academy.'

'Well *that's* interesting,' she said. 'Cheating on claims is a better sign than anything. Anyway, you liked the picture well enough to keep it and frame it. Or did your friend make the frame too?'

He smiled. 'No, I did,' he said. 'You didn't miss a thing.'

'We turn here, to the right.'

'Are you an adviser?'

'Me? Hate, no.'

'But you can pull histories?'

'Sometimes.'

'Are you at the Institute?'

'Don't ask so many questions,' she said. 'Listen, what do you want us to call you? Instead of Li RM.'

'Oh,' he said. 'Chip.'

' "Chip?" No,' she said, 'don't just say the first thing that comes into your mind. You ought to be something like "Pirate" or "Tiger". The others are King and Lilac and Leopard and Hush and Sparrow.'

'Chip's what I was called when I was a boy,' he said. 'I'm used to it.'

'All right,' she said, 'but it's not what *I* would have chosen. Do you know where we are?'

'No.'

'Fine. Left now.'

They went through a door, up steps, through another door, and into an echoing hall of some kind, where they walked and turned, walked and turned, as if by-passing a number of irregularly placed objects. They walked up a stopped escalator and along a corridor that curved towards the right.

She stopped him and asked for his bracelet. He raised his wrist, and his bracelet was pressed tight and rubbed. He touched it; there was smoothness instead of his nameber. That and his sightlessness made him suddenly feel disembodied; as if he were about to drift from the floor, drift right out through whatever walls were around him and up into space, dissolve there and become nothing.

She took his arm again. They walked farther and stopped. He heard a knock and two more knocks, a door opening, voices stilling. 'Hi,' she said, leading him forward. 'This is Chip. He insists on it.'

Chairs scuffed against the floor, voices gave greetings. A hand took his and shook it. 'I'm King,' a member said, a man. 'I'm glad you decided to come.'

'Thanks,' he said.

Another hand gripped his harder. 'Snowflake says you're quite an artist' – an older man than King. 'I'm Leopard.'

Other hands came quickly, women: 'Hello, Chip; I'm Lilac.' 'And I'm Sparrow. I hope you'll become a regular.' 'I'm Hush, Leopard's wife. Hello.' The last one's hand and voice were old; the other two were young.

He was led to a chair and sat in it. His hands found table-top before him, smooth and bare, its edge slightly curving; an oval table or a large round one. The others were sitting down; Snowflake on his right, talking; someone else on his left. He smelled something burning, sniffed to make sure. None of the others seemed aware of it. 'Something's burning,' he said.

'Tobacco,' the old woman, Hush, said on his left.

'Tobacco?' he said.

'We smoke it,' Snowflake said. 'Would you like to try some?'

'No,' he said.

Some of them laughed. 'It's not really deadly,' King said, farther away on his left. 'In fact, I suspect it may have some beneficial effects.'

'It's very pleasing,' one of the young women said, across the table from him.

'No, thanks,' he said.

They laughed again, made comments to one another, and one by one grew silent. His right hand on the tabletop was covered by Snowflake's hand; he wanted to draw it away but restrained himself. He had been stupid to come. What was he doing, sitting there sightless among those sick false-named members? His own abnormality was nothing next to theirs. Tobacco! The stuff had been extincted a hundred years ago; where the hate had they got it?

'We're sorry about the bandage, Chip,' King said. 'I assume Snowflake's explained why it's necessary.'

'She has,' Chip said, and Snowflake said, 'I did.' Her hand left Chip's; he drew his from the tabletop and took hold of his other in his lap.

'We're abnormal members, which is fairly obvious,' King said. 'We do a great many things that are generally considered sick. We think they're not. We *know* they're not.' His voice was strong and deep and authoritative; Chip visualized him as large and powerful, about forty. 'I'm not going to go into too many details,' he said, 'because in your present condition you would be shocked and upset, just as you're obviously shocked and upset by the fact that we smoke tobacco. You'll learn the details for yourself in the future, if there *is* a future as far as you and we are concerned.'

'What do you mean,' Chip said, '"in my present condition"?'

There was silence for a moment. A woman coughed. 'While you're dulled and normalized by your most recent treatment,' King said.

Chip sat still, facing in King's direction, stopped by the irrationality of what he had said. He went over the words and answered them: 'I'm not dulled and normalized'.

'But you are,' King said.

'The whole Family is,' Snowflake said, and from beyond her came 'Everyone, not just you' – in the old man's voice of Leopard.

'What do you think a treatment consists of?' King asked.

Chip said, 'Vaccines, enzymes, the contraceptive, sometimes a tranquillizer—'

'*Always* a tranquillizer,' King said. 'And LPK, which minimizes aggressiveness and also minimizes joy and perception and every other fighting thing the brain is capable of.'

'And a sexual depressant,' Snowflake said.

'That too,' King said. 'Ten minutes of automatic sex once a week is barely a fraction of what's possible.'

'I don't believe it,' Chip said. 'Any of it.'

60

They told him it was true. 'Its true, Chip.' 'Really, it's the truth.' 'It's true!'

'You're in genetics,' King said; 'isn't that what genetic engineering is working towards? – removing aggressiveness, controlling the sex drive, building in helpfulness and docility and gratitude? Treatments are doing the job in the meantime, while genetic engineering gets past size and skin colour.'

'Treatments help us,' Chip said.

'They help Uni,' the woman across the table said.

'And the Wei-worshippers who programmed Uni,' King said. 'But they don't help *us*, at least not as much as they hurt us. They make us into machines.'

Chip shook his head, and shook it again.

'Snowflake told us' – it was Hush, speaking in a dry quiet voice that accounted for her name – 'that you have abnormal tendencies. Haven't you ever noticed that they're stronger just before a treatment and weaker just after one?'

Snowflake said, 'I'll bet you made that picture frame a day or two *before* a treatment, not a day or two after one.'

He thought for a moment. 'I don't remember,' he said, 'but when I was a boy and thought about classifying myself after treatments it seemed stupid and pre-U, and before treatments it was – exciting.'

'There you are,' King said.

'But it was *sick* excitement!'

'It was healthy,' King said, and the woman across the table said, 'You were alive, you were feeling something. Any feeling is healthier than no feeling at all.'

He thought about the guilt he had kept secret from his advisers since Karl and the Academy. He nodded. 'Yes,' he said, 'yes, that could be.' He turned his face towards King, towards the woman, towards Leopard and Snowflake, wishing he could open his eyes and see them. 'But I don't understand this,' he said. 'You get treatments, don't you? Then aren't *you*—'

'Reduced ones,' Snowflake said.

'Yes, we get treatments,' King said, 'but we've managed to have them reduced, to have certain components of them reduced, so that we're a little more than the machines Uni thinks we are.'

61

'And that's what we're offering *you*,' Snowflake said; 'a way to see more and feel more and do more and enjoy more.'

'And to be more unhappy; tell him that too.' It was a new voice, soft but clear, the other young woman. She was across the table and to Chip's left, close to where King was.

'That isn't so,' Snowflake said.

'Yes it is,' the clear voice said – a girl's voice almost; she was no more than twenty, Chip guessed. 'There'll be days when you'll *hate* Christ, Marx, Wood, and Wei,' she said, 'and want to take a torch to Uni. There'll be days when you'll want to tear off your bracelet and run to a mountaintop like the old incurables, just to be able to do what you want to do and make your own choice and live your own life.'

'Lilac,' Snowflake said.

'There'll be days when you'll hate *us*,' she said, 'for waking you up and making you *not* a machine. Machines are at home in the universe; people are aliens.'

'Lilac,' Snowflake said, 'we're trying to get Chip to join us; we're not trying to scare him away.' To Chip she said, 'Lilac is *really* abnormal.'

'There's truth in what Lilac says,' King said. 'I think we all have moments when we wish there were someplace we could go, some settlement or colony where we could be our own master—'

'Not me,' Snowflake said.

'And since there isn't such a place,' King said, 'yes, we're sometimes unhappy. Not you, Snowflake; I know. With rare exceptions like Snowflake, being able to feel happiness seems to mean being able to feel *un*happiness as well. But as Sparrow said, any feeling is better and healthier than none at all; and the unhappy moments aren't that frequent, really.'

'They are,' Lilac said.

'Oh, cloth,' Snowflake said. 'Let's *stop* all this talk about unhappiness.'

'Don't worry, Snowflake,' the woman across the table, Sparrow, said; 'if he gets up and runs you can trip him.'

'Ha, ha, hate, hate,' Sparrow said.

'Snowflake, Sparrow,' King said. 'Well, Chip, what's your answer? Do you want to get your treatments reduced? It's done by steps; the first one is easy, and if you don't like the

62

way you feel a month from now, you can go to your adviser and tell him you were infected by a group of very sick members who you unfortunately can't identify.'

After a moment Chip said, 'All right. What do I do?' His arm was squeezed by Snowflake. 'Good,' Hush whispered.

'Just a moment, I'm lighting my pipe,' King said.

'Are you all smoking?' Chip asked. The burning smell was intense, drying and stinging his nostrils.

'Not right now,' Hush said. 'Only King, Lilac, and Leopard.'

'We've all *been* doing it though,' Snowflake said. 'It's not a continuous thing; you do it awhile and then stop awhile.'

'Where do you get the tobacco?'

'We grow it,' Leopard said, sounding pleased. 'Hush and I. In parkland.'

'In *parkland?*'

'That's right,' Leopard said.

'We have two patches,' Hush said, 'and last Sunday we found a place for a third.'

'Chip?' King said, and Chip turned towards him and listened. 'Basically, step one is just a matter of acting as if you're being *over*treated,' King said; 'slowing down at work, at games, at everything – slowing down *slightly*, not conspicuously. Make a small mistake at your work, and another one a few days later. And don't do well at sex. The thing to do there is masturbate before you meet your girlfriend; that way you'll be able to fail convincingly.'

'Masturbate?'

'Oh, fully treated, fully satisfied member,' Snowflake said.

'Bring yourself to an orgasm with your hand,' King said. 'And then don't be too concerned when you don't have one later. Let you girlfriend tell *her* adviser; don't you tell yours. Don't be too concerned about anything, the mistakes you make, lateness for appointments or whatever; let others do the noticing and reporting.'

'Pretend to doze off during TV,' Sparrow said.

'You're ten days from your next treatment,' King said. 'At your next week's adviser meeting, if you've done what I've told you, your adviser will sound you out about your general

63

torpor. Again, no concern on your part. Apathy. If you do the whole thing well, the depressants in your treatment will be slightly reduced, enough so that a month from now you'll be anxious to hear about step two.'

'It sounds easy enough,' Chip said.

'It is,' Snowflake said, and Leopard said, 'We've all done it; you can too.'

'There's one danger,' King said. 'Even though your treatment may be slightly weaker than usual, its effects in the first few days will still be strong. You'll feel a revulsion against what you've done and an urge to confess to your adviser and get stronger treatments than ever. There's no way of telling whether or not you'll be able to resist the urge. We did, but others haven't. In the past year we've given this talk to two other members; they did the slowdown but then confessed within a day or two after being treated.'

'Then won't my adviser be suspicious when I do the slowdown? He must have heard about those others.'

'Yes,' King said, 'but there are legitimate slowdowns, when a member's need for depressants has lessened, so if you do the job convincingly you'll get away with it. It's the urge to confess that you have to worry about.'

'Keep telling yourself' – it was Lilac speaking – 'that it's a chemical that's making you think you're sick and in need of help, a chemical that was infused into you without your consent.'

'My consent?' Chip said.

'Yes,' she said. 'Your body is yours, not Uni's.'

'Whether you'll confess or hold out,' King said, 'depends on how strong your mind's resistance is to chemical alteration, and there's not much you can do about it one way or the other. On the basis of what we know of you, I'd say you have a good chance.'

They gave him some more pointers on slowdown technique – to skip his midday cake once or twice, to go to bed before the last chime – and then King suggested that Snowflake take him back to where they had met. 'I hope we'll be seeing you again, Chip,' he said. 'Without the bandage.'

'I hope so,' Chip said. He stood and pushed back his chair. 'Good luck,' Hush said; Sparrow and Leopard said it too. Lilac said it last: 'Good luck, Chip.'

'What happens,' he asked, 'if I resist the urge to confess?'

'We'll know,' King said; 'and one of us will get in touch with you about ten days after the treatment.'

'How will you know?'

'We'll know.'

His arm was taken by Snowflake's hand. 'All right,' he said. 'Thank you, all of you.'

They said 'Don't mention it,' and 'you're welcome, Chip,' and 'Glad to be of help'. Something sounded strange, and then – as Snowflake led him from the room – he realized what it was: the not-being-said of 'Thank Uni'.

They walked slowly, Snowflake holding his arm not like a nurse but like a girl walking with her first boyfriend.

'It's hard to believe,' he said, 'that what I can feel now and see now – isn't all there is.'

'It isn't,' she said. 'Not even half. You'll find out.'

'I hope so.'

'You will. I'm sure of it.'

He smiled and said, 'Were you sure about those two who tried and didn't make it?'

'No,' she said. Then, 'Yes, I was sure of one, but not of the other.'

'What's step two?' he asked.

'First get through step one.'

'Are there more than two?'

'No. Two, if it works, gets you a major reduction. That's when you *really* come alive. And speaking of steps, there are three right ahead of us, going up.'

They went up the three steps and walked on. They were back in the plaza. It was perfectly silent, with even the breeze gone.

'The fucking's the best part,' Snowflake said. 'It gets much better, much more intense and exciting, and you'll be able to do it almost every night.'

'It's incredible.'

'And please remember,' she said, 'that I'm the one who found you. If I catch you even *looking* at Sparrow I'll kill you.'

Chip started, and told himself not to be foolish.

'Excuse me,' she said; 'I'll act aggressively towards you. Maxi-aggressively.'

'It's all right,' he said. 'I'm not shocked.'

'Not much.'

'What about Lilac?' he said. 'May I look at her?'

'All you want; she loves King.'

'Oh?'

'With a pre-U passion. He's the one who started the group; first her, then Leopard and Hush, then me, then Sparrow.'

Their footsteps became louder and resonant. She stopped him. 'We're here,' she said. He felt her fingers picking at the side of the bandage; he lowered his head. She began unwinding, peeling bandage from margins of skin that turned instantly cool. She unwound more and more and finally took the cotton from his eyes. He blinked them and stretched them wide.

She was close to him and moonlit, looking at him in a way that seemed challenging while she thrust the bandage into her medicentre coveralls. Somehow she had got her pale maşk back on – but it wasn't a mask, he saw with a shock; it was her face. She was light. Lighter than any member he had ever seen, except a few near-sixty ones. She was almost white. Almost as white as snow.

'Mask neatly in place,' she said.

'I'm sorry,' he said.

'That's all right,' she said, and smiled. 'We're all odd in one way or another. Look at that eye.' She was thirty-five or so, sharp-featured and intelligent-looking, her hair freshly clipped.

'I'm sorry,' he said again.

'I said it's all right.'

'Are you supposed to let me see what you look like?'

'I'll tell you something,' she said. 'If you don't come through I don't give a fight if the whole bunch of us get normalized. In fact, I think I'd prefer it.' She took his head in both hands and kissed him, her tongue prying at his lips. It slid in and flickered in his mouth. She held his head tight, pushed her groin against his, and rubbed circularly. He felt a responsive stiffening and put his hands to her back. He worked his tongue tentatively against hers.

66

She withdrew her mouth. 'Considering that it's the middle of the week,' she said, 'I'm encouraged.'

'Christ, Marx, Wood, and Wei,' he said. 'Is that how you all kiss?'

'Only me, brother,' she said, 'only me.'

They did it again.

'Go on home now,' she said. 'Don't touch scanners.'

He backed away from her. 'I'll see you next month,' he said.

'You fighting well better had,' she said. 'Good luck.'

He went out into the plaza and headed towards the Institute. He looked back once. There was only empty passageway between the blank moon-white buildings.

TWO

Bob RO, seated behind his desk, looked up and smiled. 'You're late,' he said.

'I'm sorry,' Chip said. He sat down.

Bob closed a white folder with a red file tab on it. 'How are you?' he asked.

'Fine,' Chip said.

'Have a good week?'

'Mm-hmm.'

Bob studied him for a moment, his elbow on his chair arm, his fingers rubbing the side of his nose. 'Anything in particular you want to talk about?' he asked.

Chip was silent, and then shook his head. 'No,' he said.

'I hear you spent half of yesterday afternoon doing somebody else's work.'

Chip nodded. 'I took a sample from the wrong section of the IC box,' he said.

'I see,' Bob said, and smiled and grunted.

Chip looked questioningly at him.

'Joke,' Bob said. 'IC, I see.'

'Oh,' Chip said, and smiled.

Bob propped his jaw on his hand, the side of a finger lying against his lips. 'What happened Friday?' he asked.

67

'Friday?'

'Something about using the wrong microscope.'

Chip looked puzzled for a moment. 'Oh,' he said. 'Yes. I didn't really use it. I just went into the chamber. I didn't change any of the settings.'

Bob said, 'It looks like it *wasn't* such a good week.'

'No, I guess it wasn't,' Chip said.

'Peace SK says you had trouble Saturday night.'

'Trouble?'

'Sexually.'

Chip shook his head. 'I didn't have any trouble,' he said. 'I just wasn't in the mood, that's all.'

'She says you tried and couldn't erect.'

'Well I felt I *ought* to do it, for *her* sake, but I just wasn't in the mood.'

Bob watched him, not saying anything.

'I was tired,' Chip said.

'It seems you've been tired a lot lately. Is that why you weren't at your photography club meeting Friday night?'

'Yes,' he said. 'I turned in early.'

'How do you feel now? Are you tired now?'

'No. I feel fine.'

Bob looked at him, then straightened in his chair and smiled. 'Okay, brother,' he said, 'touch and go.'

Chip put his bracelet to the scanner of Bob's telecomp and stood up.

'See you next week,' Bob said.

'Yes.'

'On time.'

Chip, having turned way, turned back and said, 'Beg pardon?'

'On time next week,' Bob said.

'Oh,' Chip said. 'Yes.' He turned and went out of the cubicle.

He thought he had done it well but there was no way of knowing, and as his treatment came nearer he grew increasingly anxious. The thought of a significant rise in sensation became more intriguing by the hour, and Snowflake, King, Lilac, and the others became more attractive and admirable. So what if they smoked tobacco? They were happy and healthy members – no, *people*, not members! – who had found an escape from sterility and sameness and universal mechanical efficiency. He wanted to see them and be with them. He wanted to kiss and embrace Snowflake's unique lightness; to talk with King as an equal, friend to friend; to hear more of Lilac's strange but provocative ideas. 'Your body is yours, not Uni's' – what a disturbing pre-Uni thing to say! If there were any basis for it, it could have implications that might lead him to – he couldn't think what; a jolting change of some sort in his attitude towards everything!

That was the night before his treatment. He lay awake for hours, then climbed with bandaged hands up a snow-covered mountaintop, smoked tobacco pleasurably under the guidance of a friendly smiling King, opened Snowflake's coveralls and found her snow-white with a throat-to-groin red cross, drove an early wheel-steered car through the hall-ways of a huge Genetic Suffocation Centre, and had a new bracelet inscribed *Chip* and a window in his room through which he watched a lovely nude girl watering a lilac bush. She beckoned impatiently and he went to her – and woke feeling fresh and energetic and cheerful, despite those dreams, more vivid and convincing than any of the five or six he had had in the past.

That morning, a Friday, he had his treatment. The tickle-buzz-sting seemed to last a fraction of a second less than usual, and when he left the unit, pushing down his sleeve, he still felt good and himself, a dreamer of vivid dreams, a cohort of unusual people, an outwitter of Family and Uni. He walked falsely-slowly to the Centre. It struck him that this of all times was when he should go on with the slow-down, to justify the even greater reduction that step two, whatever it was and whenever he took it, would be aimed at achieving. He was pleased with himself for having realized this, and wondered why King and the others hadn't suggested it. Perhaps they had thought he wouldn't be able to do anything after his treatment. Those other two members had apparently fallen apart completely, unlucky brothers.

He made a good small mistake that afternoon, started to type a report with the mike held wrongside up while another 663B was looking. He felt a bit guilty about doing it, but he did it anyway.

That evening, to his surprise, he really dozed off during TV, although it was something fairly interesting, a tour of a new radio telescope in Isr. And later, during the house photography club meeting, he could hardly keep his eyes open. He excused himself early and went to his room. He undressed without bothering to chute his used coveralls, got into bed without putting on pyjamas, and tapped out the light. He wondered what dreams he would have.

He woke feeling frightened, suspecting that he was sick and in need of help. What was wrong? Had he done something he shouldn't have?

It came to him, and he shook his head, scarcely able to believe it. Was it real? Was it possible? Had he been so – so contaminated by the group of pitiably sick members that he had purposely made mistakes, had tried to deceive Bob RO (and maybe succeeded!), had thought thoughts hostile to his entire loving Family? Oh, Christ, Marx, Wood, and Wei!

He thought of what the young one, 'Lilac', had told him: to remember that it was a chemical that was making him think he was sick, a chemical that had been infused into him without his consent. His consent! As if *consent* had anything to do with a treatment given to preserve one's health and well-being, an integral part of the health and well-being of the entire Family! Even before the Unification, even in the chaos and madness of the twentieth century, a member's consent wasn't asked before he was treated against typhic or typho or whatever it was. Consent! And he had listened without challenging her!

The first chime sounded and he jumped from his bed, anxious to make up for his unthinkable wrongs. He chuted the day before's coveralls, urined, washed, cleaned his teeth, evened up his hair, put on fresh coveralls, made his bed. He went to the dining-hall and claimed his cake and tea, sat among other members and wanted to help them, to give them something, to demonstrate that he was loyal and loving, not the sick offender he had been the day before. The member on his left ate the last of his cake. 'Would you like some of mine?' Chip asked.

The member looked embarrassed. 'No, of course not,' he said. 'But thanks, you're very kind.'

'No I'm not,' Chip said, but he was glad the member had said he was.

He hurried to the Centre and got there eight minutes early. He drew a sample from his own section of the IC box, not somebody else's, and took it to his own microscope; put on his glasses the right way and followed the OMP to the letter. He drew data from Uni respectfully (*Forgive my offences, Uni who knows everything*) and fed it new data humbly (*Here is exact and truthful information about gene sample NF5049*).

The section head looked in. 'How's it going?' he asked.

'Very well, Bob.'

'Good.'

At midday he felt worse, though. What about *them*, those sick ones? Was he to leave them to their sickness, their tobacco, their reduced treatments, their pre-Uni thoughts? He had no choice. They had bandaged his eyes. There was no way of finding them.

But that wasn't so; there *was* a way. Snowflake had shown him her face. How many almost-white members, women of her age, could there be in the city? Three? Four? Five? Uni, if Bob asked it, could output their namebers in an instant. And when she was found and properly treated, she would give the namebers of some of the others; and they, the namebers of the ones remaining. The whole group could be found and helped within a day or two.

The way he had helped Karl.

That stopped him. He had helped Karl and felt guilt – guilt he had clung to for years and years, and now it persisted, a part of him. Oh Jesus Christ and Wei Li Chun, how sick beyond imagining he was!

'Are you all right, brother?'

It was the member across the table, an elderly woman.

'Yes,' he said. 'I'm fine,' and smiled and put his cake to his lips.

'You looked so *troubled* for a second,' she said.

'I'm fine, he said. 'I thought of something I forgot to do.'

'Ah,' she said.

To help them or not to help them? Which was wrong,

71

which was right? He *knew* which was wrong: not to help them, to abandon them as if he weren't his brother's keeper at all.

But he wasn't sure that helping them wasn't wrong too, and how could both be wrong?

He worked less zealously in the afternoon, but well and without mistakes, everything done properly. At the end of the day he went back to his room and lay on his back on his bed, the heels of his hands pressing into his shut eyes and making pulsing auroras there. He heard the voices of the sick ones, saw himself taking the sample from the wrong section of the box and cheating the Family of time and energy and equipment. The supper chime sounded but he stayed as he was, too tangled in himself for eating.

Later Peace SK called. 'I'm in the lounge,' she said. 'It's ten to eight. I've been waiting twenty minutes.'

'I'm sorry,' he said. 'I'll be right down.'

They went to a concert and then to her room.

'What's the *matter*?' she said.

'I don't know,' he said. 'I've been – upset the last few days.'

She shook her head and plied his slack penis more briskly. 'It doesn't make sense,' she said. 'Didn't you tell your adviser? I told mine.'

'Yes, I did. Look' – he took her hand away – 'a whole group of new members came in on sixteen the other day. Why don't you go to the lounge and find somebody else?'

She looked unhappy. 'Well I think I ought to,' she said.

'I do too,' he said. 'Go ahead.'

'It just doesn't make any sense,' she said, getting up from the bed.

He dressed and went back to his room and undressed again. He thought he would have trouble falling asleep but he didn't.

On Sunday he felt even worse. He began to hope that Bob would call, would see that he wasn't well and draw the truth out of him. That way there would be no guilt or responsibility, only relief. He stayed in his room, watching the phone screen. Someone on the soccer team called; he said he wasn't feeling well.

At noon he went to the dining-hall, ate a cake quickly, and

returned to his room. Someone from the Centre called, to find out if he knew someone else's nameber.

Hadn't Bob been told by now that he wasn't acting normally? Hadn't Peace said anything? Or the caller from the soccer team? And that member across the table at lunch yesterday, hadn't she been smart enough to see through his excuse and get his nameber? (Look at him, expecting others to help *him*; who in the Family was he helping?) Where *was* Bob? What kind of adviser was he?

There were no more calls, not in the afternoon, not in the evening. The music stopped once for a starship bulletin.

Monday morning, after breakfast, he went down to the medicentre. The scanner said *no*, but he told the attendant that he wanted to see his adviser; the attendant telecomped, and then the scanners said *yes*, *yes*, *yes*, all the way into the advisory offices, which were half empty. It was only 7.50.

He went into Bob's empty cubicle and sat down and waited for him, his hands on his knees. He went over in his mind the order in which he would tell: first about the intentional slowdown; then about the group, what they said and did and the way they could all be found through Snowflake's lightness; and finally about the sick and irrational guilt-feeling he had concealed all the years since he had helped Karl. One, two, three. He would get an extra treatment to make up for anything he mightn't have got on Friday, and he would leave the medicentre sound in mind and sound in body, a healthy contented member.

Your body is yours, not Uni's.

Sick, pre-U. Uni was the will and wisdom of the entire Family. It had *made* him; had granted him his food, his clothing, his housing, his training. It had granted even the permission for his very conception. Yes, it had made him, and from now on he would be—

Bob came in swinging his telecomp and stopped short. 'Li,' he said. 'Hello. Is anything wrong?'

He looked at Bob. The *name* was wrong. He was Chip, not Li. He looked down at his bracelet: Li RM35M4419. He had expected it to say *Chip*. When had he had one that said *Chip*? In a dream, a strange happy dream, a girl beckoning . . .

'Li?' Bob said, putting his telecomp on the floor.

Uni had made him *Li*. For Wei. But he was Chip, chip off the old block. Which one was he? Li? Chip? Li?

'What is it, brother?' Bob asked, leaning close, taking his shoulder.

'I wanted to see you,' he said.

'About what?'

He didn't know what to say. 'You said I shouldn't be late,' he said. He looked at Bob anxiously. 'Am I on time?'

'On time?' Bob stepped back and squinted at him. 'Brother, you're a day early,' he said. 'Tuesday's your day, not Monday.'

He stood up. 'I'm sorry,' he said. 'I'd better get over to the Centre' – and started to go.

Bob caught his arm. 'Hold on,' he said, his telecomp falling on its side, slamming the floor.

'I'm all right,' Chip said. 'I got mixed up. I'll come tomorrow.' He went from Bob's hand, out of the cubicle.

'Li,' Bob called.

He kept going.

He watched TV attentively that evening – a track meet in Arg, a relay from Venus, the news, a dance programme, and *Wei's Living Wisdom* – and then he went to his room. He tapped the light button but something was covering it and it didn't work. The door closed sharply, had been closed by someone who was near him in the dark, breathing. 'Who is it?' he asked.

'King and Lilac,' King said.

'What happened this morning?' Lilac asked, somewhere over by the desk. 'Why did you go to your adviser?'

'To tell,' he said.

'But you didn't.'

'I should have,' he said. 'Get out of here, please.'

'You see?' King said.

'We have to try,' Lilac said.

'Please go,' Chip said. 'I don't want to get involved with you again, with any of you. I don't know what's right or wrong any more. I don't even know who I am.'

'You've got about ten hours to find out,' King said. 'Your adviser's coming here in the morning to take you to Medicentre Main. You're going to be examined there. It wasn't

74

supposed to happen for three weeks or so, after some more slowing down. It would have been step two. But it's happening tomorrow, and it'll probably be step minus-one.'

'It doesn't have to be, though,' Lilac said. 'You can still make it step two if you do what we tell you.'

'I don't want to hear,' he said. 'Just go, please.'

They didn't say anything. He heard King make a movement.

'Don't you understand?' Lilac said. 'If you do what we tell you, your treatments will be reduced as much as ours are. If you don't they'll be put back to where they were. In fact, they'll probably be increased beyond that, won't they, King?'

'Yes,' said King.

'To "protect" you,' Lilac said. 'So that you'll never again even *try* to get out from under. Don't you see, Chip?' Her voice came closer. 'It's the only chance you'll ever have. For the rest of your life you'll be a machine.'

'No, not a machine, a member,' he said. 'A healthy member doing his assignment; *helping* the Family, not cheating it.'

'You're wasting your breath, Lilac,' King said. 'If it were a few days later you might be able to get through, but it's too soon.'

'Why didn't you tell this morning?' Lilac asked him. 'You went to your adviser; why didn't you tell? Others have.'

'I was going to,' he said.

'Why didn't you?'

He turned away from her voice. 'He called me Li,' he said. 'And I thought I was Chip. Everything got – unsettled.'

'But you *are* Chip,' she said, coming still closer. 'Someone with a name different from the nameber Uni gave him. Somebody who thought of picking his own classification instead of letting Uni do it.'

He moved away, perturbed, then turned and faced their dim coverall shapes – Lilac, small, opposite him and a couple of metres away; King to his right against the light-outlined door. '*How can you speak against Uni?*' he asked. 'It's granted us everything!'

'Only what we've given it to grant us,' Lilac said. 'It's denied us a hundred times more.'

'It let us be born!'

'How many,' she said, 'will it *not* let be born? Like your children. Like mine.'

'What do you mean?' he said. 'That anyone who *wants* children – should be allowed to have them?'

'Yes,' she said. 'That's what I mean.'

Shaking his head, he backed to his bed and sat down. She came to him; crouched and put her hands on his knees. 'Please, Chip,' she said, 'I shouldn't say such things when you're still the way you are, but please, please, believe me. Believe *us*. We are *not sick*, we are *healthy*. It's the world that's sick – with chemistry, and efficiency, and humility, and helpfulness. Do what we tell you. Become healthy. Please, Chip.'

Her earnestness held him. He tried to see her face. 'Why do you care so much?' he asked. Her hands on his knees were small and warm, and he felt an impulse to touch them, to cover them with his own. Faintly he found her eyes, large and less slanted than normal, unusual and lovely.

'There are so few of us,' she said, 'and I think that maybe, if there were more, we could do something; get away somehow and make a place for ourselves.'

'Like the incurables,' he said.

'That's what we learn to call them,' she said. 'Maybe they were really the unbeatables, the undruggables.'

He looked at her trying to see more of her face.

'We have some capsules,' she said, 'that will slow down your reflexes and lower your blood pressure, put things in your blood that will make it look as if your treatments are too strong. If you take them tomorrow morning, before your adviser comes, and if you behave at the medicentre as we tell you and answer certain questions as we tell you – then tomorrow will be step two, and you'll take it and be healthy.'

'And unhappy,' he said.

'Yes,' she said, a smile coming into her voice, 'unhappy too, though not as much as I said. I sometimes get carried away.'

'About every five minutes,' King said.

She took her hands from Chip's knees and stood up. 'Will you?' she asked.

76

He wanted to say yes to her, but he wanted to say no too. He said, 'Let me see the capsules.'

King, coming forward, said, 'You'll see them after we leave. They're in here.' He put into Chip's hand a small smooth box. 'The red one has to be taken tonight and the other two as soon as you get up.'

'Where did you get them?'

'One of the group works in a medicentre.'

'Decide,' Lilac said. 'Do you want to hear what to say and do?'

He shook the box but it made no sound. He looked at the two dim figures waiting before him. He nodded. 'All right,' he said.

They sat and spoke to him, Lilac on the bed beside him, King on the drawn-over desk chair. They told him about a trick of tensing his muscles before the metabolic examination and one of looking above the objective during the depth-perception test. They told him what to say to the doctor who had charge of him and the senior adviser who interviewed him. They told him about tricks that might be played on him: sudden sounds behind his back; being left all alone, but not really, with the doctor's report form conveniently at hand. Lilac did most of the talking. Twice she touched him, once on his leg and once on his forearm; and once, when her hand lay by his side, he brushed it with his own. Hers moved away in a movement that might have begun before the contact.

'That's terrifically important,' King said.

'I'm sorry, what was that?'

'Don't ignore it completely,' King said. 'The report form.'

'Notice it,' Lilac said. 'Glance at it and then act as if it really isn't worth the bother of picking up and reading. As if you don't much care one way or the other.'

It was late when they finished; the last chime had sounded half an hour before. 'We'd better go separately,' King said. 'You go first. Wait by the side of the building.'

Lilac stood up and Chip stood too. Her hand found his. 'I know you're going to make it, Chip,' she said.

'I'll try,' he said. 'Thanks for coming.'

'You're welcome,' she said, and went to the door. He thought he would see her by the light in the hallway as she

77

went out, but King got up and was in the way and the door closed.

They stood silently for a moment, he and King, facing each other.

'Don't forget,' King said. 'The red capsule now and the other two when you get up.'

'Right,' Chip said, feeling for the box in his pocket.

'You shouldn't have any trouble.'

'I don't know; there's so much to remember.'

They were silent again.

'Thank you very much, King,' Chip said, holding out his hand in the darkness.

'You're a lucky man,' King said. 'Snowflake is a very passionate woman. You and she are going to have a lot of good times together.'

Chip didn't understand why he had said that. 'I hope so,' he said. 'It's hard to believe it's possible to have more than one orgasm a week.'

'What we have to do now,' King said, 'is find a man for Sparrow. Then everyone will have someone. It's better that way. Four couples. No friction.'

Chip lowered his hand. He suddenly felt that King was telling him to stay away from Lilac, was defining who belonged with whom and telling him to obey the definition. Had King somehow seen him touching Lilac's hand?

'I'm going now,' King said. 'Turn around, please.'

Chip turned around and heard King moving away. The room appeared dimly as the door was opened, a shadow swept across it, and it disappeared again with the door's closing.

Chip turned. How strange it was to think of someone loving one member in particular so much as to want no one else to touch her! Would he be that way too if his treatments were reduced? It was – like so many other things – hard to believe.

He went to the light button and felt what was covering it: tape, with something square and flat underneath. He picked at the tape, peeled it away, and tapped the button. He shut his eyes against the ceiling's glare.

When he could see he looked at the tape; it was skin-coloured, with a square of blue cardboard stuck to it. He dropped it down the chute and took the box from his pocket. It was white plastic with a hinged lid. He opened it. A red capsule, a white one, and one that was half white and half yellow lay bedded on a cotton filling.

He took the box into the bathroom and tapped on the light. Setting the open box on the edge of the sink, he turned on the water and pulled a cup from the slot and filled it. He turned the water off.

He started to think, but before he could think too much he picked up the red capsule, put it far back on his tongue, and drank the water.

Two doctors, not one, had charge of him. They led him in a pale blue smock from examination room to examination room, conferred with examining doctors, conferred with each other, and made checks and notations on a clipboarded report form that they handed back and forth between them. One was a woman in her forties, the other a man in his thirties. The woman sometimes walked with her arm around Chip's shoulders, smiling and calling him 'young brother'. The man watched him impassively, with eyes that were smaller and set closer together than normal. He had a fresh scar on his cheek, running from the temple to the corner of his mouth and dark bruises on his cheek and his forehead. He never took his eyes off Chip except to look at the report form. Even when conferring with doctors he kept watching him. When the three of them walked to the next examination room he usually dropped behind Chip and the smiling woman doctor. Chip expected him to make a sudden sound, but he didn't.

The interview with the senior adviser, a young woman, went well, Chip thought, but nothing else did. He was afraid to tense his muscles before the metabolic examination because of the doctor watching him, and he forgot about looking above the objective in the depth-perception test until it was too late.

'Too bad you're missing a day's work,' the watching doctor said.

'I'll make it up,' he said, and realized as he said it that it was a mistake. He should have said *It's all for the best* or *Will I be here all day?* or simply a dull overtreated *Yes*.

79

At midday he was given a glass of bitter white liquid to drink instead of totalcake and then there were more tests and examinations. The woman doctor went away for half an hour but not the man.

Around three o'clock they seemed to be finished and went into a small office. The man sat down behind the desk and Chip sat opposite him. The woman said, 'Excuse me, I'll be back in two seconds'. She smiled at Chip and went out.

The man studied the report form for a minute or two, running a fingertip back and forth along his scar, and then he looked at the clock and put down the clipboard. 'I'll go get her,' he said, and got up and went out, closing the door part-way.

Chip sat still and sniffed and looked at the clipboard. He leaned over and twisted his head, read on the report form the words *cholinesterase absorption factor*, *unamplified*, and sat back in his chair again. Had he looked too long? – he wasn't sure. He rubbed his thumb and examined it, then looked at the room's pictures, *Marx Writing* and *Wood Presenting the Unification Treaty*.

They came back in. The woman doctor sat down behind the desk and the man sat in a chair near her side. The woman looked at Chip. She wasn't smiling. She looked worried.

'Young brother,' she said, 'I'm worried about you. I think you've been trying to fool us.'

Chip looked at her. 'Fool you?' he said.

'There are sick members in this town,' she said; 'do you know that?'

He shook his head.

'Yes,' she said. 'As sick as can be. They cover members' eyes and take them some place, and tell them to slow down and make mistakes and pretend they've lost their interest in sex. They try to make other members as sick as they are. Do you know any such members?'

'No,' Chip said.

'Anna,' the man said, 'I've *watched* him. There's no reason to think there's anything wrong beyond what showed on the tests.' He turned to Chip and said, 'Very easily corrected; nothing for you to think about.'

The woman shook her head. 'No,' she said. 'No, it doesn't

feel right. Please, young brother, you want us to help you, don't you?'

'Nobody told me to make mistakes,' Chip said. 'Why? Why should I?'

The man tapped the report form. 'Look at the enzymological breakdown,' he said to the woman.

'I've looked at it, I've looked at it.'

'He's been badly OT'ed there, there, there, and there. Let's give the data to Uni and get him fixed up again.'

'I want Jesus HL to see him.'

'Why?'

'Because I'm *worried*.'

'I don't know any sick members,' Chip said. 'If I did I would tell my adviser.'

'Yes,' the woman said, 'and why did you want to see him yesterday morning?'

'Yesterday?' Chip said. 'I thought it was my day. I got mixed up.'

'Please, let's go,' the woman said, standing up holding the clipboard.

They left the office and walked down the hallway outside it. The woman put her arm around Chip's shoulders but she didn't smile. The man dropped behind.

They came to the end of the hallway, where there was a door marked 600A with a brown white-lettered plaque on it: *Chief, Chemotherapeutics Division.* They went in, to an anteroom where a member sat behind a desk. The woman doctor told her that they wanted to consult Jesus HL about a diagnostic problem, and the member got up and went out through another door.

'A waste of time all around,' the man said.

The woman said, 'Believe me, I hope so'.

There were two chairs in the anteroom, a bare low table, and *Wei Addressing the Chemotherapists.* Chip decided that if they made him tell he would try not to mention Snowflake's light skin and Lilac's less-slanted-than-normal eyes.

The member came back and held the door open.

They went into a large office. A gaunt grey-haired member in his fifties – Jesus HL – was seated behind a large untidy desk. He nodded to the doctors as they approached, and

81

looked absently at Chip. He waved a hand towards a chair facing the desk. Chip sat down in it.

The woman doctor handed Jesus HL the clipboard. 'This doesn't feel right to me,' she said. 'I'm afraid he's malingering.'

'Contrary to the enzymological evidence,' the other doctor said.

Jesus HL leaned back in his chair and studied the report form. The doctors stood by the side of the desk, watching him. Chip tried to look curious but not concerned. He watched Jesus HL for a moment, and then looked at the desk. Papers of all sorts were piled and scattered on it and lay drifted over an old-style telecomp in a scuffed case. A drink container jammed with pens and rulers stood beside a framed snapshot of Jesus HL, younger, smiling in front of Uni's dome. There were two souvenir paperweights, an unusual square one from CHI61332 and a round one from ARG-20400, neither of them on paper.

Jesus HL turned the clipboard end for end and peeled the form down and read the back of it.

'What I would like to do, Jesus,' the woman doctor said, 'is keep him here overnight and run some of the tests again tomorrow.'

'Wasting—' the man said.

'Or better still,' the woman said, louder, 'question him now under TP.'

'Wasting time and supplies,' the man said.

'What are we, doctors or efficiency analysers?' the woman asked him sharply.

Jesus HL put down the clipboard and looked at Chip. He got up from his chair and came around the side of the desk, the doctors stepping back quickly to let him pass. He came and stood directly in front of Chip's chair, tall and thin, his red-crossed coveralls stained with yellow spots.

He took Chip's hands from the chair arms, turned them over, and looked at the palms, which glistened with sweat.

He let one hand go, and held the wrist of the other, his fingers at the pulse. Chip made himself look up, unconcernedly. Jesus HL looked quizzically at him for a moment and then suspected – no, *knew* – and smiled his knowledge contemptuously. Chip felt hollow, beaten.

Jesus HL took hold of Chip's chin, bent over, and looked closely at his eyes. 'Open your eyes as wide as you can,' he said. His voice was King's. Chip stared at him.

'That's right,' he said. 'Stare at me as if I've said something shocking.' It was *King's voice*, unmistakable. Chip's mouth opened. 'Don't speak, please,' King=Jesus HL said, squeezing Chip's jaw painfully. He stared into Chip's eyes, turned his head to one side and then the other, and then released it and stepped back. He went around the desk and sat down again. He picked up the clipboard, glanced at it, and handed it to the woman doctor, smiling. 'You're mistaken, Anna,' he said. 'You can put your mind at rest. I've seen many members who were malingering; this one isn't. I commend you on your concern, though.' To the man he said, 'She's right, you know, Jesus; we mustn't be efficiency analysers. The Family can afford a little waste where a member's health is involved. What is the Family, after all, except the sum of it's members?'

'Thank you, Jesus,' the woman said, smiling. 'I'm glad I was wrong.'

'Give that data to Uni,' King said, turning and looking at Chip, 'so our brother here can be properly treated from now on.'

'Yes, right away.' The woman beckoned to Chip. He got up from the chair.

They left the office. In the doorway Chip turned. 'Thank you,' he said.

King looked at him from behind his littered desk – only looked, with no smile, no glimmer of friendship. 'Thank Uni,' he said.

Less than a minute after he got back to his room Bob called. 'I just got a report from Medicentre Main,' he said. 'Your treatments have been slightly out of line but from now on they're going to be exactly right.'

'Good,' Chip said.

'This confusion and tiredness you've been feeling will gradually pass away during the next week or so, and then you'll be your old self.'

'I hope so.'

'You will. Listen, do you want me to squeeze you in

tomorrow, Li, or shall we just let it go till next Tuesday?'

'Next Tuesday's all right.'

'Fine,' Bob said. He grinned. 'You know what?' he said. 'You look better already.'

'I feel a little better,' Chip said.

THREE

He felt a little better every day, a little more awake and alert, a little more sure that sickness was what he had had and health was what he was growing towards. By Friday – three days after the examination – he felt the way he usually felt on the day before a treatment. But his last treatment was only a week behind him; three weeks and more lay ahead, spacious and unexplored, before the next one. The slow-down had worked; Bob had been fooled and the treatment reduced. And the next one, on the basis of the examination, would be reduced even further. What wonders of feeling would he be feeling in five, in six weeks' time?

That Friday night, a few minutes after the last chime Snowflake came into his room. 'Don't mind me,' she said, taking off her coveralls. 'I'm just putting a note in your mouthpiece.'

She got into bed with him and helped him off with his pyjamas. Her body to his hands and lips was smooth, pliant, and more rousing than Peace SK's or anyone else's; and his own, as she stroked and kissed and licked it, was more shudderingly reactive than ever before, more strainingly in want. He eased himself into her – deeply, snugly in – and would have driven them both to immediate orgasm, but she slowed him, stopped him, made him draw out and come in again, putting herself into one strange but effective position and then another. For twenty minutes or more they worked and contrived together, keeping as noiseless as they could because of the members beyond the wall and on the floor below.

When they were done and apart she said, 'Well?'

'Well it was top speed, of course,' he said, 'but frankly, from what you said, I expected even more.'

84

'Patience, brother,' she said. 'You're still an invalid. The time will come when you'll look back on this as the night we shook hands.'

He laughed.

'Shh.'

He held her and kissed her. 'What does it say?' he asked. 'The note in my mouthpiece.'

'Sunday night at eleven, the same place as last time.'

'But no bandage.'

'No bandage,' she said.

He would see them all, Lilac and all the others. 'I've been wondering when the next meeting would be,' he said.

'I hear you whooshed through step two like a rocket.'

'Stumbled through it, you mean. I wouldn't have made it at all if not for—' Did she know who King really was? Was it all right to speak of it?

'If not for what?'

'If not for King and Lilac,' he said. 'They came here the night before and prepped me.'

'Well of course,' she said. 'None of us would have made it if not for the capsules and all.'

'I wonder where they get them.'

'I think one of them works in a medicentre.'

'Mm, that would explain it,' he said. She didn't know. Or she knew but didn't know that *he* knew. Suddenly he was annoyed by the need for carefulness that had come between them.

She sat up. 'Listen,' she said, 'it pains me to say this, but don't forget to carry on as usual with your girlfriend. Tomorrow night, I mean.'

'She's got someone new,' he said. 'You're my girlfriend.'

'No I'm not,' she said. 'Not on Saturday nights anyway. Our advisers would wonder why we took someone from a different house. I've got a nice normal Bob down the hall from me, and you find a nice normal Yin or Mary. But if you give her more than a little quick one I'll break your neck.'

'Tomorrow night I won't even be able to give her that.'

'That's all right,' she said, 'you're still supposed to be recovering.' She looked sternly at him. 'Really,' she said, 'you have to remember not to get too passionate, except with me. And to keep a contented smile in place between the first chime and the last. And to work hard at your assignment but not *too* hard. It's just as tricky to *stay* undertreated as it is to get that way.' She lay back down beside him and drew his arm around her. 'Hate,' she said, 'I'd give anything for a smoke now.'

'Is it really so enjoyable?'

'Mm'hmm. Especially at times like this.'

'I'll have to try it.'

They lay talking and caressing each other for a while, and then Snowflake tried to rouse him again – 'Nothing ventured, nothing gained,' she said – but everything she did proved unavailing. She left around twelve or so. 'Sunday at eleven,' she said by the door. 'Congratulations.'

Saturday evening in the lounge Chip met a member named Mary KK whose boyfriend had been transferred to Can earlier in the week. The birth-year part of her nameber was 38, making her twenty-four.

They went to a pre-Marxmas sing in Equality Park. As they sat waiting for the amphitheatre to fill, Chip looked at Mary closely. Her chin was sharp but otherwise she was normal: tan skin, upslanted brown eyes, clipped black hair, yellow coveralls on her slim spare frame. One of her toenails, half covered by sandal strap was discoloured a bluish purple. She sat smiling, watching the opposite side of the amphitheatre.

'Where are you from?' he asked her.

'Rus,' she said.

'What's your classification?'

'One-forty B.'

'Ophthalmologic technician.'

'What do you do?'

She turned to him. 'I attach lenses,' she said. 'In the children's section.'

'Do you enjoy it?'

'Of course.' She looked uncertainly at him. 'Why are you asking me so many questions?' she asked. 'And why are you looking at me so – as if you've never seen a member before?'

'I've never seen *you* before,' he said. 'I want to know you.'

86

'I'm no different from any other member,' she said. 'There's nothing unusual about me.'

'Your chin is a little sharper than normal.'

She drew back, looking hurt and confused.

'I didn't mean to hurt you,' he said. 'I just meant to point out that there is something unusual about you, even if it isn't something important.'

She looked searchingly at him then looked away, at the opposite side of the amphitheatre again. She shook her head. 'I don't understand you,' she said.

'I'm sorry,' he said. 'I was sick until last Tuesday. But my adviser took me to Medicentre Main and they fixed me up fine. I'm getting better now. Don't worry.'

'Well that's good,' she said. After a moment she turned and smiled cheerfully at him. 'I forgive you,' she said.

'Thank you,' he said, suddenly feeling sad for her.

She looked away again. 'I hope we sing "The Freeing of the Masses",' she said.

'We will,' he said.

'I love it,' she said, and smiling, she began to hum it.

He kept looking at her, trying to do so in a normal-seeming way. What she had said was true: she was no different from any other member. What did a sharp chin or a discoloured toenail signify? She was exactly the same as every Mary and Anna and Peace and Yin who had ever been his girlfriend: humble and good, helpful and hard-working. Yet she made him feel sad. Why? And could all the others have done so, had he looked at them closely as he was looking at her, had he listened as closely to what they said?

He looked at the members on the other side of him, at the scores in the tiers below, the scores in the tiers above. They were all like Mary KK, all smiling and ready to sing their favourite Marxmas songs, and all saddening; everyone in the amphitheatre, the hundreds, the thousands, the tens of thousands. Their faces lined the mammoth bowl like tan beads strung away in immeasurable close-laid ovals.

Spotlights struck the gold cross and red sickle at the bowl's centre. Four familiar trumpet notes blasted, and everybody sang:

> One mighty Family,
> A single perfect breed,
> Free of all selfishness,
> Aggressiveness and greed;
>> Each member giv-ing all he has to give
>> And get-ting all he needs to live!

But they weren't a mighty Family, he thought. They were a weak Family, a saddened and pitiable one, dulled by chemicals and dehumanized by bracelets. It was Uni that was mighty.

> One mighty Family,
> A single noble race,
> Sending its sons and daughters
> Bravely into space ...

He sang the words automatically, thinking that Lilac had been right: reduced treatments brought new unhappiness.

Sunday night at eleven he met Snowflake between the buildings on Lower Christ Plaza. He held her and kissed her gratefully, glad of her sexuality and humour and pale skin and bitter tobacco taste – all the things that were she and nobody else. 'Christ and Wei, I'm glad to see you,' he said.

She gave him a tighter hug and smiled happily at him. 'It gets to be a shut-off being with normals, doesn't it?' she said.

'And how,' he said. 'I wanted to kick the soccer team instead of the ball this morning.'

She laughed.

He had been depressed since the sing; now he felt released and happy and taller. 'I found a girlfriend,' he said, 'and guess what; I fucked her without the least bit of trouble.'

'Hate.'

'Not as extensively or as satisfyingly as we did, but with no trouble at all, not twenty-four hours later.'

'I can live without the details.'

He grinned and ran his hands down her sides and clasped her hipbones. 'I think I might even manage to do it again tonight,' he said, teasing her with his thumbs.

'Your ego is growing by leaps and bounds.'

'My everything is.'

'Come on, brother,' she said, prying his hands away and holding on to one, 'we'd better get you indoors before you start singing.'

They went into the plaza and crossed it diagonally. Flags and sagging Marxmas bunting hung motionless above it, dim in the glow of distant walkways. 'Where are we going anyway?' he asked, walking happily. 'Where's the secret meeting place of the diseased corrupters of healthy young members?'

'The Pre-U,' she said.

'The *Museum?*'

'That's right. Can you think of a better place for a group of Uni-cheating abnormals? It's exactly where we belong. Easy,' she said, tugging at his hand; 'don't walk so energetically.'

A member was coming into the plaza from the walkway they were going towards. A briefcase or telecomp was in his hand.

Chip walked more normally alongside Snowflake. The member, coming closer – it was a telecomp he had – smiled and nodded. They smiled and nodded in return as they passed him.

They went down steps and out of the plaza.

'Besides,' Snowflake said, 'it's empty from eight to eight and it's an endless source of pipes and funny costumes and unusual beds.'

'You take things?'

'We leave the beds,' she said. 'But we make use of them now and again. Meeting solemnly in the staff conference room was just for your benefit.'

'What else do you do?'

'Oh, sit around and complain a little. That's Lilac's and Leopard's department mostly. Sex and smoking is enough for me. King does funny versions of some of the TV programmes; wait till you find out how much you can laugh.'

'The making use of the beds,' Chip said; 'is it done on a group basis?'

'Only by two's, dear; we're not *that* pre-U.'

'Who did *you* use them with?'

89

'Sparrow, obviously. Necessity is the mother of et cetera. Poor girl, I feel sorry for her now.'

'Of course you do.'

'I do! Oh well, there's an artificial penis in Nineteenth Century Artifacts. She'll survive.'

'King says we should find a man for her.'

'We should. It would be a much better situation, having four couples.'

'That's what King said.'

As they were crossing the ground floor of the museum – lighting their way through the strange-figured dark with a flashlight that Snowflake had produced – another light struck them from the side and a voice nearby said, 'Hello there!' They started. 'I'm sorry,' the voice said. 'It's me, Leopard.'

Snowflake swung her light on to the twentieth-century car, and a flashlight inside it went off. They went over to the glinting metal vehicle. Leopard, sitting behind the steering wheel, was an old round-faced member wearing a hat with an orange plume. There were several dark brown spots on his nose and cheeks. He put his hand, also spotted, through the car's window frame. 'Congratulations, Chip,' he said. 'I'm glad you came through.'

'Going for a ride?' Snowflake asked.

'I've been for one,' he said. 'To Jap and back. Volvo's out of fuel now. And thoroughly wet too, come to think of it.'

They smiled at him and at each other.

'Fantastic, isn't it?' he said, turning the wheel and working a lever that projected from its shaft. 'The driver was in complete control from start to finish, using both hands and both feet.'

'It must have been awfully bumpy,' Chip said, and Snowflake said, 'Not to mention dangerous.'

'But fun too,' Leopard said. 'It must have been an adventure, really; choosing your destination, figuring out which roads to take you there, gauging your movements in relation to the movements of other cars—'

'Gauging wrong and dying,' Snowflake said.

'I don't think that really happened as often as we're told it did,' Leopard said. 'If it had, they would have made the front parts of the cars much thicker.'

Chip said, 'But that would have made them heavier and they would have gone even slower.'

'Where's Hush?' Snowflake asked.

'Upstairs with Sparrow,' Leopard said. He opened the car's door, and coming out of it with a flashlight in his hand, said, 'They're setting things up. Some more stuff was put in the room.' He cranked the window of the door halfway up and closed the door firmly. A wide brown belt decorated with metal studs was fastened about his coveralls.

'King and Lilac?' Snowflake asked.

'They're around some place.'

Chip thought, *Making use of one of the beds* – as the three of them went on through the museum.

He had thought about King and Lilac a good deal since seeing King and seeing how old he was – fifty-two or -three or even more. He had thought about the difference between the ages of the two – thirty years, surely, at the very least – and about the way King had told him to stay away from Lilac; and about Lilac's large less-slanted-than-normal eyes and her hands that had rested small and warm on his knees as she crouched before him urging him toward greater life and awareness.

They went up the steps of the unmoving central escalator and across the museum's second floor. The two flashlights, Snowflake's and Leopard's, danced over the guns and daggers, the bulbed and wired lamps, the bleeding boxers, the kings and queens in their jewels and fur-trimmed robes, and the three beggars, filthy and crippled, parading their disfigurements and thrusting out their cups. The partition behind the beggars had been slid aside, opening a narrow passageway that extended farther into the building, its first few metres lit by light from a doorway in the left-hand wall. A woman's voice spoke softly. Leopard went on ahead and through the doorway, while Snowflake, standing beside the beggars, sprung pieces of tape from a first-aid-kit cartridge. 'Snowflake's here with Chip,' Leopard said inside the room. Chip laid a piece of tape over his bracelet plaque and rubbed it down firmly.

They went to the doorway and into a tobacco-smelling

stuffiness where an old woman and a young one sat close together on pre-U chairs, with two knives and a heap of brown leaves on a table before them. Hush and Sparrow; they shook Chip's hand and congratulated him. Hush was crinkle-eyed and smiling; Sparrow, large-limbed and embarrassed-looking, her hand hot and moist. Leopard stood by Hush, holding a heat coil in the bowl of a curved black pipe and blowing out smoke around the sides of its stem.

The room, a fairly large one, was a storeroom, its farther reaches filled with a ceiling-high mass of pre-U relics, late and early: machines and furniture and paintings and bundles of clothing; swords and wood-handled implements; a statue of a member with wings, an 'angel'; half a dozen crates, opened, unopened, stencilled IND26110 and pasted at their corners with square yellow stickers. Looking around, Chip said, 'There are enough things here for another museum.'

'All genuine too,' Leopard said. 'Some of the things on display aren't, you know.'

'I didn't.'

A varied lot of chairs and benches had been set about the forward part of the room. Paintings leaned against the walls, and there were cartons of smaller relics and piles of mouldering books. A painting of an enormous boulder caught Chip's eye. He moved a chair to get a full view of it. The boulder, a mountain almost, floated above the earth in a blue sky, meticulously painted and jarring to senses. 'What an odd picture,' he said.

'A lot of them are odd,' Leopard said.

'The ones of Christ,' Hush said, 'show him with a light around his head, and he doesn't look human at all.'

'I've seen those,' Chip said, looking at the boulder, 'but I've never seen anything like this. It's fascinating; real and unreal at the same time.'

'You can't take it,' Snowflake said. 'We can't take anything that might be missed.'

Chip said, 'There's no place I could put it anyway.'

'How do you like being undertreated?' Sparrow asked.

Chip turned. Sparrow looked away, at her hands holding a roll of leaves and a knife. Hush was at the same task, chopping rapidly at a roll of leaves, cutting it into thin shreds that

92

piled before her knife. Snowflake was sitting with a pipe in her mouth; Leopard was holding the heat coil in the bowl of it. 'It's wonderful,' Chip said. 'Literally. Full of wonders. More of them every day. I'm grateful to all of you.'

'We only did what we're told to,' Leopard said, smiling. 'We helped a brother.'

'Not exactly in the approved way,' Chip said.

Snowflake offered him her pipe. 'Are you ready to try a puff?' she asked.

He went to her and took it. The bowl of it was warm, the tobacco in it grey and smoking. He hesitated for a moment, smiled at them watching him, and put the stem to his lips. He sucked briefly at it and blew out smoke. The taste was strong but pleasant, surprisingly so. 'Not bad,' he said. He did it again with more assurance. Some of the smoke went into his throat and he coughed.

Leopard, going smiling to the doorway, said, 'I'll get you one of your own,' and went out.

Chip returned the pipe to Snowflake and, clearing his throat, sat down on a bench of dark worn wood. He watched Hush and Sparrow cutting the tobacco. Hush smiled at him. He said, 'Where do you get the seeds?'

'From the plants themselves,' she said.

'Where did you get the ones you started with?'

'King had them.'

'What did I have?' King asked, coming in, tall and lean and bright-eyed, a gold medallion chain-hung on his coveralled chest. He had Lilac behind him, his hand holding hers. Chip stood up. She looked at him, unusual, dark, beautiful, young.

'The tobacco seeds,' Hush said.

King offered his hand to Chip, smiling warmly. 'It's good to see you here,' he said. Chip shook his hand; its grip was firm and hearty. 'Really good to see a new face in the group,' King said. 'Especially a male one, to help me keep these pre-U women in their proper place!'

'Huh,' Snowflake said.

'It's good to be here,' Chip said, pleased by King's friendliness. His coldness when Chip left his office must have been only a pretence, for the sake, of course, of the onlooking

93

doctors. 'Thank you,' Chip said. 'For everything. Both of you.'

Lilac said, 'I'm very glad, Chip.' Her hand was still held by King's. She was darker than normal, a lovely near-brown touched with rose. Her eyes were large and almost level, her lips pink and soft-looking. She turned away and said, 'Hello, Snowflake.' She drew her hand from King's and went to Snowflake and kissed her cheek.

She was twenty or twenty-one, no more. The upper pockets of her coveralls had something in them, giving her the breasted look of the women Karl had drawn. It was a strange, mysteriously alluring look.

'Are you beginning to feel different now, Chip?' King asked. He was at the table, bending and putting tobacco into the bowl of a pipe.

'Yes, enormously,' Chip said. 'It's everything you said it would be.'

Leopard came in and said, 'Here you are, Chip.' He gave him a yellow thick-bowled pipe with an amber stem. Chip thanked him and tried the feel of it; it was comfortable in his hand and comfortable to his lips. He took it to the table, and King, his gold medallion swinging, showed him the right way to fill it.

Leopard took him through the staff section of the museum, showing him other storerooms, the conference room, and various offices and workrooms. 'It's a good idea,' he said, 'for someone to keep rough track of who goes where during these get-togethers, and then check around later and make sure nothing is conspicuously out of place. The girls could be a little more careful than they are. I generally do it, and when I'm gone perhaps you'll take over the job. Normals aren't quite as unobservant as we'd like them to be.'

'Are you being transferred?' Chip asked.

'Oh no,' Leopard said. 'I'll be dying soon. I'm over sixty-two now, by almost three months. So is Hush.'

'I'm sorry,' Chip said.

'So are we,' Leopard said, 'but nobody lives for ever. Tobacco ashes are a danger, of course, but everyone's good about that. You don't have to worry about the smell; the air conditioning goes on at seven-forty and whips it right out; I stayed one morning and made sure. Sparrow's going to take over the tobacco growing. We dry the leaves right here, in back of the hot-water tank; I'll show you.'

When they got back to the storeroom, King and Snowflake were sitting opposite each other astride a bench, playing intently at a mechanical game of some kind that lay between them. Hush was dozing in her chair and Lilac was crouched at the verge of a mass of relics, taking books one at a time from a carton, looking at them, and putting them in a pile on the floor. Sparrow wasn't there.

'What's that?' Leopard asked.

'New game that came in,' Snowflake said, not looking up.

There were levers that they pressed and released, one for each hand, making little paddles hit a rusted ball back and forth on a rimmed metal board. The paddles, some of them broken, squeaked as they swung. The ball bounded this way and that and came to a stop in a depression at King's end of the board. 'Five!' Snowflake cried. 'There you are brother!'

Hush opened her eyes, looked at them, and closed them again.

'Losing's the same as winning,' King said, lighting his pipe with a metal lighter.

'Like hate it is,' Snowflake said. 'Chip? Come on, you're next.'

'No, I'll watch,' he said smiling.

Leopard declined to play too, and King and Snowflake began another match. At a break in the play, when King had scored a point against Snowflake, Chip said, 'May I see the lighter?' and King gave it to him. A bird in flight was painted on the side of it; a duck, Chip thought. He had seen lighters in museums but had never worked one. He opened the hinged top and pushed his thumb against the ridged wheel. On the second try the wick flamed. He closed the lighter, looked at it all over, and at the next break handed it back to King.

He watched them play for another few moments and then moved away. He went over to the mass of relics and looked at it, and then moved nearer to Lilac. She looked up at him and smiled, putting a book on one of several piles beside her. 'I keep hoping to find one in the language,' she said, 'but they're always in the old ones.'

He crouched and picked up the book she had just put down. On the spine of it were small letters: *Bädda fördöd*. 'Hmm,' he said, shaking his head. He glanced through the old brown pages, at strange words and phrases: *allvarlig, lögnerska, dök ner på brickorna*. The double dots and little circles were over many of the letters.

'Some of them are enough like the language so that you can understand a word or two,' she said, 'but some of them are – well look at this one.' She showed him a book on which backward N's and rectangular open-bottomed characters were mixed in with ordinary P's and E's and O's. 'Now what does *that* mean?' she said, putting it down.

'It would be interesting to find one we could read,' he said, looking at her cheek's rose-brown smoothness.

'Yes, it would,' she said, 'but I think they were screened before they were sent here and that's why we can't.'

'You think they were screened?'

'There ought to be lots of them in the language,' she said. 'How could it have *become* the language if it wasn't the one most widely used?'

'Yes, of course,' he said. 'You're right.'

'I keep hoping, though,' she said, 'that there was a slip in the screening.' She frowned at a book and put it on a pile.

Her filled pockets stirred with her movements, and suddenly they looked to Chip like empty pockets lying against round breasts, breasts like the ones Karl had drawn; the breasts, almost, of a pre-U woman. It was possible, considering her abnormal darkness and the various physical abnormalities of the lot of them. He looked at her face again, so as not to embarrass her if she really had them.

'I thought I was double-checking this carton,' she said, 'but I have a funny feeling I'm triple-checking it.'

'But *why* should the books have been screened?' he asked her.

She paused, with her dark hands hanging empty and her elbows on her knees, looking at him gravely with her large, level eyes. 'I think we've been taught things that aren't true,' she said. 'About the way life was before the Unification. In the *late* pre-U, I mean, not the early.'

'What things?'

'The violence, the aggressiveness, the greed, the hostility.

There was some of it, I suppose, but I can't believe there was nothing else, and that's what we're taught, really. And the "bosses" punishing the "workers", and all the sickness and alcohol=drinking and starvation and self-destruction. Do *you* believe it?'

He looked at her. 'I don't know,' he said. 'I haven't thought much about it.'

'I'll tell you what *I* don't believe,' Snowflake said. She had risen from the bench, the game with King evidently finished. 'I don't believe that they cut off the baby boys' foreskins,' she said. 'In the early pre-U, maybe – in the early, *early* pre-U – but not in the late; it's just too incredible. I mean, they had *some* kind of intelligence, didn't they?'

'It's incredible, all right,' King said, hitting his pipe against his palm, 'but I've seen photographs. Alleged photographs, anyway.'

Chip shifted around and sat on the floor. 'What do you mean?' he said. 'Can photographs be – not genuine?'

'Of course they can,' Lilac said. 'Take a close look at some of the ones inside. Parts of them have been drawn in. And parts have been drawn out.' She began putting books back into the carton.

'I had no idea it was possible,' Chip said.

'It is with the flat ones,' King said.

'What we're probably given,' Leopard said – he was sitting in a gilded chair, toying with the orange plume of the hat he had worn – 'is a mixture of truth and untruth. It's anybody's guess as to which part is which and how much there is of each.'

'Couldn't we study these books and learn the languages?' Chip asked. 'One would be all we'd really need.'

'For what?' Snowflake asked.

'To find out,' he said. 'What's true and what isn't.'

'I tried it,' Lilac said.

'She certainly did,' King said to Chip, smiling. 'A while back she wasted more nights than I care to remember beating her pretty head against one of those nonsensical jumbles. Don't *you* do it, Chip; I beg you.'

'Why not?' Chip asked. 'Maybe I'll have better luck.'

'And suppose you do?' King asked. 'Suppose you decipher a language and read a few books in it and find out that we *are* taught things that are untrue. Maybe *everything*'s untrue. Maybe life in AD 2000 was one endless orgasm, with everyone choosing the right classification and helping his brothers and loaded to the ears with love and health and life's necessities. So what? You'll still be right here, in 162 Y.U., with a bracelet and an adviser and a monthly treatment. You'll only be unhappier. We'll *all* be unhappier.'

Chip frowned and looked at Lilac. She was packing books into the carton, not looking at him. He looked back at King and sought words. 'It would still be worth knowing,' he said. 'Being happy or unhappy – is that really the most important thing? Knowing the truth would be a different kind of happiness – a more satisfying kind, I think, even if it turned out to be a sad kind.'

'A sad kind of happiness?' King said, smiling. 'I don't see that at all.' Leopard looked thoughtful.

Snowflake, gesturing to Chip to get up, said, 'Come on, there's something I want to show you.'

He climbed to his feet. 'But we'd probably only find that things have been exaggerated,' he said; 'that there was hunger but not so *much* hunger, aggressiveness but not so *much* aggressiveness. Maybe some of the minor things have been made up, like the foreskin-cutting and the flag-worship.'

'If you feel that way, then there's *certainly* no point in bothering,' King said. 'Do you have any idea what a job it would be? It would be staggering.'

Chip shrugged. 'It would be good to *know*, that's all,' he said. He looked at Lilac; she was putting the last few books into the carton.

'Come on,' Snowflake said, and took his arm. 'Save us some tobacco, you mems.'

They went out and into the dark of the exhibit hall. Snowflake's flashlight lit their way. 'What is it?' Chip asked. 'What do you want to show me?'

'What do you think?' she said. 'A bed. Certainly not more books.'

They generally met two nights a week, Sundays and Woods or Thursdays. They smoked and talked and idled with relics and exhibits. Sometimes Sparrow sang songs that she wrote, accompanying herself on a lap-held instrument whose strings at her fingers made pleasing antique music. The songs were short and sad, about children who lived and died on starships, lovers who were transferred, the eternal sea. Sometimes King re-enacted the evening's TV, comically mocking a lecturer on climate control or a fifty-member chorus singing 'My Bracelet'. Chip and Snowflake made use of the seventeenth-century bed and the nineteenth-century sofa, the early pre-U farm wagon and the late Pre-U plastic rug. On nights between meetings they sometimes went to one or the other's room. The nameber on Snowflake's door was Anna PY24A9155; the 24, which Chip couldn't resist working out, made her thirty-eight, older than he had thought her to be.

Day by day his senses sharpened and his mind grew more alert and restless. His treatment caught him back and dulled him, but only for a week or so; then he was awake again, alive again. He went to work on the language Lilac had tried to decipher. She showed him the books she had worked from and the lists she had made. *Momento* was moment; *silenzio*, silence. She had several pages of easily recognized translations; but there were words in the books' every sentence that could only be guessed at and the guesses tried elsewhere. Was *allora* 'then' or 'already'? What were *quale* and *sporse* and *rimanesse*? He worked with the books for an hour or so at every meeting. Sometimes she leaned over his shoulder and looked at what he was doing – said 'Oh, of course!' or 'Couldn't that be one of the days of the week?' – but most of the time she stayed near King, filling his pipe for him and listening while he talked. King watched Chip working and, reflected in glass panes of pre-U furniture, smiled at the others and raised his eyebrows.

Chip saw Mary KK on Saturday nights and Sunday afternoons. He acted normal with her, smiled through the Amusement Gardens and fucked her simply and without passion. He acted normal at his assignment following the established procedures. Acting normal began to irritate him, more and more as week followed week.

In July, Hush died. Sparrow wrote a song about her, and when Chip returned to his room after the meeting at which she had sung it, she and Karl (Why hadn't he thought of him sooner?) suddenly came together in his mind. Sparrow was large and awkward but lovely when she sang, twenty-five or so and lonely. Karl presumably had been 'cured' when Chip 'helped' him, but might he not have had the strength or the genetic capacity or the whatever-it-was to resist the cure, at least to a degree? Like Chip he was a 663; there was a chance that he was right there at the Institute somewhere, an ideal prospect for being led into the group and an ideal match for Sparrow. It was certainly worth a try. What a pleasure it would be to *really* help Karl! Undertreated, he would draw – well what *wouldn't* he draw? – pictures such as no one had ever imagined! As soon as he got up the next morning he got his last nameber book out of his take-along kit, touched the phone, and read out Karl's nameber. But the screen stayed blank and the phone voice apologized; the member he had called was out of reach.

Bob RO asked him about it a few days later, just as he was getting up from the chair. 'Oh, say,' Bob said, 'I meant to ask you; how come you wanted to call this Karl WL?'

'Oh,' Chip said, standing by the chair. 'I wanted to see how he was. Now that I'm all right, I guess I wanted to be sure that everyone else is.'

'Of course he is,' Bob said. 'It's an odd thing to do, after so many years.'

'I just happened to think of him,' Chip said.

He acted normal from the first chime to the last and met with the group twice a week. He kept working at the language – Italiano, it was called – although he suspected that King was right and there was no point in it. It was something to do, though, and seemed more worthwhile than playing with mechanical toys. And once in a while it brought Lilac to him, leaning over to look, with one hand on the leather-topped table he worked at and the other on the back of his chair. He could smell her – it wasn't his imagination; she actually smelled of flowers – and he could look at her dark cheek and neck and the chest of her coveralls pushed taut by two mobile round protrusions. They were breasts. They were definitely breasts.

FOUR

One night late in August, while looking for more books in
Italiano, he found one in a different language whose title,
Vers l'avenir, was similar to the Italiano words *verso* and
avvenire and apparently meant *Towards the Future*. He
opened the book and thumbed its pages, and *Wei Li Chun*
caught his eye, printed at the tops of twenty or thirty of
them. Other names were at the tops of other clusters of pages,
Mario Sofik, A. F. Liebman. The book, he realized, was a
collection of short pieces by various writers, and two of the
pieces were indeed by Wei. The title of one of them, *Le pas
prochain en avant*, he recognized (*pas* would be *passo*; *avant*,
avanti) as 'The Next Step Forward', in Part One of *Wei's
Living Wisdom*.

The value of what he had found, as he began to perceive
it, held him motionless. Here in this small brown book, its
cover clinging by threads, were twelve or fifteen pre-U-
language pages of which he had an exact translation waiting
in his night-table drawer. Thousands of words, of verbs in
their bafflingly changing forms; instead of guessing and
groping as he had done for his near-useless fragments of
Italiano, he could gain a solid footing in this second language
in a matter of hours!

He said nothing to the others; slipped the book into his
pocket and joined them; filled his pipe as if nothing were out
of the ordinary. *Le pas*-whatever-it-was-*avant* might not be
'The Next Step Forward' after all. But it *was*, it had to be.

It was; he saw it as soon as he compared the first few
sentences. He sat up in his room all that night, carefully
reading and comparing, with one finger at the lines in the
pre-U-language and another at the lines translated. He
worked his way twice through the fourteen-page essay, and
then began making alphabetical word lists.

The next night he was tired and slept, but the following
night, after a visit from Snowflake, he stayed up and worked
again.

He began going to the museum on nights between meetings.

There he could smoke while he worked, could look for other Français books – Français was the language's name; the hook below the C was a mystery – and could roam the halls by flashlight. On the third floor he found a map from 1951, artfully patched in several places, where Eur was 'Europe', with the division called 'France' where Français had been used, and all its strangely and appealingly named cities: 'Paris' and 'Nantes' and 'Lyon' and 'Marseille'.

Still he said nothing to the others. He wanted to confound King with a language fully mastered, and delight Lilac. At meetings he no longer worked at Italiano. One night Lilac asked him about it, and he said, truthfully, that he had given up trying to unravel it. She turned away, looking disappointed, and he was happy, knowing the surprise he was preparing for her.

Saturday nights were wasted, lying by Mary KK, and meeting nights were wasted too; although now, with Hush dead, Leopard sometimes didn't come, and when he didn't, Chip stayed on at the museum to straighten up and stayed still later to work.

In three weeks he could read Français rapidly, with only a word here and there that was indecipherable. He found several Français books. He read one whose title, translated, was *The Purple Sickle Murders*; and another, *The Pygmies of the Equatorial Forest*; and another, *Father Goriot*.

He waited until a night when Leopard wasn't there, and then he told them. King looked as if he had heard bad news. His eyes measured Chip and his face was still and controlled, suddenly older and more gaunt. Lilac looked as if she had been given a longed-for gift. 'You've read *books* in it?' she said. Her eyes were wide and shining and her lips stayed parted. But neither one's reaction could give Chip the pleasure he had looked forward to. He was grave with the weight of what he now knew.

'Three of them,' he said to Lilac. 'And I'm halfway through a fourth.'

'That's marvellous, Chip!' Snowflake said. 'What did you keep it a secret for?' And Sparrow said, 'I didn't think it was possible.'

'Congratulations, Chip,' King said, taking out his pipe. 'It's

102

an achievement, even with the help of the essay. You've really put me in my place.' He looked at his pipe, working the stem of it to get it straight. 'What have you found out so far?' he asked. 'Anything interesting?'

Chip looked at him. 'Yes,' he said. 'A lot of what we're told is true. There was crime and violence and stupidity and hunger. There was a lock on every door. Flags were important, and the borders of territories. Children waited for their parents to die so they could inherit their money. The waste of labour and material was fantastic.'

He looked at Lilac and smiled consolingly at her; her longed-for gift was breaking. 'But with it all,' he said, 'members seem to have felt stronger and happier than we do. Going where they wanted, doing what they wanted, "earning" things, "owning" things, choosing, always choosing – it made them somehow more *alive* than members today.'

King reached for tobacco. 'Well that's pretty much what you expected to find, isn't it?' he said.

'Yes, pretty much,' Chip said. 'And there's one thing more.'

'What's that?' Snowflake asked.

Looking at King, Chip said, 'Hush didn't have to die.'

King looked at him. The others did too. 'What are you talking about?' King said, his fingers stopped in pipe-filling.

'Don't you know?' Chip asked him.

'No,' he said. 'I don't understand.'

'What do you mean?' Lilac asked.

'Don't you know, King?' Chip said.

'No,' King said. 'What are – I haven't the faintest idea of what you're getting at. How could pre-U books tell you anything about *Hush*? And why should I be expected to know what it is if they could?'

'Living to the age of sixty-two,' Chip said, 'is no marvel of chemistry and breeding and totalcakes. Pygmies of the equatorial forests, whose life was hard even by pre-U standards, lived to be fifty-five and sixty. A member named Goriot lived to seventy-three and nobody thought it was terribly unusual, and that was in the early nineteenth century. Members lived to their eighties, even to their nineties!'

'That's impossible,' King said. 'The body wouldn't last that long; the heart, the lungs—'

'The book I'm reading now,' Chip said, 'is about some members who lived in 1991. One of them has an artificial heart. He gave money to doctors and they put it into him in place of his own.'

'Oh for—' King said. 'Are you sure you really understand that Frandaze?'

'Français,' Chip said. 'Yes, I'm positive. Sixty-two isn't a long life; it's a relatively short one.'

'But that's when we *die*,' Sparrow said. 'Why *do* we, if it isn't – when we have to?'

'We *don't* die ...' Lilac said, and looked from Chip to King.

'That's right,' Chip said. 'We're *made* to die. By Uni. It's programmed for efficiency, for efficiency first, last, and always. It's scanned all the data in its memory banks – which aren't the pretty pink toys you've seen if you've made the visit; they're ugly steel monsters – and it's decided that sixty-two is the optimum dying time, better than sixty-one or sixty-three and better than bothering with artificial hearts. If sixty-two isn't a new high in longevity that we're lucky to have reached – and it *isn't*, I *know* it isn't – then that's the only answer. Our replacements are trained and waiting, and off we go, a few months early or late so that everything isn't too suspiciously tidy. Just in case anyone is sick enough to be able to *feel* suspicion.'

'Christ, Marx, Wei,' Snowflake said.

'Yes,' Chip said. 'Especially Wood and Wei.'

'King?' Lilac said.

'I'm staggered,' King said. 'I see now, Chip, why you thought I'd know.' To Snowflake and Sparrow he said, 'Chip knows that I'm in chemotherapy.'

'And don't you know?' Chip said.

'I don't.'

'Is there or is there not a poison in the treatment units?' Chip asked. 'You *must* know *that*.'

'Gently, brother, I'm an old member,' King said. 'There's no poison as such, no; but almost any compound in the set-up *could* cause death if too much of it were infused.'

'And you don't know how much of the compounds are infused when a member hits sixty-two?'

'No,' King said. 'Treatments are formulated by impulses

104

that go directly from Uni to the units, and there's no way of monitoring them. I can *ask* Uni, of course, what any particular treatment consisted of or is going to consist of, but if what you're saying is true' – he smiled – 'it's going to lie to me, isn't it?'

Chip drew a breath, and let it go. 'Yes,' he said.

'And when a member dies,' Lilac said, 'the symptoms are the ones of old age?'

'They're the ones I was *taught* are of old age,' King said. 'They could very well be the ones of something entirely different.' He looked at Chip. 'Have you found any medical books in that language?' he asked.

'No,' Chip said.

King took out his lighter and thumbed it open. 'It's possible,' he said. 'It's very possible. It never even crossed my mind. Members live to sixty-two; it used to be less, some day it'll be more; we have two eyes, two ears, one nose. Established facts.' He lit the lighter and put the flame to his pipe.

'It *must* be true,' Lilac said. 'It's the final logical end of Wood's and Wei's thinking. Control everyone's life and you eventually get around to controlling everyone's death.'

'It's awful,' Sparrow said. 'I'm glad Leopard's not here. Can you imagine how he'd feel? Not only Hush, but he himself any day now. We mustn't say anything to him; let him think it's going to happen naturally.'

Snowflake looked bleakly at Chip. 'What did you have to tell *us* for?' she said.

King said, 'So that we can experience a happy kind of sadness. Or was it a sad kind of happiness, Chip?'

'I thought you would want to know,' he said.

'Why?' Snowflake said. 'What can we do about it? Complain to our advisers?'

'I'll tell you one thing we can do,' Chip said. 'Start getting more members into this group.'

'Yes!' Lilac said.

'And where do we find them?' King said. 'We can't just grab any Karl or Mary off the walkways, you know.'

Chip said, 'Do you mean to say that in your assignment you can't pull a print-out on local members with abnormal tendencies?'

'Not without giving Uni a good reason, I can't,' King said. 'One fuzzy note, brother, and the doctors will be examining *me*. Which would also mean, incidentally, that they'd be *re*examining *you*.'

'Other abnormals are around,' Sparrow said. '*Somebody* writes "Fight Uni" on the backs of buildings.'

'We've got to figure out a way to get *them* to find *us*,' Chip said. 'A signal of some kind.'

'And then what?' King said. 'What do we do when we're twenty or thirty strong? Claim a group visit and blow Uni to pieces?'

'The idea has occurred to me,' Chip said.

'Chip!' Snowflake said. Lilac stared at him.

'First of all,' King said, smiling, 'it's impregnable. And second of all, most of us have already been there, so we wouldn't be granted another visit. Or would we *walk* from here to Eur? And what would we do with the world once everything was uncontrolled – once the factories were clogged and the cars had crashed and the chimes had all stopped chiming – get really pre-U and say a prayer for it?'

'If we could find members who know computer and microwave theory,' Chip said, 'members who know *Uni*, maybe we could work out a way to change its programming.'

'If we could find those members,' King said. 'If we could get them with us. If we could get to Eur-zip-one. Don't you see what you're asking for? The impossible, that's all. *This* is why I told you not to waste time with those books. There's nothing we can do about *anything*. This is Uni's world, will you get that through your head? It was handed over to it fifty years ago, and it's going to do its assignment – spread the fighting Family through the fighting universe – and *we're* going to do *our* assignments, including dying at sixty-two and not missing TV. This is it right here, brother: all the freedom we can hope for – a pipe and a few jokes and some extra fucking. Let's not lose what we've got, all right?'

'But if we get other—'

'Sing a song, Sparrow,' King said.

'I don't want to,' she said.

'Sing a song!'

'All right, I will.'

Chip glared at King and got up and strode from the room.

He strode into the dark exhibit hall, banged his hip against hardness, and strode on, cursing. He went far from the passageway and the storeroom; stood rubbing his forehead and rocking on the balls of his feet before the jewel-glinting kings and queens, mute darker-than-darkness watchers. 'King,' he said. 'Thinks he really is, the brother-fighting ...'

Sparrow's singing came faintly, and the string-tinkle of her pre-U instrument. And footsteps, coming closer. 'Chip?' It was Snowflake. He didn't turn. His arm was touched. 'Come on back,' she said.

'Leave me alone, will you?' he said. 'Just leave me alone for a couple of minutes.'

'Come on,' she said. 'You're being childish.'

'Look,' he said, turning to her. 'Go listen to Sparrow, will you? Go smoke your pipe.'

She was silent, and then said, 'All right,' and went away.

He turned back to the kings and queens, breathing deeply. His hip hurt and he rubbed it. It was infuriating the way King cut off his every idea, made everyone do exactly as he—

She was coming back. He started to tell her to get the hate away but checked himself. He took a clenched-teeth breath and turned around.

It was King coming towards him, his grey hair and coveralls catching the dim glow from the passageway. He came close and stopped. They looked at each other, and King said, 'I didn't intend to speak quite that sharply.'

'How come you haven't taken one of these crowns?' Chip asked. 'And a robe. Just that medallion – hate, that's not enough for a real pre-U king.'

King stayed silent for a moment, and then said, 'My apologies.'

Chip drew a breath and held it, then let it go. 'Every member we can get to join us,' he said, 'would mean new ideas, new information we can draw on, possibilities that maybe we haven't thought of.'

'New risks too,' King said. 'Try to see it from my viewpoint.'

'I can't,' Chip said. 'I'd rather go back to full treatments than settle for just this.'

' "Just this" seems very nice to a member of my age.'

'You're twenty or thirty years closer to sixty-two than I

107

am; *you* should be the one who wants to change things.'

'If change were possible, maybe I would be,' King said. 'But chemotherapy plus computerization equals no change.'

'Not necessarily,' Chip said.

'It does,' King said, 'and I don't want to see "just this" go down the drain. Even your coming here on off nights is an added risk. But don't take offence' – he raised a hand – 'I'm not telling you to stay away.'

'I'm not going to,' Chip said; and then, 'Don't worry, I'm careful.'

'Good,' King said. 'And we'll go on carefully looking for abnormals. Without signals.' He held out his hand.

After a moment Chip shook it.

'Come on back in now,' King said. 'The girls are upset.'

Chip went with him towards the passageway.

'What was that you said before, about the memory banks being "steel monsters"?' King asked.

'That's what they are,' Chip said. 'Enormous frozen blocks, thousands of them. My grandfather showed them to me when I was a boy. He helped build Uni.'

'The brother-fighter.'

'No, he was sorry. He wished he hadn't. Christ and Wei, if he were alive he'd be a marvellous member to have with us.'

The following night Chip was sitting in the storeroom reading and smoking when 'Hello, Chip,' Lilac said, and was standing in the doorway with a flashlight at her side.

Chip stood up, looking at her.

'Do you mind my interrupting you?' she asked.

'Of course not, I'm glad to see you,' he said. 'Is King here?'

'No,' she said.

'Come on in,' he said.

She stayed in the doorway. 'I want you to teach me that language,' she said.

'I'd like to,' he said. 'I was going to ask you if you wanted the lists. Come on in.'

He watched her come in, then found his pipe in his hand, put it down, and went to the mass of relics. Catching the legs of one of the chairs they used, he tossed it right side up and brought it back to the table. She had pocketed her flashlight and was looking at the open pages of the book he had been reading. He put the chair down, moved his chair to the side, and put the second chair next to it.

She turned up the front part of the book and looked at its cover.

'It means *A Motive for Passion*,' he said. 'Which is fairly obvious. Most of it isn't.'

She looked at the open pages again. 'Some of it looks like Italiano,' she said.

'That's how I got on to it,' he said. He held the back of the chair he had brought for her.

'I've been sitting all day,' she said. 'You sit down. Go ahead.'

He sat and got his folded lists out from under the stacked Français books. 'You can keep these as long as you want,' he said, opening them and spreading them out on the table. 'I know it all pretty well by heart now.'

He showed her the way the verbs fell into groups, following different patterns of change to express time and subject, and the way the adjectives took one form or another depending on the nouns they were applied to. 'It's complicated,' he said, 'but once you get the hang of it, translation's fairly easy.' He translated a page of *A Motive for Passion* for her. Victor, a trader in shares of various industrial companies – the member who had had the artificial heart put into him – was rebuking his wife, Caroline, for having been unfriendly to an influential lawmaker.

'It's fascinating,' Lilac said.

'What amazes me,' Chip said, 'is how many non-productive members there were. These share-traders and lawmakers; the soldiers and policemen, bankers, tax-gatherers ...'

'They weren't non-productive,' she said. 'They didn't produce *things* but they made it possible for members to live the way they did. They produced the *freedom*, or at least they maintained it.'

'Yes,' he said. 'I suppose you're right.'

'I am,' she said, and moved restlessly from the table.

He thought for a moment, 'Pre-U members,' he said, 'gave up efficiency – in exchange for freedom. And we've done the reverse.'

'*We* haven't done it,' Lilac said. 'It was done *for* us.' She turned and faced him, and said, 'Do you think it's possible that the incurables are still alive?'

He looked at her.

'That their descendants have survived somehow,' she said, 'and have a – a society somewhere? On an island or in some area that the Family isn't using?'

'Wow,' he said, and rubbed his forehead. 'Sure it's possible,' he said. 'Members survived on islands *before* the Unification; why not after?'

'That's what *I* think,' she said, coming back to him. 'There have been five generations since the last ones—'

'Battered by disease and hardship—'

'But reproducing at will!'

'I don't know about a *society*,' he said, 'but there might be a colony—'

'A city,' she said. 'They were the smart ones, the strong ones.'

'What an idea,' he said.

'It's possible, isn't it?' She was leaning towards him, hands on the table, her large eyes questioning, her cheeks flushed to a rosier darkness.

He looked at her. 'What does King think?' he asked. She drew back a bit and he said, 'As if I can't guess.'

She was angry suddenly, fierce-eyed. 'You were *terrible* to him last night!' she said.

'Terrible? *I* was? To *him*?'

'Yes!' She whirled from the table. 'You questioned him as if you were— How could you even *think* he would know about Uni killing us and not tell us?'

'I still think he knew.'

She faced him angrily. 'He didn't!' she said. 'He doesn't keep secrets from me!'

'What are you, his adviser?'

'Yes!' she said. 'That's *exactly* what I am, in case you want to know.'

'You're not,' he said.

'I am.'

'Christ and Wei,' he said. 'You really are? You're an adviser? That's the *last classification* I would have thought of. How *old* are you?'

'Twenty-four.'

110

'And you're *his?*'

She nodded.

He laughed. 'I decided that you worked in the gardens,' he said. 'You smell of flowers, do you know that? You really do.'

'I wear perfume,' she said.

'You *wear* it?'

'The perfume of flowers, in a liquid. King made it for me.'

He stared at her. 'Parfum!' he said, slapping the open book before him. 'I thought it was some kind of germicide; she put it in her bath. Of course!' He groped among the lists, took up his pen, crossed out and wrote. 'Stupid,' he said. '*Parfum* equals *perfume*. Flowers in a liquid. How did he do *that?*'

'Don't accuse him of deceiving us.'

'All right, I won't.' He put the pen down.

'Everything we've got,' she said, 'we owe to him.'

'What is it though?' he said. 'Nothing – unless we use it to try for more. And he doesn't seem to want us to.'

'He's more sensible than we are.'

He looked at her, standing a few metres away from him before the mass of relics. 'What would you do,' he asked, 'if we somehow found that there *is* a city of incurables?'

Her eyes stayed on his. 'Get to it,' she said.

'And live on plants and animals?'

'If necessary.' She glanced at the book, moved her head towards it. 'Victor and Caroline seem to have enjoyed their dinner.'

He smiled and said, 'You really are a pre-U woman, aren't you?'

She said nothing.

'Would you let me see your breasts?' he asked.

'What for?' she said.

'I'm curious, that's all.'

She pulled open the top of her coveralls and held the two sides apart. Her breasts were rose-brown soft-looking cones that stirred with her breathing, taut on their upper surfaces and rounded below. Their tips, blunt and pink, seemed to contract and grow darker as he looked at them. He felt oddly aroused, as if he were being caressed.

'They're nice,' he said.

'I know they are,' she said, closing her coveralls and pressing the closure. 'That's something else I owe King. I used to think I was the ugliest member of the entire Family.'

'You?'

'Until he convinced me I wasn't.'

'All right,' he said, 'you owe King very much. We all do. What have you come to *me* for?'

'I told you,' she said. 'To learn that language.'

'Cloth,' he said, getting up. 'You want me to start looking for places the Family isn't using, for signs that your "city" exists. Because I'll do it and he won't; because I'm not "sensible", or old, or content to make fun of TV.'

She started for the door but he caught her by the shoulder and pushed her around. 'Stay here!' he said. She looked frightenedly at him and he took hold of her jaw and kissed her mouth; clamped her head in both his hands and pushed his tongue against her shut teeth. She pressed at his chest and wrenched her head. He thought she would stop, give in and take the kiss, but she didn't; she kept struggling with increasing vigour, and finally he let go and she pushed away from him.

'That's – that's *terrible*!' she said. 'Forcing me! That's – I've never been *held* that way!'

'I love you,' he said.

'Look at me, I'm shaking,' she said. 'Wei Li Chun, is *that* how you love, by becoming an animal? That's *awful*!'

'A human,' he said, 'like you.'

'No,' she said. 'I wouldn't hurt anyone, hold anyone that way!' She held her jaw and moved it.

'How do you think incurables kiss?' he said.

'Like humans, not like animals.'

'I'm sorry,' he said. 'I love you.'

'Good,' she said. 'I love you too – the way I love Leopard and Snowflake and Sparrow.'

'That's not what I mean,' he said.

'But it's what I mean,' she said, looking at him. She went sideways to the doorway and said, 'Don't do that again. That's terrible!'

'Do you want the lists?' he asked.

She looked as if she was going to say no, hesitated, and then said, 'Yes. That's what I came for.'

He turned and gathered the lists on the table, folded them

together, and took *Père Goriot* from the stack of books. She came over and he gave them to her.

'I didn't mean to hurt you,' he said.

'All right,' she said. 'Just don't do it again.'

'I'll look for places the Family isn't using,' he said. 'I'll go over the maps at the MFA and see if—'

'I've done that,' she said.

'Carefully?'

'As carefully as I could.'

'I'll do it again,' he said. 'It's the only way to begin. Millimetre by millimetre.'

'All right,' she said.

'Wait a second, I'm going now too.'

She waited while he put away his smoking things and got the room back the way it belonged, and then they went out together through the exhibit hall and down the escalator.

'A city of incurables,' he said.

'It's possible,' she said.

'It's worth looking for anyway,' he said.

They went out on to the walkway.

'Which way do you go?' he asked.

'West,' she said.

'I'll go a few blocks with you.'

'No,' she said. 'Really, the longer you're out, the more chances there are for someone to see you not touching.'

'I touch the rim of the scanner and block it with my body. Very tricky.'

'No,' she said. 'Please, go your own way.'

'All right,' he said. 'Goodnight.'

'Goodnight.'

He put his hand on her shoulder and kissed her cheek.

She didn't move away; she was tense and waiting under his hand.

He kissed her lips. They were warm and soft, slightly parted, and she turned and walked away.

'Lilac,' he said, and went after her.

She turned and said, 'No. Please, Chip, go,' and turned and walked away again.

He stood uncertainly. Another member was in the distance, coming towards them.

He watched her go, hating her, loving her.

FIVE

Evening after evening he ate quickly (but not *too* quickly), then railed to the Museum of the Family's Achievements and studied its maze of ceiling-high illuminated maps until the ten-of-TV closing. One night he went there after the last chime – an hour-and-a-half walk – but found that the maps were unreadable by flashlight, their markings lost in glare; and he hesitated to put on their internal lights, which, tied in as they seemed to be with the lighting of the entire hall, might have produced a Uni-alerting overdraft of power. One Sunday he took Mary KK there, sent her off to see the Universe of Tomorrow exhibit, and studied the maps for three hours straight.

He found nothing: no island without its city or industrial installation; no mountaintop that wasn't spacewatch or climatonomy centre; no square kilometre of land – or of ocean floor, for that matter – that wasn't being mined or harvested or used for factories or houses or airports or parkland by the Family's eight billion. The gold-lettered legend suspended at the entrance of the map area – *The Earth Is Our Heritage; We Use It Wisely and Without Waste* – seemed true, so true that there was no place left for even the smallest non-Family community.

Leopard died and Sparrow sang. King sat silently, picking at the gears of a pre-U gadget, and Snowflake wanted more sex.

Chip said to Lilac, 'Nothing. Nothing at all.'

'There must have been hundreds of little colonies to begin with,' she said. 'One of them *must* have survived.'

'Then it's half a dozen members in a cave somewhere,' he said.

'Please, keep looking,' she said. 'You can't have checked *every* island.'

He thought about it, sitting in the dark in the twentieth-century car, holding its steering wheel, moving its different knobs and levers; and the more he thought about it, the less

114

possible a city or even a colony of incurables came to seem. Even if he had overlooked an unused area on the maps, could a community exist without Uni learning of it? People made marks on their environment; a thousand people, even a hundred, would raise an area's temperature, soil its streams with their wastes, and its air perhaps with their primitive fires. The land or sea for kilometres around would be affected by their presence in a dozen detectable ways.

So Uni would have long since known of the theoretical city's existence, and having known, would have – done what? Dispatched doctors and advisers and portable treatment units; would have 'cured' the incurables and made them into 'healthy' members.

Unless of course, they had defended themselves ... Their ancestors had fled the Family soon after the Unification, when treatments were optional, or later, when they were compulsory but not yet at present-day effectiveness; surely some of *those* incurables must have defended their retreats by force, with deadly weapons. Wouldn't they have handed on the practice, and the weapons too, to succeeding generations? What would Uni do today, in 162, facing an armed, defensive community with an unarmed, unaggressive Family? What would it have done five or twenty-five years ago, detecting the signs of it? Let it be? Leave its inhabitants to their 'sickness' and their few square kilometres of the world? Spray the city with LPK? But what if the city's weapons could bring down planes? Would Uni decide in its cold steel blocks that the cost of the 'cure' outweighed its usefulness?

He was two days from a treatment, his mind as active as it ever got. He wished it could get still more active. He felt that there was something he wasn't thinking of, just beyond the rim of his awareness.

If Uni let the city be, rather than sacrifice members and time and technology to the 'helping' of it – then *what*? There was *something else*, a next idea to be picked and pried out of that one.

He called the medicentre on Thursday, the day before his treatment, and complained of a toothache. He was offered a Friday-morning appointment, but he said that he was coming in on Saturday morning for his treatment and couldn't he catch two birds with one net? It wasn't a severe tooth-ache, just a slight throb.

He was given an appointment for Saturday morning at 8.15.

Then he called Bob RO and told him that he had a dental appointment at 8.15 on Saturday. Did he think it would be a good idea if he got his treatment then too? Catch two birds with one net.

'I guess you might as well,' Bob said. 'Hold on' – and switched on his telecomp. 'You're Li RM—'

'Thirty-five M4419.'

'Right,' Bob said, tapping keys.

Chip sat and watched unconcernedly.

'Saturday morning at 8.05,' Bob said.

'Fine,' Chip said. 'Thanks.'

'Thank Uni,' Bob said.

Which gave him a day longer between treatments than he'd had before.

That night, Thursday, was a rainy night, and he stayed in his room. He sat at his desk with his forehead on his fists, thinking, wishing he were in the museum and able to smoke.

If a city of incurables existed, and Uni knew about it and was leaving it to its armed defenders – then – then—

Then Uni wasn't letting the Family know – and be troubled or in some instances tempted – *and it was feeding concealing data to the mapmaking equipment.*

Of course! How could supposedly unused areas be shown on beautiful Family maps? 'But look at that place there, Daddy!' a child visiting the MFA exclaims. 'Why aren't we Using Our Heritage Wisely and Without Waste?' And Daddy replies, 'Yes that *is* odd ...' So the city would be labelled IND99999 or Enormous Desk Lamp Factory, and no one would ever be passed within five kilometres of it. If it were an island it wouldn't be shown at all; blue ocean would replace it.

And looking at maps was therefore useless. There could be cities of incurables here, there, everywhere. Or – there could be none at all. The maps proved or disproved nothing.

Was this the great revelation he had racked his brain for – that his map-examining had been stupidity from the beginning? That there was no way at all of finding the city, except possibly by walking everywhere on Earth?

Fight Lilac, with her maddening ideas!

No, not really.

Fight *Uni*.

For half an hour he drove his mind against the problem – how do you find a theoretical city in an untravellable world? – and finally he gave up and went to bed.

He thought then of Lilac, of the kiss she had resisted and the kiss she had allowed, and the strange arousal he had felt when she showed him her soft-looking conical breasts ...

On Friday he was tense and on edge. Acting normal was unendurable; he held his breath all day long at the Centre, and through dinner, TV, and Photography Club. After the last chime he walked to Snowflake's building – 'Ow,' she said, 'I'm not going to be able to *move* tomorrow!' and then to the Pre-U. He circled the halls by flashlight, unable to put the idea aside. The city might exist, it might even be somewhere near. He looked at the money display and the prisoner in his cell. (*The two of us, brother*) and the locks and the flat-picture cameras.

There was *one* answer that he could see, but it involved getting dozens of members into the group. Each could then check out the maps according to his own limited knowledge. He himself, for instance, could verify the genetics labs and research centres and the cities he had seen or heard spoken of by other members. Lilac could verify the advisory establishments and other cities ... But it would take for ever, and an army of undertreated accomplices. He could hear King raging.

He looked at the 1951 map, and marvelled as he always did at the strange names and the intricate networks of borders. Yet members then could go where they wanted, more or less! Thin shadows moved in response to his light at the edges of the map's neat patches, cut to fit precisely into the crosslines of the grid. If not for the moving flashlight the blue rectangles would have been com—

Blue rectangles ...

If the city were an island it wouldn't be shown; blue ocean would replace it.

And would have to replace it on pre-U maps as well.

He didn't let himself get excited. He moved the flashlight slowly back and forth over the glass-covered map and counted the shadow-moving patches. There were eight of them, all blue. All in the oceans, evenly distributed. Five of them covered single rectangles of the grid, and three covered pairs of rectangles. One of the one-rectangle patches was right there off Ind, in 'Bay of Bengal' – Stability Bay.

He put the flashlight on a display case and took hold of the wide map by both sides of its frame. He lifted it free of its hook, lowered it to the floor, leaned its glassed face against his knee, and took up the flashlight again.

The frame was old, but its grey-paper backing looked relatively new. The letters EV were stamped at the bottom of it.

He carried the map by its wire across the hall, down the escalator, across the second-floor hall, and into the storeroom. Tapping on the light, he brought the map to the table and laid it carefully face-down.

With the corner of a fingernail he tore the taut paper backing along the bottom and sides of the frame, pulled it out from under the wire, and pressed it back so that it stayed. White cardboard lay in the frame, pinned down by ranks of short brads.

He searched in the cartons of smaller relics until he found a rusted pair of pincers with a yellow sticker around one handle. He used the pincers to pull the brads from the frame, then lifted out the cardboard and another piece of cardboard that lay beneath it.

The back of the map was brown-blotched but untorn, with no holes that would have justified the patching. A line of brown writing was faintly visible: *Wyndham, MUS–2161–* some kind of early nameber.

He picked at the map's edges and lifted it from the glass, turned it over and raised it sagging above his head against the white light of the ceiling. Islands showed through all the patches: here a large one, 'Madagascar'; here a cluster of small ones, 'Azores'. The patch in Stability Bay showed a line of four small ones, 'Andaman Islands'. He remembered none of the patch-covered islands from the maps at the MFA.

He put the map back down in the frame, face-up, and leaned his hands on the table and looked at it, grinned at its pre-U oddity, its eight blue almost-invisible rectangles. *Lilac!* he thought. *Wait till I tell you!*

With the head of the frame propped on piles of books and his flashlight standing under the glass, he traced on a sheet of paper the four small 'Andaman Islands' and the shoreline of 'Bay of Bengal'. He copied down the names and locations of the other islands and traced the map's scale, which was in 'miles' rather than kilometres.

One pair of medium-sized islands, 'Falkland Islands', was off the coast of Arg ('Argentina') opposite 'Santa Cruz', which seemed to be ARG20400. Something teased his memory in that, but he couldn't think what.

He measured the Andaman Islands; the three that were closest together were about a hundred and twenty 'miles' in overall length – somewhere around two hundred kilometres, if he remembered correctly; big enough for several cities! The shortest approach to them would be from the other side of Stability Bay, SEA77122, if he and Lilac (and King? Snowflake? Sparrow?) were to go there. *If* they were to go? Of course they would go, now that he had found the islands. They'd manage it somehow; they *had* to.

He turned the map face-down in the frame, put back the pieces of cardboard, and pushed the brads back into their holes with a handle-end of the pincers – wondering as he did so why ARG20400 and the 'Falkland Islands' kept poking at his memory.

He slipped the frame's backing in under the wire – Sunday night he would bring tape and make a better job of it – and carried the map back up to the third floor. He hung it on its hook and made sure the loose backing didn't show from the sides.

ARG20400 ... A new zinc mine being cut underneath it had been shown recently on TV; was that why it seemed significant? He'd certainly never been there ...

He went down to the basement and got three tobacco leaves from behind the hot-water tank. He brought them up to the storeroom, got his smoking things from the carton he kept them in, and sat down at the table and began cutting the leaves.

Could there possibly be another reason why the islands were covered and unmapped? And who did the covering?

Enough. He was tired of thinking. He let his mind go – to the knife's shiny blade, to Hush and Sparrow cutting tobacco the first time he'd seen them. He had asked Hush where the seeds had come from, and she'd said that King had had them.

And he remembered where he had seen ARG20400 – the nameber, not the city itself.

A screaming woman in torn coveralls was being led into Medicentre Main by red-crossed-coveralled members on either side of her. They held her arms and seemed to be talking to her, but she kept on screaming – short sharp screams, each the same as the others, that screamed again from building walls and screamed again from farther in the night. The woman kept on screaming and the walls and the night kept screaming with her.

He waited until the woman and the members leading her had gone into the building, waited longer while the far-off screams lessened to silence, and then he slowly crossed the walkway and went in. He lurched against the admission scanner as if off balance, clicking his bracelet below the plate on metal, and went slowly and normally to an up-gliding escalator. He stepped on to it and rode with his hand on the rail. Somewhere in the building the woman still screamed, but then she stopped.

The second floor was lighted. A member passing in the hallway with a tray of glasses nodded to him. He nodded back.

The third and fourth floors were lighted too, but the escalator to the fifth floor wasn't moving and there was darkness above. He walked up the steps, to the fifth floor and the sixth.

He walked by flashlight down the sixth-floor hallway – quickly now, not slowly – past the doors he had gone through with the two doctors, the woman who had called him 'young brother' and the scar-cheeked man who had watched him. He walked to the end of the hallway, shining his light on the door marked 600A and *Chief, Chemotherapeutics Division.*

He went through the anteroom and into King's office. The large desk was neater than before: the scuffed telecomp, a pile of folders, the container of pens – and the two paperweights, the unusual square one and the ordinary round one. He picked up the round one – ARG20400 was inscribed on it – and held its cool plated-metal weight on his palm for a moment. Then he put it down, next to King's young smiling snapshot at Uni's dome.

He went around behind the desk, opened the centre drawer, and searched in it until he found a plastic-coated section roster. He scanned the half column of Jesuses and found Jesus HL09E6290. His classification was 080A; his residence, G35, room 1744.

He paused outside the door for a moment, suddenly realizing that Lilac might be there too, dozing next to King under his outstretched possessing arm. *Good!* he thought. *Let her hear it at first hand!* He opened the door, went in, and closed it softly behind him. He aimed his flashlight towards the bed and switched it on.

King was alone, his grey head encircled by his arms.

He was glad and sorry. More glad, though. He would tell her later, come to her triumphantly and tell her all he had found.

He tapped on the light, switched off the flashlight, and put it in his pocket, 'King,' he said.

The head and the pyjamaed arms stayed unmoving.

'King,' he said, and went and stood beside the bed. 'Wake up, Jesus HL,' he said.

King rolled on to his back and laid a hand over his eyes. Fingers chinked and an eye squinted between them.

'I want to speak to you,' Chip said.

'What are you doing here?' King asked. 'What time is it?'

Chip glanced at the clock. 'Four-fifty,' he said.

King sat up, palming at his eyes. 'What the hate's going on?' he said. 'What are you doing here?'

Chip got the desk chair and put it near the foot of the bed and sat down. The room was untidy, coveralls caught in the chute, tea stains on the floor.

King coughed into the side of a fist, and coughed again. He kept the fist at his mouth, looking red-eyed at Chip, his hair pressed to his scalp in patches.

Chip said, 'I want to know what it's like on the Falkland Islands.'

121

King lowered his hand. 'On what islands?' he said.

'Falkland,' Chip said. 'Where you got the tobacco seeds. And the perfume you gave Lilac.'

'I made the perfume,' King said.

'And the tobacco seeds? Did you make them?'

King said, 'Someone gave them to me.'

'In ARG20400?'

After a moment King nodded.

'Where did *he* get them?'

'I don't know.'

'You didn't ask?'

'No,' King said, 'I didn't. Why don't you get back where you're supposed to be? We can talk about this tomorrow night.'

'I'm staying,' Chip said. 'I'm staying here until I hear the truth. I'm due for a treatment at 8.05. If I don't take it on time, everything's going to be finished – me, you, the group. You're not going to be king of anything.'

'You brother fighter,' King said, 'get out of here.'

'I'm staying,' Chip said.

'I've *told* you the truth.'

'I don't believe it.'

'Then go fight yourself,' King said, and lay down and turned over on to his stomach.

Chip stayed where he was. He sat looking at King and waiting.

After a few minutes King turned over again and sat up. He threw aside the blanket, swung his legs around, and sat with his bare feet on the floor. He scratched with both hands at his pyjamaed thighs. '"Americanueva,"' he said, 'not "Falkland". They come ashore and trade. Hairy-faced creatures in cloth and leather.' He looked at Chip. 'Diseased, disgusting savages,' he said, 'who speak in a way that's barely understandable.'

'They exist, they've survived.'

'That's *all* they've done. Their hands are like wood from working. They steal from one another and go hungry.'

'But they haven't come back to the Family.'

'They'd be better off if they did,' King said. 'They've still got religion going. And alcohol-drinking.'

'How long do they live?' Chip asked.

King said nothing.

'Past sixty-two?' Chip asked.

King's eyes narrowed coldly. 'What's so magnificent about living,' he said, 'that it has to be prolonged indefinitely? What's so fantastically beautiful about life here or life there that makes sixty-two not enough of it instead of too fighting much? Yes, they live past sixty-two. One of them claimed to be eighty, and looking at him, I believed it. But they die *younger* too, in their thirties, even in their twenties – from work and filth and defending their "money".'

'That's only one group of islands,' Chip said. 'There are seven others.'

'They'll all be the same,' King said. 'They'll all be the same.'

'How do you know?'

'How can they *not* be?' King asked. 'Christ and Wei, if I'd thought a halfway-human life was possible I'd have said something!'

'You should have said something anyway,' Chip said. 'There are islands right here in Stability Bay. Leopard and Hush might have got to them and still be living.'

'They'd be dead.'

'Then you should have let them choose where they died,' Chip said. 'You're not Uni.'

He got up and put the chair back by the desk. He looked at the phone screen, reached over the desk, and took the adviser's-nameber card from under the rim of it: *Anna SG38P2823.*

'You mean you don't know her nameber?' King said. 'What do you do, meet in the dark? Or haven't you worked your way out to her extremities yet?'

Chip put the card in his pocket. 'We don't meet at all,' he said.

'Oh come on,' King said, 'I know what's been going on. What do you think I am, a dead body?'

'Nothing's been going on,' Chip said. 'She came to the museum once and I gave her the word lists for Français, that's all.'

'I can just imagine,' King said. 'Get out of here, will you? I need my sleep.' He lay back on the bed, put his legs in under the blanket, and spread the blanket up over his chest.

'Nothing's been going on,' Chip said. 'She feels that she owes you too much.'

With his eyes closed, King said, 'But we'll soon take care of that, won't we?'

Chip said nothing for a moment, and then he said, 'You should have told us. About Americanova.'

'Americaneuva,' King said, and then said nothing more. He lay with his eyes closed, his blanketed chest rising and falling rapidly.

Chip went to the door and tapped off the light. 'I'll see you tomorrow night,' he said.

'I hope you get there,' King said. 'The two of you. To Americaneuva. You deserve it.'

Chip opened the door and went out.

King's bitterness depressed him, but after he had been walking for fifteen minutes or so he began to feel cheerful and optimistic, and elated with the results of his night of extra clarity. His right-hand pocket was crisp with a map of Stability Bay and the Andaman Islands, the names and locations of the other incurable strongholds, and Lilac's red-printed nameber card. Christ, Marx, and Wei, what would he be capable of with no treatments at all?

He took the card out and read it as he walked. *Anna SG38P2823*. He would call her after the first chime and arrange to meet her – during the free hour that evening. *Anna SG*. Not she, not an 'Anna'; a Lilac she was, fragrant, delicate, beautiful. (Who had picked the name, she or King? Incredible. The hater thought they had been meeting and fucking. If only!) *Thirty*-eight P, twenty-*eight* twenty-*three*. He walked to the swing of the nameber for a while, then realized he was walking too briskly and slowed himself, pocketing the card again.

He would be back in his building before the first chime, would shower, change, call Lilac, eat (he was starving), then get his treatment at 8.05 and keep his 8.15 dental appointment ('It feels much better today, sister. The throbbing's almost completely gone'). The treatment would dull him, fight it, but not so much that he wouldn't be able to tell Lilac about the Andaman Islands and start planning with her – and with Snowflake and Sparrow if they were interested – how they would try to get there. Snowflake would probably choose to stay. He hoped so; it would simplify things tremendously. Yes, Snowflake would stay with King, laugh and smoke and fuck with him, and play that mechanical paddle-ball game. And he and Lilac would go.

Anna SG, *thirty*-eight P, twenty-*eight* twenty-*three* ...

He got to the building at 6.22. Two up-early members were coming down his hallway, one naked, one dressed. He smiled and said, 'Good morning sisters'.

He went into his room tapped on the light, and Bob was on the bed, lifting himself up on his elbows and blinking at him. His telecomp lay open on the floor, its blue and amber lights gleaming.

SIX

He closed the door behind him.

Bob swung his legs off the bed and sat up, looking at him anxiously. His coveralls were partway open. 'Where've you been, Li?' he asked.

'In the lounge,' Chip said. 'I went back there after Photography Club – I'd left my pen there – and I suddenly got very tired. From being late on my treatment, I guess. I sat down to rest and' – he smiled – 'all of a sudden it's morning.'

Bob looked at him, still anxiously, and after a moment shook his head. 'I checked the lounge,' he said. 'And Mary KK's room, and the gym, and the bottom of the pool.'

'You must have missed me,' Chip said. 'I was in the corner behind—'

'I *checked* the *lounge*, Li,' Bob said. He pressed closed his coveralls and shook his head despairingly.

Chip moved from the door, walked a slow away-from-Bob curve toward the bathroom. 'I've got to ure,' he said.

He went into the bathroom and opened his coveralls and urined, trying to find the extra mental clarity he had had before, trying to think of an explanation that would satisfy Bob or at worst seem like only a one-night aberration. Why had Bob come there anyway? How long had he been there?

'I called at eleven-thirty,' Bob said, 'and there was no answer. Where have you been between then and now?'

He closed his coveralls. 'I was walking around,' he said – loudly, to reach Bob in the room.

'Without touching scanners?' Bob said.

Christ and Wei.

'I must have forgot,' he said, and turned on the water and rinsed his fingers. 'It's this toothache,' he said. 'It's gotten worse. The whole side of my head aches.' He wiped his fingers, looking in the mirror at Bob on the bed looking back at him. 'It was keeping me awake,' he said, 'so I went out and walked around. I told you that story about the lounge because I know I should have gone right down to the—'

'It was keeping *me* awake too,' Bob said, 'that "toothache" of yours. I saw you during TV and you looked tense and abnormal. So finally I pulled the nameber of the dental-appointment clerk. You were offered a Friday appointment but you said your treatment was on Saturday.'

Chip put the towel down and turned and stood facing Bob in the doorway.

The first chime sounded, and 'One Mighty Family' began to play.

Bob said, 'It was all an act, wasn't it, Li – the slowdown last spring, the sleepiness and overtreatedness.'

After a moment Chip nodded.

'Oh, brother,' Bob said. 'What have you been doing?'

Chip didn't say anything.

'Oh, brother,' Bob said, and bent over and switched his telecomp off. He closed its cover and snapped the catches. 'Are you going to forgive me?' he asked. He stood the telecomp on end and steadied the handle between the fingers of both hands, trying to get it to stay standing up. 'I'll tell you something very funny,' he said. 'I have a streak of vanity in me. I do. Correction, I did. I thought I was one of the two or three best advisers in the house. In the house, hate; in the *city*. Alert, observant, *sensitive* ... "Comes the rude awakening."' He had the handle standing, and slapped it down and smiled dryly at Chip. 'So you're not the only sick one,' he said, 'if that's any consolation.'

'I'm not sick, Bob,' Chip said. 'I'm healthier than I've been in my entire life.'

Still smiling, Bob said, 'That's kind of contrary to the evidence, isn't it?' He picked up the telecomp and stood up.

'You can't see the evidence,' Chip said. 'You've been dulled by your treatments.'

Bob beckoned with his head and moved towards the door. 'Come on,' he said, 'let's go get you fixed up.'

Chip stayed where he was. Bob opened the door and stopped, looking back.

Chip said, 'I'm perfectly healthy.'

Bob held out his hand sympathetically. 'Come on, Li,' he said.

After a moment Chip went with him. Bob took his arm and they went out into the hallway. Doors were open and members were about, talking quietly, walking. Four or five were gathered at the bulletin board, reading the day's notices.

'Bob,' Chip said, 'I want you to listen to what I'm going to say to you.'

'Don't I always listen?' Bob said.

'I want you to try to open your mind,' Chip said. 'Because you're not a stupid member, you're bright, and you're good-hearted and you want to help me.'

Mary KK came towards them from the escalators, holding a pack of coveralls with a bar of soap on top of it. She smiled and said, 'Hi,' and to Chip, 'Where were you?'

'He was in the lounge,' Bob said.

'In the middle of the night?' Mary said.

Chip nodded and Bob said, 'Yes,' and they went on to the escalators, Bob keeping his hand lightly on Chip's arm.

They rode down.

'I know you think your mind is open already,' Chip said, 'but will you try to open it even more, to listen and think for a few minutes as if I'm just as healthy as I say I am?'

'All right, Li, I will,' Bob said.

'Bob,' Chip said, 'we're not free. None of us is. Not one member of the Family.'

'How can I listen as if you're healthy' Bob said, 'when you say something like that? Of course we're free. We're free of war and want and hunger, free of crime, violence, aggressiveness, sel—'

'Yes, yes, we're free *of* things,' Chip said, 'but we're not free to *do* things. Don't you see that, Bob? Being "free of" really has nothing to do with being free at all.'

Bob frowned. 'Being free to do what?' he said.

They stepped off the escalator and started around towards the next one. 'To choose our own classifications,' Chip said, 'to have children when we want, to go where we want and do what we want, to refuse treatments if we want . . .'

Bob said nothing.

They stepped on to the next escalator. 'Treatments really do dull us, Bob,' Chip said. 'I know that from my own experience. There are things in them that "make us humble, make us good" – like in the rhyme, you know? I've been undertreated for half a year now' – the second chime sounded – 'and I'm more awake and alive than I've *ever* been. I think more clearly and feel more deeply. I fuck four or five times a week, would you believe that?'

'No,' Bob said, looking at his telecomp riding on the handrail.

'It's true,' Chip said. 'You're more sure than ever that I'm sick now, aren't you. Love of Family, I'm not. There are others like me, thousands, maybe millions. There are islands all over the world, there may be cities on the mainland too' – they were walking around to the next escalator – 'where people live in true freedom. I've got a list of the islands right here in my pocket. They're not on maps because Uni doesn't want us to know about them, because they're *defended* against the Family and the people there won't *submit* to being treated. Now, you want to help me, don't you? To *really* help me?'

They stepped on to the next escalator. Bob looked grievingly at him. 'Christ and Wei,' he said, 'can you doubt it, brother?'

'All right, then,' Chip said, 'this is what I'd like you to do for me: when we get to the treatment room tell Uni that I'm okay, that I fell asleep in the lounge the way I told you. Don't input anything about my not touching scanners or the way I made up the toothache. Let me get just the treatment I would have got yesterday, all right?'

'And that would be helping you?' Bob said.

'Yes, it would,' Chip said. 'I know you don't think so, but

I ask you as my brother and my friend to – to respect what I think and feel. I'll get away to one of these islands somehow and I won't harm the Family in any way. What the Family has given me, I've given back to it in the work I've done, and I didn't ask for it in the first place, and I had no choice about accepting it.'

They walked around to the next escalator.

'All right,' Bob said when they were riding down, 'I listened to *you*, Li; now *you* listen to *me*.' His hand above Chip's elbow tightened slightly. 'You're very, very sick,' he said, 'and it's entirely my fault and I feel miserable about it. There are no islands that aren't on maps; and treatments don't dull us; and if we had the kind of "freedom" you're thinking about we'd have disorder and overpopulation and want and crime and war. Yes, I'm going to help you, brother. I'm going to tell Uni everything, and you'll be cured and you'll thank me.'

They walked around to the next escalator and stepped on to it. *Third floor – Medicentre*, the sign at the bottom said. A red-cross-coveralled member riding towards them on the up escalator smiled and said, 'Good morning, Bob'.

Bob nodded to him.

Chip said, 'I don't *want* to be cured.'

'That's proof that you need to be,' Bob said. 'Relax and trust me, Li. No, why the hate should you? Trust Uni, then; will you do that? Trust the members who programmed Uni.'

After a moment Chip said, 'All right, I will.'

'I feel awful,' Bob said, and Chip turned to him and struck away his hand. Bob looked at him, startled, and Chip put both hands at Bob's back and swept him forward. Turning with the movement, he grasped the handrail – hearing Bob tumble, his telecomp clatter – and climbed out on to the up-moving central incline. It wasn't moving once he was on it; he crept sideways, clinging with fingers and knees to metal ridges; crept sideways to the up-escalator handrail, caught it, and flung himself over and down into the sharp-staired trench of humming metal. He quickly got to his feet – 'Stop him!' Bob shouted below – and ran up the upgoing steps taking two in each stride. The red-crossed member at the top, off the escalator, turned. 'What are you—' and Chip took him by the shoulders – elderly wide-eyed member

– and swung him aside and pushed him away.

He ran down the hallway. 'Stop him!' someone shouted, and other members: 'Catch that member!' 'He's sick; stop him!'

Ahead was the dining-hall, members on line turning to look. He shouted, 'Stop that member!' running at them and pointing; 'Stop him!' and ran past them. 'Sick member in there!' he said, pushing past the ones at the doorway, past the scanner. 'Needs help in there! Quickly!'

In the dining-hall he looked, and ran to the side, through a swing-door to the behind-the-dispensers section. He slowed, walked quickly, trying to still his breathing, past members loading stacks of cakes between vertical tracks, members looking down at him while dumping tea powder into steel drums. A cart filled with boxes marked *Napkins*; he took the handle of it, swung it around, and pushed it before him, past two members standing eating, two more gathering cakes from a broken carton.

Ahead was a door market *Exit*, the door to one of the corner stairways. He pushed the cart towards it, hearing raised voices behind him. He rammed the cart against the door, butted it open, and went with the cart out on to the landing; closed the door and brought the cart handle back against it. He backed down two steps and pulled the cart sideways to him, wedged it tight between the door and the stair-rail post with one black wheel turning in air.

He hurried down the stairs.

He had to get out, out of the building and on to the walk-ways and plazas. He would walk to the museum – it wouldn't be open yet – and hide in the storeroom or behind the hot-water tank until tomorrow night, when Lilac and the others would be there. He should have grabbed some cakes just now. Why hadn't he thought of it? Hate!

He left the stairway at the ground floor and walked quickly along the hallway, nodded at an approaching member. She looked at his legs and bit her lip worriedly. He looked down and stopped. His coveralls were torn at the knees and his right knee was bruised, with blood in small beads on the surface.

'Can I do anything?' the member asked.

'I'm on my way to the medicentre now,' he said. 'Thanks,

sister.' He went on. There was nothing he could do about it; he would have to take his chances. When he got outside, away from the building, he would tie a tissue around the knee and fix the coveralls as best he could. The knee began to sting, now that he knew about it. He walked faster.

He turned into the back of the lobby and paused, looked at the escalators planing down on either side of him and, up ahead, the four glass scanner-posted doors with the sunny walkway beyond them. Members were talking and going out, a few coming in. Everything looked ordinary; the murmur of voices was low, unalarmed.

He started towards the doors, walking normally, looking straight ahead. He would do his scanner trick – the knee would be an excuse for the stumbling if anyone noticed – and once he was out on – The music stopped, and 'Excuse me,' a woman's voice loudspeakered, 'would everyone please stay exactly where he is for a moment? Would everyone please stop moving?'

He stopped, in the middle of the lobby.

Everyone stopped, looked around questioningly and waited. Only the members on the escalators kept moving, and then they stopped too and looked down at their feet. One member walked down steps. 'Don't move!' several members called to her and she stopped and blushed.

He stood motionless, looking at the huge stained-glass faces above the doors: bearded Christ and Marx, hairless Wood, smiling slit-eyed Wei. Something slipped down his shin: a drop of blood.

'Brothers, sisters,' the woman's voice said, 'an emergency has arisen. There's a member in the building who's sick, very sick. He's acted aggressively and ran away from his adviser' – members drew breath – 'and he needs everyone of us to help find him and get him to the treatment room as quickly as possible.'

'Yes!' a member behind Chip said, and another said, 'What do we do?'

'He's believed to be somewhere below the fourth floor,' the woman said; 'a twenty-seven-year-old—' A second voice spoke to her, a man's voice, quick and unintelligible. A member about to step on the nearest escalator was looking at Chip's knees. Chip looked at the picture of Wood. 'He'll probably try to leave the building,' the woman said, 'so the two members nearest each exit will move to it and block it, please. No one else move; only the two members nearest each exit.'

The members near the doors looked at one another, and two moved to each door and put themselves uneasily side by side in line with the scanners. 'It's awful!' someone said. The member who had been looking at Chip's knees was looking now at his face. Chip looked back at him, a man of forty or so; he looked away.

'The member we're looking for,' a man's voice on the speaker said, 'is a twenty-seven-year-old male, nameber Li RM35M4419. That's Li, Rm, 35M, 4419. First we'll check among ourselves and then we'll search the floors we're on. Just a minute, just a minute please. UniComp says the member is the only Li RM in the building, so we can forget the rest of his nameber. All we have to look for is Li RM. Li RM. Look at the bracelets of the members around you. We're looking for Li RM. Be sure that every member within your sight is checked by at least one other member. Members who are in their rooms will come out now into the hallways. Li RM. We're looking for Li RM.'

Chip turned to a member near him, took his hand and looked at his bracelet. 'Let me see yours,' the member said. Chip raised his wrist and turned away, went towards another member. 'I didn't see it,' the member said. Chip took the other member's hand. His arm was touched by the first member, saying, 'Brother, I didn't see.'

He ran for the doors. He was caught and arm-pulled around – by the member who had been looking at him. He clenched his hand to a fist and hit the member in the face and he fell away.

Members screamed. 'It's him!' they cried. 'There he is!' 'Help him!' 'Stop him!'

He ran to a door and fist-hit one of the members there. His arm was grabbed by the other, saying in his ear, 'Brother, brother!' His other arm was caught by other members; he was clutched around the chest from behind.

'We're looking for Li RM,' the man on the speaker said. 'He may act aggressively when we find him but we mustn't

132

be afraid. He's depending on us for our help and our understanding.'

'Let go of me!' he cried, trying to pull himself free of the arms tightly holding him.

'Help him!' members cried. 'Get him to the treatment room!' 'Help him!'

'Leave me alone!' he cried. 'I don't *want* to be helped! Leave me *alone*, you brother-fighting haters!'

He was dragged up escalator steps by members panting and flinching, one of them with tears in his eyes. 'Easy, easy,' they said, 'we're helping you. You'll be all right, we're helping you.' He kicked, and his legs were caught and held. 'I don't *want* to be helped!' he cried. 'I want to be left alone! I'm healthy! I'm healthy! I'm not sick!'

He was dragged past members who stood with hands over ears, with hands pressed to mouths below staring eyes.

'*You're* sick,' he said to the member whose face he had hit. Blood was leaking from his nostrils, and his nose and cheek were swollen; Chip's arm was locked under his. 'You're dulled and you're drugged,' Chip said to him. 'You're dead. You're a dead man. You're *dead!*'

'Shh, we love you, we're helping you,' the member said.

'*Christ and Wei, let GO of me!*'

He was dragged up more steps.

'He's been found,' the man on the speaker said. 'Li RM has been found, members. He's being brought to the medicentre. Let me say that again: Li RM has been found, and is being brought to the medicentre. The emergency is over, brothers and sisters, and you can go on now with what you were doing. Thank you; thank you for your help and co-operation. Thank you on behalf of the Family, thank you on behalf of Li RM.'

He was dragged along the medicentre hallway.

Music started in mid-melody.

'You're all dead,' he said. 'The whole Family's dead. Uni's alive, only Uni. But there are islands where *people* are living! Look at the map! Look at the map in the Pre-U Museum!'

He was dragged into the treatment room. Bob was there, pale and sweating, with a bleeding cut over his eyebrow; he

133

was jabbing at the keys of his telecomp, held for him by a girl in a blue smock.'

'Bob,' he said, 'Bob, do me a favour, will you? Look at the map in the Pre-U Museum. Look at the map from 1951.'

He was dragged to a blue-lighted room. He grabbed the edge of the opening, but his thumb was pried up and his hand forced in; his sleeve torn back and his arm shoved in all the way to the shoulder.

His cheek was soothed – by Bob, trembling. 'You'll be all right, Li,' he said. 'Trust Uni.' Three lines of blood ran from the cut into his eyebrow hairs.

His bracelet was caught by the scanner, his arms touched by the infusion disc. He clamped his eyes shut. *I will not be made dead!* he thought. *I will not be made dead! I'll remember the islands, I'll remember Lilac! I will not be made dead! I will not be made dead!* He opened his eyes, and Bob smiled at him. A strip of skin-coloured tape was over his eyebrow. 'They *said* three o'clock and they *meant* three o'clock,' he said.

'What do you mean?' he asked. He was lying in a bed and Bob was sitting beside it.

'That's when the doctors said you'd wake up,' Bob said. 'Three o'clock. And that's what it is. Not 2.59, not 3.01, but three o'clock. These mems are so clever it scares me.'

'Where am I?' he asked.

'In Medicentre Main.'

And then he remembered – remembered the things he had thought and said, and worst of all, the things he had done. 'Oh Christ,' he said. 'Oh, Marx. Oh, Christ and Wei.'

'Take it easy, Li,' Bob said, touching his hand.

'Bob,' he said, 'oh Christ and Wei, Bob, I – I pushed you down the—'

'Escalator,' Bob said. 'You certainly did, brother. That was the most surprised moment in my life. I'm fine though.' He tapped the tape above his eyebrow. 'All closed up and good as new, or will be in a day or two.'

'I *hit* a member! With my hand!'

'He's fine too,' Bob said. 'Two of those are from him.' He nodded across the bed, at red roses in a vase on a table. 'And two from Mary KK, and two from the members in your section.'

He looked at the roses, sent to him by the members he had hit and deceived and betrayed, and tears came into his eyes and he began to tremble.

'Hey, easy there, come on,' Bob said.

But Christ and Wei, he was thinking only of himself! 'Bob, listen,' he said, turning to him, getting up on an elbow, backhanding at his eyes.

'Take it easy,' Bob said.

'Bob, there are *others*,' he said, 'others who're just as sick as I was! We've got to find them and help them!'

'We know.'

'There's a member called "Lilac", Anna SG38P2823, and another one—'

'We know, we know,' Bob said. 'They've already been helped. They've all been helped.'

'They have?'

Bob nodded. 'You were questioned while you were out,' he said. 'It's Monday. Monday afternoon. They've already been found and helped – Anna SG; and the one you called "Snowflake", Anna PY; and Yin GU, "Sparrow".'

'And King,' he said. 'Jesus HL; he's right here in this building; he's—'

'No,' Bob said, shaking his head. 'No, we were too late. That one – that one is dead.'

'He's dead?'

Bob nodded. 'He hung himself,' he said.

Chip stared at him.

'From his shower, with a strip of blanket,' Bob said.

'Oh, Christ and Wei,' Chip said, and lay back on the pillow. Sickness, sickness, sickness; and he had been part of it.

'The others are all fine though,' Bob said, patting his hand. 'And you'll be fine too. You're going to a rehabilitation centre, brother. You're going to have yourself a week's vacation. Maybe even more.'

'I feel so ashamed, Bob,' he said, 'so fighting ashamed of myself ...'

'Come on,' Bob said. 'You wouldn't feel ashamed if you'd slipped and broken an ankle, would you? It's the same thing. I'*m* the one who should feel ashamed, if anyone should.'

'I *lied* to you!'

'I let myself be lied to,' Bob said. 'Look, nobody's really responsible for anything. You'll see that soon.' He reached down, brought up a take-along kit, and opened it on his lap. 'This is yours,' he said. 'Tell me if I missed anything. Mouthpiece, clippers, snapshots, nameber books, picture of a horse, your—'

'That's sick,' he said. 'I don't want it. Chute it.'

'The picture?'

'Yes.'

Bob drew it from the kit and looked at it. 'It's nicely done,' he said. 'It's not accurate, but it's – nice in a way.'

'It's sick,' he said. 'It was done by a sick member. Chute it.'

'Whatever you say,' Bob said. He put the kit on the bed and got up and crossed the room; opened the chute and dropped the picture down.

'There are islands full of sick members,' Chip said. 'All over the world.'

'I know,' Bob said. 'You told us.'

'Why can't we help them?'

'That I *don't* know,' Bob said. 'But Uni does. I told you before, Li : trust Uni.'

'I will,' he said, 'I will,' and tears came into his eyes again.

A red-cross-coveralled member came into the room. 'How are we feeling?' he asked.

Chip looked at him.

'He's pretty low,' Bob said.

'That's to be expected,' the member said. 'Don't worry; we'll get him evened up.' He went over and took Chip's wrist.

'Li, I have to go now,' Bob said.

'All right,' Chip said.

Bob went over and kissed his cheek. 'In case you're not sent back here, goodbye, brother,' he said.

'Goodbye, Bob,' Chip said. 'Thanks. Thanks for everything.'

'Thank Uni,' Bob said, and squeezed his hand and smiled. He nodded at the red-crossed member and went out.

The member took an infusion syringe from his pocket and snapped off its cap. 'You'll be feeling perfectly normal in no time at all,' he said.

Chip lay still and closed his eyes, wiped with one hand at tears while the member pushed up his other sleeve. 'I was so sick,' he said. 'I was so sick.'

'Shh, don't think about it,' the member said, gently infusing him. 'It's nothing to think about. You'll be fine in no time.'

PART THREE

GETTING AWAY

ONE

Old cities were demolished; new cities were built. The new cities had taller buildings, broader plazas, larger parks, monorails whose cars flew faster though less frequently.

Two more starships were launched, towards Sirius B and 61 Cygni. The Mars colonies, repopulated and safeguarded now against the devastation of 152, were expanding daily; so too were the colonies on Venus and the Moon, the outposts on Titan and Mercury.

The free hour was extended by five minutes. Voice-input telecomps began to replace key-input ones, and totalcakes came in a pleasant second flavour. Life expectancy increased to 62.4.

Members worked and ate, watched TV and slept. They sang and went to museums and walked in amusement gardens.

On the two-hundredth anniversary of Wei's birth, in the parade in a new city, a huge portrait banner of smiling Wei was carried at one of its poles by a member of thirty or so who was ordinary in every respect except that his right eye was green instead of brown. Once long ago this member had been sick, but now he was well. He had his assignment and his room, his girlfriend and his adviser. He was relaxed and content.

A strange thing happened during the parade. As this member marched along, smiling, holding the banner pole, he began to hear a nameber saying itself over and over in his head: Anna SG, thirty-eight P, twenty-eight twenty-three; Anna SG, thirty-eight P, twenty-eight twenty-three. It kept repeating itself to him, in time with his marching. He wondered who the nameber belonged to, and why it should be repeating itself in his head that way.

Suddenly he remembered: it was from his sickness! It was the nameber of one of the other sick ones, the one called 'Lovely' – no, 'Lilac'. Why, after so long, had her nameber come back to him? He stamped his feet down harder, trying not to hear it, and was glad when the signal to sing was given.

He told his adviser. 'It's nothing to think about,' she said. 'You probably saw something that reminded you of her. Maybe you even saw *her*. There's nothing to be afraid of in remembering – unless, of course, it becomes bothersome. Let me know if it happens again.'

But it didn't happen again. He was well, thank Uni.

One Christmas Day, when he had another assignment, was living in another city, he bicycled with his girlfriend and four other members to the outlying parkland. They brought cakes and cokes with them, and lunched on the ground near a grove of trees.

He had set his coke container on an almost-level stone and, reaching for it while talking, knocked it over. The other members refilled his container from theirs.

A few minutes later, while folding his cake wrapper, he noticed a flat leaf lying on the wet stone, drops of coke shining on its back, its stem curled upwards like a handle. He took the stem and lifted the leaf, and the stone underneath it was dry in the leaf's oval shape. The rest of the stone was wet-black, but where the leaf had been it was dry-grey. Something about the moment seemed significant to him, and he sat silently, looking at the leaf in his one hand, the folded cake wrapper in his other, and the dry leaf shape on the stone. His girlfriend said something to him and he took himself away from the moment, put the leaf and the wrapper together and gave them to the member who had the litter bag.

The image of the dry leaf shape on the stone came into his mind several times that day, and on the next day too. Then he had his treatment and he forgot about it. In a few weeks, though, it came into his mind again. He wondered why. Had he lifted a leaf from a wet stone that way sometime before? If he had, he didn't remember it ...

Every now and then, while he was walking in a park or, oddly enough, waiting on line for his treatment, the image of the dry leaf shape came into his mind and made him frown.

There was an earthquake. (His chair flung him off it; glass

broke in the microscope and the loudest sound he had ever heard roared from the depths of the lab.) A seismovalve half the continent away had jammed and gone undetected, TV explained a few nights later. It hadn't happened before and it wouldn't happen again. Members must mourn, of course, but it was nothing to think about in the future.

Dozens of buildings had collapsed, hundreds of members had died. Every medicentre in the city was overloaded with the injured, and more than half the treatment units were damaged; treatments were delayed up to ten days.

A few days after he was to have had his, he thought of Lilac and how he had loved her differently and more – more *excitingly* – than he loved everyone else. He had wanted to tell her something. What was it? Oh yes, about the islands. The islands he had found hidden on the pre-U map. The islands of incurables ...

His adviser called him. 'Are you all right?' he asked.

'I don't think so, Karl,' he said. 'I need my treatment.'

'Hold on a minute,' his adviser said, and turned away and spoke softly to his telecomp. After a moment he turned back. 'You can get it tonight at seven-thirty,' he said, 'but you'll have to go to the medicentre in T24.'

He stood on a long line at seven-thirty, thinking about Lilac, trying to remember exactly what she looked like. When he got near the treatment units, the image of a dry leaf shape on a stone came into his mind.

Lilac called him (she was right there in the same building) and he went to her room, which was the storeroom in the Pre-U. Green jewels hung from her earlobes and glittered around her rose-brown throat; she was wearing a gown of gleaming green cloth that exposed her pink-tipped soft-cone breasts. 'Bon soir, Chip,' she said, smiling. 'Comment vas-tu? Je m'ennuyais tellement de toi.' He went to her and took her in his arms and kissed her – her lips were warm and soft, her mouth opening – and he awoke to darkness and disappointment; it was a dream, it had only been a dream.

But strangely, frighteningly, everything was in him: the smell of her perfume (parfum) and the taste of tobacco and the sound of Sparrow's songs, and desire for Lilac and anger at King and resentment of Uni and sorrow for the Family and happiness in feeling, in being alive and awake.

And in the morning he would have a treatment and it would all be gone. At eight o'clock. He tapped on the light, squinted at the clock: 4.54. In a little more than three hours ...

He tapped the light off again and lay open-eyed in the dark. He didn't want to lose it. Sick or not, he wanted to keep his memories and the capacity to explore and enjoy them. He didn't want to think about the *islands* – no, never; that was *real* sickness – but he wanted to think about Lilac, and the meetings of the group in the relic-filled storeroom, and once in a while, maybe, to have another dream.

But the treatment would come in three hours and everything would be gone. There was nothing he could do – except hope for another earthquake, and what chance was there of that? The seismovalves had worked perfectly in the years since and they would go on working perfectly in the years ahead. And what short of an earthquake could postpone his treatment? Nothing. Nothing at all. Not with Uni knowing that he had lied for a postponement once before.

A dry leaf shape on stone came into his mind but he chased it away to think of Lilac, to see her as he had seen her in the dream, not to waste his three short hours of aliveness. He had forgotten how large her eyes were, how lovely her smile and her rose-brown skin, how moving her earnestness. He had forgotten so fighting much: the pleasure of smoking, the excitement of deciphering Français ...

The dry leaf shape came back, and he thought about it, irritated, to find out why his mind hung on to it, to get rid of it once and for all. He thought back to the ridiculously meaningless moment; saw again the leaf, with the drops of coke shining on it; saw his fingers lifting it by its stem, and his other hand holding the folded foil cake wrapper, and the dry grey oval on the black coke-wet stone. He had spilled the coke, and the leaf had been lying there, and the stone underneath it had—

He sat up in bed and clasped his hand to his pyjamaed right arm. 'Christ and Wei,' he said, frightened.

He got up before the first chime and dressed and made the bed.

He was the first one in the dining-room; ate and drank, and went back to his room with a cake wrapper folded loosely in his pocket.

He opened the wrapper, put it on the desk, and smoothed it down flat with his hand. He folded the square of foil neatly in half, and the half into thirds. He pressed the packet flat and held it; it was thin despite its six layers. Too thin? He put it down again.

He went into the bathroom and, from the cabinet's first-aid kit, got cotton and the cartridge of tape. He brought them back to the desk.

He put a layer of cotton on the foil packet – a layer smaller than the packet itself – and began covering the cotton and the packet with long overlapping strips of skin-coloured tape. He stuck the tape ends lightly to the desk-top.

The door opened and he turned, hiding what he was doing and putting the tape cartridge into his pocket. It was Karl TK from next door. 'Ready to eat?' he asked.

'I already have,' he said.

'Oh,' Karl said. 'See you later.'

'Right,' he said, and smiled.

Karl closed the door.

He finished the taping and then peeled the tape ends from the desk and carried the bandage he had made into the bathroom. He laid it foil-side up on the edge of the sink and pushed up his sleeve.

He took the bandage and put the foil carefully against the inner surface of his arm, where the infusion disc would touch him. He clasped the bandage and pressed its tape border tightly to his skin.

A leaf. A shield. Would it work?

If it did, he would think only of Lilac, not of the islands. If he found himself thinking of the islands, he would tell his adviser.

He drew down his sleeve.

At eight o'clock he joined the line in the treatment room. He stood with his arms folded and his hand over the sleeve-covered bandage – to warm it in case the infusion disc was temperature-sensitive.

I'm sick, he thought. *I'll get all the diseases: cancer, smallpox, cholera, everything. Hair will grow on my face!*

145

He would do it just this once. At the first sign of anything wrong he would tell his adviser.

Maybe it wouldn't work.

His turn came. He pushed his sleeve to his elbow, put his hand wrist-deep into the unit's rubber-rimmed opening, and then pushed his sleeve to his shoulder and in the same moment slid his arm all the way in.

He felt the scanner finding his bracelet, and the infusion disc's slight pressure against the cotton-packed bandage ... Nothing happened.

'You're done,' a member said behind him.

The unit's blue light was on.

'Oh,' he said, and pushed down his sleeve as he drew out his arm.

He had to go right to his assignment.

After lunch he went back to his room and, in the bathroom, pushed up his sleeve and pulled the bandage from his arm. The foil was unbroken, but so was skin after a treatment. He tore the foil packet from the tape.

The cotton was greyish and matted. He squeezed the bandage over the sink, and a trickle of waterlike liquid ran from it.

Awareness came, more of it each day. Memory came, in sharper, more anguished detail.

Feeling came. Resentment of Uni grew into hatred; desire for Lilac grew into hopeless hunger.

Again he played the old deceptions; was normal at his assignment, normal with his adviser; normal with his girlfriend. But day by day the deceptions grew more irritating to maintain, more infuriating.

On his next treatment day he made another bandage of cake wrapper, cotton, and tape; and squeezed from it another trickle of waterlike liquid.

Black specks appeared on his chin and cheeks and upper lip – the beginnings of hair. He took apart his clippers, wired the cutter blade to one of the handles, and before the first chime each morning, rubbed soap on his face and shaved the specks away.

He dreamed every night. Sometimes the dreams brought orgasms.

146

More and more maddening it became, to pretend relaxation and contentment, humility, goodness. On Marxmas Day, at a beach, he trotted along the shore and then ran, ran from the members trotting with him, ran from the sunbathing, cake-eating Family. He ran till the beach narrowed into tumbled stone, and ran on through surf and over slippery ancient abutments. Then he stopped, and alone and naked between ocean and soaring cliffs, clenched his hands into fists and hit at the cliffs; cried 'Fight it!' at the clear blue sky and wrenched and tore at the untearable chain of his bracelet.

It was 169, the fifth of May. Six and a half years he had lost. *Six and a half years!* He was thirty-four. He was in USA90058.

And where was she? Still in Ind, or was she somewhere else? Was she on Earth or on a starship?

And was she alive, as he was, or was she dead, like everyone else in the Family?

TWO

It was easier now, now that he had bruised his hands and shouted; easier to walk slowly with a contented smile, to watch TV and the screen of his microscope, to sit with his girlfriend at amphitheatre concerts.

Thinking all the while of what to do ...

'Any friction?' his adviser asked.

'Well, a little,' he said.

'I thought you didn't look right. What is it?'

'Well, you know, I was pretty sick a few years ago—'

'I know.'

'And now one of the members I was sick with, the one who got me sick, in fact, is right here in the building. Could I possibly be moved somewhere else?'

His adviser looked doubtfully at him. 'I'm a little surprised,' he said, 'that UniComp's put the two of you together again.'

'So am I,' Chip said. 'But she's here. I saw her in the dining-hall last night and again this morning.'

'Did you speak to her?'

'No.'

'I'll look into it,' his adviser said. 'If she is here and it makes you uncomfortable, of course we'll get you moved. Or get *her* moved. What's her nameber?'

'I don't remember all of it,' Chip said. 'Anna ST38P.'

His adviser called him early the next morning. 'You were mistaken, Li,' he said. 'It wasn't that member you saw. And by the way, she's Anna SG, not ST.'

'Are you sure she's not here?'

'Positive. She's in Afr.'

'That's a relief,' Chip said.

'And Li, instead of having your treatment Thursday, you're going to have it today.'

'I am?'

'Yes. At one-thirty.'

'All right,' he said. 'Thank you, Jesus.'

'Thank Uni.'

He had three cake wrappers folded and hidden in the back of his desk drawer. He took one out, went into the bathroom, and began making a bandage.

She was in Afr. It was nearer than Ind but still an ocean away. And the width of Usa besides.

His parents were there, in '71334; he would wait a few weeks and then claim a visit. It was a little under two years since he had seen them last; there was a fair chance that the claim would be granted. Once in Afr he could call her – pretend to have an injured arm, get a child to touch the plate of an outdoor phone for him – and find out her exact location. *Hello, Anna SG. I hope you're as well as I am. What city are you in?*

And then what? Walk there? Claim a car ride to some place near, an installation involved with genetics in one way or another? Would Uni realize what he was up to?

But even if it all happened, even if he got to her, what would he do *then*? It was too much to hope that she too had lifted a leaf from a wet stone one day. No, fight it, she would be a normal member, as normal as he himself had been

148

until a few months ago. And at his first abnormal word she would have him in a medicentre. Christ, Marx, Wood and Wei, what could he *do*?

He could forget about her, that was one answer; strike out on his own, now, for the nearest free island. There would be women there, probably a lot of them, and some of them would probably have rose-brown skin and large less-slanted-than-normal eyes and soft-looking conical breasts. Was it worth risking his own aliveness on the slim chance of awakening hers?

Though *she* had awakened *his*, crouching before him with her hands on his knees ...

Not at the risk of her own, though. Or at least not at as *great* a risk.

He went to the Pre-U Museum; went the old way, at night, without touching scanners. It was the same as the one in IND26110. Some of the exhibits were slightly different, standing in different places.

He found another pre-U map, this one made in 1937, with the same eight blue rectangles pasted to it. Its backing had been cut and crudely taped; someone else had been at it before him. The thought was exciting; someone else had found the islands, was maybe on the way to one at that very moment.

In another storeroom – this one with only a table and a few cartons and a curtained boothlike machine with rows of small levers – he again held a map to the light, again saw the hidden islands. He traced on paper the nearest one, 'Cuba,' off Usa's southeast tip. And in case he decided to risk seeing Lilac, he traced the shape of Afr and the two islands near it, 'Madagascar' to the east and little 'Majorca' to the north.

One of the cartons held books; he found one in Français, *Spinoza et ses contemporains*. Spinoza and his contemporaries. He looked through it and took it.

He put the reframed map in its place and browsed through the museum. He took a wrist-strap compass that still seemed to be working, and a bone-handled 'razor' and the stone for sharpening it.

'We're going to be reassigned soon,' his section head said at lunch one day. 'GL4 is taking over our work.'

'I hope I go to Afr,' he said. 'My parents are there.'

It was a risky thing to say, slightly unmemberlike, but maybe the section head had an indirect influence on who went where.

His girlfriend was transferred and he went with her to the airport to see her off – and to see whether it was possible to get aboard a plane without Uni's permission. It didn't seem to be; the close single line of boarding members would allow no false touching of the scanner, and by the time the last member in the line was touching, a member in orange coveralls was at his side ready to stop the escalator and sink it in its pit. Getting off a plane presented the same difficulty : the last member out touched the scanner, while two orange-coveralled members looked on; they reversed the escalator, touched, and went aboard with steel containers for the cake and drink dispensers. He might manage to get on a plane waiting in the hangar area – and hide in it, although he didn't recall any hiding place in planes – but how could he know where it would eventually go?

Flying was impossible, till Uni said he could fly.

He claimed a visit to his parents. It was denied.

New assignments were posted for his section. Two 66's were sent to Afr, but not he; he was sent to USA36104. During the flight he studied the plane. There was no hiding place. There was only the long seat-filled hull, the bathroom at the front, the cake and drink dispensers at the back, and the TV screens, with an actor playing Marx on all of them.

USA36104 was in the southeast, close to Usa's tip and Cuba beyond it. He could go bicycling one Sunday and keep bicycling; go from city to city, sleeping in the parkland between them and going into the cities at night for cakes and drinks; it was twelve hundred kilometres by the MFA map. At '33037 he could find a boat, or traders coming ashore like the ones in ARG20400 that King had spoken of.

Lilac, he thought, *what else can I do?*

He claimed the visit to Afr again, and again it was denied.

He began bicycling on Sundays and during the free hour, to ready his legs. He went to the '36104 pre-U and found a better compass and a tooth-edged knife he could use for cutting branches in the parkland. He checked the map there; this one's backing was intact, unopened. He wrote on it, *Yes, there are islands where members are free. Fight Uni!*

Early one Sunday morning he set out for Cuba, with the compass and a map he had drawn in one of his pockets. In the bike's basket, *Wei's Living Wisdom* lay on a folded blanket along with a container of coke and a cake; within the blanket was his take-along kit, and in that were his razor and its sharpening stone, a bar of soap, his clippers, two cakes, the knife, a flashlight, cotton, a cartridge of tape a snapshot of his parents and Papa Jan, and an extra set of coveralls. Under his right sleeve there was a bandage on his arm, though if he were taken for treatment it would almost certainly be found. He wore sunglasses and smiled, pedalling southeast among other cyclists on the path towards '36081. Cars skimmed past in rhythmic sequence over the roadway that paralleled the path. Pebbles kicked by the cars' airjets pinged now and then against the metal divider.

He stopped every hour or so and rested for a few minutes. He ate half a cake and drank some of the coke. He thought about Cuba, and what he would take from '33037 to trade there. He thought about the women on Cuba. Probably they would be attracted by a new arrival. They would be completely untreated, passionate beyond imagining, as beautiful as Lilac or even more beautiful ...

He rode for five hours, and then he turned around and rode back.

He forced his mind to his assignment. He was the staff 663 in a medicentre's paediatrics division. It was boring work, endless gene examinations with little variation, and it was the sort of assignment from which one was seldom transferred. He would be there for the rest of his life.

Every four or five weeks he claimed a visit to his parents in Afr.

In February of 170 the claim was granted.

He got off the plane at four in the morning Afr time and went into the waiting-room, holding his right elbow and looking uncomfortable, his kit slung on his left shoulder. The member who had got off the plane behind him, and who had helped him up when he had fallen, put her bracelet to a phone for him. 'Are you sure you're all right?' she asked.

'I'm fine,' he said, smiling. 'Thanks, and enjoy your visit.'

To the phone he said, 'Anna SG38P2823.' The member went away.

The screen flashed and patterned as the connexion was made, and then it went dark and stayed dark. *She's been transferred*, he thought; *she's off the continent*. He waited for the phone to tell him. But she said, 'Just a second, I can't—' and was there, blurry-close. She sat back down on the edge of her bed, rubbing her eyes, in pyjamas. 'Who is it?' she asked. Behind her a member turned over. It was Saturday night. Or was she married?

'Who?' she asked. She looked at him and leaned closer, blinking. She was more beautiful. Were there ever such eyes?

'Li RM,' he said, making himself be only courteous, memberlike. 'Don't you remember? From IND26110, back in 162.'

Her brow contracted uneasily for an instant. 'Oh yes, of course,' she said, and smiled. 'Of course I remember. How are you, Li?'

'Very well,' he said. 'How are you?'

'Fine,' she said, and stopped smiling.

'Married?'

'No,' she said. 'I'm glad you called, Li. I want to thank you. You know, for helping me.'

'Thank Uni,' he said.

'No, no,' she said. 'Thank you. Belatedly.' She smiled again.

'I'm sorry to call at this hour,' he said. 'I'm passing through Afr on a transfer.'

'That's all right,' she said. 'I'm glad you did.'

'Where are you?' he asked.

'In '14509.'

'That's where my sister lives.'

'Really?' she said.

'Yes,' he said. 'Which building are you in?'

'P51.'

'She's in A-something.'

The member behind her sat up and she turned and said something to him. He smiled at Chip. She turned and said, 'This is Li XE.'

'Hello,' Chip said, thinking '14509, P51; '14509, P51.

'Hello, brother,' Li XE's lips said; his voice didn't reach the phone.

'Is something wrong with your arm?' Lilac asked.

He was still holding it. He let it go. 'No,' he said. 'I fell etting off the plane.'

'Oh, I'm sorry,' she said. She glanced beyond him. 'There's member waiting,' she said. 'We'd better say goodbye now.'

'Yes,' he said. 'Goodbye. It was nice seeing you. You naven't changed at all.'

'Neither have you,' she said. 'Goodbye, Li.' She rose and reached forward and was gone.

He tapped off and gave way to the member behind him.

She was dead; a normal healthy member lying down now beside her boyfriend in '14509, P51. How could he risk talking to her of anything that wasn't as normal and healthy as she was? He should spend the day with his parents and fly back to Usa; go bicycling next Sunday and this time not turn back.

He walked around the waiting-room. There was an outline map of Afr on one wall, with lights at the major cities and thin orange lines connecting them. Near the north was '14510, near where she was. Half the continent from '71330, where he was. An orange line connected the two lights.

He watched the flight-schedule signboard flashing and blinking, revising the *Sunday 18 Feb* schedule. A plane for '14510 was leaving at 8.20 in the evening, forty minutes before his own flight for USA33100.

He went to the glass that faced the field and watched members single-filing on to the escalator of the plane he had left. An orange-coveralled member came and waited by the scanner.

He turned back to the waiting-room. It was nearly empty. Two members who had been on the plane with him, a woman holding a sleeping infant and a man carrying two kits, put their wrists and the infant's wrist to the scanner at the door to the carport – *yes*, it greened three times – and went out. An orange-coveralled member, on his knees by a water fountain, unscrewed a plate at its base; another pushed a floor polisher to the side of the waiting-room, touched a scanner – *yes* – and pushed the polisher out through a swing-door.

He thought for a moment, watching the member working

at the fountain, and then he crossed the waiting-room, touched the carport-door scanner – *yes* – and went out. A car for '71334 was waiting, three members in it. He touched the scanner – *yes* – and got into the car, apologizing to the members for having kept them waiting. The door closed and the car started. He sat with his kit in his lap, thinking.

When he got to his parents' apartment he went in quietly, shaved, and then woke them. They were pleased, even happy, to see him.

The three of them talked and ate breakfast and talked more. They claimed a call to Peace, in Eur, and it was granted; they talked with her and her Karl, her ten-year-old Bob and her eight-year-old Yin. Then, at his suggestion, they went to the Museum of the Family's Achievements.

After lunch he slept for three hours and then they railed to the Amusement Gardens. His father joined a volleyball game, and he and his mother sat on a bench and watched. 'Are you sick again?' she asked him.

He looked at her. 'No,' he said. 'Of course not. I'm fine.'

She looked closely at him. She was fifty-seven now, grey-haired, her tan skin wrinkled. 'You've been thinking about something,' she said. 'All day.'

'I'm well,' he said. 'Please. You're my mother; believe me.'

She looked into his eyes with concern.

'I'm well,' he said.

After a moment she said, 'All right, Chip.'

Love for her suddenly filled him; love, and gratitude, and a boylike feeling of oneness with her. He clasped her shoulder and kissed her cheek. 'I love you, Suzu,' he said.

She laughed. 'Christ and Wei,' she said, 'what a memory you have!'

'That's because I'm healthy,' he said. 'Remember that, will you? I'm healthy and happy. I want you to remember that.'

'Why?'

'Because,' he said.

He told them that his plane left at eight. 'We'll say goodbye at the carport,' he said. 'The airport will be too crowded.'

His father wanted to come along anyway, but his mother said no, they would stay in '334; she was tired.

At seven-thirty he kissed them goodbye – his father and

154

then his mother, saying in her ear, 'Remember' – and got on line for a car to the '71330 airport. The scanner, when he touched it, said *yes*.

The waiting-room was even more crowded than he had hoped it would be. Members in white and yellow and pale blue walked and stood and sat and waited in line, some with kits and some without. A few members in orange moved among them.

He looked at the signboard; the 8.20 flight for '14510 would load from lane two. Members were in line there, and beyond the glass, a plane was swinging into place against a rising escalator. Its door opened and a member came out, another behind him.

Chip made his way through the crowd to the swing-door at the side of the room, false-touched its scanner, and pushed through: into a depot area where crates and cartons stood ranked under white light, like Uni's memory banks. He unslung his kit and jammed it between a carton and the wall.

He walked ahead normally. A cart of steel containers crossed his path, pushed by an orange-coveralled member who glanced at him and nodded.

He nodded back, kept walking, and watched the member push the cart out through a large open portal on to the flood-lit field.

He went in the direction from which the member had come, into an area where members in orange were putting steel containers on the conveyor of a washing-machine and filling other containers with coke and steaming tea from the taps of giant drums. He kept walking.

He false-touched a scanner and went into a room where coveralls, ordinary ones, hung on hooks, and two members were taking off orange ones. 'Hello,' he said.

'Hello,' they both said.

He went to a closet door and slid it open; a floor polisher and bottles of green liquid were inside. 'Where are the cuvs?' he asked.

'In there,' one of the members said, nodding at another closet.

He went to it and opened it. Orange coveralls were on

155

shelves; orange toeguards, pairs of heavy orange gloves.

'Where did you come from?' the member asked.

'RUS50937,' he said, taking a pair of coveralls and a pair of toeguards. 'We kept the cuvs in there.'

'They're supposed to be in *there*,' the member said, closing white coveralls.

'I've been in Rus,' the other member, a woman, said. 'I had two assignments there; first four years and then three years.'

He took his time putting on the toeguards, finishing as the two members chuted their orange coveralls and went out.

He pulled the orange coveralls on over his white ones and closed them all the way to his throat. They were heavier than ordinary coveralls and had extra pockets.

He looked in other closets, found a wrench and a good-sized piece of yellow paplon.

He went back to where he had left his kit, got it out, and wrapped the paplon around it. The swing-door bumped him. 'Sorry,' a member said, coming in. 'Did I hurt you?'

'No,' he said, holding the wrapped kit.

The orange-coveralled member went on.

He waited for a moment, watching him, and then he tucked the kit under his left arm and got the wrench from his pocket. He gripped it in his right hand, in a way that he hoped looked natural.

He followed after the member, then turned and went to the portal that opened on to the field.

The escalator leaning against the flank of the lane-two plane was empty. A cart, probably the one he had seen pushed out, stood at the foot of it, beside the scanner.

Another escalator was sinking into the ground, and the plane it had served was on its way towards the runways. There was an 8.10 flight to Chi, he recalled.

He crouched on one knee, put his kit and the wrench down on concrete, and pretended to have trouble with his toeguard. Everyone in the waiting-room would be watching the plane for Chi when it lifted; that was when he would go on to the escalator. Orange legs rustled past him, a member walking towards the hangars. He took off his toeguard and put it back on, watching the plane pivot ...

It raced forward. He gathered his kit and the wrench,

stood up, and walked normally. The brightness of the flood-lights unnerved him, but he told himself that no one was watching him, everyone was watching the plane. He walked to the escalator, false-touched the scanner – the cart beside it helped, justifying his awkwardness – and stepped on to the upgoing stairs. He clutched his paplon-wrapped kit and the damp-handled wrench as he rose quickly towards the open plane door. He stepped off the escalator and into the plane.

Two members in orange were busy at the dispensers. They looked at him and he nodded. They nodded back. He went down the aisle towards the bathroom.

He went into the bathroom, leaving the door open, and put his kit on the floor. He turned to a sink, worked its faucets, and tapped them with the wrench. He got down on his knees and tapped the drainpipe. He opened the jaws of the wrench and put them around the pipe.

He heard the escalator stop, and then start again. He leaned over and looked out the door. The members were gone.

He put down the wrench, got up, closed the door, and pulled open the orange coveralls. He took them off, folded them lengthwise, and rolled them into as compact a bundle as he could. Kneeling, he unwrapped his kit and opened it. He squeezed in the coveralls, and folded the yellow paplon and put that in too. He took the toeguards off his sandals, nested them together, and tucked them into one of the kit's corners. He put the wrench in, stretched the cover tight, and pressed it closed.

With the kit slung on his shoulder, he washed his hands and face with cold water. His heart was beating quickly but he felt good, excited, alive. He looked in the mirror at his one-green-eyed self. *Fight Uni!*

He heard the voices of members coming aboard the plane. He stayed at the sink, wiping his already-dry hands.

The door opened and a boy of ten or so came in.

'Hi,' Chip said, wiping his hands. 'Did you have a nice day?'

'Yes,' the boy said.

Chip chuted the towel. 'First time you've flown?'

'No,' the boy said, opening his coveralls. 'I've done it lots of times.' He sat down on one of the toilets.

157

'See you inside,' Chip said, and went out.

The plane was about a third filled, with more members filing in. He took the nearest empty aisle seat, checked his kit to make sure it was securely closed, and stowed it below.

It would be the same at the other end. When everyone was leaving the plane he would go into the bathroom and put on the orange coveralls. He would be working at the sink when the members came aboard with the refill containers and he would leave after they left. In the depot area behind a crate or in a closet, he would get rid of the coveralls, the toeguards, and the wrench; and then he would false-touch out of the airport and walk to '14509. It was eight kilometres east of '510; he had checked on a map at the MFA that morning. With luck he would be there by midnight or half past.

'Isn't that odd,' the member next to him said.

He turned to her.

She was looking towards the back of the plane. 'There's no seat for that member,' she said.

A member was walking slowly up the aisle, looking to one side and then the other. All the seats were taken. Members were looking about, trying to be of help to him.

'There *must* be one,' Chip said, lifting himself in his seat and looking about. 'Uni couldn't have made a mistake.'

'There's isn't,' the member next to him said. 'Every seat is filled.'

Conversation rose in the plane. There was indeed no seat for the member. A woman took a child on to her lap and called to him.

The plane began moving and the TV screens went on, with a programme about Afr's geography and resources.

He tried to pay attention to it, thinking there might be information in it that would be useful to him, but he couldn't. If he were found and treated now, he would never get alive again. This time Uni would make certain that he would see no meaning in even a thousand leaves on a thousand wet stones.

He got to '14509 at twenty past midnight. He was wide awake, still on Usa time, with afternoon energy.

First he went to the pre-U, and then to the bike station on

the plaza nearest building P51. He made two trips to the bike station, and one to P51's dining-hall and its supply centre.

At three o'clock he went into Lilac's room. He looked at her by flashlight while she slept – looked at her cheek, her neck, her dark hand on the pillow – and then he went to the desk and tapped on the lamp.

'Anna,' he said, standing at the foot of the bed. 'Anna, you have to get up now.'

She mumbled something.

'You have to get up now, Anna,' he said. 'Come on, get up.'

She raised herself with a hand at her eyes, making little sounds of complaint. Sitting, she drew the hand away and peered at him; recognized him and frowned bewilderedly.

'I want you to come for a ride with me,' he said. 'A bike ride. You mustn't talk loud and you mustn't call for help.' He reached into his pocket and took out a gun. He held it the way it seemed meant to be held, with his first finger across the trigger, the rest of his hand holding the handle, and the front of it pointed at her face. 'I'll kill you if you don't do what I tell you,' he said. 'Don't shout now, Anna.'

THREE

She stared at the gun, and at him.

'The generator's weak,' he said, 'but it made a hole a centi-metre deep in the wall of the museum and it'll make a deeper one in you. So you'd better obey me. I'm sorry to frighten you, but eventually you'll understand why I'm doing it.'

'This is terrible!' she said. 'You're still sick!'

'Yes,' he said, 'and I've gotten worse. So do as I say or the Family will lose two valuable members; first you, and then me.'

'How can you *do* this, Li?' she said. 'Can't you see yourself – with a *weapon* in your hand, *threatening* me?'

'Get up and get dressed,' he said.

'Please, let me call—'

'Get dressed,' he said. 'Quickly!'

'All right,' she said, turning aside the blanket. 'All right, I'll do exactly as you say.' She got up and opened her pyjamas.

He backed away, watching her, keeping the gun pointed at her.

She took off her pyjamas, let them fall, and turned to the shelf for a set of coveralls. He watched her breasts and the rest of her body, which in subtle ways – a fullness of the buttocks, a roundness of the thighs – was different too from the normal. How beautiful she was!

She stepped into the coveralls and put her arms into the sleeves. 'Li, I beg you,' she said, looking at him, 'let's go down to the medicentre and—'

'Don't talk,' he said.

She closed the coveralls and put her feet into her sandals. 'Why do you want to go *bicycling*?' she said. 'It's the middle of the night.'

'Pack your kit,' he said.

'My take-along?'

'Yes,' he said. 'Put in another set of cuvs and your first-aid kit and your clippers. And anything that's important to you that you want to keep. Do you have a flashlight?'

'What are you planning to *do*?' she asked.

'Pack your kit,' he said.

She packed her kit,' and when she had closed it he took it and slung it on his shoulder. 'We're going to go around behind the building,' he said. 'I've got two bikes there. We're going to walk side by side and I'll have the gun in my pocket. If we pass a member and you give any indication that anything's wrong, I'll kill you *and* the member, do you understand?'

'Yes,' she said.

'Do whatever I tell you. If I say stop and fix your sandal, stop and fix your sandal. We're going to pass scanners without touching them. You've done that before; now you're going to do it again.'

'We're not coming back here?' she said.

'No. We're going far away.'

'Then there's a snapshot I'd like to take.'

'Get it,' he said. 'I told you to take whatever you wanted to keep.'

160

She went to the desk, opened the drawer, and rummaged in it. *A snapshot of King?* he wondered. No, King was part of her 'sickness'. Probably one of her family. 'It's in here somewhere,' she said, sounding nervous, not right.

He hurried to her and pushed her aside. *Li RM gun 2 bicy* was written on the bottom of the drawer. A pen was in her hand. 'I'm trying to help you,' she said.

He felt like hitting her but stopped himself; but stopping was wrong, she would know he wouldn't hurt her; he hit her face with his open hand, stingingly hard. 'Don't try to trick me!' he said. 'Don't you realize how sick I am? *You'll* be dead and maybe a dozen *other* members will be dead if you do something like this again!'

She stared wide-eyed at him, trembling, her hand at her cheek.

He was trembling too, knowing he had hurt her. He snatched the pen from her hand, made zigzags over what she had written, and covered it with papers and a nameber book. He threw the pen in the drawer and closed it, took her elbow and pushed her towards the door.

They went out of her room and down the hallway, walking side by side. He kept his hand in his pocket, holding the gun. 'Stop shaking,' he said. 'I won't hurt you if you do what I tell you.'

They rode down escalators. Two members came towards them, riding up. 'You and them,' he said. 'And anyone else who comes along.'

She said nothing.

He smiled at the members. They smiled back. She nodded at them.

'This is my second transfer this year,' he said to her.

They rode down more escalators, and stepped on to the one leading to the lobby. Three members, two with tele-comps, stood talking by the scanner at one of the doors. 'No tricks now,' he said.

They rode down, reflected at a distance in dark-outside glass. The members kept talking. One of them put his tele-comp on the floor.

They stepped off the escalator. 'Wait a minute, Anna,' he said. She stopped and faced him. 'I've got an eyelash in my eye,' he said. 'Do you have a tissue?'

She reached into her pocket and shook her head.

He found one under the gun and took it out and gave it to her. He stood facing the members and held his eye wide open, his other hand in his pocket again. She held the tissue to his eye. She was still trembling. 'It's only an eyelash,' he said. 'Nothing to be nervous about.'

Beyond her the member had picked up his telecomp and the three were shaking hands and kissing. The two with telecomps touched the scanner. Yes, it winked, yes. They went out. The third member came towards them, a man in his twenties.

Chip moved Lilac's hand away. 'That's it,' he said, blinking. 'Thanks, sister.'

'Can I be of help?' the member asked. 'I'm a 101.'

'No, thanks, it was just an eyelash,' Chip said. Lilac moved. Chip looked at her. She put the tissue in her pocket.

The member, glancing at the kit, said, 'Have a good trip.'

'Thanks,' Chip said. 'Goodnight.'

'Goodnight,' the member said, smiling at them.

'Goodnight,' Lilac said.

They went towards the doors and saw in them the reflection of the member stepping on to an upgoing escalator. 'I'm going to lean close to the scanner,' Chip said. 'Touch the side of it, not the plate.'

They went outside. 'Please, Li,' Lilac said, 'for the sake of the Family, let's go back in and go up to the medicentre.'

'Be quiet,' he said.

They turned into the passageway between the building and the next one. The darkness grew deeper and he took out his flashlight.

'What are you going to do to me?' she asked.

'Nothing,' he said, 'unless you try to trick me again.'

'Then what do you want me for?' she asked.

He didn't answer.

There was a scanner at the cross-passage behind the buildings. Lilac's hand went up; Chip said, 'No!' They passed it without touching, and Lilac made a distressed sound and said under her breath, 'Terrible.'

The bikes were leaning against the wall where he had left them. His blanket-wrapped kit was in the basket of one, with cakes and drink containers squeezed in with it. A blanket was draped over the basket of the other; he put Lilac's kit down into it and closed the blanket around it, tucking it snugly. 'Get on,' he said, holding the bike upright for her.

She got on and held the handlebars.

'We'll go straight along between the buildings to the East Road,' he said. 'Don't turn or stop or gear up unless I tell you to.'

He got astride the other bike. He pushed the flashlight down into the side of the basket, with the light shining out through the mesh at the pavement ahead.

'All right, let's go,' he said.

They pedalled side by side down the straight passage that was all darkness except for columns of lesser darkness between buildings, and far above a narrow strip of stars, and far ahead the pale blue spark of a single walkway light.

'Gear up a little,' he said.

They rode faster.

'When are you due for your next treatment?' he asked.

She was silent, and then said, 'Marx eighth.'

Two weeks, he thought. Christ and Wei, why couldn't it have been tomorrow or the next day? Well, it could have been worse; it could have been *four* weeks.

'Will I be able to get it?' she asked.

There was no point in disturbing her more than he had already. 'Maybe,' he said. 'We'll see.'

He had intended to go a short distance every day, during the free hour when cyclists would attract no attention. They would go from parkland to parkland, passing one city or perhaps two, and make their way by small steps to '12082 on Afr's north coast, the city nearest Majorca.

That first day, though, in the parkland north of '14509, he changed his mind. Finding a hiding place was harder than he expected; not until long after sunrise – around eight o'clock, he guessed – were they settled under a rock-ledge canopy fronted by a thicket of saplings whose gaps he had filled with cut branches. Soon after, they heard a copter's hum; it passed and repassed above them while he pointed the gun at Lilac and she sat motionless, watching him, a half-eaten cake in her hands. At midday they heard branches

163

cracking, leaves slashing, and a voice no more than twenty metres away. It spoke unintelligibly, in the slow flat way one addressed a telephone or a voice-input telecomp.

Either Lilac's desk-drawer message had been found or, more likely, Uni had put together his disappearance, her disappearance, and two missing bicycles. So he changed his mind and decided that having been looked for and missed, they would stay where they were all week and ride on Sunday. They would make a sixty- or seventy-kilometre hop – not directly to the north but to the northeast – then settle and hide for another week. Four or five Sundays would bring them in a curving path to '12082, and each Sunday Lilac would be more herself and less Anna SG, more helpful or at least less anxious to see him 'helped'.

Now, though, she was Anna SG. He tied and gagged her with blanket strips and slept with the gun at his hand till the sun went down. In the middle of the night he tied and gagged her again, and carried away his bike. He came back in a few hours with cakes and drinks and two more blankets, towels and toilet paper, a 'wristwatch' that had already stopped ticking, and two Français books. She was lying awake where he had left her, her eyes anxious and pitying. Held captive by a sick member, she suffered his abuses forgivingly. She was sorry for him.

But in daylight she looked at him with revulsion. He touched his cheek and felt two days' stubble. Smiling, slightly embarrassed, he said, 'I haven't had a treatment in almost a year.'

She lowered her head and put a hand over her eyes. 'You've made yourself into an animal,' she said.

'That's what we are, really,' he said. 'Christ, Marx, Wood, and Wei made us into something dead and unnatural.'

She turned away when he began to shave, but she glanced over her shoulder, glanced again, and then turned and watched distastefully. 'Don't you cut your skin?' she asked.

'I did in the beginning,' he said, pressing taut his cheek and working the razor easily, watching it in the side of his flashlight propped on a stone. 'I had to keep my hand at my face for days.'

'Do you always use tea?' she asked.

He laughed. 'No,' he said. 'It's a substitute for water. To-

164

night I'm going to go looking for a pond or a stream.'

'How often do you – do that?' she asked.

'Every day,' he said. 'I missed yesterday. It's a nuisance, but it's only for a few more weeks. At least I hope so.'

'What do you mean?' she said.

He said nothing, kept shaving.

She turned away.

He read one of the Français books, about the cause of a war that lasted thirty years. Lilac slept, and then she sat on a blanket and looked at him and at the trees and at the sky.

'Do you want me to teach you this language?' he asked.

'What for?' she said.

'Once you wanted to learn it,' he said. 'Do you remember? I gave you lists of words.'

'Yes,' she said, 'I remember. I learned them, but I've forgotten them. I'm well now; what would I want to learn it now for?'

He did callisthenics and made her do them too, so that they would be ready for Sunday's long ride. She followed his directions unprotestingly.

That night he found, not a stream, but a concrete-banked irrigation channel about two metres wide. He bathed in its slow-flowing water, then brought filled drink containers back to the hiding place and woke Lilac and untied her. He led her through the trees and stood and watched while she bathed. Her wet body glistened in the faint light of the quarter moon.

He helped her up on to the bank, handed her a towel, and stayed close to her while she dried herself. 'Do you know why I'm doing this?' he asked her.

She looked at him.

'Because I love you,' he said.

'Then let me go,' she said.

He shook his head.

'Then how can you say you love me?'

'I do,' he said.

She bent over and dried her legs. 'Do you want me to get sick again?' she asked.

'Yes,' he said.

'Then you *hate* me,' she said, 'you don't love me.' She stood up straight.

He took her arm, cool and moist, smooth. 'Lilac,' he said. 'Anna.'

He tried to kiss her lips but she turned her head and drew away. He kissed her cheek.

'Now point your gun at me and "rape" me,' she said.

'I won't do that,' he said. He let go of her arm.

'I don't know why not,' she said, getting into her coveralls. She closed them fumblingly. 'Please, Li,' she said, 'let's go back to the city. I'm *sure* you can be cured, because if you were really sick, *incurably* sick, you *would* "rape" me. You'd be much less kind than you are.'

'Come on,' he said, 'let's get back to the place.'

'Please, Li—' she said.

'*Chip*,' he said. 'My name is *Chip*. Come on.' He jerked his head and they started through the trees.

Towards the end of the week she took his pen and the book he wasn't reading and drew pictures on the inside of the book's cover – near-likenesses of Christ and Wei, groups of buildings, her left hand, and a row of shaded crosses and sickles. He looked to make sure she wasn't writing messages that she would try to give to someone on Sunday.

Later he drew a building and showed it to her.

'What is it?' she asked.

'A building,' he said.

'No it isn't.'

'It is,' he said. 'They don't all have to be blank and rectangular.'

'What are the ovals?'

'Windows.'

'I've never seen a building like this one,' she said. 'Not even in the pre-U. Where is it?'

'Nowhere,' he said. 'I made it up.'

'Oh,' she said. 'Then it isn't a building, not really. How can you draw things that aren't real?'

'I'm sick, remember?' he said.

She gave the book back to him, not looking at his eyes. 'Don't joke about it,' she said.

He hoped – well, didn't *hope*, but thought it might possibly happen – that Saturday night, out of custom or desire

166

or even only memberlike kindness, she would show a willingness for him to come close to her. She didn't, though. She was the same as she had been every other night, sitting silently in the dusk with her arms around her knees, watching the band of purpling sky between the shifting black treetops and the black rock ledge overhead.

'It's Saturday night,' he said.

'I know,' she said.

They were silent for a few moments, and then she said, 'I'm not going to be able to have my treatment, am I?'

'No,' he said.

'Then I might get pregnant,' she said. 'I'm not supposed to have children and neither are you.'

He wanted to tell her that they were going some place where Uni's decisions were meaningless, but it was too soon; she might become frightened and unmanageable. 'Yes, I suppose you're right,' he said.

When he had tied her and covered her, he kissed her cheek. She lay in the darkness and said nothing, and he got up from his knees and went to his own blankets.

Sunday's ride went well. Early in the day a group of young members stopped them, but it was only to ask their help in repairing a broken drive chain, and Lilac sat on the grass away from the group while Chip did the job. By sundown they were in the parkland north of '14266. They had gone about seventy-five kilometres.

Again it was hard to find a hiding place, but the one Chip finally found – the broken walls of a pre-U or early-U building, roofed with a sagging mass of vines and creepers – was larger and more comfortable than the one they had used the week before. The same night, despite the day's riding, he went into '266 and brought back a three-day supply of cakes and drinks.

Lilac grew irritable that week. 'I want to clean my *teeth*,' she said, 'and I want to take a shower. How long are we going to go on this way? For ever? You may enjoy living like an animal but I don't; I'm a human being. And I can't sleep with my hands and feet tied.'

'You slept all right last week,' he said.

'Well I can't now!'

'Then lie quietly and let *me* sleep,' he said.

When she looked at him it was with annoyance, not with pity. She made disapproving sounds when he shaved and when he read; answered curtly or not at all when he spoke. She balked at doing callisthenics, and he had to take out the gun and threaten her.

It was getting close to Marx eighth, her treatment day, he told himself, and this irritability, a natural resentment of captivity and discomfort, was a sign of the healthy Lilac who was buried in Anna SG. It ought to have pleased him, and when he thought about it, it did. But it was much harder to live with than the previous week's sympathy and member-like docility.

She complained about insects and boredom. There was a rain night and she complained about the rain.

One night Chip woke and heard her moving. He shone his flashlight at her. She had untied her wrists and was untying her ankles. He retied her and struck her.

That Saturday night they didn't speak to each other.

On Sunday they rode again. Chip stayed close to her side and watched her carefully when members came towards them. He reminded her to smile, to nod, to answer greetings, to act as if nothing was wrong. She rode in grim silence, and he was afraid that despite the threat of the gun she might call out for help at any moment or stop and refuse to go on. 'Not just you,' he said; 'everyone in sight. I'll kill them all, I swear I will.' She kept riding. She smiled and nodded resentfully. Chip's gearshift jammed and they went only forty kilometres.

Towards the end of the third week her irritation subsided. She sat frowning, picking at blades of grass, looking at her fingertips, turning her bracelet around and around her wrist. She looked at Chip curiously, as if he were someone strange whom she hadn't seen before. She followed his instructions slowly, mechanically.

He worked on his bike, letting her awaken in her own time.

One evening in the fourth week she said, 'Where are we going?'

He looked at her for a moment – they were eating the

day's last cake — and said, 'To an island called Majorca. In the Sea of Eternal Peace.'

' "Majorca"?' she said.

'It's an island of incurables,' he said. 'There are seven others all over the world. More than seven, really, because some of them are groups. I found them on a map in the Pre-U, back in Ind. They were covered over and they're not shown on MFA maps. I was going to tell you about them the day I was — "cured".'

She was silent, and then she said, 'Did you tell King?'

It was the first time she had mentioned him. Should he tell her that King hadn't needed to be told, that he had known all along and withheld it from them? What for? King was dead; why diminish her memory of him? 'Yes, I did,' he said. 'He was amazed, and very excited. I don't understand why he — did what he did. You know about it, don't you?'

'Yes, I know,' she said. She took a small slice of cake and ate it, not looking at him. 'How do they live on this island?' she asked.

'I have no idea,' he said. 'It might be very rough, very primitive. Better than this, though.' He smiled. 'Whatever it's like,' he said, 'it's a free life. It might be highly civilized. The first incurables must have been the most independent and resourceful members.'

'I'm not sure that I want to go there,' she said.

'Just think about it,' he said. 'In a few days you'll be sure. You're the one who had the idea that incurable colonies might exist, do you remember? You asked me to look for them.'

She nodded. 'I remember,' she said.

Later in the week she took a new Français book that he had found and tried to read it. He sat beside her and translated it for her.

That Sunday, while they were riding along, a member pedalled up on Chip's left and stayed even with them. 'Hi,' he said.

'Hi,' Chip said.

'I thought all the old bikes had been phased out,' he said.

'So did I,' Chip said, 'but these are what was there.'

The member's bike had a thinner frame and a thumb-knob gear control. 'Back in '935?' he asked.

'No, '939,' Chip said.

'Oh,' the member said. He looked at their baskets, filled with their blanket-wrapped kits.

'We'd better speed up, Li,' Lilac said. 'The others are out of sight.'

'They'll wait for us,' Chip said. 'They have to; we have the cakes and blankets.'

The member smiled.

'No, come on, let's go faster,' Lilac said. 'It's not fair to make them wait around.'

'All right,' Chip said, and to the member, 'Have a good day.'

'You too,' he said.

They pedalled faster and pulled ahead.

'Good for you,' Chip said. 'He was just going to ask why we're carrying so much.'

Lilac said nothing.

They went about eighty kilometres that day and reached the parkland northwest of '12471, within another day's ride of '082. They found a fairly good hiding place, a triangular cleft between high rock spurs overhung with trees. Chip cut branches to close off the front of it.

'You don't have to tie me any more,' Lilac said. 'I won't run away and I won't try to attract anyone. You can put the gun in your kit.'

'You want to go?' Chip asked. 'To Majorca?'

'Of course,' she said. 'I'm anxious to. It's what I've always wanted – when I've been myself, I mean.'

'All right,' he said. He put the gun in his kit and that night he didn't tie her.

Her casual matter-of-factness didn't seem right to him. Shouldn't she have shown more enthusiasm? Yes, and gratitude too; that was what he had expected, he admitted to himself : gratitude, expressions of love. He lay awake listening to her slow soft breathing. Was she really asleep or was she only pretending? Could she be tricking him in some unimaginable way? He shone his flashlight at her. Her eyes were closed, her lips, parted, her arms together under the blanket as if she were still tied.

It was only Marx twentieth, he told himself. In another week or two she would show more feeling. He closed his eyes. When he awoke she was picking stones and twigs from the ground. 'Good morning,' she said pleasantly.

They found a narrow trickle of stream nearby, and a green-fruited tree that he thought was an 'olivier'. The fruit was bitter and strange-tasting. They both preferred cakes.

She asked him how he had avoided his treatments, and he told her about the leaf and the wet stone and the bandages he had made. She was impressed. It was clever of him, she said.

They went into '12471 one night for cakes and drinks, towels, toilet paper, coveralls, new sandals; and to study, as well as they could by flashlight, the MFA map of the area.

'What will we do when we get to '082?' she asked the next morning.

'Hide by the shore,' he said, 'and watch every night for traders.'

'Would they do that?' she asked. 'Risk coming ashore?'

'Yes,' he said, 'I think they would, away from the city.'

'But wouldn't they be more likely to go to Eur? It's nearer.'

'We'll just have to hope they come to Afr too,' he said. 'And I want to get some things from the city for *us* to trade when we get *there*, things that they're likely to put a value on. We'll have to think about that.'

'Is there any chance that we can find a boat?' she asked.

'I don't think so,' he said. 'There aren't any offshore islands, so there aren't likely to be any powerboats around. Of course, there are always amusement-garden rowboats, but I can't see us rowing two hundred and eighty kilometres; can you?'

'It's not impossible,' she said.

'No,' he said, 'if worse comes to worst. But I'm counting on traders, or maybe even some kind of organized rescue operation. Majorca has to defend itself, you see, because Uni knows about it; it knows about all the islands. So the members there might keep a lookout for newcomers, to increase their population, increase their strength.'

'I suppose they might,' she said.

There was another rain night, and they sat together with

171

a blanket around them in the inmost narrow corner of their place, tight between the high rock spurs. He kissed her and tried to work open the top of her coveralls, but she stopped his hand with hers. 'I know it doesn't make sense,' she said, 'but I still have a little of that only-on-Saturday-night feeling. Please? Could we wait till then?'

'It *doesn't* make sense,' he said.

'I know,' she said, 'but please? Could we wait?'

After a moment he said, 'Sure, if you want to.'

'I do, Chip,' she said.

They read, and decided on the best things to take from '082 for trading. He checked over the bikes and she did callisthenics, did them longer and more purposefully than he did.

On Saturday night he came back from the stream and she stood holding the gun, pointing it at him, her eyes narrowed hatingly. 'He called me before he did it,' she said.

He said, 'What are you—' and 'King!' she cried. 'He called me! You lying, hating—' She squeezed the gun's trigger. She squeezed it again harder. She looked at the gun and looked at him.

'There's no generator,' he said.

She looked at the gun and looked at him, drawing a deep breath through flaring nostrils.

'Why the hate do you—' she said, and she swept back the gun and threw it at him; he raised his hands and it hit him in the chest, making pain and no air in him.

'Go with you?' she said. '*Fuck* with you? After you killed him? Are you – are you *fou*, you green-eyed *cochon*, *chien*, *bâtard*!'

He held his chest, found breath. 'Didn't kill him!' he said. 'He killed *himself*, Lilac! Christ and—'

'Because you lied to him! Lied about us! Told him we'd been—'

'That was *his* idea; I told him it wasn't true! I told him and he wouldn't believe me!'

'You *admitted* it,' she said. 'He said he didn't care, we deserved each other, and then he tapped off and—'

'Lilac,' he said, 'I swear by my love of the Family, I told him it wasn't true!'

'*Then why did he kill himself?*'

172

'Because he knew!'

'Because you told him!' she said, and turned and grabbed up her bike – its basket was packed – and rammed it against the branches piled at the place's front.

He ran and caught the back of the bike, held it with both hands. 'You stay here!' he said.

'Let go of it!' she said, turning.

He took the bike at its middle, wrenched it away from her, and flung it aside. He grabbed her arm. She hit at him but he held her. 'He knew about the *islands*!' he said. 'The *islands*! He'd *been* near one, traded with the members! That's how I know they come ashore!'

She stared at him. 'What are you talking about?' she said.

'He'd had an assignment near one of the islands,' he said. 'The Falklands, off Arg. And he'd met the members and traded with them. He hadn't told us because he knew we would want to go, and *he didn't* want to! That's why he killed himself! He knew you were going to find out, from me, and he was ashamed of himself, and tired, and he wasn't going to be "King" any more.'

'You're lying to me the way you lied to him,' she said, and tore her arm free, her coveralls splitting at the shoulder.

'That's how he got the perfume and tobacco seeds,' he said.

'I don't want to hear you,' she said. 'Or see you. I'm going by myself.' She went to her bike, picked up her kit and the blanket trailing from it.

'Don't be stupid,' he said.

She righted the bike, dumped the kit in the basket, and jammed the blanket in on top of it. He went to her and held the bike's seat and handlebar. 'You're not going alone,' he said.

'Oh yes I am,' she said, her voice quavering. They held the bike between them. Her face was blurred in the growing darkness.

'I'm not going to let you,' he said.

'I'll do what *he* did before I go with *you*.'

'You listen to me, you—' he said. 'I could have been on one of the islands half a year ago! I was on my way and I turned back, because I didn't want to leave you dead and

173

brainless!' He put his hand on her chest and pushed her hard, sent her back flat against rock wall and slung the bike rolling and bumping away. He went to her and held her arms against the rock. 'I came all the way from Usa,' he said, 'and I haven't enjoyed this animal life any more than you have. I don't give a fight whether you love me or hate me' – 'I hate you,' she said – 'you're going to stay with me! The gun doesn't work but other things do, like rocks and hands. You won't have to kill yourself because—' Pain burst in his groin – her knee – and she was away from him and at the branches, a pale yellow shape, thrashing, pushing.

He went and caught her by the arm, swung her around, and threw her shrieking to the ground. '*Bâtard!*' she shrieked. '*You sick aggressive*—' and he dived on to her and clapped his hand over her mouth, clamped it down as tight as he could. Her teeth caught the skin of his palm and bit it, bit it harder. Her legs kicked and her fisted palms hit his head. He got a knee on her thigh, a foot on her other ankle; caught her wrist, let her other hand hit him, her teeth go on biting. 'Someone might be here!' he said. 'It's Saturday night! Do you want to get us *both* treated, you stupid garce?' She kept hitting him, biting his palm.

The hitting slowed and stopped; her teeth parted, let go. She lay panting, watching him. 'Garce!' he said. She tried to move the leg under his foot, but he bore down harder against it. He kept holding her wrist and covering her mouth. His palm felt as if she had bitten flesh out of it.

Having her under him, having her subdued, with her legs held apart, suddenly excited him. He thought of tearing off her coveralls and 'raping' her. Hadn't she said they should wait till Saturday night? And maybe it would stop all the cloth about King, and her hating him; stop the fighting – that was what they had been doing, *fighting* – and the Français hate-names.

Her eyes looked at him.

He let go of her wrist and took her coveralls where they were split at the shoulder. He tore them down across her chest and she began hitting him again and straining her legs and biting his palm.

He tore the coveralls away in stretching splitting pieces until her whole front was open, and then he felt her; felt

174

her soft fluid breasts and her stomach's smoothness, her mound with a few close-lying hairs on it, the moist lips below. Her hands hit his head and clutched at his hair; her teeth bit his palm. He kept feeling her with his other hand – breasts, stomach, mound, lips; stroking, rubbing, fingering, growing more excited – and then he opened his coveralls. Her leg wrenched out from under his foot and kicked. She rolled, trying to throw him off her, but he pressed her back down, held her thigh, and threw his leg over hers. He mounted squarely atop her, his feet on her ankles locking her legs bent outward around his knees. He ducked his loins and thrust himself at her; caught one of her hands and fingers of the other. 'Stop,' he said, 'stop,' and kept thrusting. She bucked and squirmed, bit deeper into his palm. He found himself partway inside her; pushed, and was all the way in. 'Stop,' he said, 'stop.' He moved his length slowly; let go of her hands and found her breasts beneath him. He caressed their softness, and stiffening nipples. She bit his hand and squirmed. 'Stop,' he said, 'stop it, Lilac.' He moved himself slowly in her, then faster and harder.

He got up on to his knees and looked at her. She lay with one arm over her eyes and the other thrown back, her breasts rising and falling.

He stood up and found one of his blankets, shook it out and spread it over her up to her arms. 'Are you all right?' he asked, crouching beside her.

She didn't say anything.

He found his flashlight and looked at his palm. Blood was running from an oval of bright wounds. 'Christ and Wei,' he said. He poured water over it, washed it with soap, and dried it. He looked for the first-aid kit and couldn't find it. 'Did you take the first-aid kit?' he asked.

She didn't say anything.

Holding his hand up, he found her kit on the ground and opened it and got out the first-aid kit. He sat on a stone and put the kit in his lap and the flashlight on another stone alongside.

'Animal,' she said.

'I don't bite,' he said. 'And I also don't try to kill. Christ and Wei, you thought the gun was working.' He sprayed healer on his palm; a thin coat and then a thicker one.

'Cochon,' she said.

'Oh come on,' he said, 'don't start that again.'

He unwrapped a bandage and heard her getting up, heard her coveralls rustling as she took them off. She came over nude and took the flashlight and went to her kit; took out soap, a towel, and coveralls, and went to the back of the place, where he had piled stones between the spurs, making steps leading out towards the stream.

He put the bandage on in the dark and then found her flashlight on the ground near her bike. He put the bike with his, gathered blankets and made the two usual sleeping places, put her kit by hers, and picked up the gun and the pieces of her coveralls. He put the gun in his kit.

The moon slid over one of the spurs behind leaves that were black and motionless.

She didn't come back and he began to worry that she had gone away on foot.

Finally, though, she came. She put the soap and towel into her kit and switched off the flashlight and got between her blankets.

'I got excited having you under me that way,' he said. 'I've always wanted you, and these last few weeks have been just about unbearable. You know I love you, don't you?'

'I'm going alone,' she said.

'When we get to Majorca,' he said, 'if we get there, you can do what you want; but until we get there we're staying together. That's it, Lilac.'

She didn't say anything.

He woke hearing strange sounds, squeals and pained whimpers. He sat up and shone the light on her; her hand was over her mouth, and tears were running down her temple from her closed eyes.

He hurried to her and crouched beside her, touching her head. 'Lilac, don't,' he said. 'Don't cry, Lilac, please don't.' She was doing it, he thought, because he had hurt her, maybe internally.

She kept crying.

'Oh Lilac, I'm sorry!' he said. 'I'm sorry, love! Oh Christ and Wei, I wish the gun had been working!'

She shook her head, holding her mouth.

'Isn't that why you're crying?' he said. 'Because I hurt you? Then why? If you don't want to go with me, you don't really have to.'

She shook her head again and kept crying.

He didn't know what to do. He stayed beside her, caressing her head and asking her why she was crying and telling her not to, and then he got his blankets, spread them alongside her, and lay down and turned her to him and held her. She kept crying, and he woke up and she was looking at him, lying on her side with her head propped on her hand. 'It doesn't make sense for us to go separately,' she said, 'so we'll stay together.'

He tried to recall what they had said before sleeping. As far as he could remember, nothing; she had been crying. 'All right,' he said, confused.

'I feel awful about the gun,' she said. 'How could I have done that? I was sure you had lied to King.'

'I feel awful about what I did,' he said.

'Don't,' she said. 'I don't blame you. It was perfectly natural. How's your hand?'

He took it out from under the blanket and flexed it; it hurt badly. 'Not bad,' he said.

She took it in her hand and looked at the bandage. 'Did you spray it?' she asked.

'Yes,' he said.

She looked at him, still holding his hand. Her eyes were large and brown and morning-bright. 'Did you really start for one of the islands and turn back?' she asked.

He nodded.

She smiled. 'You're très fou,' she said.

'No, I'm not,' he said.

'You are,' she said, and looked at his hand again. She took it to her lips and kissed his fingertips one by one.

FOUR

They didn't get started until mid-morning, and then they rode quickly for a long while to make up for their laxness. It was an odd day, hazy and heavy-aired, the sky greenish grey and the sun a white disc that could be looked at with fully opened eyes. It was a freak of climate control; Lilac remembered a similar day in Chi when she was twelve or thirteen. ('Is that where you were born?' 'No, I was born in Mex.' 'You were? I was too!') There were no shadows, and bikes coming towards them seemed to ride above the ground like cars. Members glanced at the sky apprehensively, and coming nearer, nodded without smiling.

When they were sitting on the grass, sharing a container of cake, Chip said, 'We'd better go slowly from now on. There are liable to be scanners in the path and we want to be able to pick the right moment for passing them.'

'Scanners because of us?' she said.

'Not necessarily,' he said. 'Just because it's the city nearest to one of the islands. Wouldn't you set up extra safeguards if you were Uni?'

He wasn't as much afraid of scanners as he was that a medical team might be waiting ahead.

'What if there are members watching for us?' she said. 'Advisers or doctors, with pictures of us.'

'It's not very likely after all this time,' he said. 'We'll have to take our chances. I've got the gun, and the knife too.' He touched his pocket.

After a moment she said, 'Would you use it?'

'Yes,' he said. 'I think so.'

'I hope we don't have to,' she said.

'So do I.'

'You'd better put your sunglasses on,' she said.

'Today?' He looked at the sky.

'Because of your eye.'

'Oh,' he said. 'Of course.' He took his glasses out and put them on, looked at her and smiled. 'There's not much that you can do,' he said, 'except exhale.'

'What do you mean?' she said, then flushed and said, 'They're not noticeable when I'm dressed.'

'First thing I saw when I looked at you,' he said. 'First things I saw.'

'I don't believe you,' she said. 'You're lying. You are. Aren't you?'

He laughed and poked her on the chin.

They rode slowly. There were no scanners in the path. No medical team stopped them.

All the bicycles in the area were new ones, but nobody remarked on their old ones.

By late afternoon they were in '12082. They rode to the west of the city, smelling the sea, watching the path ahead carefully.

They left their bikes in parkland and walked back to a canteen where there were steps leading down to the beach. The sea was far below them, spreading away smooth and blue, away and away into greenish-grey haze.

'Those members didn't touch,' a child said.

Lilac's hand tightened on Chip's. 'Keep going,' he said. They walked down concrete steps jutting from rough cliff-face.

'Say, you there!' a member called, a man. 'You two members!'

Chip squeezed Lilac's hand and they turned around. The member was standing behind the scanner at the top of the steps, holding the hand of a naked girl of five or six. She scratched her head with a red shovel, looking at them.

'Did you touch just now?' the member asked.

They looked at each other and at the member. 'Of course we did,' Chip said. 'Yes, of course,' Lilac said.

'It didn't say yes,' the girl said.

'It did sister,' Chip said gravely. 'If it hadn't we wouldn't have gone on, would we?' He looked at the member and let a smile show. The member bent and said something to the girl.

'No I *didn't*,' she said.

'Come on,' Chip said to Lilac, and they turned and walked downwards again.

'Little hater,' Lilac said, and Chip said, 'Just keep going.'

They went all the way down and stopped at the bottom to take off their sandals. Chip, bending, looked up: the member and the girl were gone; other members were coming down.

The beach was half empty under the strange hazy sky. Members sat and lay on blankets, many of them in their coveralls. They were silent or talked softly, and the music of the speakers – 'Sunday, Fun Day' – sounded loud and unnatural. A group of children jumped rope by the water's edge: 'Christ, Marx, Wood, and Wei, led us to this perfect day; Marx, Wood, Wei, and Christ—'

They walked westward, holding hands and holding their sandals. The narrow beach grew narrower, emptier. Ahead a scanner stood flanked by cliff and sea. Chip said, 'I've never seen one on a beach before.'

'Neither have I,' Lilac said.

They looked at each other.

'This is the way we'll go,' he said. 'Later.'

She nodded and they walked closer to the scanner.

'I've got a fou impulse to touch it,' he said. ' "Fight you, Uni; here I am." '

'Don't you dare,' she said.

'Don't worry,' he said, 'I won't.'

They turned around and walked back to the centre of the beach. They took their coveralls off, went into the water, and swam far out. Treading with their backs to the sea, they studied the shore beyond the scanner, the grey cliffs lessening away into greenish-grey haze. A bird flew from the cliffs, circled, and flew back. It disappeared, gone in a hairline cranny.

'There are probably caves where we can stay,' Chip said.

A lifeguard whistled and waved at them. They swam back to the beach.

'It's five to five, members,' the speakers said. 'Litter and towels in the baskets, please. Be mindful of the members around you when you shake out your blankets.'

They dressed, went back up the steps, and walked to the grove of trees where they had left their bikes. They carried them farther in and sat down to wait. Chip cleaned the compass and the flashlights and the knife, and Lilac packed the other things they had into a single bundle.

An hour or so after dark they went to the canteen and gathered a carton of cakes and drinks and went down to the beach again. They walked to the scanner and beyond it. The night was moonless and starless; the haze of the day was still above. In the water's lapping edge phosphorescent sparks glittered now and then; otherwise there was only darkness. Chip held the carton of cakes and drinks under his arm and shone his flashlight ahead of them every few moments. Lilac carried the blanket-bundle.

'Traders won't come ashore on a night like this,' she said.

'Nobody else will be on the beach either,' Chip said. 'No sex-wild twelve-year-olds. It's a good thing.'

But it wasn't, he thought; it was a bad thing. What if the haze remained for days, for nights, blocking them at the very brink of freedom? Was it possible that Uni had *created* it, intentionally, for just that purpose? He smiled at himself. He was très fou, exactly as Lilac had said.

They walked until they guessed themselves to be midway between '082 and the next city to the west, and then they put down the carton and the bundle and searched the cliff face for a usable cave. They found one within minutes; a low-roofed sand-floored burrow littered with cake wrappers and, intriguingly, two pieces – a green 'Egypt', a pink 'Ethip' – torn from a pre-U map. They brought the carton and the bundle into the cave, spread their blankets, ate, and lay down together.

'Can you?' Lilac said. 'After this morning and last night?'

'Without treatments,' Chip said, 'all things are possible.'

'It's fantastic,' Lilac said.

Later Chip said, 'Even if we don't get any farther than this, even if we're caught and treated five minutes from now, it'll have been worth it. We've been ourselves, alive, for a few hours at least.'

'I want all of my life, not just a little of it,' Lilac said.

'You'll have it,' Chip said. 'I promise you.' He kissed her lips, caressing her cheek in the darkness. 'Will you stay with me?' he asked. 'On Majorca?'

'Of course,' she said. 'Why shouldn't I?'

'You weren't going to,' he said. 'Remember? You weren't even going to come this far with me.'

'Christ and Wei, that was *last night*,' she said, and kissed him. 'Of course I'm going to stay,' she said. 'You woke me up and now you're stuck with me.'

They lay holding each other and kissing each other.

'Chip!' she cried – in reality, not in his dream.

She was beside him. He sat up and banged his head on stone, groped for the knife he had left stuck in the sand.

'Chip! Look!' – as he found it and threw himself over on to knees and one hand. She was a dark shape crouched at the cave's blinding blue opening. He raised the knife, ready to slash whoever was coming.

'No, no,' she said, laughing. 'Come look! Come on! You won't believe it!'

Squinting at the brilliance of sky and sea, he crawled over to her. 'Look,' she said happily, pointing up the beach.

A boat sat on the sand about fifty metres away, a small two-rotor launch, old, with a white hull and a red skirting. It sat just clear of the water, tipped slightly forward. There were white splatters on the skirting and the windscreen, part of which seemed to be missing.

'Let's see if it's good!' Lilac said. With her hand on Chip's shoulder she started to rise from the cave; he dropped the knife, caught her arm, and pulled her back. 'Wait a minute,' he said.

'What for?' She looked at him.

He rubbed his head where he had bumped it, and frowned at the boat – so white and red and empty and convenient in the bright morning haze-free sun. 'It's a trick of some kind,' he said. 'A trap. It's too convenient. We go to sleep and wake up and a boat's been delivered for us. You're right, I don't believe it.'

'It wasn't "delivered" for us,' she said. 'It's been here for weeks. Look at the bird stuff on it, and how deep in the sand the front of it is.'

'Where did it come from?' he asked. 'There are no islands nearby.'

'Maybe traders brought it from Majorca and got caught on shore,' she said. 'Or maybe they left it behind on purpose for members like us. You said there might be a rescue operation.'

'And nobody's seen it and reported it in the time it's been here?'

'Uni hasn't let anyone on to this part of the beach.'

'Let's wait,' he said. 'Let's just watch and wait a while.'

Reluctantly she said, 'All right.'

'It's too convenient,' he said.

'Why must everything be inconvenient?'

They stayed in the cave. They ate and rebundled the blankets, always watching the boat. They took turns crawling to the back of the cave, and buried their wastes in sand.

Wave edges slipped under the back of the boat's skirting, then fell away towards low tide. Birds circled and landed on the windscreen and handrail, four that were sea gulls and two smaller brown ones.

'It's getting filthier every minute,' Lilac said. 'And what if it's *been* reported and today's the day it's going to be taken away?'

'Whisper, will you?' Chip said. 'Christ and Wei, I wish I'd brought a telescope.'

He tried to improvise one from the compass lens, a flashlight lens, and a rolled flap of the food carton, but he couldn't make it work.

'How long are we going to wait?' she asked.

'Till after dark,' he said.

No one passed on the beach, and the only sounds were the waves' lapping and the wingbeats and cries of the birds.

He went to the boat alone, slowly and cautiously. It was older than it had looked from the cave; the hull's flaking white paint showed repair scars, and the skirting was dented and cracked. He walked around it without touching it, looking with his flashlight for signs – he didn't know what form they would take – of deception, of danger. He didn't see any; he saw only an old boat that had been inexplicably abandoned, its centre seats gone, a third of its windscreen broken away, and all of it spattered with dried white birdwaste. He switched his light off and looked at the cliff – touched the boat's handrail and waited for an alarm. The cliff stayed dark and deserted in pale moonlight.

He stepped on to the skirting, climbed into the boat and shone his light on its controls. They seemed simple enough: on-off switches for the propulsion rotors and the lift rotor, a speed-control knob calibrated to 100 KPH, a steering lever, a few gauges and indicators, and a switch marked *Controlled* and *Independent* that was set in the independent position. He found the battery housing on the floor between the front seats and unlatched its cover; the battery's fade-out date was April 171, a year away.

He shone his light at the rotor housings. Twigs were piled in one of them. He brushed them out, picked them all out,

183

and shone the light on the rotor within; it was new, shiny. The other rotor was old, its blades nicked and one missing.

He sat down at the controls and found the switch that lighted them. A miniature clock said 5.11 Fri 27 Aug 169. He switched on one propulsion rotor and then the other; they scraped but then hummed smoothly. He switched them off, looked at the gauges and indicators, and switched the control lights off.

The cliff was the same as before. No members had sprung from hiding. He turned to the sea behind him; it was empty and flat, silvered in a narrowing path that ended under the nearly full moon. No boats were flying towards him.

He sat in the boat for a few minutes, and then he climbed out of it and walked back to the cave.

Lilac was standing outside it. 'Is it all right?' she asked.

'No, it's not,' he said. 'It wasn't left by traders because there's no message or anything in it. The clock stopped last year but it has a new rotor. I didn't try the lift rotor because of the sand, but even if it works, the skirting is cracked in two places and it may just wallow and get nowhere. On the other hand it may take us directly into '082 – to a little seaside medicentre – even though it's supposed to be off telecontrol.'

Lilac stood looking at him.

'We might as well try it though,' he said. 'If traders didn't leave it, they're not going to come ashore while it's sitting here. Maybe we're just two very lucky members.' He gave the flashlight to her.

He got the carton and the blanket-bundle from the cave and held one under each arm. They started walking towards the boat. 'What about the things to trade?' she said.

'We'll have it,' he said. 'A boat must be worth a hundred times more than cameras and first-aid kits.' He looked towards the cliff. 'All right, doctors!' he called. 'You can come out now!'

'Shh, *don't*!' she said.

'We forgot the sandals,' he said.

'They're in the carton.'

He put the carton and the bundle into the boat and they scraped the birdwaste from the broken windscreen with pieces of shell. They lifted the front of the boat and hauled

184

it around towards the sea, then lifted the back and hauled again.

They kept lifting and hauling at either end and finally they had the boat down in the surf, bobbing and veering clumsily. Chip held it while Lilac climbed aboard, and then he pushed it farther out and climbed in with her.

He sat down at the controls and switched on their lights. She sat in the seat beside him, watching. He glanced at her – she looked anxiously at him – and he switched on the propulsion rotors and then the lift rotor. The boat shook violently, flinging them from side to side. Loud clankings banged from beneath it. He caught the steering lever, held it, and turned the speed-control knob. The boat splashed forward and the shaking and clanging lessened. He turned the speed higher, to twenty, twenty-five. The clanking stopped and the shaking subsided to a steady vibration. The boat scuffed along on the water's surface.

'It's not lifting,' he said.

'But it's moving,' she said.

'For how long though? It's not built to hit the water this way and the skirting's cracked already.' He turned the speed higher and the boat splashed through the crests of swells. He tried the steering lever; the boat responded. He steered north, got out his compass, and compared its reading with the direction indicator's. 'It's not taking us into '082,' he said. 'At least not yet.'

She looked behind them, and up at the sky. 'No one's coming,' she said.

He turned the speed higher and got a little more lift, but the impact when they scraped the swells was greater. He turned the speed back down. The knob was at fifty-six. 'I don't think we're doing more than forty,' he said. 'It'll be light when we get there, if we get there. It's just as well, I suppose; I won't get us on to the wrong island. I don't know how much this is throwing us off course.'

Two other islands were near Majorca: EUR91766, forty kilometres to the northeast, the site of a copper-production complex; and EUR91603, eighty-five kilometres to the southwest, where there was an algae-processing complex and a climatonomy sub-centre.

Lilac leaned close to Chip, avoiding the wind and spray

from the broken part of the windscreen. Chip held the steering lever. He watched the direction indicator and the moonlit sea ahead and the stars that shone above the horizon.

The stars dissolved, the sky began to lighten, and there was no Majorca. There was only the sea, placid and endless all around them.

'If we're doing forty,' Lilac said, 'it should have taken seven hours. It's been more than that, hasn't it?'

'Maybe we haven't been doing forty,' Chip said.

Or maybe he had compensated too much or too little for the eastward drift of the sea. Maybe they had passed Majorca and were heading towards Eur. Or maybe Majorca didn't exist – had been blanked from pre-U maps because pre-U members had 'bombed' it to nothing and why should the Family be reminded again of folly and barbarism?

He kept the boat headed a hairline west of north, but slowed it down a little.

The sky grew lighter and still there was no island, no Majorca. They scanned the horizon silently, avoiding each other's eyes.

One final star glimmered above the water in the northeast. No, glimmered *on* the water. No – 'There's a light over there,' he said.

She looked where he pointed, held his arm.

The light moved in an arc from side to side, then up and down as if beckoning. It was a kilometre or so away.

'Christ and Wei,' Chip said softly, and steered towards it.

'Be careful,' Lilac said. 'Maybe it's—'

He changed hands on the steering lever and got the knife from his pocket, laid it in his lap.

The light went out and a small boat was there. Someone sat waving in it, waving a pale thing that he put on his head – a hat – and then waving his empty hand and arm.

'One member,' Lilac said.

'One *person*,' Chip said. He kept steering towards the boat – a rowboat, it looked like – with one hand on the lever and the other on the speed-control knob.

'Look at him!' Lilac said.

The waving man was small and white-bearded, with a

ruddy face below his broad-brimmed yellow hat. He was wearing a blue-topped white legged garment.

Chip slowed the boat, steered it near the rowboat, and switched all three rotors off.

The man – old past sixty-two and blue-eyed, fantastically blue-eyed – smiled with brown teeth and gaps where teeth were missing and said, 'Running from the dummies, are you? Looking for liberty?' His boat bobbed in their side-waves. Poles and nets shifted in it – fish-catching equipment.

'Yes,' Chip said. 'Yes, we are! We're trying to find Majorca.'

'Majorca?' the man said. He laughed and scratched his beard. 'Myorca,' he said. 'Not Majorca, Myorca! But *Liberty* is what it's called now. It hasn't been called Myorca for – God knows, a hundred years, I guess! Liberty, it is.'

'Are we near it?' Lilac asked, and Chip said, 'We're friends. We haven't come to – interfere in any way, to try to "cure" you or anything.'

'We're incurables ourselves,' Lilac said.

'You wouldn't be coming this way if you wasn't,' the man said. 'That's what I'm here for, to watch for folks like you and help them into port. Yes, you're near it. That's it over there.' He pointed to the north.

And now on the horizon a dark green bar lay low and clear. Pink streaks glowed above its western half – mountains lit by the sun's first rays.

Chip and Lilac looked at it, and looked at each other, and looked again at Majorca-Myorca-Liberty.

'Hold fast,' the man said, 'and I'll tie on to your stern and come aboard.'

They turned in their seats and faced each other. Chip took the knife from his lap, smiled, and tossed it to the floor. He took Lilac's hands.

They smiled at each other.

'I thought we'd gone past it,' she said.

'So did I,' he said. 'Or that it didn't even exist any more.'

They smiled at each other, and leaned forward and kissed each other.

'Hey, give me a hand here will you?' the man said looking at them over the back of the boat, clinging with dirty-nailed fingers.

They got up quickly and went to him. Chip kneeled on the back seat and helped him over.

His clothes were made of cloth, his hat woven of flat strips of yellow fibre. He was half a head shorter than they and smelled strangely and strongly. Chip grasped his hard-skinned hand and shook it. 'I'm Chip,' he said, 'and this is Lilac.'

'Glad to meet you,' the bearded blue-eyed old man said, smiling his ugly-toothed smile. 'I'm Darren Costanza.' He shook Lilac's hand.

'Darren Costanza?' Chip said.

'That's the name.'

'It's beautiful!' Lilac said.

'You've got a good boat here,' Darren Costanza said, looking about.

'It doesn't lift,' Chip said, and Lilac said, 'But it got us here. We were lucky to find it.'

Darren Costanza smiled at them 'And your pockets are filled with cameras and things?' he said.

'No,' Chip said, 'we decided not to take anything. The tide was in and—'

'Oh, that was a mistake,' Darren Costanza said. 'Didn't you take *anything*?'

'A gun without a generator,' Chip said, taking it from his pocket. 'And a few books and a razor in the bundle there.'

'Well, this is worth something,' Darren Costanza said, taking the gun and looking at it, thumbing its handle.

'We'll have the boat to trade,' Lilac said.

'You should have taken more,' Darren Costanza said, turning from them and moving away. They glanced at each other and looked at him again, about to follow, but he turned, holding a gun. He pointed it at them and put Chip's gun into his pocket. 'This old thing shoots bullets,' he said, backing farther away to the front seats. 'Doesn't need a generator,' he said. 'Bang, bang. Into the water now, real quick. Go on. Into the water.'

They looked at him.

'*Get in the water, you dumb steelies!*' he shouted. 'You want a bullet in your head?' He moved something at the back of the gun and pointed it at Lilac.

188

Chip pushed her to the side of the boat. She clambered over the rail and on to the skirting – saying 'What is he doing this for?' – and slipped down into the water. Chip jumped in after her.

'Away from the boat!' Darren Costanza shouted. 'Clear away! Swim!'

They swam a few metres, their coveralls ballooning around them, then turned, treading water.

'What are you *doing* this for?' Lilac asked.

'Figure it out for yourself, steely!' Darren Costanza said, sitting at the boat's controls.

'We'll drown if you leave us!' Chip cried. 'We can't swim that far!'

'Who told you to come here?' Darren Costanza said, and the boat rushed splashing away, the rowboat dragging from its back carving up fins of foam.

'You fighting brother-hater!' Chip shouted. The boat turned towards the eastern tip of the far-off island.

'He's taking it himself!' Lilac said. '*He's* going to trade it!'

'The sick selfish pre-U—' Chip said. 'Christ, Marx, Wood, and Wei, I had the knife in my hand and I threw it on the floor! "Waiting to help us into port"! He's a *pirate*, that's what he is, the fighting—'

'Stop! Don't!' Lilac said, and looked at him despairingly.

'Oh Christ and Wei,' he said.

They pulled open their coveralls and squirmed themselves out of them. 'Keep them!' Chip said. 'They'll hold air if we tie the openings!'

'Another boat!' Lilac said.

A speck of white was speeding from west to east, midway between them and the island.

She waved her coveralls.

'Too far!' Chip said. 'We've got to start swimming!'

They tied the sleeves of their coveralls around their necks and swam against the chilly water. The island was impossibly far away – twenty or more kilometres.

If they could take short rests against the inflated coveralls, Chip thought, they could get far enough in so that another boat might see them. But who would be on it? Members like Darren Costanza? Foul-smelling *pirates* and

189

murderers? Had King been right? *'I hope you get there,'* King said, lying in his bed with his eyes closed. *'The two of you. You deserve it.'* Fight that brother-hater!

The second boat had got near their pirated one, which was heading farther east as if to avoid it.

Chip swam steadily, glimpsing Lilac swimming beside him. Would they get enough rest to go on, to make it? Or would they drown, choke, slide languidly downward through darkening water ... He drove the image from his mind; swam and kept swimming.

The second boat had stopped; their own was farther from it than before. But the second boat seemed bigger now, and bigger still.

He stopped and caught Lilac's leg. She looked around, gasping, and he pointed.

The boat hadn't stopped; it had turned and was coming towards them.

They tugged at the coverall sleeves at their throats, loosed them and waved the light blue, the bright yellow.

The boat turned slightly away, then back, then away in the other direction.

'Here!' they cried, *'Help! Help! Help!'* – waving the coveralls, straining high in the water.

The boat turned back and away again, then sharply back. It stayed pointed at them, enlarging, and a horn sounded – loud, loud, loud, loud, loud.

Lilac sank against Chip, coughing water. He ducked his shoulder under her arm and supported her.

The boat came skimming to full-size white closeness – I.A. was painted large and green on its hull; it had one rotor – and splatted to a stop with a wave that washed over them. 'Hang on!' a member cried, and something flew in the air and splashed beside them: a floating white ring with a rope. Chip grabbed it and the rope sprang taut, pulled by a member, young, yellow-haired. He drew them through the water. 'I'm all right,' Lilac said in Chip's arm. 'I'm all right.'

The side of the boat had rungs going up it. Chip pulled Lilac's coveralls from her hand, bent her fingers around a rung, and put her other hand to the rung above. She climbed. The member, leaning over and stretching, caught her hand and helped her. Chip guided her feet and climbed up after her.

They lay on their backs on warm firm floor under scratchy blankets, hand in hand, panting. Their heads were lifted in turn and a small metal container was pressed to their lips. The liquid in it smelled like Darren Costanza. It burned in their throats, but once it was down it warmed their stomachs surprisingly.

'Alcohol?' Chip said.

'Don't worry,' the young yellow-haired man said, smiling down at them with normal teeth as he screwed the container on to a flask, 'one sip won't rot your brain.' He was about twenty-five, with a short beard that was yellow too, and normal eyes and skin. A brown belt at his hips held a gun in a brown pocket; he wore a white cloth shirt without sleeves and tan cloth trousers patched with blue that ended at his knees. Putting the flask on a seat, he unfastened the front of his belt. 'I'll get your coveralls,' he said. 'Catch your breath.' He put the gun-belt with the flask and climbed over the side of the boat. A splash sounded and the boat swayed.

'At least they're not all like that other one,' Chip said.

'He has a gun,' Lilac said.

'But he left it here,' Chip said. 'If he were – sick, he would have been afraid to.'

They lay silently hand in hand under the scratchy blankets, breathing deeply, looking at the clear blue sky.

The boat tilted and the young man climbed back aboard with their dripping coveralls. His hair, which hadn't been clipped in a long time, clung to his head in wet rings. 'Feeling better?' he asked, smiling at them.

'Yes,' they both said.

He shook the coveralls over the side of the boat. 'I'm sorry I wasn't here in time to keep that lunky away from you,' he said. 'Most immigrants come from Eur, so I generally stay to the north. What we need are two boats, not one. Or a longer-range spotter.'

'Are you a – policeman?' Chip asked.

'Me?' The young man smiled. 'No,' he said, 'I'm with Immigrants' Assistance. That's an agency we've been generously allowed to set up, to help new immigrants get oriented.

And get ashore without being drowned.' He hung the coveralls over the boat's railing and pulled apart their clinging folds.

Chip raised himself on his elbows. 'Does this happen often?' he asked.

'Stealing immigrants' boats is a popular local pastime,' the young man said. 'There are others that are even more fun.'

Chip sat up, and Lilac sat up beside him. The young man faced them, pink sunlight gleaming on his side.

'I'm sorry to disappoint you,' he said, 'but you haven't come to any paradise. Four-fifths of the island's population is descended from families who were here before the Unification or who came here right after; they're inbred, ignorant, mean, self-satisfied – and they despise immigrants. "Steelies", they call us. Because of the bracelets. Even after we take them off.'

He took his gun-belt from the seat and put it around his hips. 'We call them "lunkies",' he said, fastening the belt's buckle. 'Only don't ever say it out loud or you'll find five or six of them stamping on your ribs. That's another of their pastimes.'

He looked at them again. 'The island is run by a General Costanza,' he said, 'with the—'

'That's who took the boat!' they said. 'Darren Costanza!'

'I doubt it,' the young man said, smiling. 'The General doesn't get up this early. Your lunky must have been pulling your leg.'

Chip said, 'The brother-hater!'

'General Costanza,' the young man said, 'has the Church and the Army behind him. There's very little freedom even for lunkies, and for us there's virtually none. We have to live in specified areas, "Steelytowns", and we can't step outside them without a good reason. We have to show identity cards to every lunky cop, and the only jobs we can get are the lowest, most back-breaking ones.' He took up the flask. 'Do you want some more of this?' he asked. 'It's called "whisky".'

Chip and Lilac shook their heads.

The young man unscrewed the container and poured amber liquid into it. 'Let's see, what have I left out?' he said. 'We're not allowed to own land or weapons. I turn in my gun when I set foot on shore.' He raised the container and looked at them. 'Welcome to Liberty,' he said, and drank.

They looked disheartenedly at each other, and at the young man.

'That's what they call it,' he said. 'Liberty.'

'We thought they would welcome newcomers,' Chip said. 'To help keep the Family away.'

The young man, screwing the container back on to the flask, said, 'Nobody comes here except two or three immigrants a month. The last time the Family tried to treat the lunkies was back when there were five computers. Since Uni went into operation not one attempt has been made.'

'Why not?' Lilac asked.

The young man looked at them. 'Nobody knows,' he said. 'There are different theories. The lunkies think that either "God" is protecting them or the Family is afraid of the Army, a bunch of drunken incapable louts. Immigrants think – well, some of them think that the island is so depleted that treating everyone on it simply isn't worth Uni's while.'

'And others think—' Chip said.

The young man turned away and put the flask on a shelf below the boat's controls. He sat down on the seat and turned to face them. 'Others,' he said, 'and I'm one of them, think that Uni is *using* the island, *and* the lunkies, and *all* the hidden islands all over the world.'

'*Using* them?' Chip said, and Lilac said, 'How?'

'As prisons for *us*,' the young man said.

They looked at him.

'Why is there always a boat on the beach?' he asked. '*Always*, in Eur and in Afr – an old boat that's still good enough to get here. And why are there those handy patched-up maps in museums? Wouldn't it be easier to make *fake ones* with the islands *really* omitted?'

They stared at him.

'What do you do,' he said, looking at them intently, 'when you're programming a computer to maintain a perfectly efficient, perfectly stable, perfectly co-operative society? How do you allow for biological freaks, "incurables", possible trouble-makers?'

They said nothing, staring at him.

He leaned closer to them. 'You leave a few "un-unified"

islands all around the world,' he said. 'You leave maps in museums and boats on beaches. The computer doesn't have to weed out your bad ones; *they do the weeding themselves*. They wiggle their way happily into the nearest isolation ward, and *lunkies* are waiting, with a General Costanza in charge, to take their boats, jam them into Steelytowns, and keep them helpless and harmless – in ways that high-minded disciples of Christ, Marx, Wood, and Wei would never *dream* of stooping to.'

'It can't *be*,' Lilac said.

'A lot of us think it can,' the young man said.

Chip said, 'Uni *let us* come here?'

'No,' Lilac said. 'It's too – twisted.'

The young man looked at Chip.

Chip said, 'I thought I was being so fighting clever !'

'So did I,' the young man said, sitting back. 'I know just how you feel.'

'No, it can't be,' Lilac said.

There was silence for a moment, and then the young man said, 'I'll take you in now. IA will take off your bracelets and get you registered and lend you twenty-five bucks to get started.' He smiled. 'As bad as it is,' he said, 'it's better than being with the Family. Cloth is more comfortable than paplon – really – and even a rotten fig tastes better than totalcakes. You can have children, a drink, a cigarette – a couple of rooms if you work hard. Some steelies even get rich – entertainers, mostly. If you "sir" the lunkies and stay in Steelytown, it's all right. No scanners, no advisers, and not one "Life of Marx" in a whole year's TV.'

Lilac smiled. Chip smiled too.

'Put the coveralls on,' the young man said. 'Lunkies are horrified by nakedness. It's "ungodly".' He turned to the boat's controls.

They put aside the blankets and got into their moist coveralls, then stood behind the young man as he drove the boat towards the island. It spread out green and gold in the radiance of the just-risen sun, crested with mountains and dotted with bits of white, yellow, pink, pale blue.

'It's beautiful,' Lilac said determinedly.

Chip, with his arm about her shoulders, looked ahead with narrowed eyes and said nothing.

FIVE

They lived in a city called Pollensa, in half a room in a cracked and crumbling Steelytown building with intermittent power and brown water. They had a mattress and a table and a chair, and a box for their clothing that they used as a second chair. The people in the other half of the room, the Newmans – a man and woman in their forties with a nine-year-old daughter – let them use their stove and TV and a shelf in the 'fridge' where they stored their food. It was the Newmans' room; Chip and Lilac paid four dollars a week for their half of it.

They earned nine dollars and twenty cents a week between them. Chip worked in an iron mine, loading ore into carts with a crew of other immigrants alongside an automatic loader that stood motionless and dusty, unrepairable. Lilac worked in a clothing factory, attaching fasteners to shirts. There too a machine stood motionless, furred with lint.

Their nine dollars and twenty cents paid for the week's rent and food and railfare, a few cigarettes, and a newspaper called the *Liberty Immigrant*. They saved fifty cents towards clothing replacement and emergencies that might arise, and gave fifty cents to Immigrants' Assistance as partial repayment of the twenty-five-dollar loan they had been given on their arrival. They ate bread and fish and potatoes and figs. At first these foods gave them cramps and constipation, but they soon came to like them, to relish the different tastes and consistencies. They looked forward to meals, although the preparation and the cleaning up afterwards became a bother.

Their bodies changed. Lilac's bled for a few days, which the Newmans assured them was natural in untreated women, and it grew more rounded and supple as her hair grew longer. Chip's body hardened and strengthened from his work in the mine. His beard grew out black and straight, and he trimmed it once a week with the Newmans' scissors.

They had been given names by a clerk at the Immigration Bureau. Chip was named Eiko Newmark, and Lilac, Grace

Newbridge. Later, when they married – with no application to Uni, but with forms and a fee and vows to 'God' – Lilac's name was changed to Grace Newmark. They still called themselves Chip and Lilac, however.

They got used to handling coins and dealing with shop-keepers, and to travelling on Pollensa's rundown over-crowded monorail. They learned how to sidestep natives and avoid offending them; they memorized the Vow of Loyalty and saluted Liberty's red-and-yellow flag. They knocked on doors before opening them, said *Wednesday* instead of *Woodsday*, *March* instead of *Marx*. They reminded them-selves that *fight* and *hate* were acceptable words but *fuck* was a 'dirty' one.

Hassan Newman drank a great deal of whisky. Soon after coming home from his job – in the island's largest furniture factory – he would be playing loud games with Gigi, his daughter, and fumbling his way through the room's divid-ing curtain with a bottle clutched in his three-fingered saw-damaged hand. 'Come on, you sad steelies,' he would say, 'where the hate are your glasses? Come on, have a little cheer.' Chip and Lilac drank with him a few times, but they found that whisky made them confused and clumsy and they usually declined his offer. 'Come on,' he said one even-ing. 'I know I'm the landlord, but I'm not exactly a lunky, am I? Or what is it? Do you think I'll expect you to receep – to reciprocate? I know you like to watch the pennies.'

'It's not that,' Chip said.

'Then what is it?' Hassan asked. He swayed and steadied himself.

Chip didn't say anything for a moment, and then he said, 'Well, what's the point in getting away from treatments if you're going to dull yourself with whisky? You might as well be back in the Family.'

'Oh,' Hassan said. 'Oh sure, I get you.' He looked angrily at them, a broad, curly-bearded, bloodshot-eyed man. 'Just wait,' he said. 'Wait till you've been here a little longer. Just wait till you've been here a little longer, that's all.' He turned around and groped his way through the curtain, and they heard him muttering, and his wife, Ria, speaking placatingly.

Almost everyone in the building seemed to drink as much whisky as Hassan did. Loud voices, happy or angry, sounded through the walls at all hours of the night. The elevator and the hallways smelled of whisky, and of fish, and of sweet perfumes that people used against the whisky and fish smells.

Most evenings, after they had finished whatever cleaning had to be done, Chip and Lilac either went up to the roof for some fresh air or sat at their table reading the *Immigrant* or books they had found on the monorail or borrowed from a small collection at Immigrants' Assistance. Sometimes they watched TV with the Newmans – plays about foolish misunderstandings in native families, with frequent stops for announcements about different makes of cigarettes and disinfectants. Occasionally there were speeches by General Costanza or the head of the Church, Pope Clement – disquieting speeches about shortages of food and space and resources, for which immigrants alone weren't to be blamed. Hassan, belligerent with whisky, usually switched them off before they were over; Liberty TV, unlike the Family's, could be switched on and off at one's choosing.

One day in the mine, towards the end of the fifteen-minute lunch break, Chip went over to the automatic loader and began examining it, wondering whether it was in fact unrepairable or whether some part of it that couldn't be replaced might not be by-passed or substituted for in some way. The native in charge of the crew came over and asked him what he was doing. Chip told him, taking care to speak respectfully, but the native got angry. 'You fucking steelies all think you're so God-damned smart!' he said, and put his hand on his gun handle. 'Get over there where you belong and stay there!' he said. 'Try to figure out a way to eat less food if you've got to have something to think about!'

All natives weren't quite that bad. The owner of their building took a liking to Chip and Lilac and promised to let them have a room for five dollars a week as soon as one became available. 'You're not like some of these others,' he said. 'Drinking, walking around the hallways stark naked – I'd rather take a few cents less and have your kind.'

Chip, looking at him, said, 'There are reasons why immigrants drink, you know.'

197

'I know, I know,' the owner said. 'I'm the first one to say it; it's terrible the way we treat you. But still and all, do *you* drink? Do *you* walk around stark naked?'

Lilac said, 'Thank you, Mr Corsham. We'll be grateful if you can get a room for us.'

They caught 'colds' and 'the flu'. Lilac lost her job at the clothing factory but found a better one in the kitchen of a native restaurant within walking distance of the house. Two policemen came to the room one evening, checking identity cards and looking for weapons. Hassan muttered something as he showed his card and they clubbed him to the floor. They stuck knives into the mattresses and broke some of the dishes.

Lilac didn't have her 'period', her monthly few days of vaginal bleeding, and that meant she was pregnant.

One night on the roof Chip stood smoking and looking at the sky to the northeast, where there was a dull orange glow from the copper-production complex on EUR91766. Lilac who had been taking washed clothes from a line where she had hung them to dry, came over to him and put her arm around him. She kissed his cheek and leaned against him. 'It's not so bad,' she said. 'We've got twelve dollars saved, we'll have a room of our own any day now, and before you know it we'll have a baby.'

'A steely,' Chip said.

'No,' Lilac said. 'A baby.'

'It stinks,' Chip said. 'It's rotten. It's inhuman.'

'It's all there is,' Lilac said. 'We'd better get used to it.'

Chip said nothing. He kept looking at the orange glow in the sky.

The *Liberty Immigrant* carried weekly articles about immigrant singers and athletes, and occasionally scientists, who earned forty or fifty dollars a week and lived in good apartments, who mixed with influential and enlightened natives, and who were hopeful about the chances of a more equitable relationship developing between the two groups. Chip read these articles with scorn – they were meant by the newspaper's native owners to lull and pacify immigrants, he felt – but Lilac accepted them at face value, as evidence that their own lot would ultimately improve.

One week in October, when they had been on Liberty for a little over six months, there was an article about an artist named Morgan Newgate, who had come from Eur eight years before and who lived in a four-room apartment in New Madrid. His paintings, one of which, a scene of the Crucifixion, had just been presented to Pope Clement, brought him as much as a hundred dollars each. He signed them with an A, the article explained, because his nickname was Ashi.

'Christ and Wei,' Chip said.

Lilac said, 'What is it?'

'I was at academy with this "Morgan Newgate",' Chip said, showing her the article. 'We were good friends. His name was Karl. You remember that picture of the horse I had back in Ind?'

'No,' she said, reading.

'Well, he drew it,' Chip said. 'He used to sign everything with an A in a circle.' And yes, he thought, 'Ashi' seemed like the name Karl had mentioned. Christ and Wei, so he had got away too! – had 'got away', if you could call it that, to Liberty, to Uni's isolation ward. At least he was doing what he'd always wanted; for him Liberty really *was* liberty.

'You ought to call him,' Lilac said, still reading.

'I will,' Chip said.

But maybe he wouldn't. Was there any point, really, in calling 'Morgan Newgate', who painted Crucifixions for the Pope and assured his fellow immigrants that conditions were getting better every day? But maybe Karl hadn't said that; maybe the *Immigrant* had lied.

'Don't just say it,' Lilac said. 'He could probably help you get a better job.'

'Yes,' Chip said, 'he probably could.'

She looked at him. 'What's the matter?' she said. 'Don't you want a better job?'

'I'll call him tomorrow, on the way to work,' he said.

But he didn't. He swung his shovel into ore and lifted and heaved, swung and lifted and heaved. *Fight them all*, he thought: *the steelies who drink, the steelies who think things are getting better; the lunkies, the dummies; fight Uni.*

On the following Sunday morning Lilac went with him to

199

a building two blocks from theirs where there was a working telephone in the lobby, and she waited while he paged through the tattered directory. *Morgan* and *Newgate* were names commonly given to immigrants, but few immigrants had phones; there was only one *Newgate, Morgan* listed, and that one in New Madrid.

Chip put three tokens into the phone and spoke the number. The screen was broken, but it didn't make any difference since Liberty phones no longer transmitted pictures anyway.

A woman answered, and when Chip asked if Morgan Newgate was there, said he was, and then nothing more. The silence lengthened, and Lilac, a few metres away beside a Sani-Spray poster, waited and then came close. 'Isn't he there?' she asked in a whisper. 'Hello?' a man's voice said.

'Is this Morgan Newgate?' Chip asked.

'Yes. Who's this?'

'It's Chip,' Chip said. 'Li RM, from the Academy of the Genetic Sciences.'

There was silence, and then, 'My God,' the voice said, 'Li! You got pads and charcoal for me!'

'Yes,' Chip said. 'And I told my adviser you were sick and needed help.'

Karl laughed. 'That's right, you did, you bastard!' he said. 'This is great! When did you get over?'

'About six months ago,' Chip said.

'Are you in New Madrid?'

'Pollensa.'

'What are you doing?'

'Working in a mine,' Chip said.

'Christ, that's a shut-off,' Karl said, and after a moment, 'It's hell here, isn't it?'

'Yes,' Chip said, thinking *He even uses their words. Hell. My God I'll bet he says prayers.*

'I wish these phones were working so I could get a look at you,' Karl said.

Suddenly Chip was ashamed of his hostility. He told Karl about Lilac and about her pregnancy; Karl told him that he had been married in the Family but had come over alone. He wouldn't let Chip congratulate him on his success. 'The things I sell are awful,' he said. 'Appealing little lunky children. But I manage to do my own work three days a week, so I can't complain. Listen, Li – no, what is it, Chip? Chip, listen we've got to get together. I've got a motorbike; I'll come down one evening. No wait,' he said, 'are you doing anything next Sunday, you and your wife?'

Lilac looked anxiously at Chip. He said, 'I don't think so. I'm not sure.'

'I'm having some friends over,' Karl said. 'You come too, all right? Around six o'clock.'

With Lilac nodding at him, Chip said, 'We'll try. We'll probably be able to make it.'

'See that you do,' Karl said. He gave Chip his address. 'I'm glad you got over,' he said. 'It's better than *there* anyway, isn't it?'

'A little,' Chip said.

'I'll expect you next Sunday,' Karl said. 'So long, brother.'

'So long,' Chip said, and tapped off.

Lilac said, 'We're going, aren't we?'

'Do you have any idea what the railfare's going to be?' Chip said.

'Oh, Chip . . .'

'All right,' he said. 'All right, we'll go. But I'm not taking any favours from him. And you're not *asking* for any. You remember that.'

Every evening that week Lilac worked on the best of their clothes, taking off the frayed sleeves of a green dress, remending a trouser leg so that the mend was less noticeable.

The building, at the very edge of New Madrid's Steelytown, was in no worse condition than many native buildings. Its lobby was swept, and smelled only slightly of whisky and fish and perfume, and the elevator worked well.

A pushbutton was set in new plaster next to Karl's door : a bell to be rung. Chip pressed it. He stood stiffly, and Lilac held his arm.

'Who is it?' a man's voice asked.

'Chip Newmark,' Chip said.

The door was unlocked and opened, and Karl – a thirty-five-year-old bearded Karl with the long-ago Karl's sharp-focused eyes – grinned and grabbed Chip's hand and said, 'Li! I thought you weren't coming!'

'We ran into some good-natured lunkies,' Chip said.

'Oh Christ,' Karl said, and let them in.

He locked the door and Chip introduced Lilac. She said, 'Hello, Mr Newgate,' and Karl, taking her held-out hand and looking at her face, said, 'It's Ashi. Hello Lilac.'

'Hello, Ashi,' she said.

To Chip, Karl said, 'Did they hurt you?'

'No,' Chip said. 'Just "recite the Vow" and that kind of cloth.'

'Bastards,' Karl said. 'Come on, I'll give you a drink and you'll forget about it.' He took their elbows and led them into a narrow passage walled with frame-to-frame paintings. 'You look great, Chip,' he said.

'So do you,' Chip said. 'Ashi.'

They smiled at each other.

'Seventeen years, brother,' Karl said.

Men and women were sitting in a smoky brown-walled room, ten or twelve of them, talking and holding cigarettes and glasses. They stopped talking and turned expectantly.

'This is Chip and this is Lilac,' Karl said to them. 'Chip and I were at academy together; the Family's two worst genetics students.'

The men and women smiled, and Karl began pointing to them in turn and saying their names. 'Vito, Sunny, Ria, Lars ...' Most of them were immigrants, bearded men and long-haired women with the Family's eyes and colouring. Two were natives: a pale erect beak-nosed woman of fifty or so, with a gold cross hanging against her black empty-looking dress ('Julia,' Karl said, and she smiled with closed lips); and an overweight red-haired younger woman in a tight dress glazed with silvery beads. A few of the people could have been either immigrants or natives: a grey-eyed beardless man named Bob, a blonde woman, a young blue-eyed man.

'Whisky or wine?' Karl asked. 'Lilac?'

'Wine, please,' Lilac said.

They followed him to a small table set out with bottles and glasses, plates holding a slice or two of cheese and meat, and packets of cigarettes and matches. A souvenir paperweight sat on a pile of napkins. Chip picked it up and looked at it; it was from AUS21989. 'Make you homesick?' Karl asked, pouring wine.

Chip showed it to Lilac and she smiled. 'Not very,' he said, and put it down.

'Chip?'

'Whisky.'

The red-haired native woman in the silvery dress came over smiling and holding an empty glass in a ring-fingered hand. To Lilac she said, 'You're absolutely beautiful. Really,' and to Chip, 'I think all you people are beautiful. The Family may not have any freedom but it's way ahead of us in physical appearance. I'd give anything to be lean and tan and slant-eyed.' She talked on – about the Family's sensible attitude towards sex – and Chip found himself with a glass in his hand and Karl and Lilac talking to other people and the woman talking to him. Lines of black paint edged and extended her brown eyes. 'You people are so much more open than we are,' she said. 'Sexually, I mean, You enjoy it more.'

An immigrant woman came over and said, 'Isn't Heinz coming, Marge?'

'He's in Palama,' the woman said, turning. 'A wing of the hotel collapsed.'

'Would you excuse me, please?' Chip said, and side-stepped away. He went to the other end of the room, nodded at people sitting there, and drank some of his whisky, looking at a painting on the wall – slabs of brown and red on a white background. The whisky tasted better than Hassan's. It was less bitter and searing; lighter and more pleasant to drink. The painting with its brown and red slabs was only a flat design, interesting to look at for a moment but with nothing in it connected to life. Karl's (no, Ashi's!) A-in-a-circle was in one of its bottom corners. Chip wondered whether it was one of the bad paintings he sold or, since it was hanging there in his living-room, part of his 'own work' that he had spoken of with satisfaction. Wasn't he still doing the beautiful unbraceleted men and women he had drawn back at the Academy?

He drank some more of the whisky and turned to the people sitting near him: three men and a woman, all immigrants. They were talking about furniture. He listened for a few minutes, drinking, and moved away.

Lilac was sitting next to the beak-nosed native woman –

Julia. They were smoking and talking, or rather Julia was talking and Lilac was listening.

He went to the table and poured more whisky into his glass. He lit a cigarette.

A man named Lars introduced himself. He ran a school for immigrant children there in New Madrid. He had been brought to Liberty as a child, and had been there for forty-two years.

Ashi came, holding Lilac by the hand. 'Chip, come see my studio,' he said.

He led them from the room into the passage walled with paintings. 'Do you know who you were speaking to?' he asked Lilac.

'Julia?' she said.

'Julia *Costanza*,' he said. 'She's the General's cousin. Despises him. She was one of the founders of Immigrants' Assistance.'

His studio was large and brilliantly lighted. A half-finished painting of a native woman holding a kitten stood on an easel; on another easel stood a canvas painted with slabs of blue and green. Other paintings stood against the walls: slabs of brown and orange, blue and purple, purple and black, orange and red.

He explained what he was trying to do, pointing out balances, and opposing thrusts, and subtle shadings of colour.

Chip looked away and drank his whisky.

'Listen, you steelies!' he said, loudly enough so they all could hear him. 'Stop talking about *furniture* for a minute and listen! You know what we've got to do? Fight Uni! I'm not being *rude*, I mean it literally. Fight Uni! Because it's Uni who's to blame – for everything! For lunkies, who're what they are because they don't have enough food, or space, or *connexion with any outside world*; and for dummies, who're what they are because they're LPK'ed that way and tranquillized that way; and for *us*, who're what *we* are because Uni put us here to get rid of us! It's *Uni* who's to blame – it's frozen the world so there's no more change – and we've got to fight it! We've got to get up off our stupid beaten behinds and FIGHT IT!'

Ashi, smiling, slapped at his cheek. 'Hey, brother,' he said, 'you've had a little too much, you know that? Hey, Chip, you hear me?'

Of course he'd had too much; of course, of course, of course. But it hadn't dulled him, it had freed him. It had opened up everything that had been inside him for months and months. Whisky was *good!* Whisky was *marvellous!*

He stopped Ashi's slapping hand and held it. 'I'm okay, Ashi,' he said. 'I know what I'm talking about.' To the others, sitting and swaying and smiling, he said, 'We can't just give up and accept things, *adjust ourselves* to this prison! Ashi, you used to draw members without bracelets, and they were so beautiful! And now you're painting colour, slabs of *colour!*'

They were trying to get him to sit down, Ashi on one side of him and Lilac on the other, Lilac looking anxious and embarrassed. 'You too, love,' he said. 'You're accepting, adjusting.' He let them seat him, because standing hadn't been easy and sitting was better, more comfortable and sprawly. 'We've got to fight, not adjust,' he said. 'Fight, fight, fight. We've got to fight,' he said to the grey-eyed beardless man sitting next to him.

'By God, you're right!' the man said. 'I'm with you all the way! Fight Uni! What'll we do? Go over in boats and take the Army along for good measure? But maybe the sea is monitored by satellite and doctors'll be waiting with clouds of LPK. I've got a better idea; we'll get a plane – I hear there's one on the island that actually flies – and we'll—'

'Don't tease him, Bob,' someone said. 'He just came over.'

'That's obvious,' the man said, getting up.

'There's a way to do it,' Chip said. 'There has to be. There's a way to do it.' He thought about the sea and the island in the middle of it, but he couldn't think as clearly as he wanted. Lilac sat where the man had been and took his hand. 'We've got to *fight*,' he said to her.

'I know, I know,' she said, looking at him sadly.

Ashi came and put a warm cup to his lips. 'It's coffee,' he said. 'Drink it.'

It was very hot and strong; he swallowed a mouthful, then pushed the cup away. 'The copper complex,' he said. 'On

205

'91766. The copper must get ashore. There must be boats or barges; we could—'

'It's been done before,' Ashi said.

Chip looked at him, thinking he was tricking him, making fun of him in some way, like the grey-eyed beardless man.

'Everything you're saying,' Ashi said, 'everything you're thinking – "fight Uni" – it's been said before and thought before. And tried before. A dozen times.' He put the cup to Chip's lips. 'Take some more,' he said.

Chip pushed the cup away, staring at him, and shook his head. 'It's not true,' he said.

'It is, brother. Come on, take a—'

'It isn't!' he said.

'It is;' a woman said across the room. 'It's true.'

Julia. It was Julia, General's-cousin-Julia, sitting erect and alone in her black dress with her little gold cross.

'Every five or six years,' she said, 'a group of people like you – sometimes only two or three, sometimes as many as ten – sets out to destroy UniComp. They go in boats, in submarines that they spend years building; they go on board the barges you just mentioned. They take guns, explosives, gas masks, gas bombs, gadgets; they have plans that they're sure will work. They never come back. I financed the last two parties and am supporting the families of men who were in them, so I speak with authority. I hope you're sober enough to understand, and to spare yourself useless anguish. Accepting and adjusting is all that's possible. Be grateful for what you have: a lovely wife, a child on the way, and a small amount of freedom that we hope in time will grow larger. I might add that in no circumstances whatsoever will I finance another such party. I am not as rich as certain people think I am.'

Chip sat looking at her. She looked at him with small black eyes above her pale beak of nose.

'They never come back, Chip,' Ashi said.

Chip looked at him.

'Maybe they get to shore,' Ashi said; 'maybe they get to '001. Maybe they even get into the dome. But that's as far as they get, because they're gone, every one of them. And Uni is still working.'

Chip looked at Julia. She said, 'Men and women exactly

like you. As far back as I can remember.'

He looked at Lilac, holding his hand. She squeezed it looking compassionately at him.

He looked at Ashi, who held the cup of coffee towards him.

He blocked the cup and shook his head. 'No, I don't want coffee,' he said.

He sat motionless, with sudden sweat on his forehead, and then he leaned forward and began vomiting.

He was in bed, and Lilac was lying beside him sleeping. Hassan was snoring on the other side of the curtain. A sour taste was in his mouth, and he remembered vomiting. Christ and Wei! And on carpet – the first he'd seen in half a year!

Then he remembered what had been said to him by that woman, Julia, and by Karl – by Ashi.

He lay still for a while, and then he got up and tiptoed around the curtain and past the sleeping Newmans to the sink. He got a drink of water, and because he didn't want to go all the way down the hall, urinated quietly in the sink and rinsed it out thoroughly.

He got back down beside Lilac and drew the blanket over him. He felt a little drunk again and his head hurt, but he lay on his back with his eyes closed, breathing lightly and slowly, and after a while he felt better.

He kept his eyes closed and thought about things.

After half an hour or so Hassan's alarm clock jangled. Lilac turned. He stroked her head and she sat up. 'Are you all right?' she asked.

'Yes, sort of,' he said.

The light went on and they winced. They heard Hassan grunting and getting up, yawning, farting. 'Get up, Ria,' he said. 'Gigi? It's time to get up.'

Chip stayed on his back with his hand on Lilac's cheek. 'I'm sorry, darling,' he said. 'I'll call him today and apologize.'

She took his hand and turned her lips to it. 'You couldn't help it,' she said. 'He understood.'

'I'm going to ask him to help me find a better job,' Chip said.

Lilac looked at him questioningly.

'It's all out of me,' he said. 'Like the whisky. All out. I'm going to be an industrious, optimistic steely. I'm going to accept and adjust. We're going to have a bigger apartment than Ashi some day.'

'I don't want that,' she said. 'I would love to have two rooms, though.'

'We will,' he said. 'In two years. Two rooms in two years; that's a promise.'

She smiled at him.

He said, 'I think we ought to think about moving to New Madrid where our rich friends are. That man Lars runs a school, did you know that? Maybe you could teach there. And the baby could go there when it's old enough.'

'What could I teach?' she said.

'Something,' he said. 'I don't know.' He lowered his hand and stroked her breasts. 'How to have beautiful breasts, maybe,' he said.

Smiling, she said, 'We've got to get dressed.'

'Let's skip breakfast,' he said, drawing her down. He rolled on to her and they embraced and kissed.

'Lilac?' Ria called. 'How was it?'

Lilac freed her mouth. 'Tell you later!' she called.

While he was walking down the tunnel into the mine he remembered the tunnel into Uni, Papa Jan's tunnel down which the memory banks had been rolled.

He stopped still.

Down which the *real* memory banks had been rolled. And above them were the false ones, the pink and orange toys that were reached through the dome and the elevators, and which everyone thought was Uni itself; everyone including – it had to be! – all those men and women who had gone out to fight it in the past. But Uni, the real Uni, was on the levels below, and could be reached through the tunnel, through Papa Jan's tunnel from behind Mount Love.

It would still be there – closed at its mouth, probably, maybe even sealed with a metre of concrete – but it would still be there; because nobody fills in all of a long tunnel, especially not an efficient computer. And there was space cut out below for more memory banks – Papa Jan had said so – so the tunnel would be needed again some day.

It was there, behind Mount Love.

A tunnel into Uni.

With the right maps and charts, someone who knew what he was doing could probably work out its exact location, or very nearly.

'You there! Get moving!' someone shouted.

He walked ahead quickly, thinking about it, thinking about it.

It was there. The tunnel.

SIX

'If it's money, the answer is no,' Julia Costanza said, walking briskly past clattering looms and immigrant women glancing at her. 'If it's a job,' she said, 'I might be able to help you.'

Chip, walking along beside her, said, 'Ashi's already got me a job.'

'Then it's money,' she said.

'Information first,' Chip said, 'then maybe money.' He pushed open a door.

'No,' Julia said, going through. 'Why don't you go to IA? That's what it's there for. What information? About what?' She glanced at him as they started up a spiral stairway that shifted with their weight.

Chip said, 'Can we sit down somewhere for five minutes?'

'If I sit down,' Julia said, 'half this island will be naked tomorrow. That's probably acceptable to you but it isn't to me. What information?'

He held in his resentment. Looking at her beak-nosed profile, he said, 'Those two attacks on Uni you—'

'No,' she said. She stopped and faced him, one hand holding the stairway's centrepost. 'If it's about *that* I really won't listen,' she said. 'I knew it the minute you walked into that living-room, the disapproving air you had. No. I'm not interested in any more plans and schemes. Go talk to somebody else.' She went up the stairs.

He went quickly and caught up with her. 'Were they planning to use a tunnel?' he asked. 'Just tell me that; were they going in through a tunnel from behind Mount Love?'

She pushed open the door at the head of the stairway; he held it and went through after her, into a large loft where a few machine parts lay. Birds rose fluttering to holes in the peaked roof and flew out.

'They were going in with the other people,' she said, walking straight through the loft towards a door at its far end. 'The sightseers. At least that was the plan. They were going to go down in the elevators.'

'And then?'

'There's no *point* in—'

'Just answer me, will you, please?' he said.

She glanced at him, angrily, and looked ahead. 'There's supposed to be a large observation window,' she said. 'They were going to smash it and throw in explosives.'

'Both groups?'

'Yes.'

'They may have succeeded,' he said.

She stopped with her hand on the door and looked at him, puzzled.

'That's not really Uni,' he said. 'It's a display for the sightseers. And maybe it's also meant as a false target for attackers. They could have blown it up and nothing would have happened – except that they would have been grabbed and treated.

She kept looking at him.

'The real thing is farther down,' he said. 'On three levels. I was in it once when I was ten or eleven years old.'

She said, 'Digging a tunnel is the most ri—'

'It's there already,' he said. 'It doesn't have to be dug.'

She closed her mouth, looked at him, and turned quickly away and pushed open the door. It led to another loft, brightly lit, where a row of presses stood motionless with layers of cloth on their beds: Water was on the floor, and two men were trying to lift the end of a long pipe that had apparently fallen from the wall and lay across a stopped conveyor belt piled with cut cloth pieces. The wall end of the pipe was still anchored, and the men were trying to lift its other end and get it off the belt and back up against the wall. Another man, an immigrant, waited on a ladder to receive it.

'Help them,' Julia said, and began gathering pieces of cloth from the wet floor.

'If that's how I spend my time, nothing's going to be changed,' Chip said. 'That's acceptable to you, but it isn't to me.'

'Help them!' Julia said. 'Go on! We'll talk later! You're not going to get anywhere by being cheeky!'

Chip helped the men get the pipe secured against the wall, and then he went out with Julia on to a railed landing on the side of the building. New Madrid stretched away below them, bright in the mid-morning sun. Beyond it lay a strip of blue-green sea dotted with fishing boats.

'Every day it's something else,' Julia said, reaching into the pocket of her grey apron. She took out cigarettes, offered Chip one, and lit them with ordinary cheap matches.

They smoked, and Chip said, 'The tunnel's there. It was used to bring in the memory banks.'

'Some of the groups I wasn't involved with may have known about it,' Julia said.

'Can you find out?'

She drew on her cigarette. In the sunlight she was older-looking, the skin of her face and neck netted with wrinkles. 'Yes,' she said. 'I suppose so. How do *you* know about it?'

He told her. 'I'm sure it's not filled in,' he said. 'It must be fifteen kilometres long. And besides, it's going to be used again. There's space cut out for more banks for when the Family gets bigger.'

She looked questioningly at him. 'I thought the colonies had their own computers,' she said.

'They do,' he said, not understanding. And then he understood. It was only in the colonies that the Family was growing; on Earth, with two children per couple and not every couple allowed to reproduce, the Family was getting smaller, not bigger. He had never connected that with what Papa Jan had said about the space for more memory banks. 'Maybe they'll be needed for more telecontrolled equipment,' he said.

'Or maybe,' Julia said, 'your grandfather wasn't a reliable source of information.'

'He was the one who had the idea for the tunnel,' Chip said. 'It's there; I know it is. And it may be a way, the *only* way, that Uni can be gotten at. I'm going to try it, and I

211

want your help, as much of it as you can give me.'

'You want my *money*, you mean,' she said.

'Yes,' he said. 'And your help. In finding the right people with the right skills. And in getting information that we'll need, and equipment. And in finding people who can teach us skills that we don't have. I want to take this very slowly and carefully. I want to come back.'

She looked at him with her eyes narrowed against her cigarette smoke. 'Well, you're not an absolute imbecile,' she said. 'What kind of job has Ashi found for you?'

'Washing dishes at the Casino.'

'God in heaven!' she said. 'Come here tomorrow morning at a quarter to eight.'

'The casino leaves my mornings free,' he said.

'Come here!' she said. 'You'll get the time you need.'

'All right,' he said, and smiled at her. 'Thanks,' he said.

She turned away and looked at her cigarette. She crushed it against the railing. 'I'm not going to pay for it,' she said. 'Not all of it. I can't. You have no idea how expensive it's going to be. Explosives, for instance: last time they cost over two thousand dollars, and that was five years ago; God knows what they'll be today.' She scowled at her cigarette stub and threw it away over the railing. 'I'll pay what I can,' she said, 'and I'll introduce you to people who'll pay the rest if you flatter them enough.'

'Thank you,' Chip said. 'I couldn't ask for more. Thank you.'

'God in heaven, here I go again,' Julia said. She turned to Chip. 'Wait, you'll find out,' she said: 'the older you get, the more you stay the same. I'm an only child who's used to having her way, that's my trouble. Come on, I've got work to do.'

They went down stairs that led from the landing. 'Really,' Julia said. 'I have all kinds of noble reasons for spending my time and money on people like you – a Christian urge to help the Family, love of justice, freedom, democracy – but the truth of the matter is, I'm an only child who's used to having her way. It *maddens* me, it absolutely *maddens* me, that I can't go anywhere I please on this planet! Or off it, for that matter! You have no idea how I *resent* that damned computer!'

Chip laughed. 'I *do!*' he said. 'That's just the way I feel.'

'It's a monster straight out of hell,' Julia said.

They walked around the building. 'It's a monster, all right,' Chip said, throwing away his cigarette. 'At least the way it is now. One of the things I want to try to find out is whether, if we got the chance, we could change its programme instead of destroying it. If the *Family* were running it, instead of vice versa, it wouldn't be so bad. Do you really believe in heaven and hell?'

'Let's not get into religion,' Julia said, 'or you're going to find yourself washing dishes at the Casino. How much are they paying you?'

'Six-fifty a week.'

'Really?'

'Yes.'

'I'll give you the same,' Julia said, 'but if anyone around here asks, say you're getting five.'

He waited until Julia had questioned a number of people without learning of any attack party that had known about the tunnel, and then, confirmed in his decision, he told his plans to Lilac.

'You *can't!*' she said. 'Not after all those other people went!'

'They were aiming at the wrong target,' he said.

She shook her head, held her brow, looked at him. 'It's – I don't know what to *say*,' she said. 'I thought you were – done with all this. I thought we were *settled*.' She threw her hands out at the room around them, their New Madrid room, with the walls they had painted, the bookshelf he had made, the bed, the refrigerator, Ashi's sketch of a laughing child.

Chip said, 'Honey, I may be the only person on any of the islands who knows about the tunnel, about the real Uni. I *have* to make use of that. How can I *not* do it?'

'All right, *make* use of it,' she said. 'Plan, help *organize* a party – fine! I'll help you! But why do you have to *go*? *Other* people should do it, people without families.'

'I'll be here when the baby's born,' he said. 'It's going to take longer than that to get everything ready. And then I'll only be gone for – maybe as little as a week.'

She stared at him. 'How can you *say* that?' she said. 'How can you say you'll – you could be gone for ever! You could be caught and treated!'

'We're going to learn how to fight,' he said. 'We're going to have guns and—'

'Others should go!' she said.

'How can I ask them, if I'm not going myself?'

'Ask them, that's all. Ask them.'

'No,' he said. '*I've* got to go too.'

'You *want* to go, that's what it is,' she said. 'You don't *have* to go; you *want* to.'

He was silent for a moment, and then he said, 'All right, I want to. Yes. I can't think of not being there when Uni is beaten. I want to throw the explosive myself, or pull the switch myself, or do whatever it is that's finally done – myself.'

'You're sick,' she said. She picked up the sewing in her lap and found the needle and started to sew. 'I mean it,' she said. 'You're sick on the subject of Uni. It didn't *put* us here; we're lucky to have got here. Ashi's right: it would have killed us the way it kills people at sixty-two; it wouldn't have wasted boats and islands. We got away from it; it's *already* been beaten; and you're sick to want to go back and beat it again.'

'It put us here,' Chip said, 'because the programmers couldn't justify killing people who were still young.'

'Cloth,' Lilac said. 'They justified killing old people, they'd have justified killing *infants*. We got away. And now you're going back.'

'What about our parents?' he said. '*They're* going to be killed in a few more years. What about Snowflake and Sparrow – the whole Family, in fact?'

She sewed, jabbing the needle into green cloth – the sleeves from her green dress that she was making into a shirt for the baby. 'Others should go,' she said. 'People without families.'

Later, in bed, he said, 'If anything *should* go wrong, Julia will take care of you. And the baby.'

'That's a great comfort,' she said. 'Thanks. Thanks very much. Thank Julia too.'

It stayed between them from that night on: resentment on her part and refusal to be moved by it on his.

PART FOUR

FIGHTING BACK

ONE

He was busy, busier than he'd been in his entire life: planning, looking for people and equipment, travelling, learning, explaining, pleading, devising, deciding. And working at the factory too, where Julia, despite the time off she allowed him, made sure she got her six-fifty-a-week's worth out of him in machinery repair and production speed-up. And with Lilac's pregnancy advancing, he was doing more of the at-home chores too. He was more exhausted than he'd ever been, and more wide awake; more sick of everything one day and more sure of everything the next; more alive.

It, the plan, the project, was like a machine to be assembled, with all the parts to be found or made, and each dependent for its shape and size on all the others.

Before he could decide on the size of the party, he had to have a clearer idea of its ultimate aim; and before he could have that, he had to know more about Uni's functioning and where it could be most effectively attacked.

He spoke to Lars Newman, Ashi's friend who ran a school. Lars sent him to a man in Andrait, who sent him to a man in Manacor.

'I knew those banks were too small for the amount of insulation they seemed to have,' the man in Manacor said. His name was Newbrook and he was near seventy; he had taught in a technological academy before he left the Family. He was minding a baby granddaughter, changing her diaper and annoyed about it. 'Hold *still*, will you?' he said. 'Well, assuming you can get in,' he said to Chip, 'the power source is what you've obviously got to go for. The reactor or, more likely, the reactors.'

'But they could be replaced fairly quickly, couldn't they?' Chip said. 'I want to put Uni out of commission for a good long time, long enough for the Family to wake up and decide what it wants to do with it.'

'Damn it, hold *still*!' Newbrook said. 'The refrigerating plant, then.'

'The refrigerating plant?' Chip said.

'That's right,' Newbrook said. 'The internal temperature of the banks has to be close to absolute zero; raise it a few degrees and the grids won't – there, *you see* what you've done? – the grids won't be superconductive any more. You'll erase Uni's memory.' He picked up the crying baby and held her against his shoulder, patting her back. 'Shh, shh,' he said.

'Erase it permanently?' Chip asked.

Newbrook nodded, patting the crying baby. 'Even if the refrigeration's restored,' he said, 'all the data will have to be fed in again. It'll take years.'

'That's exactly what I'm looking for,' Chip said.

The refrigerating plant.

And the stand-by plant.

And the second stand-by plant, if there was one.

Three refrigeration plants to be put out of operation. Two men for each, he figured; one to place the explosives and one to keep members away.

Six men to stop Uni's refrigeration and then hold its entrances against the help it would summon with its thawing faltering brain. Could six men hold the elevators and the tunnel? (And had Papa Jan mentioned other shafts in the other cut-out space?) But six was the minimum, and the minimum was what he wanted, because if any man was caught while they were on their way, he would tell the doctors everything and Uni would be expecting them at the tunnel. The fewer the men, the less the danger.

He and five others.

The yellow-haired young man who ran the IA patrol boat – Vito Newcome, but he called himself Dover – painted the boat's railing while he listened, and then, when Chip spoke about the tunnel and the real memory banks, listened without painting; crouched on his heels with the brush hanging in his hand, squinted up at Chip with flecks of white in his short beard and on his chest. 'You're sure of it?' he asked.

'Positive,' Chip said.

'It's about time somebody took another crack at that brother-fighter.' Dover Newcome looked at his thumb, white-smeared, and wiped it on his trouser thigh.

Chip crouched beside him. 'Do you want to be in on it?' he asked.

Dover looked at him and, after a moment, nodded. 'Yes,' he said. 'I certainly do.'

Ashi said no, which was what Chip had expected; he asked him only because not asking, he thought, would be a slight. 'I just don't feel it's worth the risk,' Ashi said. 'I'll help you out in any way I can, though. Julia's already hit me for a contribution and I've promised a hundred dollars. I'll make it more than that if you need it.'

'Fine,' Chip said. 'Thanks. Ashi. You *can* help. You can get into the Library, can't you? See if you can find any maps of the area around EUR-zip-one, U or pre-U. The larger the better; maps with topographical details.'

When Julia heard that Dover Newcome was to be in the group, she objected. 'We need him here, on the boat,' she said.

'You won't once we're finished,' Chip said.

'God in heaven,' Julia said. 'How do you get by with so little confidence?'

'It's easy,' Chip said. 'I have a friend who says prayers for me.'

Julia looked coldly at him. 'Don't take anyone else from IA,' she said. 'And don't take anyone from the factory. And don't take anyone with a family that I may wind up supporting!'

'How do you get by with so little faith?' Chip said.

He and Dover between them spoke to some thirty or forty immigrants without finding any others who wanted to take part in the attack. They copied names and addresses from the IA files, of men and women over twenty and under forty who had come to Liberty within the previous few years, and they called on seven or eight of them every week. Lars Newman's son wanted to be in the group, but he had been born on Liberty, and Chip wanted only people who had been raised in the Family, who were accustomed to scanners and walkways, to the slow pace and the contented smile.

He found a company in Pollensa that would make dynamite bombs with fast or slow mechanical fuses, provided they were ordered by a native with a permit. He found another company, in Calvia, that would make six gas masks, but they wouldn't guarantee them against LPK unless he gave them a sample for testing. Lilac, who was working in an immigrant clinic, found a doctor who knew the LPK formula, but none of the island's chemical companies could manufacture any; lithium was one of its chief constituents, and there hadn't been any lithium available for over thirty years.

He was running a weekly two-line advertisement in the *Immigrant*, offering to buy coveralls, sandals, and take-along kits. One day he got an answer from a woman in Andrait, and a few evenings later he went there to look at two kits and a pair of sandals. The kits were shabby and outdated, but the sandals were good. The woman and her husband asked why he wanted them. Their name was Newbridge and they were in their early thirties, living in a tiny wretched rat-infested cellar. Chip told them, and they asked to join the group – insisted on joining it, actually. They were perfectly normal-looking, which was a point in their favour, but there was a feverishness about them, a keyed-up tension, that bothered Chip a little.

He went to see them again a week later, with Dover, and that time they seemed more relaxed and possibly suitable. Their names were Jack and Ria. They had had two children, both of whom had died in their first few months. Jack was a sewer worker and Ria worked in a toy factory. They said they were healthy and seemed to be.

Chip decided to take them – provisionally, at least and he told them the details of the plan as it was taking shape.

'We ought to blow up the whole fucking thing, not just the refrigerating plants,' Jack said.

'One thing has to be very clear,' Chip said. 'I'm going to be in charge. Unless you're prepared to do exactly as I say every step of the way, you'd better forget the whole thing.'

'No, you're absolutely right,' Jack said. 'There *has* to be one man in charge of an operation like this; it's the only way it can work.'

'We can offer suggestions, can't we?' Ria said.

'The more the better,' Chip said. 'But the decisions are going to be mine, and you've got to be ready to go along with them.'

Jack said, 'I am,' and Ria said, 'So am I.'

Locating the entrance of the tunnel turned out to be more difficult than Chip had anticipated. He collected three large-scale maps of central Eur and a highly detailed pre-U topographic one of 'Switzerland' on which he carefully transcribed Uni's site, but everyone he consulted – former engineers and geologists, native mining engineers – said that more data was needed before the tunnel's course could be projected with any hope of accuracy. Ashi became interested in the problem and spent occasional hours in the Library copying references to 'Geneva' and 'Jura Mountains' out of old encyclopedias and works on geology.

On two consecutive moonlit nights Chip and Dover went out in the IA boat to a point west of EUR91766 and watched for the copper barges. These passed, they found, at precise intervals of four hours and twenty-five minutes. Each low flat dark shape moved steadily towards the northwest at thirty kilometres an hour, its rolling afterwaves lifting the boat and dropping it, lifting it and dropping it. Three hours later a barge would come from the opposite direction, riding higher in the water, empty.

Dover calculated that the Eur-bound barges, if they maintained their speed and direction, would reach EUR91772 in a little over six hours.

On the second night he brought the boat alongside a barge and slowed to match its speed while Chip climbed aboard. Chip rode on the barge for several minutes, sitting comfortably on its flat compacted load of copper ingots in wood cribs, and then he climbed back aboard the boat.

Lilac found another man for the group, an attendant at the clinic named Lars Newstone who called himself Buzz. He was thirty-six, Chip's age, and taller than normal; a quiet and capable-seeming man. He had been on the island for nine years and at the clinic for three, during which he had picked up a certain amount of medical knowledge. He was married but living apart from his wife. He wanted to join the group, he said, because he had always felt that 'somebody ought to do something, or at least try. It's wrong,' he said, 'to let Uni – *have* the world without trying to get it back.'

'He's fine, just the man we need,' Chip said to Lilac after Buzz had left their room. 'I wish I had two more of him instead of the Newbridges. Thank you.'

Lilac said nothing, standing at the sink washing cups. Chip went to her, took her shoulders, and kissed her hair. She was in the seventh month of her pregnancy, big and uncomfortable.

At the end of March, Julia gave a dinner party at which Chip, who had by then been working four months on the plan, presented it to her guests – natives with money who could each be counted on, she had said, for a contribution of at least five hundred dollars. He gave them copies of a list he had prepared of all the cost that would be involved, and passed around his 'Switzerland' map with the tunnel drawn in its approximate position.

They weren't as receptive as he had thought they would be.

'Thirty-six hundred for explosives?' one asked.

'That's right, sir,' Chip said. 'If anyone knows where we can get them cheaper, I'll be glad to hear about it.'

'What's this "kit reinforcing"?'

'The kits we're going to carry; they're not made for heavy loads. They have to be taken apart and remade around metal frames.'

'You people can't buy guns and bombs, can you?'

'I'll do the buying,' Julia said, 'and everything will stay on my property until the party leaves. I have the permits.'

'When do you think you'll go?'

'I don't know yet,' Chip said. 'The gas masks are going to take three months from when they're ordered. And we still have one more man to find, and training to go through. I'm hoping for July or August.'

'Are you sure this is where the tunnel actually is?'

'No, we're still working on that. That's just an approximation.'

Five of the guests gave excuses and seven gave cheques that added up to only twenty-six hundred dollars, less than a quarter of the eleven thousand that was needed.

'Lunky bastards,' Julia said.

'It's a beginning, anyway,' Chip said. 'We can start ordering things. And take on Captain Gold.'

'We'll do it again in a few weeks,' Julia said. 'What were you so nervous for? You've got to speak more forcefully!'

The baby was born, a boy, and they named him Jan. Both his eyes were brown.

On Sundays and Wednesday evenings, in an unused loft in Julia's factory, Chip, Dover, Buzz, Jack, and Ria studied various forms of fighting. Their teacher was an officer in the Army, Captain Gold, a small smiling man who obviously disliked them and seemed to take pleasure in having them hit one another and throw one another to the thin mats spread on the floor. 'Hit! Hit! Hit!' he would say, bobbing before them in his undershirt and army trousers. 'Hit! Like this! *This* is hitting, not *this! This* is waving at someone! God almighty, you're hopeless, you steelies! Come on, Green-eye, *hit him!*'

Chip swung his fist at Jack and was in the air and on his back on a mat.

'Good, you!' Captain Gold said. 'That looked a little human! Get up, Green-eye, you're not dead! What did I tell you about keeping low?'

Jack and Ria learned most quickly; Buzz, most slowly.

Julia gave another dinner, at which Chip spoke more forcefully, and they got thirty-two hundred dollars.

The baby was sick – had a fever and a stomach infection – but he got better and was fine-looking and happy, sucking hungrily at Lilac's breasts. Lilac was warmer than before, pleased with the baby and interested in hearing Chip tell about the money-raising and the gradual coming-into-being of the plan.

Chip found a sixth man, a worker on a farm near Santany, who had come over from Afr shortly before Chip and Lilac had. He was a little older than Chip would have liked, forty-three, but he was strong and quick-moving, and sure that Uni could be beaten. He had worked in chromatomicrography in the Family, and his name was Morgan Newmark, though he still called himself by his Family name, Karl.

Ashi said, 'I think I could find the damned tunnel myself now,' and handed Chip twenty pages of notes that he had copied from books in the Library. Chip brought them, along with the maps, to each of the people he had consulted before, and three of them were now willing to hazard a projection of the tunnel's likeliest course. They came up, not unexpectedly, with three different places for the tunnel's entrance. Two were within a kilometre of each other and one was six kilometres away. 'This is enough if we can't do better,' Chip said to Dover.

The company that was making the gas masks went out of business – without returning the eight-hundred-dollar advance Chip had given them – and another maker had to be found.

Chip talked again with Newbrook, the former technological-academy teacher, about the type of refrigerating plants Uni would be likely to have. Julia gave another dinner and Ashi gave a party: three thousand dollars more was collected. Buzz had a run-in with a gang of natives and, though he surprised them by fighting effectively, came out of it with two cracked ribs and a fractured shinbone. Everyone began looking for another man in case he wasn't able to go.

Lilac woke Chip one night.

'What's wrong?' he said.

'Chip?' she said.

'Yes?' He could hear Jan breathing, asleep in his cradle.

'If you're right,' she said, 'and this island is a prison that Uni has put us on—'

'Yes?'

'And attacks have been made from here before—'

'Yes?' he said.

She was silent – he could see her lying on her back with her eyes open – and then she said, 'Wouldn't Uni put *other* people here, "healthy" members, to warn it of other attacks?'

He looked at her and said nothing.

'Maybe to – take part in them?' she said. 'And get everyone "helped" in Eur?'

'No,' he said, and shook his head. 'It's – no. They would have to get treatments, wouldn't they? To *stay* "healthy"?'

'Yes,' she said.

'You think there's a secret medicentre somewhere?' he asked, smiling.

'No,' she said.

'No,' he said. 'I'm sure there aren't any – "espions" here. Before Uni would go to those lengths, it *would* simply kill incurables the way you and Ashi say it would.'

'How do you *know*?' she said.

'Lilac, there *are* no espions,' he said. 'You're just looking

224

for things to worry about. Go to sleep now. Go on. Jan's going to be up in a little while. Go on.'

He kissed her and she turned over. After a while she seemed to be asleep.

He stayed awake.

It couldn't be. They would need treatments . . .

How many people had he told about the plan, the tunnel, the real memory banks? There was no counting. Hundreds! And each must have told others . . .

He'd even put the ad in the *Immigrant: Will buy kits, cuvs, sandals* . . .

Someone who was *in the group?* No. Dover? – impossible. Buzz? – no, never. Jack or Ria? – no. Karl? He didn't really know Karl that well yet – pleasant, talked a lot, drank a little more than he should have but not enough to worry about – no, Karl *couldn't* be anything but what he seemed, working on a farm out in the middle of nowhere . . .

Julia? He was out of his head. Christ and Wei! God in heaven!

Lilac was just worrying too much, that was all.

There couldn't be any espions, any people around who were secretly on Uni's side, because they would need treatments to stay that way.

He was going ahead with it no matter what.

He fell asleep.

The bombs came: bundles of thin brown cylinders taped around a central black one. They were stored in a shed behind the factory. Each had a small metal handle, blue or yellow, lying taped against its side. The blue handles were thirty-second fuses; the yellow, four-minute ones.

They tried one in a marble quarry at night; wedged it in a cleft and pulled its fuse handle, blue, with fifty metres of wire from behind a pile of cut blocks. The explosion when it came was thunderous, and where the cleft had been they found a hole the size of a doorway, running with rubble, churning with dust.

They hiked in the mountains – all except Buzz – wearing kits weighted with stones. Captain Gold showed them how to load a bullet-gun and focus an L-beam; how to draw, aim, and shoot – at planks propped against the factory's rear wall.

'Are you giving another dinner?' Chip asked Julia.

'In a week or two,' she said.

But she didn't. She didn't mention money again, and neither did he.

He spent some time with Karl, and satisfied himself that he wasn't an 'espion'.

Buzz's leg healed almost completely, and he insisted he would be able to go.

The gas masks came, and the remaining guns, and the tools and the shoes and the razors; and the plastic sheeting, the remade kits, the watches, the coils of strong wire, the inflatable raft, the shovel, the compasses, the binoculars.

'Try to hit me,' Captain Gold said, and Chip hit him and split his lip.

It took till November to get everything done, almost a year, and then Chip decided to wait and go at Christmas, to make the move to '001 on the holiday, when bike paths and walkways, carports and airports, would be at their busiest; when members would move a little less slowly than normal and even a 'healthy' one might miss the plate of a scanner.

On the Sunday before they were to go, they brought everything from the shed into the loft and packed the kits and the secondary kits they would unpack when they landed. Julia was there, and Lars Newman's son John, who was going to bring back the IA boat, and Dover's girlfriend Nella – twenty-two and yellow-haired as he, excited by it all. Ashi looked in and so did Captain Gold. 'You're nuts, you're all nuts,' Captain Gold said, and Buzz said, 'Scram, you lunky.' When they were done, when all the kits were plastic-wrapped and tied, Chip asked everyone not in the group to go outside. He gathered the group in a circle on the mats.

'I've been thinking a lot about what happens if one of us gets caught,' he said, 'and this is what I've decided. If any-one, even *one*, gets caught – the rest of us will turn around and go back.'

They looked at him. Buzz said, 'After all this?'

'Yes,' he said. 'We won't have a chance, once anyone's treated and telling a doctor that we're going in through the tunnel. So we'll go back, quickly and quietly, and find one of the boats. In fact, I want to try to spot one when we land, before we start travelling.'

'Christ and Wei!' Jack said. 'Sure, if three or four get caught, but one?'

'That's the decision,' Chip said. 'It's the right one.'

Ria said, 'What if you get caught?'

'Then Buzz is in charge,' Chip said, 'and it's up to him. But meanwhile that's the way it's going to be: if anyone gets caught we all turn back.'

Karl said, 'So let's nobody get caught.'

'Right,' Chip said. He stood up. 'That's all,' he said. 'Get plenty of sleep. Wednesday at seven.'

'Woodsday,' Dover said.

'Woodsday, Woodsday, Woodsday,' Chip said. 'Woodsday at seven.'

He kissed Lilac as if he were going out to see someone about something and would be back in a few hours. "Bye, love,' he said.

She held him and kept her cheek against his and didn't say anything.

He kissed her again, took her arms from around him, and went to the cradle. Jan was busy reaching for an empty cigarette box hanging on a string. Chip kissed his cheek and said goodbye to him.

Lilac came to him and he kissed her. They held each other and kissed, and then he went out, not looking back at her.

Ashi was waiting downstairs on his motorbike. He drove Chip to Pollensa and the pier.

They were all in the IA office by a quarter to seven, and while they were clipping one another's hair the truck came. John Newman and Ashi and a man from the factory loaded the kits and the raft on to the boat, and Julia unpacked sandwiches and coffee. The men clipped their hair and shaved their faces bare.

They put bracelets on and closed links that looked like ordinary ones. Chip's bracelet said Jesus AY31G6912.

He said goodbye to Ashi, and kissed Julia. 'Pack your kit and get ready to see the world,' he said.

'Be careful,' she said. 'And try praying.'

He got on the boat, sat on the deck in front of the kits

227

with John Newman and the others – Buzz and Karl, Jack and Ria; strange-looking and Family-like with their clipped hair, their beardless similar faces.

Dover started the boat and steered it out of the harbour, then turned it towards the faint orange glow that came from '91766.

TWO

In pallid pre-dawn light they slipped from the barge and pushed the kit-loaded raft away from it. Three of them pushed and three swam along beside, watching the black high-cliffed shore. They moved slowly, keeping about fifty metres out. Every ten minutes or so they changed places; the ones who had been swimming pushed, the ones who had been pushing swam.

When they were well below '91772 they turned and pushed the raft in. They beached it in a small sandy cove with towering rock walls, and unloaded the kits and unwrapped them. They opened the secondary kits and put on coveralls; pocketed guns, watches, compasses, maps; then dug a hole and packed into it the two emptied kits and all the plastic wrappings, the deflated raft, their Liberty clothing, and the shovel they had used for digging. They filled the hole and stamped it level, and with kits slung on their shoulders and sandals in their hands, began walking in single file down the narrow strip of beach. The sky lightened and their shadows appeared before them, sliding in and out over rocky cliff-base. Near the back of the line Karl started whistling 'One Mighty Family'. The others smiled, and Chip, at the front, joined in. Some of the others did too.

Soon they came to a boat – an old blue boat lying on its side, waiting for incurables who would think themselves lucky. Chip turned, and walking backwards, said, 'Here it is, if we need it,' and Dover said, 'We won't,' and Jack after Chip had turned and they had passed it picked up a stone, turned, threw it at the boat, and missed.

They switched their kits from one shoulder to the other

as they walked. In a little less than an hour they came to a scanner with its back to them. 'Home again,' Dover said, and Ria groaned, and Buzz said, 'Hi, Uni, how are you?' – patting the scanner's top as he passed it. He was walking without limping; Chip had looked around a few times to check.

The strip of beach began to widen, and they came to a litter basket and more of them, and then lifeguard platforms, speakers and a clock – 6.54 *Thu 25 Dec 171 Y.U.* – and a stairway zigzagging up the cliff with red and green bunting wound around some of its railing supports.

They put their kits down, and their sandals, and took their coveralls off and spread them out. They lay down on them and rested under the sun's growing warmth. Chip mentioned things that he thought they should say when they spoke to the Family – afterwards – and they talked about that and about the extent to which Uni's stopping would block TV and how long the restoring of it would take.

Karl and Dover fell asleep.

Chip lay with his eyes closed and thought about some of the problems the Family would face as it awakened, and different ways of dealing with them.

'Christ, Who Taught Us' began on the speakers at eight o'clock, and two red-capped lifeguards in sunglasses came walking down the zigzag stairs. One of them came to a platform near the group. 'Merry Christmas,' he said.

'Merry Christmas,' they said to him.

'You can go in now if you want,' he said, climbing up on to the platform.

Chip and Jack and Dover got up and went into the water. They swam around for a while, watching members come down the stairs, and then they went out and lay down again.

When there were thirty-five or forty members on the beach, at 8.22, the six got up and began putting on their coveralls and shouldering their kits.

Chip and Dover went up the stairs first. They smiled and said 'Merry Christmas' to members coming down, and easily false-touched the scanner at the top. The only members nearby were at the canteen with their backs turned.

They waited by a water fountain, and Jack and Ria came up, and then Buzz and Karl.

They went to the bike racks, where twenty or twenty-five

229

bikes were lined up in the nearest slots. They took the last six, put their kits in the baskets, mounted, and rode to the entrance of the bike path. They waited there, smiling and talking, until no cyclists and no cars were going by, and then they passed the scanner in a group, touching their bracelets to the side of it in case someone could see them from a distance.

They rode towards EUR91770 singly and in twos, spaced out widely along the path. Chip went first, with Dover behind him. He watched the cyclists who approached them and the occasional cars that rushed past. *We're going to do it,* he thought. *We're going to do it.*

They went into the airport separately and gathered near the flight-schedule signboard. Members pressed them close together; the red-and-green-streamered waiting-room was densely crowded, and so voice-filled that Christmas music could only intermittently be heard. Beyond the glass, large planes turned and moved ponderously, took members on from three escalators at once, let lines of members off, rolled to and from the runways.

It was 9.35. The next flight to EUR00001 was at 11.48.

Chip said, 'I don't like the idea of staying here so long. The barge either used extra power or came in late, and if the difference was conspicuous, Uni may have figured out what caused it.'

'Let's go now,' Ria said, 'and get as close to '001 as we can and then bike again.'

'We'll get there a lot sooner if we wait,' Karl said. 'This isn't such a bad hiding place.'

'No,' Chip said, looking at the signboard, 'let's go – on the 10.06 to '00020. That's the soonest we can manage it, and it's only about fifty kilometres from '001. Come on, the door's over that way.'

They made their way through the crowd to the swing-door at the side of the room and clustered around its scanner. The door opened and a member in orange came out. Excusing himself, he reached between Chip and Dover to touch the scanner – *yes*, it winked – and went on.

Chip slipped his watch from his pocket and checked it against a clock. 'It's lane six,' he said. 'If there's more than one escalator, be on line for the one at the back of the plane; and make sure you're near the end of the line but with at least six members behind you. Dover?' He took Dover's elbow and they went through the door into the depot area. A member in orange standing there said, 'You're not supposed to be in here.'

'Uni okayed it,' Chip said. 'We're in airport design.'

'Three-thirty-seven A,' Dover said.

Chip said, 'This wing is being enlarged next year.'

'I see what you meant about the ceiling,' Dover said, look-in up at it.

'Yes,' Chip said. 'It could easily go up another metre.'

'Metre and a half,' Dover said.

'Unless we run into trouble with the ducts,' Chip said.

The member left them and went out through the door.

'Yes, all the ducts,' Dover said. 'Big problem.'

'Let me show you where they lead,' Chip said. 'It's interesting.'

'It certainly is,' Dover said.

They went into the area where members in orange were readying cake and drink containers, working more quickly than members usually did.

'Three-thirty-seven A?' Chip said.

'Why not?' Dover said, and pointed at the ceiling as they separated for a member pushing a cart, 'You see the way the ducts run?' he said.

'We're going to have to change the whole setup,' Chip said. 'In here too.'

They false-touched and went into the room where coveralls hung on hooks. No one was in it. Chip closed the door and pointed to the closet where the orange coveralls were kept.

They put orange coveralls on over their yellow ones, and toeguards on their sandals. They tore openings inside the pockets of the orange coveralls so that they could reach into the pockets of the inner ones.

A member in white came in. 'Hello,' he said. 'Merry Christmas.'

'Merry Christmas,' they said.

'I was sent up from '765 to help out,' he said. He was about thirty.

'Good, we can use it,' Chip said.

231

The member, opening his coveralls, looked at Dover, who was closing his. 'What have you got the other ones on underneath for?' he asked.

'It's warmer that way,' Chip said, going to him.

He turned to Chip, puzzled. 'Warmer?' he said. 'What do you want to be warmer for?'

'I'm sorry, brother,' Chip said, and hit him in the stomach. He bent forward, grunting, and Chip swung his fist up under his jaw. The member straightened and fell backwards; Dover caught him under the arms and lowered him to the floor. He lay with his eyes closed, as if sleeping.

Chip, looking down at him, said, 'Christ and Wei, it works.'

They tore up a set of coveralls and tied the member's wrists and ankles and knotted a sleeve between his teeth; then lifted him and put him into the closet where the floor polisher was.

The clock's 9.51 became 9.52.

They wrapped their kits in orange coveralls and went out of the room and past the members working at the cake and drink containers. In the depot area they found a half-empty carton of towels and put the wrapped kits into it. Carrying the carton between them, they went out through the portal on to the field.

A plane was opposite lane six, a large one, with members leaving it on two escalators. Members in orange waited at each escalator with a container cart.

They went away from the plane, towards the left; crossed the field diagonally with the carton between them, skirting a slow-moving maintenance truck and approaching the hangars that lay in a flat-roofed wing extending towards the runways.

They went into a hangar. A smaller plane was there, with members in orange underneath it, lowering a square black housing from it. Chip and Dover carried the carton to the back of the hangar where there was a door in the side wall. Dover opened it, looked in, and nodded to Chip.

They went in and closed the door. They were in a supply room: racks of tools, rows of wood crates, black metal drums marked *Lub Oil SG*. 'Couldn't be better,' Chip said as they put the carton on the floor.

Dover went to the door and stood at its hinge side. He took out his gun and held it by its barrel.

Chip, crouching, unwrapped a kit, opened it, and took out a bomb, one with a yellow four-minute handle.

He separated two of the oil drums and put the bomb on the floor between them, with its taped-down handle facing up. He took his watch out and looked at it. Dover said, 'How long?' and he said, 'Three minutes'.

He went back to the carton and, still holding the watch, closed the kit and rewrapped it and closed the carton's leaves.

'Is there anything we can use?' Dover asked, nodding at the tool racks.

Chip went to one and the door of the room opened and a member in orange came in. 'Hello,' Chip said, and took a tool from the rack and put the watch in his pocket. 'Hello,' the member said, coming to the other side of the rack. She glanced over it at Chip. 'Who're you?' she asked.

'Li RP,' he said. 'I was sent up from '765 to help.' He took another tool from the rack, a pair of callipers.

'It's not as bad as Wei's Birthday,' the member said.

Another member came to the door. 'We've got it, Peace,' he said. 'Li had it.'

'I asked him and he said he didn't,' the first member said.

'Well he did,' the second member said, and went away.

The first member went after him. 'He was the first one I asked,' she said.

Chip stood and watched the door as it slowly closed. Dover, behind it, looked at him and closed it all the way, softly. Chip looked back at Dover, and then at his hand holding the tools. It was shaking. He put the tools down, let his breath out, and showed his hand to Dover, who smiled and said, 'Very unmemberlike'.

Chip drew a breath and got the watch from his pocket. 'Less than a minute,' he said, and went to the drums and crouched. He pulled the tape from the bomb's handle.

Dover put his gun into his pocket – poked it into the inner one – and stood with his hand on the doorknob.

Chip looking at the watch and holding the fuse handle, said, 'Ten seconds'. He waited, waited, waited – and then pulled the handle up and stood as Dover opened the door. They picked up the carton and carried it from the room and pulled the door closed.

They walked with the carton through the hangar – 'Easy, easy,' Chip said – and across the field towards the plane opposite lane six. Members were filing on to the escalators, riding up.

'What's that?' a member in orange with a clipboard asked, walking along with them.

'We were told to bring it over there,' Chip said.

'Karl?' another member said at the other side of the one with the clipboard. He stopped and turned, saying 'Yes?' and Chip and Dover kept walking.

They brought the carton to the plane's rear escalator and put it down. Chip stayed opposite the scanner and looked at the escalator controls; Dover slipped through the line and stood at the scanner's back. Members passed between them, touching their bracelets to the green-winking scanner and stepping on to the escalator.

A member in orange came to Chip and said, 'I'm on this escalator.'

'Karl just told me to take it,' Chip said. 'I was sent up from '765 to help.'

'What's wrong?' the member with the clipboard asked, coming over. 'Why are there three of you here?'

'I thought I was on this escalator,' the other member said. The air shuddered and a loud roar clapped from the hangars.

A black pillar, vast and growing, stood on the wing of hangars, and rolling orange fire was in the black. A black and orange rain fell on the roof and the field, and members in orange came running from the hangars, running and slowing and looking back up at the fiery pillar on the roof.

The member with the clipboard stared, and hurried forward. The other member hurried after him.

The members on the line stood motionless, looking upwards towards the hangars. Chip and Dover caught at their arms and drew them forward. 'Don't stop,' they said. 'Keep moving, please. There's no danger. The plane is waiting. Touch and step on. Keep moving, please.' They herded the members past the scanner and on to the escalator and one was Jack – 'Beautiful,' he said, gazing past Chip as he false-

234

touched; and Ria, who looked as excited as she had the first time Chip had seen her; and Karl, looking awed and sombre; and Buzz, smiling. Dover moved to the escalator after Buzz; Chip thrust a wrapped kit to him and turned to the other members on line, the last seven or eight, who stood looking towards the hangars. 'Keep moving, please,' he said. 'The plane is waiting for you. Sister!'

'There is no cause for alarm,' a woman's voice loud-speakered. 'There has been an accident in the hangars but everything is under control.'

Chip urged the members to the escalator. 'Touch and step on,' he said. 'The plane's waiting.'

'Departing members, please resume your places in line,' the voice said. 'Members who are boarding planes, continue to do so. There will be no interruption of service.'

Chip false-touched and stepped on to the escalator behind the last member. Riding upwards with his wrapped kit under his arm, he glanced towards the hangars: the pillar was black and smudging; there was no more fire. He looked ahead again, at pale blue coveralls. 'All personnel except forty-sevens and forty-nines, resume your assigned duties,' the woman's voice said. 'All personnel except forty-sevens and forty-nines, resume your assigned duties. Everything is under control.' Chip stepped into the plane and the door slid down behind him. 'There will be no interruption of—' Members stood confusedly, looking at filled seats.

'There are extra passengers because of the holiday,' Chip said. 'Go forward and ask members with children to double up. It can't be helped.'

The members moved down the aisle, looking from one side of the plane to the other.

The five were sitting in the last row, next to the dispensers. Dover took his wrapped kit from the aisle seat and Chip sat down. Dover said, 'Not bad.'

'We're not up yet,' Chip said.

Voices filled the plane: members telling members about the explosion, spreading the news from row to row. The clock said 10.06 but the plane wasn't moving.

The 10.06 became 10.07.

The six looked at one another, and looked forward, normally.

235

The plane moved; swung gently to the side and then pulled forward. It moved faster. The light dimmed and the TV screens flicked on.

They watched *Christ's Life* and a years-old *Family at Work*. They drank tea and coke but couldn't eat; there were no cakes on the plane, because of the hour, and though they had foil-wrapped rounds of cheese in their kits, they would have been seen eating them by the members who came to the dispensers. Chip and Dover sweated in their double coveralls. Karl kept dozing off, and Ria and Buzz on either side of him nudged him to keep him awake and watching.

The flight took forty minutes.

When the location sign said EURooo2o, Chip and Dover got up from their seats and stood at the dispensers, pressing the buttons and letting tea and coke flow down the drains. The plane landed and rode and stopped, and members began filing off. After a few dozen had gone through the doorway nearby, Chip and Dover lifted the emptied containers from the dispensers, set them on the floor and raised their covers, and Buzz put a wrapped kit into each. Then Buzz, Karl, Ria, and Jack got up and the six went to the doorway. Chip, carrying a container against his chest, said, 'Would you excuse us, please?' to an elderly member and went out. The others followed close behind him. Dover, carrying the other container said to the member, 'You'd better wait till I'm off the escalator,' and the member nodded, looking confused.

At the bottom of the escalator Chip leaned his wrist towards the scanner and then stood opposite it, blocking it from the members in the waiting-room. Buzz, Karl, Ria, and Jack passed in front of him, false-touching, and Dover leaned against the scanner and nodded to the member waiting above.

The four went towards the waiting-room, and Chip and Dover crossed the field to the portal and went through it into the depot area. Setting down the containers, they took the kits out of them and slipped between two rows of crates. They found a cleared space near the wall and took off the orange coveralls and pulled the toeguards from their sandals.

They left the depot area through the swing-door, their kits slung on their shoulders. The others were waiting around the scanner. They went out of the airport by twos it was almost as crowded as the one in '91770 – and gathered again at the bike racks.

By noon they were north of '00018. They ate their rounds of cheese between the bike path and the River of Freedom, in a valley flanked by mountains that rose to awesome snow-streaked heights. While they ate they looked at their maps. By nightfall, they calculated, they could be in parkland a few kilometres from the tunnel's entrance.

A little after three o'clock, when they were nearing '00013, Chip noticed an approaching cyclist, a girl in her early teens, who was looking at the faces of the northbound cyclists – his own as she passed him – with an expression of concern, of memberlike wanting-to-help. A moment later he saw another approaching cyclist looking at faces in the same slightly anxious way, an elderly woman with flowers in her basket. He smiled at her as she passed, then looked ahead. There was nothing out of the ordinary in the path and the road beside it; a few hundred metres ahead both path and road turned to the right and disappeared behind a power station.

He rode on to grass, stopped, and looking back, signalled to the others as they came along.

They pushed their bikes farther on to the grass. They were on the last stretch of parkland before the city: a span of grass, then picnic tables and a rising slope of trees.

'We're never going to make it if we stop every half hour,' Ria said.

They sat down on the grass.

'I think they're checking bracelets up ahead,' Chip said. 'Telecomps and red-crossed coveralls. I noticed two members coming this way who looked as if they were trying to spot the sick one. They had that how-can-I-help look.'

'Hate,' Buzz said.

Jack said, 'Christ and Wei, Chip, if we're going to start worrying about members' *facial expressions*, we might as well just turn around and go home.'

Chip looked at him and said, 'A bracelet check isn't so unlikely, is it? Uni must know by now that the explosion at '91770 was no accident, and it must have figured out exactly why it happened. This is the shortest route from '020 to

Uni – and we're coming to the first sharp turn in about twelve kilometres.'

'All right, so they're checking bracelets,' Jack said. 'What the hate are we carrying guns for?'

'Yes!' Ria said.

Dover said, 'If we shoot our way through we'll have the whole bike path after us.'

'So we'll drop a bomb behind us,' Jack said. 'We've got to move fast, not sit on our asses as if we're in a chess game. These dummies are half dead anyway; what difference does it make if we kill a few of them? We're going to help all the rest, aren't we?'

'The guns and bombs are for when we need them,' Chip said, 'not for when we can avoid using them.' He turned to Dover. 'Take a walk in the woods there,' he said. 'See if you can get a look at what's past the turn.'

'Right,' Dover said. He got up and crossed the grass, picked something up and brought it to a litter basket, and went in among the trees. His yellow coveralls became bits of yellow that vanished up the slope.

They turned from watching him. Chip took out his map.

'Shit,' Jack said.

Chip said nothing. He looked at the map.

Buzz rubbed his leg and took his hand from it abruptly.

Jack tore bits of grass from the ground. Ria, sitting close to him, watched him. 'What's your suggestion,' Jack said, 'if they *are* checking bracelets?'

Chip looked up from the map and, after a moment, said, 'We'll go back a little way and cut east and by-pass them.'

Jack tore up more grass and then threw it down. 'Come on,' he said to Ria, and stood up. She sprang up beside him, bright-eyed.

'Where are you going?' Chip said.

'Where we planned to go,' Jack said, looking down at him. 'The parkland near the tunnel. We'll wait for you until it gets light.'

'Sit down, you two,' Karl said.

Chip said, 'You'll go with all of us when I say we'll go. You agreed to that at the beginning.'

'I've changed my mind,' Jack said. 'I don't like taking

orders from you any more than I like taking them from Uni.'

'You're going to ruin everything,' Buzz said.

Ria said, 'You are! Stopping, turning back, by-passing – if you're going to do a thing, do it!'

'Sit down and wait till Dover gets back,' Chip said.

Jack smiled. 'You want to make me?' he said. 'Right out here in front of the Family?' He nodded to Ria and they picked up their bikes and steadied the kits in the baskets.

Chip got up, putting the map in his pocket. 'We can't break the group in two in this way,' he said. 'Stop and think for a minute, will you, Jack? How will we know if—'

'You're the stopper-and-thinker,' Jack said. 'I'm the one who's going to walk down that tunnel.' He turned and pushed his bike away. Ria pushed hers along with him. They went towards the path.

Chip took a step after them and stopped, his jaw tight, his hands fisted. He wanted to shout at them, to take his gun out and force them back – but there were cyclists passing, members on the grass nearby.

'There's nothing you can do, Chip,' Karl said, and Buzz said, 'The brother-fighters.'

At the edge of the path Jack and Ria mounted their bikes. Jack waved. 'So long!' he called. 'See you in the lounge at TV!' Ria waved too and they pedalled away.

Buzz and Karl waved after them.

Chip snatched up his kit from his bike and slung it on his shoulder. He took another kit and tossed it in Buzz's lap. 'Karl, you stay here,' he said. 'Buzz, come on with me.'

He went into the woods and realized he had moved quickly, angrily, abnormally, but thought Fight it! He went up the slope in the direction Dover had taken. God DAMN them!

Buzz caught up with him 'Christ and Wei,' he said, 'don't throw the kits!'

'God damn them!' Chip said. 'The first time I saw them I knew they were no good! But I shut my eyes because I was so fighting – God damn me!' he said. 'It's my fault. Mine.'

'Maybe there's no bracelet check and they'll be waiting in the parkland,' Buzz said.

Yellow flickered among the trees ahead: Dover coming

down. He stopped, then saw them and came on. 'You're right,' he said. 'Doctors on the ground, doctors in the air—'

'Jack and Ria have gone on,' Chip said.

Dover looked at him wide-eyed and said, 'Didn't you stop them?'

'How?' Chip said. He caught Dover's arm and turned him around. 'Show us the way,' he said.

Dover led them quickly up the slope through the trees. 'They'll never get through,' he said. 'There's a whole medi-centre and barriers to prevent bikes from turning.'

They came out of the trees on to an incline of rock. Buzz last and hurrying. Dover said, 'Get down or we'll be seen.'

They dropped to their stomachs and crawled up the incline to its rim. Beyond lay the city, '00013, its white slabs standing clean and bright in the sunlight, its interweaving rails glittering, its border of roadways flashing with cars. The river curved before it and continued to the north, blue and slender, with sightseeing boats drifting slowly and a long line of barges passing under bridges.

Below, they looked into a rock-walled half bowl whose floor was a semicircular plaza where the bike path branched; it came down from the north around the power station, and half of it turned, passed over the car-rushing road, and bridged to the city, while the other half went on across the plaza and followed the river's curving eastern bank with the road coming up to rejoin it. Before it branched, barriers channelled the oncoming cyclists into three lanes, each of them passing before a group of red-cross-coveralled members standing beside a short unusual-looking scanner. Three members in anitgrav gear hovered face-down in the air, one over each group. Two cars and a copter were in the nearer part of the plaza, and more members in red-crossed coveralls stood by the line of cyclists who were leaving the city, hurrying them along when they slowed to look at the ones who were touching the scanners.

'Christ, Marx, Wood, and Wei,' Buzz said.

Chip, while he looked, pulled his kit open at his side. 'They must be in the line somewhere,' he said. He found his binoculars and put them to his eyes and focused them.

'They are,' Dover said. 'See the kits in the baskets?'

240

Chip swept the line and found Jack and Ria; they were pedalling slowly, side by side in wood-barriered lanes. Jack was looking ahead and his lips were moving. Ria nodded. They were steering with their left hands only; their right hands were in their pockets.

Chip passed the binoculars to Dover and turned to his kit. 'We've got to help them get through,' he said. 'If they make it over the bridge they may be able to lose themselves in the city.'

'They're going to shoot when they get to the scanners,' Dover said.

Chip gave Buzz a blue-handled bomb and said, 'Take off the tape and pull when I tell you. Try to get it near the copter; two birds with one net.'

'Do it before they start shooting,' Dover said.

Chip took the binoculars back from him and looked through them and found Jack and Ria again. He scanned the lines ahead of them; about fifteen bikes were between them and the groups at the scanners.

'Do they have bullets or L-beams?' Dover asked.

'Bullets,' Chip said. 'Don't worry, I'll time it right.' He watched the lines of slow-moving bikes, gauging their speed.

'They'll probably shoot anyway,' Buzz said. 'Just for fun. Did you see that look in Ria's eyes?'

'Get ready,' Chip said. He watched until Jack and Ria were five bikes from the scanners. 'Pull,' he said.

Buzz pulled the handle and threw the bomb underhanded to the side. It hit stone, tumbled downward, bounded off a projection, and landed near the side of the copter. 'Get back,' Chip said. He took another look through the binoculars, at Jack and Ria two bikes from the scanners looking tense but confident, and slipped back between Buzz and Dover. 'They look as if they're going to a party,' he said.

They waited, their cheeks on stone, and the explosion roared and the incline shuddered. Metal crashed and grated below. There was silence, and the bomb's bitter smell; and then voices, murmuring and rising louder. 'Those two!' someone shouted

They edged forward to the rim.

Two bikes were racing on to the bridge. All the others had

241

stopped, their riders standing one-footed, facing towards the copter – tipped to its side below and smoking – and turning now towards the two bikes speeding and the red-cross-coveralled members running after them. The three members in the air veered and flew towards the bridge.

Chip raised the binoculars – to Ria's bent back and Jack's ahead of her. They pedalled rapidly in depthless flatness, seeming to get no farther away. A glittering mist appeared, partly obscuring them.

Above, a hovering member downpointed a cylinder gushing thick white gas.

'He's got them!' Dover said.

Ria stood astride her bike; Jack looked over his shoulder at her.

'Ria, not Jack,' Chip said.

Jack stopped and turned with his gun aimed upward. It jerked, and jerked again.

The member in the air went limp (*crack* and *crack*, the shots sounded), the white-gushing cylinder falling from his hand.

Members fleeing the bridge bicycled in both directions, ran wide-eyed on the flanking walkways.

Ria sat by her bike. She turned her head, and her face was moist and glittering. She looked troubled. Red-crossed coveralls blurred over her.

Jack stared, holding his gun, and his mouth opened big and round, closed and opened again in glittering mist. ('Ria!' Chip heard, small and far away.) Jack raised his gun (Ria!') and fired, fired, fired.

Another member in the air (*crack, crack, crack*) went limp and dropped his cylinder. Red spattered on the walkway below him, and more red.

Chip lowered the binoculars.

'Your *gas mask!*' Buzz said. He had binoculars too.

Dover was lying with his face in his arms.

Chip sat up and looked with only his eyes: at the narrow emptied bridge with a faraway cyclist in pale blue wobbling down the middle of it and a member in the air following him at a distance; at the two dead or dying members, turning slowly in the air, drifting; at the red-cross-coveralled members, walking now in a bridge-wide line, and one of them helping a member in yellow by a fallen bike, taking her about the shoulders and leading her back towards the plaza.

The cyclist stopped and looked back towards the red-cross-coveralled members, then turned and bent forward over the front of his bike. The member in the air flew quickly closer and pointed his arm; a thick white feather grew from it and brushed the cyclist.

Chip raised the binoculars.

Jack, grey-snouted in his gas mask, leaned to his left in glittering mist and put a bomb on the bridge. Then he pedalled, skidded, sideslipped, and fell. He raised himself on one arm with the bike lying between his legs. His kit, spilled from the bike's basket, lay by the bomb.

'Oh Christ and Wei,' Buzz said.

Chip took down the binoculars, looked at the bridge, and then wound the binoculars' neckstrap tightly around their middle.

'How many?' Dover asked, looking at him.

Chip said, 'Three'.

The explosion was bright, loud, and long. Chip watched Ria, walking from the bridge with the red-cross-coveralled member leading her. She didn't turn around.

Dover, up on his knees and looking, turned to Chip.

'His whole kit,' Chip said. 'He was sitting next to it.' He put the binoculars into his kit and closed it. 'We've got to get out of here,' he said. 'Put them away, Buzz. Come on.'

He meant not to look, but before they left the incline he did.

The middle of the bridge was black and rubbled, and its sides were burst outwards. A bicycle wheel lay outside the blackened area, and there were other smaller things towards which the red-cross-coveralled members slowly moved. Pieces of pale blue were on the bridge and floating on the river.

They went back to Karl and told him what had happened, and the four of them got on their bikes and rode south for a few kilometres and went into parkland. They found a stream and drank from it and washed.

'And now we turn back?' Dover said.

'No,' Chip said, 'not all of us.'

They looked at him.

'I said we would,' he said, 'because if anyone got caught, I wanted him to believe it, and say it when he was questioned. The way Ria's probably saying it right now.' He took a cigarette that they were passing around – despite the risk of the smoke smell travelling – and drew on it and passed it to Buzz. 'One of us is going to go back,' he said. 'At least I hope only one will go – to set off a bomb or two between here and the coast and take a boat, to make it look as if we've stuck to the plan. The rest of us will hide in parkland, work our way closer to '001, and go for the tunnel in two weeks or so.'

'Good,' Dover said, and Buzz said, 'I never thought it made sense to give up so easily.'

'Will three of us be enough?' Karl asked.

'We won't know till we try,' Chip said. 'Would six have been enough? Maybe it can be done by one, and maybe it can't be done by a dozen. But after coming this far, I fighting well mean to find out.'

'I'm with you; I was just asking,' Karl said. Buzz said, 'I'm with you too,' and Dover said, 'So am I.'

'Good,' Chip said. 'Three stand a better chance than one, that I do know. Karl, you're the one who goes back.'

Karl looked at him. 'Why me?' he asked.

'Because you're forty-three,' Chip said. 'I'm sorry, brother, but I can't think of any other basis for deciding.'

'Chip,' Buzz said, 'I think I'd better tell you: my leg has been hurting me for the past few hours. I can make it back or I can go on, but – well, I thought you ought to know.'

Karl gave Chip the cigarette. It was down to a couple of centimetres; he snuffed it into the ground. 'All right, Buzz, you'd better be the one,' he said. 'Shave first. We'd all better shave in case we run into anyone.'

They shaved, and then Chip and Buzz worked out a route for Buzz to the nearest part of the coast, about three hundred kilometres away. He would set off a bomb at the airport at '00015 and another when he was near the sea. He kept two extra in case he needed them and gave his others to Chip. 'With luck you'll be on a boat by tomorrow night,' Chip said. 'Make sure there's nobody counting heads when you take it. Tell Julia, and Lilac too, that we'll be hiding for at least two weeks, maybe longer.'

Buzz shook hands with all of them, wished them luck, and took his bike and left.

'We'll stay right here for a while and take turns getting some sleep,' Chip said. 'Tonight we'll go into the city for cakes and cuvs.'

'Cakes,' Karl said, and Dover said, 'It's going to be a long two weeks.'

'No it isn't,' Chip said. 'That was in case *he* gets caught. We're going to do it in four or five days.'

'Christ and Wei,' Karl said, smiling, 'you're really being cagey.'

THREE

They stayed where they were for two days – slept and ate and shaved and practised fighting, played children's word games, talked about democratic government and sex and the pygmies of the equatorial forests – and on the third day, Sunday, they bicycled north. Outside of '00013 they stopped and went up on to the incline overlooking the plaza and the bridge. The bridge was partly repaired and closed off by barriers. Lines of cyclists crossed the plaza in both directions; there were no doctors, no scanners, no copter, no cars. Where the copter had been, there was a rectangle of fresh pink paving.

Early in the afternoon they passed '001 and glimpsed at a distance Uni's white dome beside the Lake of Universal brotherhood. They went into the parkland beyond the city.

The following evening, at dusk, with their bikes hidden in a branch-covered hollow and their kits on their shoulders, they passed a scanner at the parkland's farther border and went out on to the grassy slopes that approached Mount Love. They walked briskly, in shoes and green coveralls, with binoculars and gas masks hung about their necks. They held their guns, but as the darkness grew deeper and the slope more rocky and irregular, they pocketed them. Now and then they paused, and Chip put a hand-covered flashlight to his compass.

They came to the first of the three presumed locations of the tunnel's entrance, and separated and looked for it, using their flashlights guardedly. They didn't find it.

They started for the second location, a kilometre to the northeast. A half moon came over the shoulder of the mountain, wanly lighting it, and they searched its base carefully as they crossed the rock-slope before it.

The slope became smooth, but only in the strip where they were walking – and they realized that they were on a road, old and scrub-patched. Behind them it curved away towards the parkland; ahead it led into a fold in the mountain.

They looked at one another, and took out their guns. Leaving the road, they moved close to the side of the mountain and edged slowly in single file – first Chip, then Dover, then Karl – holding their kits to keep them from bumping, holding their guns.

They came to the fold, and waited against the mountainside, listening.

No sound came from within.

They waited and listened, and then Chip looked back at the others and raised his gas mask and fastened it.

They did the same.

Chip stepped out into the opening of the fold, his gun before him. Dover and Karl stepped out beside him.

Within was a deep and level clearing; and opposite, at the base of sheer mountain wall, the black round flat-bottomed opening of a large tunnel.

It appeared to be completely unprotected.

They lowered their masks and looked at the opening through their binoculars. They looked at the mountain above it and, taking a few steps forward, looking at the fold's outcurving walls and the oval of sky that roofed it.

'Buzz must have done a good job,' Karl said.

'Or a bad one and got caught,' Dover said.

Chip swung his binoculars back to the opening. Its rim had a glassy sheen, and pale green scrub lay along its bottom. 'It feels like the boats on the beaches,' he said. 'Sitting there wide open ...'

'Do you think it leads back to Liberty?' Dover asked, and Karl laughed.

Chip said, 'There could be fifty traps that we won't see until it's too late.' He lowered his binoculars.

Karl said, 'Maybe Ria didn't say anything.'

'When you're questioned at a medicentre you say *everything*,' Chip said. 'But even if she didn't, wouldn't it at least be closed? That's what we've got the tools for.'

Karl said, 'It must be still in use.'

Chip stared at the opening.

'We can always go back,' Dover said.

'Sure, let's,' Chip said.

They looked all around them, and raised their masks into place, and walked slowly across the clearing. No gas jetted, no alarms sounded, no members in antigrav gear appeared in the sky.

They walked to the opening of the tunnel and shone their flashlights into it. Light shimmered and sparked in high plastic-lined roundness, all the way to the place where the tunnel seemed to end, but no, was bending to its downward angle. Two steel tracks reached into it, wide and flat, with a couple of metres of unplasticked black rock between them.

They looked back at the clearing and up at the opening's rim. They stepped inside the tunnel, looked at one another, lowered their masks and sniffed.

'Well,' Chip said. 'Ready to walk?'

Karl nodded, and Dover, smiling, said, 'Let's go.'

They stood for a moment and then walked ahead on the smooth black rock between the tracks.

'Will the air be all right?' Karl asked.

'We've got the masks if it isn't,' Chip said. He shone his flashlight on his watch. 'It's a quarter to ten,' he said. 'We should be there around one.'

'Uni'll be up,' Dover said.

'Till we put it to sleep,' Karl said.

The tunnel bent to a slight incline, and they stopped and looked – at plastic roundness glimmering away and away and away into blackest black.

'Christ and Wei,' Karl said.

They started walking again, at a brisker pace, side by side

247

between the tracks. 'We should have brought the bikes,' Dover said. 'We could have coasted.'

'Let's keep the talk to a minimum,' Chip said. 'And just one light at a time. Yours now, Karl.'

They walked without talking, behind the light of Karl's flashlight. They took their binoculars off and put them in their kits.

Chip felt that Uni was listening to them, was recording the vibrations of their footsteps or the heat of their bodies. Would they be able to overcome the defences it surely was readying, outfight its members, resist its gases? (Were the gas masks any good? Had Jack fallen because he had got his on too late, or would getting it on sooner have made no difference?)

Well, the time for questioning was over, he told himself. This was the time for going ahead. They would meet whatever was waiting for them and do their best to get to the refrigerating plants and blast them.

How many members would they have to hurt, to kill? Maybe none, he thought; maybe the threat of their guns would be enough to protect them. (Against helpful unselfish members seeing Uni in danger? No, never.)

Well, it had to be; there was no other way.

He turned his thoughts to Lilac – to Lilac and Jan and their room in New Madrid.

The tunnel grew cold but the air stayed good.

They walked on, into plastic roundness that glimmered away into blackest black with the tracks reaching into it. *We're here*, he thought. Now. *We're doing it.*

At the end of an hour they stopped to rest. They sat on the tracks and divided a cake among them and passed a container of tea around. Karl said, 'I'd give my arm for some whisky.'

'I'll buy you a case when we get back,' Chip said.

'You heard him,' Karl said to Dover.

They sat for a few minutes and then they got up and started walking again. Dover walked on a track. 'You look pretty confident,' Chip said, flashing his light at him.

'I am,' Dover said. 'Aren't you?'

'Yes,' Chip said, shining his light ahead again.

'I'd feel better if there were six of us,' Karl said.

'So would I,' Chip said.

It was funny about Dover: he had hidden his face in his arms when Jack had started shooting, Chip remembered, and now, when *they* would soon be shooting, perhaps killing, he seemed cheerful and carefree. But maybe it was a cover-up, to hide anxiety. Or maybe it was just being twenty-five or twenty-six, however old he was.

They walked, shifting their kits from one shoulder to the other.

'Are you sure this thing ends?' Karl said.

Chip flicked the light at his watch. 'It's eleven-thirty,' he said. 'We should be past the halfway mark.'

They kept walking into the plastic roundness. It grew a little less cold.

They stopped again at a quarter to twelve, but they found themselves restless and got up in a minute and went on.

Light glinted far away in the centre of the blackness, and Chip pulled out his gun. 'Wait,' Dover said, touching his arm, 'it's *my* light. Look!' He switched his flashlight off and on, off and on, and the glint in the darkness went and came back with it. 'It's the end,' he said. 'Or something on the tracks.'

They walked on, more quickly. Karl took his gun out too. The glint, moving slightly up and down, seemed to stay the same distance from them, small and faint.

'It's moving away from us,' Karl said.

But then, abruptly, it grew brighter, was nearer.

They stopped and raised their masks, fastened them, and walked on.

Towards a disc of steel, a wall that sealed the tunnel to its rim.

They went close to it but didn't touch it. It would slide upwards, they saw; bands of fine vertical scratches ran down it and its bottom was shaped to fit over the tracks.

They lowered their masks and Chip put his watch to Dover's light. 'Twenty to one,' he said. 'We made good time.'

'Or else it goes on on the other side,' Karl said.

'You would think of that,' Chip said, pocketing his gun and unslinging his kit. He put it down on the rock, got on one knee beside it, and pulled it open. 'Come closer with the light, Dover,' he said. 'Don't touch it, Karl.'

Karl, looking at the wall, said, 'Do you think it's electrified?'

'Dover?' Chip said.

'Hold on,' Dover said.

He had backed a few metres into the tunnel and was shining his light at them. The tip of his L-beam protruded into it. 'Don't panic, you're not going to be hurt,' he said. 'Your guns don't work. Drop yours, Karl. Chip, let me see your hands, then put them on your head and stand up.'

Chip stared above the light. There was a glistening line: Dover's clipped blond hair.

Karl said, 'Is this a joke or what?'

'Drop it, Karl,' Dover said. 'Put down your kit too. Chip, let me see your hands.'

Chip showed his empty hands and put them on his head and stood up. Karl's gun clattered on the rock, and his kit bumped. 'What is this?' he said, and to Chip, 'What's he doing?'

'He's an espion,' Chip said.

'A what?'

Lilac had been right. An espion in the group. But *Dover?* It was impossible. It couldn't be.

'Hands on your head, Karl,' Dover said. 'Now turn around, both of you, and face the wall.'

'You brother-fighter,' Karl said.

They turned around and faced the steel wall with their hands on their heads.

'Dover,' Chip said. 'Christ and Wei—'

'You little bastard,' Karl said.

'You're not going to be hurt,' Dover said. The wall slid upwards – and a long concrete-walled room extended before them, with the tracks going halfway into it and ending. A pair of steel doors were at the room's far end.

'Six steps forward and stop,' Dover said. 'Go on. Six steps.'

They walked six steps forward and stopped.

Kit-strap fittings clinked behind them. 'The gun is still on you,' Dover said – from lower down; he was crouching. They glanced at each other. Karl's eyes questioned; Chip shook his head.

'All right,' Dover said, his voice coming from his standing height again. 'Straight ahead.'

They walked through the concrete-walled room, and the steel doors at the end of it slid apart. White-tiled wall stood beyond.

'Through and to the right,' Dover said.

They went through the doorway and turned to the right. A long white-tiled corridor stretched before them, ending at a single steel door with a scanner beside it. The right-hand wall of the corridor was solid tile; the left was broken by evenly spaced steel doors, ten or twelve of them, each with its scanner, about ten metres apart.

Chip and Karl walked side by side down the corridor with their hands on their heads. *Dover!* Chip thought. The first person he had gone to! And why not? So bitterly anti-Uni he had sounded, that day on the IA boat! It was Dover who had told him and Lilac that Liberty was a prison, that Uni had let them get to it! 'Dover!' he said. 'How the hate can you—'

'Just keep walking,' Dover said.

'You're not dulled, you're not treated!'

'No.'

'Then – *how? Why?*'

'You'll see in a minute,' Dover said.

They neared the door at the end of the corridor and it slid abruptly open. Another corridor stretched beyond it: wider, less brightly lit, dark-walled, not tiled.

'Keep going,' Dover said.

They went through the doorway and stopped, staring.

'Go ahead,' Dover said.

They walked on.

What kind of corridor was this? The floor was carpeted, with a gold-coloured carpet thicker and softer than any Chip had ever seen or walked on. The walls were lustrous polished wood, with numbered gold-knobbed doors (12, 11) on both sides. Paintings hung between the doors, beautiful paintings that were surely pre-U: a woman sitting with folded hands smiling knowingly; a hillside city of windowed buildings under a strange black-clouded sky; a garden; a woman reclining; a man in armour. A pleasant odour spiced the air; tangy, dry, impossible to name.

'Where *are* we?' Karl asked.

'In Uni,' Dover said.

Ahead of them double doors stood open; a red-draped room lay beyond.

'Keep going,' Dover said.

They went through the doorway and into the red-draped room; it spread away on both sides, and members, people, were sitting and smiling and starting to laugh, were laughing and rising and some were applauding; young people, old people, were rising from chairs and sofas, laughing and applauding; applauding, applauding, *they all were applauding!*; and Chip's arm was pulled down – by Dover laughing – and he looked at Karl, who looked at him, stupefied; and still they were applauding, men and women, fifty, sixty of them alert- and alive-looking, in coveralls of silk not paplon, green-gold-blue-white-purple; a tall and beautiful woman, a black-skinned man, a woman who looked like Lilac, a man with white hair who must have been over ninety; applauding, applauding, laughing, applauding ...

Chip turned, and Dover grinning, said, 'You're awake,' and to Karl, 'It's real, it's happening.'

'*What* is?' Chip said. 'What the hate *is* this? Who *are* they?'

Laughing, Dover said, 'They're the *programmers*, Chip! And that's what *you're* going to be! Oh if you could only see your faces!'

Chip stared at Karl, and at Dover again. 'Christ and Wei, what are you *talking* about?' he said. 'The programmers are *dead!* Uni's – it goes on by *itself*, it doesn't have—'

Dover was looking past him, smiling. Silence had spread through the room.

Chip turned around.

A man in a smiling mask that looked like Wei (Was this really happening?) was coming to him, moving springily in red silk high-collared coveralls. 'Nothing goes on by itself,' he said in a voice that was high-pitched but forceful, his smiling mask-lips moving like real ones. (But was it a mask – the yellow skin shrunken tight over the sharp cheekbones, the glinting slit-eyes, the wisps of white hair on the shining yellow head?) 'You must be "Chip" with the one green eye,' the man said, smiling and holding out his hand. 'You'll have

252

to tell me what was wrong with the name "Li" that inspired you to change it.' Laughter lifted around them.

The outstretched hand was normal-coloured and youthful. Chip took it (*I'm going mad, he thought*), and it gripped his hand strongly, squeezed his knucklebones to an instant's pain.

'And you're Karl,' the man said, turning and holding out his hand again. 'Now if *you* had changed your name I could understand it.' Laughter rose louder. 'Shake it,' the man said smiling. 'Don't be afraid.'

Karl, staring, shook the man's hand.

Chip said, 'You're—'

'Wei,' the man said, his slit-eyes twinkling. 'From here up, that is.' He touched his coverall's high collar. 'From here down,' he said, 'I'm several other members, principally Jesus RE who won the decathlon in 163.' He smiled at them. 'Didn't you ever bounce a ball when you were a child?' he asked. 'Didn't you ever jump rope? "Marx, Wood, Wei, and Christ; all but Wei were sacrificed." It's still true, you see. "Out of the mouths of babes." Come, sit down, you must be tired. Why couldn't you use the elevators like everyone else? Dover, it's good to have you back. You've done very well, except for that awful business at the '013 bridge.'

They sat in deep and comfortable red chairs, drank pale yellow tart-tasting wine from sparkling glasses, ate sweetly stewed cubes of meat and fish and who-knew-what brought on delicate white plates by young members who smiled at them admiringly – and as they sat and drank and ate, they talked with Wei.

With *Wei!*

How old was that tight-skinned yellow head, living and talking on its lithe red-coveralled body that reached easily for a cigarette, crossed its legs casually? The last anniversary of his birth had been what – the two-hundred-and-sixth, the two-hundred-and-seventh?

Wei died when he was sixty, twenty-five years after the Unification. Generations before the building of Uni, which was programmed by his 'spiritual heirs'. Who died, of course, at sixty-two. So the Family was taught.

And there he sat, drinking, eating, smoking. Men and women stood listening around the group of chairs; he seemed not to notice them. 'The islands have been all those things,' he said. 'At first they were the strongholds of the original incurables; and then, as you put it, "isolation wards" to which we let later incurables "escape", although we weren't so kind as to supply boats in those days.' He smiled and drew on his cigarette. 'Then, however,' he said, 'I found a better use for them, and now they serve as, forgive me, wildlife preserves, where natural leaders can emerge and prove themselves exactly as you have done. Now we supply boats and maps, rather obliquely, and "shepherds" like Dover who accompany returning members and prevent as much violence as they can. And prevent, of course, the final intended violence, Uni's destruction – although the visitor's display is the usual target, so there's no real danger whatsoever.'

Chip said, 'I don't know where I am.' Karl, spearing a cube of meat with a small gold fork, said, 'Asleep in the parkland,' and the men and women nearby laughed.

Wei, smiling, said, 'Yes, it's a disconcerting discovery, I'm sure. The computer that you thought was the Family's changeless and uncontrolled master is in fact the Family's servant controlled by members like yourselves – enterprising, thoughtful, and concerned. Its goals and procedures change continually, according to the decisions of a High Council and fourteen sub-councils. We enjoy luxuries, as you can see, but we have responsibilities that more than justify them. Tomorrow you'll begin to learn. Now, though' – he leaned forward and pressed his cigarette into an ashtray – 'it's very late, thanks to your partiality to tunnels. You'll be shown to your rooms; I hope you find them worth the walk.' He smiled and rose, and they rose with him. He shook Karl's hand – 'Congratulations, Karl,' he said – and Chip's. 'And congratulations to you, Chip,' he said. 'We suspected a long time ago that sooner or later you would be coming. We're glad you haven't disappointed us. I'm glad, I mean: it's hard to avoid talking as if Uni has feelings too.' He turned away and people crowded around them, shaking their hands and saying, 'Congratulations, I never thought you'd make it before Unification Day, it's awful isn't it when you come in and everyone's sitting here congratulations you'll get used to things before you congratulations.'

*　　　*　　　*

The room was large and pale blue, with a large pale-blue silken bed with many pillows, a large painting of floating water lilies, a table of covered dishes and decanters, dark green armchairs, and a bowl of white and yellow chrysanthemums on a long low cabinet.

'It's beautiful,' Chip said. 'Thank you.'

The girl who had led him to it, an ordinary-looking member of sixteen or so in white paplon, said, 'Sit down and I'll take off your—' She pointed at his feet.

'Shoes,' he said, smiling. 'No. Thanks, sister; I can do it myself.'

'Daughter,' she said.

'Daughter?'

'The programmers are our Fathers and Mothers,' she said.

'Oh,' he said. 'All right. Thanks, daughter. You can go now.'

She looked surprised and hurt. 'I'm supposed to stay and take care of you,' she said. 'Both of us.' She nodded towards a doorway beyond the bed. Light and the sound of running water came from it.

Chip went to it.

A pale-blue bathroom was there, large and gleaming; another young member in white paplon kneeled by a filling tub, stirring her hand in the water. She turned and smiled and said, 'Hello, Father'.

'Hello,' Chip said. He stood with his hand on the jamb and looked back at the first girl – drawing the cover from the bed – and back again at the second girl. She smiled up at him, kneeling. He stood with his hand on the jamb. 'Daughter,' he said.

FOUR

He was sitting in bed – had finished his breakfast and was reaching for a cigarette – when a knock at the door sounded. One of the girls went to answer it and Dover came in, smiling and clean and brisk in yellow silk. 'How you doing, brother?' he asked.

'Pretty well,' Chip said, 'pretty well.' The other girl lit his cigarette, took the breakfast tray, and asked him if he wanted more coffee. 'No, thanks,' he said. 'Do you want some coffee?'

'No, thanks,' Dover said. He sat in one of the dark green chairs and leaned back, his elbows on the chair arms, his hands meshed across his middle, his legs outstretched. Smiling at Chip, he said, 'Over the shock?'

'Hate, no,' Chip said.

'It's a long-standing custom,' Dover said. 'You'll enjoy it when the next group comes in.'

'It's cruel, really cruel,' Chip said.

'Wait, you'll be laughing and applauding with everyone else.'

'How often do groups turn up?'

'Sometimes not for years,' Dover said, 'sometimes a month apart. It averages out to one-point-something people a year.'

'And you were in contact with Uni the whole time, you brother-fighter?'

Dover nodded and smiled. 'A telecomp the size of a matchbox,' he said. 'In fact, that's what I kept it in.'

'Bastard,' Chip said.

The girl with the tray had taken it out, and the other girl changed the ashtray on the night table and took her coveralls from a chairback and went into the bathroom. She closed the door.

Dover looked after her, then looked at Chip quizzically. 'Nice night?' he asked.

'Mm-hmm,' Chip said. 'I gather they're not treated.'

'Not in all departments, that's for sure,' Dover said. 'I hope you're not sore at me for not dropping a hint somewhere along the way. The rules are ironclad: no help beyond what's asked of you, no suggestions, no nothing; stay on the sidelines as much as you can and try to prevent bloodshed. I shouldn't have even been doing that routine on the boat – about Liberty being a prison – but I'd been there for two years and nobody was even *thinking* of trying anything. You can see why I wanted to move things along.'

'Yes, I certainly can,' Chip said. He tipped ashes from his cigarette into the clean white tray.

'I'd just as soon you didn't say anything to Wei about it,' Dover said. 'You're having lunch with him at one o'clock.'

'Karl too?'

'No, just you. I think he's got you pegged as High Council material. I'll come by at ten-to and take you to him. You'll find a razor inside there – a thing that looks like a flashlight. This afternoon we'll go to the medicentre and start de-whiskerizing.'

'There's a medicentre?'

'There's everything,' Dover said. 'A medicentre, a library, a gym, a pool, a theatre – there's even a garden that you'd swear was up on top. I'll show you around later.'

Chip said 'And this is where we – stay?'

'All except us poor shepherds,' Dover said. 'I'll be going out to another island, but not for at least six months, thank Uni.'

Chip put his cigarette out. He pressed it out thoroughly. 'What if I don't want to stay?' he said.

'Don't *want* to?' Dover said.

'I've got a wife and a baby, remember?'

'Well so do lots of the others,' Dover said. 'You've got a bigger obligation here, Chip, an obligation to the whole Family, *including* the members on the islands.'

'Nice obligation,' Chip said. 'Silk coveralls and two girls at once.'

'That was for last night only,' Dover said. 'Tonight you'll be lucky to get one.' He sat up straight. 'Look,' he said, 'I know there are – surface attractions here that make it all look – questionable. But the Family *needs* Uni. Think of the way things were on Liberty! And it needs untreated programmers to run Uni and – well, Wei'll explain things better than I can. And one day a week we wear paplon anyway. And eat cakes.'

'A whole day?' Chip said. 'Really?'

'All right, all right,' Dover said, getting up. He went to a chair where Chip's green coveralls lay and picked them up and felt their pockets. 'Is everything here?' he asked.

'Yes,' Chip said. 'Including some snapshots I'd like to have.'

'Sorry, nothing you came in with,' Dover said. 'More rules.' He took Chip's shoes from the floor and stood and looked at him. 'Everyone's a little unsure at first,' he said. 'You'll be proud to stay once you've got the right slant on things. It's an obligation.'

'I'll remember that,' Chip said.

There was a knock at the door, and the girl who had taken the tray came in with blue silk coveralls and white sandals. She put them on the foot of the bed.

Dover, smiling, said, 'If you want paplon it can be arranged.'

The girl looked at him.

'Hate, no,' Chip said. 'I guess I'm as worthy of silk as anyone else around here.'

'You are,' Dover said. 'You are, Chip. I'll see you at ten to one, right?' He started to the door with the green coveralls over his arm and the shoes in his hand. The girl hurried ahead to open the door for him.

Chip said, 'What happened to Buzz?'

Dover stopped and turned, regretful-looking. 'He was caught in '015,' he said.

'And treated?'

Dover nodded.

'More rules,' Chip said.

Dover nodded again and turned and went out.

There were thin steaks cooked in a lightly spiced brown sauce, small browned onions, a sliced yellow vegetable that Chip hadn't seen on Liberty – 'Squash,' Wei said – and a clear red wine that was less enjoyable than the yellow of the night before. They ate with gold knives and forks, from plates with wide gold borders.

Wei, in grey silk, ate quickly, cutting his steak, forking it into his wrinkle-lipped mouth, and chewing only briefly before swallowng and raising his fork again. Now and then he paused sipped wine, and pressed his yellow napkin to his lips.

'These things existed,' he said. 'Would there have been any point in destroying them?'

The room was large and handsomely furnished in pre-U style: white, gold, orange, yellow. At a corner of it, two white-coveralled members waited by a wheeled serving table.

'Of course it seems wrong at first,' Wei said, 'but the ultimate decisions *have* to be made by untreated members, and untreated members can't and shouldn't live their lives on cakes and TV and *Marx Writing*.' He smiled. 'Not even on

Wei Addressing the Chemotherapists,' he said, and put steak into his mouth.

'Why can't the Family make its decisions itself?' Chip asked.

Wei chewed and swallowed. 'Because it's incapable of doing so,' he said. 'That is, of doing so reasonably. Untreated it's – well, you had a sample on your island; it's mean and foolish and aggressive, motivated more often by selfishness than by anything else. Selfishness and fear.' He put onions into his mouth.

'It achieved the Unification,' Chip said.

'Mmm, yes,' Wei said, 'but after what a struggle! And what a fragile structure the Unification was until we buttressed it with treatments! No, the Family has to be helped to full humanity – by treatments today, by genetic engineering tomorrow – and decisions have to be made for it. Those who have the means and the intelligence have the duty as well. To shirk it would be treason against the species.' He put steak into his mouth and raised his other hand and beckoned.

'And part of the duty,' Chip said, 'is to kill members at sixty-two?'

'Ah, *that*,' Wei said, and smiled. 'Always a principal question, sternly asked.'

The two members came to them, one with a decanter of wine and the other with a gold tray that he held at Wei's side. 'You're looking at only part of the picture,' Wei said, taking a large fork and spoon and lifting a steak from the tray. He held it with sauce dripping from it. 'What you're neglecting to look at,' he said, 'is the immeasurable number of members who would die far *earlier* than sixty-two if not for the peace and stability and well-being we give them. Think of the mass for a moment, not of individuals within the mass.' He put the steak on his plate. 'We add many more years to the Family's total life than we take away from it,' he said. 'Many, many more years.' He spooned sauce on to the steak and took onions and squash. 'Chip?' he said.

'No, thanks,' Chip said. He cut a piece from the half steak before him. The member with the decanter refilled his glass.

'Incidentally,' Wei said, cutting steak, 'the actual time of dying is closer now to sixty-three than sixty-two. It will

259

grow still higher as the population on Earth is gradually reduced.' He put steak into his mouth.

The members withdrew.

Chip said, 'Do you include the members who don't get born in your balance of years added and taken away?'

'No,' Wei said smiling. 'We're not that unrealistic. If those members *were* born, there would be no stability, no well-being, and eventually no Family.' He put squash into his mouth and chewed and swallowed. 'I don't expect your feelings to change in one lunch,' he said. 'Look around, talk with everyone, browse in the library – particularly in the history and sociology banks. I hold informal discussions a few evenings a week – once a teacher, always a teacher – sit in on some of them, argue, discuss.'

'I left a wife and a baby on Liberty,' Chip said.

'From which I deduce,' Wei said, smiling, 'that they weren't of overriding importance to you.'

Chip said, 'I expected to be coming back.'

'Arrangements can be made for their care if necessary,' Wei said. 'Dover told me you had already done so.'

'Will I be allowed to go back?' Chip asked.

'You won't want to,' Wei said. 'You'll come to recognize that we're right and your responsibility lies here.' He sipped wine and pressed his napkin to his lips. 'If we're wrong on minor points you can sit on the High Council some day and correct us,' he said. 'Are you interested in architecture or city planning, by any chance?'

Chip looked at him and, after a moment, said, 'I've thought once or twice about designing buildings.'

'Uni thinks you should be on the Architectural Council at present,' Wei said. 'Look in on it. Meet Madhir, the head of it.' He put onions into his mouth.

Chip said, 'I really don't *know* anything . . .'

'You can learn if you're interested,' Wei said, cutting steak. 'There's plenty of time.'

Chip looked at him. 'Yes,' he said. 'Programmers seem to live past sixty-two. Even past sixty-three.'

'Exceptional members have to be preserved as long as possible,' Wei said. 'For the Family's sake.' He put steak into his mouth and chewed, looking at Chip with his slit-eyes. 'Would you like to hear something incredible?' he said.

'Your generation of programmers is almost certain to live indefinitely. Isn't that fantastic? We old ones are going to die sooner or later – the doctors say maybe not, but Uni says we will. You younger ones though, in all probability you won't die. Ever.'

Chip put a piece of steak into his mouth and chewed it slowly.

Wei said, 'I suppose it's an unsettling thought. It'll grow more attractive as you get older.'

Chip swallowed what was in his mouth. He looked at Wei, glanced at his grey-silk chest, and looked at his face again. 'That member,' he said. 'The decathlon winner. Did he die naturally or was he killed?'

'He was killed,' Wei said. 'With his permission, given freely, even eagerly.'

'Of course,' Chip said. 'He was treated.'

'An athlete?' Wei said. 'They take very little. No, he was proud that he was going to become – allied to me. His only concern was whether I would keep him "in condition" – a concern that I'm afraid was justified. You'll find that the children, the ordinary members here, vie with one another to give parts of themselves for transplant. If you wanted to replace that eye, for instance, they'd be slipping into your room and begging you for the honour.' He put squash into his mouth.

Chip shifted in his seat. 'My eye doesn't bother me,' he said. 'I like it.'

'You shouldn't,' Wei said. 'If nothing could be done about it, then you would be justified in accepting it. But an imperfection that can be remedied? That we must *never* accept.' He cut steak. ' "One goal, one goal only, for all of us – perfection," ' he said. 'We're not there yet, but some day we will be: a Family improved genetically so that treatments no longer are needed; a corps of ever-living programmers so that the islands too can be unified; perfection, on Earth and moving "outward, outward, outward to the stars".' His fork, with steak on it, stopped before his lips. He looked ahead of him and said, 'I dreamed of it when I was young: a universe of the gentle, the helpful, the loving, the unselfish. I'll live to see it. I shall live to see it.'

Dover led Chip and Karl through the complex that afternoon – showed them the library, the gym, the pool, and the garden ('Christ and Wei.' 'Wait till you see the sunsets and the stars'); the music-room, the theatre, the lounges; the dining-room and the kitchen ('I don't know, from somewhere,' a member said, watching other members taking bundles of lettuce and lemons from a steel carrier. 'Whatever we need comes in,' she said, smiling. 'Ask Uni'). There were four levels, passed through by small elevators and narrow escalators. The medicentre was on the bottom level. Doctors named Boroviev and Rosen, young-moving men with shrunken faces as old-looking as Wei's, welcomed them and examined them and gave them infusions. 'We can replace that eye one-two-three, you know,' Rosen said to Chip, and Chip said, 'I know. Thanks, but it doesn't bother me.'

They swam in the pool. Dover went to swim with a tall and beautiful woman Chip had noticed applauding the night before and he and Karl sat on the edge of the pool and watched them. 'How do you feel?' Chip asked.

'I don't know,' Karl said. 'I'm pleased, of course, and Dover says it's all necessary and it's our duty to help, but – I don't know. Even if they're running Uni, it's Uni anyway, isn't it?'

'Yes,' Chip said. 'That's how I feel.'

'There would have been a mess up above if we'd done what we planned,' Karl said, 'but it would have been straightened out eventually, more or less.' He shook his head. 'I honestly don't know, Chip,' he said. 'Any system the Family set up on its own would certainly be a lot less *efficient* than Uni is, than these people are; you can't deny that.'

'No, you can't,' Chip said.

'Isn't it fantastic how long they live?' Karl said. 'I still can't get over the fact that – look at those breasts, will you? Christ and Wei.'

A light-skinned round-breasted woman dived into the pool from the other side.

Karl said, 'Let's talk some more later on, all right?' He slipped down into the water.

'Sure, we've got plenty of time,' Chip said.

Karl smiled at him and kicked off and swam arm-over-arm away.

The next morning Chip left his room and walked down a green-carpeted painting-hung corridor towards a steel door at the end of it. He hadn't gone very far when 'Hi, brother,' Dover said and came along and walked beside him. 'Hi,' Chip said. He looked ahead again and, walking, said, 'Am I being guarded?'

'Only when you go in this direction,' Dover said.

Chip said, 'I couldn't do anything with my bare hands even if I wanted to.'

'I know,' Dover said. 'The old man's cautious. Pre-U mind.' He tapped his temple and smiled. 'Only for a few days,' he said.

They walked to the end of the corridor and the steel door slid open. White-tiled corridor stretched beyond it; a member in blue touched a scanner and went through a doorway.

They turned and started back. The door whispered behind them. 'You'll get to see it,' Dover said. 'He'll probably give you the tour himself. Want to go to the gym?'

In the afternoon Chip looked in at the offices of the Architectural Council. A small and cheerful old man recognized him and welcomed him – Madhir, the Council's head. He looked to be over a hundred; his hands too – all of him apparently. He introduced Chip to other members of the Council: an old woman named Sylvie, a reddish-haired man of fifty or so whose name Chip didn't catch, and a short but pretty woman called Gri-gri. Chip had coffee with them and ate a piece of pastry with a cream filling. They showed him a set of plans they were discussing, layouts that Uni had made for the rebuilding of 'G-3 cities'. They talked about whether or not the layouts should be redone to different specifications, asked questions of a telecomp and disagreed on the significance of its answers. The old woman Sylvie gave a point-by-point explanation of why she felt the layouts were needlessly monotonous. Madhir asked Chip if he had an opinion; he said he didn't. The younger woman, Gri-gri, smiled at him invitingly.

There was a party in the main lounge that night – 'Happy new Year!' 'Happy U year!' – and Karl shouted in Chip's ear, 'I'll tell you one thing I don't like about this place! No whisky! Isn't that a shut-off? If wine is okay, why not whisky?' Dover was dancing with the woman who looked like Lilac (not really, not half as pretty), and there were people Chip had sat with at meals and met in the gym and the music-room, people he had seen in one part of the complex or another, people he hadn't seen before; there were more than had been there the other night when he and Karl had come in – almost a hundred of them, with white-paploned members channelling trays among them. 'Happy U year!' someone said to him, an elderly woman who had been at his lunch table, Hera or Hela. 'It's almost 172!' she said. 'Yes,' he said, 'half an hour.' 'Oh, there he is!' she said, and moved forward. Wei was in the doorway, in white with people crowding around him. He shook their hands and kissed their cheeks his shrivelled yellow face grin-split and gleaming, his eyes lost in wrinkles. Chip moved back farther into the crowd and turned away. Gri-gri waved, jumping up to see him over people between them. He waved back at her and smiled and kept moving.

He spent the next day, Unification Day, in the gym and the library.

He went to a few of Wei's evening discussions. They were held in the garden, a pleasant place to be. The grass and the trees were real, and the stars and the moon were near reality, the moon changing phase but never position. Bird warblings sounded from time to time and a gentle breeze blew. Fifteen or twenty programmers were usually at the discussions, sitting on chairs and on the grass. Wei, in a chair, did most of the talking. He expanded on quotations from the *Living Wisdom* and deftly traced the particulars of questions to their encompassing generalities. Now and then he deferred to the head of the Educational Council, Gustafsen, or to Boroviev, the head of the Medical Council, or to another of the High Council members.

At first Chip sat at the edge of the group and only listened, but then he began to ask questions – why parts, at least, of treatments couldn't be put back on a voluntary basis; whether human perfection might not include a degree of selfishness and aggressiveness; whether selfishness, in fact, didn't play a considerable part in their own acceptance of alleged 'duty' and 'responsibility'. Some of the programmers near him seemed affronted by his questions, but Wei answered them patiently and fully; seemed even to welcome them, heard his 'Wei?' over the askings of the others. He moved a little closer in from the group's edge.

One night he sat up in bed and lit a cigarette and smoked in the dark.

The woman lying beside him stroked his back. 'It's right, Chip,' she said. 'It's what's best for everyone.'

'You read minds?' he said.

'Sometimes,' she said. Her name was Deirdre and she was on the Colonial Council. She was thirty-eight, light-skinned, and not especially pretty, but sensible, shapely, and good company.

'I'm beginning to think it is what's best,' Chip said, 'and I don't know whether I'm being convinced by Wei's logic or by lobsters and Mozart and you. Not to mention the prospect of eternal life.'

'That scares me,' Deirdre said.

'Me too,' Chip said.

She kept stroking his back. 'It took me two months to cool down,' she said.

'Is that how you thought of it?' he said. 'Cooling down?'

'Yes,' she said. 'And growing up. Facing reality.'

'So why does it feel like giving in?' Chip said.

'Lie down,' Deirdre said.

He put out his cigarette, put the ashtray on the table, and turned to her, lying down. They held each other and kissed. 'Truly,' she said. 'It's best for everybody, in the long run. We'll improve things gradually, working in our own councils.'

They kissed and caressed each other, and then they kicked down the sheet and she threw her leg over Chip's hip and his hardness slipped easily into her.

He was sitting in the library one morning when a hand took his shoulder. He looked around, startled, and Wei was there. He bent, pushing Chip aside, and put his face down to the viewer hood.

After a moment he said, 'Well, you've gone to the right man.' He kept his face at the hood another moment, and then stood up and let go of Chip's shoulder and smiled at him. 'Read Liebman too,' he said. 'And Okida and Marcuse.

I'll make a list of titles and give it to you in the garden this evening. Will you be there?'

Chip nodded.

His days fell into a routine: mornings at the library, afternoons at the Council. He studied construction methods and environment planning; examined factory flow charts and circulation patterns of residential buildings. Madhir and Sylvie showed him drawings of buildings under construction and buildings planned for the future, of cities as they existed and (plastic overlay) cities as they might some day be modified. He was the eighth member of the Council; of the other seven, three were inclined to challenge Uni's designs and change them, and four, including Madhir, were inclined to accept them without question. Formal meetings were held on Friday afternoons; at other times seldom more than four or five of the members were in the offices. Once only Chip and Gri-gri were there, and they wound up locked together on Madhir's sofa.

After Council, Chip used the gym and the pool. He ate with Deirdre and Dover and Dover's woman-of-the-day and whoever else joined them – sometimes Karl, on the Transportation Council and resigned to wine.

One day in February, Chip asked Dover if it was possible to get in touch with whoever had replaced him on Liberty and find out if Lilac and Jan were all right and whether Julia was providing for them as she had said she would.

'Sure,' Dover said. 'No problem at all.'

'Would you do it then?' Chip said. 'I'd appreciate it.'

A few days later Dover found Chip in the library. 'All's well,' he said. 'Lilac is staying home and buying food and paying rent, so Julia must be coming through.'

'Thanks, Dover,' Chip said. 'I was worried.'

'The man there'll keep an eye on her,' Dover said. 'If she needs anything, money can come in the mail.'

'That's fine,' Chip said. 'Wei told me.' He smiled. 'Poor Julia,' he said, 'supporting all those families when it isn't really necessary. If she knew she'd have a fit.'

Dover smiled. 'She would,' he said. 'Of course, everyone who set out didn't get here, so in some cases it is necessary.'

'That's right,' Chip said. 'I wasn't thinking.'

266

'See you at lunch,' Dover said.

'Right,' Chip said. 'Thanks.'

Dover went, and Chip turned to the viewer and bent his face to the hood. He put his finger on the next-page button and, after a moment, pressed it.

He began to speak up at Council meetings and to ask fewer questions at Wei's discussions. A petition was circulated for the reduction of cake days to one a month; he hesitated but signed it. He went from Deirdre to Blackie to Nina and back to Deirdre; listened in the smaller lounges to sex gossip and jokes about High Council members; followed crazes for paper-aeroplane making and speaking in pre-U languages ('Français' was pronounced 'Fransay', he learned).

One morning he woke up early and went to the gym. Wei was there, jumping astride and swinging dumb-bells, shining with sweat, slab-muscled, slim-hipped; in a black supporter and something white tied around his neck. 'Another early bird, good morning,' he said, jumping his legs out and in, out and in, swinging the dumb-bells out and together over his white-wisped head.

'Good morning,' Chip said. He went to the side of the gym and took off his robe and hung it on a hook. Another robe, blue, hung a few hooks away.

'You weren't at the discussion last night,' Wei said.

Chip turned. 'There was a party,' he said, toeing off his sandals. 'Patya's birthday.'

'It's all right,' Wei said, jumping, swinging the dumb-bells. 'I just mentioned it.'

Chip walked on to a mat and began trotting in place. The white thing around Wei's neck was a band of silk, tightly knotted.

Wei stopped jumping and tossed down the dumb-bells and took a towel from one of the parallel bars. 'Madhir's afraid you're going to be a radical,' he said, smiling.

'He doesn't know the half of it,' Chip said.

Wei watched him, still smiling, wiping the towel over his big-muscled shoulders and under his arms.

'Do you work out every morning?' Chip asked.

'No, only once or twice a week,' Wei said. 'I'm not athletic by nature.' He rubbed the towel behind him.

267

Chip stopped trotting. 'Wei, there's something I'd like to speak to you about,' he said.

'Yes?' Wei said. 'What is it?'

Chip took a step towards him. 'When I first came here.' he said, 'and we had lunch together—'

'Yes?' Wei said.

Chip cleared his throat and said, 'You said that if I wanted to I could have my eye replaced. Rosen said so too.'

'Yes, of course,' Wei said. 'Do you want to have it done?'

Chip looked at him uncertainly. 'I don't know, it seems like such – vanity,' he said. 'But I've always been aware of it—'

'It's not vanity to correct a flaw,' Wei said. 'It's negligence not to.'

'Can't I get a lens put on?' Chip said. 'A brown lens?'

'Yes, you can,' Wei said, 'if you want to cover it and not correct it.'

Chip looked away and then back at him. 'All right,' he said, 'I'd like to do it, have it done.'

'Good,' Wei said, and smiled. 'I've had eye changes twice,' he said. 'There's blurriness for a few days that's all. Go down to the medicentre this morning. I'll tell Rosen to do it himself, as soon as possible.'

'Thank you,' Chip said.

Wei put his towel around his white-banded neck, turned to the parallel bars, and lifted himself straight-armed on to them. 'Keep quiet about it,' he said, hand-walking between the bars, 'or the children will start pestering you.'

It was done, and he looked in his mirror and both his eyes were brown. He smiled, and stepped back, and stepped close again. He looked at himself from one side and the other, smiling.

When he had dressed he looked again.

Deirdre, in the lounge, said, 'It's a tremendous improvement! You look wonderful! Karl, Gri-gri, look at Chip's eye!'

Members helped them into heavy green coats thickly quilted and hooded. They closed them and put on thick green gloves, and a member pulled open the door. The two of them, Wei and Chip, went in.

They walked together along an aisle between steel walls of memory banks, their breath clouding from their nostrils. Wei spoke of the banks' internal temperature and of the weight and number of them. They turned into a narrower aisle where the steel walls stretched ahead of them convergingly to a faraway crosswall.

'I was in here when I was a child,' Chip said.

'Dover told me,' Wei said.

'It frightened me then,' Chip said. 'But it has a kind of – majesty to it; the order and precision ...'

Wei nodded, his eyes glinting. 'Yes,' he said. 'I look for excuses to come in.'

They turned into another cross-aisle, passed a pillar, and turned into another long narrow aisle between back-to-back rows of steel memory banks.

In coveralls again, they looked into a vast railed pit, round and deep, where steel and concrete housings lay, linked by blue arms and sending thicker blue arms branching upwards to low brightly glowing ceiling. ('I believe you had a special interest in the refrigerating plants,' Wei said, smiling, and Chip looked uncomfortable.) A steel pillar stood beside the pit; beyond it lay a second railed and blue-armed pit, and another pillar, another pit. The room was enormous, cool and hushed. Transmitting and receiving equipment lined its two long walls, with red pinpoint lights gleaming; members in blue drew out and replaced two-handled vertical panels of speckled black and gold. Four red-dome reactors stood at one end of the room, and beyond them, behind glass, half a dozen programmers sat at a round console reading into microphones, turning pages.

'There you are,' Wei said.

Chip looked around at it all. He shook his head and blew out breath. 'Christ and Wei,' he said.

Wei laughed happily.

They stayed a while, walking about, looking, talking with some of the members, and then they left the room and walked through white-tiled corridors. A steel door slid open for them, and they went through and walked together down the carpeted corridor beyond.

FIVE

Early in September of 172, a party of seven men and women accompanied by a 'shepherd' named Anna set out from the Andaman Islands in Stability Bay to attack and destroy Uni. Announcements of their progress were made in the programmers' dining-room at each mealtime. Two members of the party 'failed' in the airport at SEA77120 (head-shakings and sighs of disappointment), and two more the following day in a carport in EUR46209 (head-shakings and sighs of disappointment). On the evening of Thursday, September tenth, the three others – a young man and woman and an older man – came single-file into the main lounge with their hands on their heads, looking angry and frightened. A stocky woman behind them, grinning, pocketed a gun.

The three stared foolishly, and the programmers rose, laughing and applauding, Chip and Deirdre among them. Chip laughed loud, applauded hard. All the programmers laughed loud and applauded hard as the newcomers lowered their hands and turned to one another and to their laughing applauding shepherd.

Wei in gold-trimmed green went to them, smiling, and shook their hands. The programmers hushed one another. Wei touched his collar and said, 'From here up, at any rate. From here down …' The programmers laughed and hushed one another. They moved closer, to hear, to congratulate.

After a few minutes the stocky woman slipped out of the crush and left the lounge. She turned to the right and went towards a narrow upgoing escalator. Chip came after her. 'Congratulations,' he said.

'Thanks,' the woman said, glancing back at him and smiling tiredly. She was about forty, with dirt on her face and dark rings under her eyes. 'When did you come in?' she asked.

'About eight months ago,' Chip said.

'Who with?' The woman stepped on to the escalator.

Chip stepped on behind her. 'Dover,' he said.

'Oh,' she said. 'Is he still here?'

'No,' Chip said. 'He was sent out last month. Your people didn't come in empty-handed, did they?'

'I wish they had,' the woman said. 'My shoulder is killing me. I left the kits by the elevator. I'm going to get them now.' She stepped off the escalator and walked back around it.

Chip went with her. 'I'll give you a hand with them,' he said.

'It's all right, I'll pick up one of the boys,' the woman said, turning to the right.

'No, I don't mind doing it,' Chip said.

They walked down the corridor past the glass wall of the pool. The woman looked in and said, 'That's where I'm going to be in fifteen minutes.'

'I'll join you,' Chip said.

The woman glanced at him. 'All right,' she said.

Boroviev and a member came into the corridor towards them. 'Anna! Hello!' Boroviev said, his eyes sparkling in his withered face. The member, a girl, smiled at Chip.

'Hello!' the woman said, shaking Boroviev's hand. 'How are you?'

'Fine!' Boroviev said. 'Oh, you look exhausted!'

'I am.'

'But everything's all right?'

'Yes,' the woman said. 'They're downstairs. I'm on my way to get rid of the kits.'

'Get some rest!' Boroviev said.

'I'm going to,' the woman said, smiling. 'Six months of it.'

Boroviev smiled at Chip, and taking the member's hand, went past them and down the corridor. The woman and Chip went ahead towards the steel door at the corridor's end. They passed the archway to the garden, where someone was singing and playing a guitar.

'What kind of bombs did they have?' Chip asked.

'Crude plastic ones,' the woman said. 'Throw and boom. I'll be glad to get them into the can.'

The steel door slid open; they went through and turned to the right. White-tiled corridor stretched before them with scanner-posted doors in the left-hand wall.

'Which council are you on?' the woman asked.

'Wait a second,' Chip said, stopping and taking her arm.

She stopped and turned and he punched her in the stomach. Catching her face in his hand, he smashed her head back hard against the wall. He let it come forward, smashed it back again, and let go of her. She slid downward – a tile was cracked – and sank heavily to the floor and fell over sideways, one knee up, eyes closed.

Chip stepped to the nearest door and opened it. A two-toilet bathroom was inside. Holding the door with his foot, he reached over and took hold of the woman under her arms. A member came into the corridor and stared at him, a boy of about twenty.

'Help me,' Chip said.

The boy came over, his face pale. 'What happened?' he asked.

'Take her legs,' Chip said. 'She passed out.'

They carried the woman into the bathroom and set her down on the floor. 'Shouldn't we take her to the medicentre?' the boy asked.

'We will in a minute,' Chip said. He got on one knee beside the woman, reached into the pocket of her yellow-paplon coveralls, and took out her gun. He aimed it at the boy. 'Turn around and face the wall,' he said. 'Don't make a sound.'

The boy stared wide-eyed at him, and turned around and faced the wall between the toilets.

Chip stood up, passed the gun between his hands, and holding it by its taped barrel, stepped astride the woman. He raised the gun and quickly swung its butt down hard on the boy's close-clipped head. The blow drove the boy to his knees. He fell forward against the wall and then sideways, his head stopping against wall and toilet pipe, red gleaming in its short black hair.

Chip looked away and at the gun. He passed it back to a shooting grip, thumbed its safety catch aside, and turned it towards the bathroom's back wall: a red thread, gone, shattered a tile and drilled dust from behind it. Chip put the gun into his pocket, and holding it, stepped over the woman and moved to the door.

He went into the corridor, pulled the door tightly closed, and walked quickly, holding the gun in his pocket. He came to the end of the corridor and followed its left turn.

A member coming towards him smiled and said, 'Hello, Father.'

Chip nodded, passing him. 'Son,' he said.

A door was ahead in the right-hand wall. He went to it, opened it, and went through. He closed the door behind him and stood in dark hallway. He took out the gun.

Opposite, under a ceiling that barely glowed, were the pink, brown, and orange memory-banks-for-visitors, the gold cross and sickle, the clock on the wall – 9.33 Thu 10 Sep 172 Y.U.

He went to the left, past the other displays, unlighted, dormant, increasingly visible in the light from an open door to the lobby.

He went to the open door.

On the floor in the centre of the lobby lay three kits, a gun, and two knives. Another kit lay near the elevator doors.

Wei leaned back, smiling, and drew on his cigarette. 'Believe me,' he said, 'that's how everybody feels at this point. But even the most stubbornly disapproving come to see that we're wise and we're right.' He looked at the programmers standing around the group of chairs. 'Isn't that so, Chip?' he said. 'Tell them.' He looked about, smiling.

'Chip went out,' Deirdre said, and someone else said 'After Anna.' Another programmer said, 'Too bad, Deirdre,' and Deirdre, turning, said, 'He didn't go out after Anna, he went out; he'll be right back.'

'A little tired, of course,' someone said.

Wei looked at his cigarette and leaned forward and pressed it out. 'Everyone here will confirm what I'm saying,' he said to the newcomers, and smiled. 'Excuse me, will you?' he said. 'I'll be back in a little while. Don't get up.' He rose, and the programmers parted for him.

Straw filled half the kit, held in place by a wood divider; on the other side, wires, tools, papers, cakes, whatnot. He brushed straw away – from more dividers that formed square straw-filled compartments. He fingered in one and found only straw and hollowness; in another, though, there was something soft-surfaced but firm. He pulled away straw and lifted out a heavy whitish ball, a claylike handful with straw stick-

273

ing to it. He put it on the floor and took out two more –
another compartment was empty – and a fourth one. He
ripped the wood framework from the kit, put it aside, and
dumped out straw, tools, everything; put the four bombs
close together in the kit, opened the other two kits and took
out their bombs and put them in with the four – five from
one kit, six from the other. Room for three more remained.

He got up and went for the fourth kit by the elevators. A
sound in the hallway spun him around – he had left the gun
by the bombs – but the doorway was empty-dark and the
sound (whisper of silk?) was no more. If it had been at all.
His own sound, it might have been, reflected back at him.

Watching the doorway, he backed to the kit, caught up its
strap, and brought it quickly to the other kits; kneeled again
and brought the gun close to his side. He opened the kit,
pulled out straw, and lifted out three bombs and fitted them
in with the others. Three rows of six. He covered them and
pressed the kit closed, then put his arm through the strap
and lodged it on his shoulder. He raised the kit carefully
against his hip. The bombs in it shifted heavily.

The gun with the kits was an L-beam too, newer-looking
than the one he had. He picked it up and opened it. A stone
was in the generator's place. He put the gun down, took one
of the knives – black-handled, pre-U, its blade worn thin but
sharp – and slipped it into his right-hand pocket. Taking the
working gun and holding the kit with his fingers under its
bottom, he got up from his knees, stepped over an empty kit,
and went quietly to the doorway.

Darkness and silence were outside it. He waited till he
could see more clearly, then walked to the left. A giant telecomp clung to the display wall (it had been broken, hadn't
it, when he had been there before?); he passed it and stopped.
Someone lay near the wall ahead, motionless.

But no, it was a stretcher, two stretchers, with pillows and
blankets. The blankets Papa Jan and he had wrapped around
them. The very same two, conceivably.

He stood for a moment, remembering.

Then he went on. To the door. The door that Papa Jan
had pushed him through. And the scanner beside it, the first
he had ever passed without touching. How frightened he had
been !

This time you don't have to push me, Papa Jan, he thought.

He opened the door a bit, looked in at the landing – brightly lit, empty – and went in.

And down the stairs into coolness. Quickly now, thinking of the boy and the woman upstairs, who might soon be coming to, crying an alarm.

He passed the door to the first level of memory banks.

And the second.

And came to the end of the stairs, the bottom-level door.

He put his right shoulder against it, held the gun ready, and turned the knob with his left hand.

He eased the door slowly open. Red lights gleamed in dimness, one of the walls of transmitting-receiving equipment. The low ceiling glowed faintly. He opened the door wider. A railed refrigerator pit lay ahead of him, blue arms upreaching; beyond it, a pillar, a pit, a pillar, a pit. The reactors were at the other end of the room, red domes doubled in the glass of the dimly lit programming room. Not a member in sight, closed doors, silence – except for a whining sound, low and steady. He opened the door wider, stepping into the room with it, and saw the second wall of equipment sparked with red lights.

He went farther into the room, caught the door edge behind him and let it pull itself away towards closing. He lowered the gun, thumbed the strap up off his shoulder, and let the kit down gently to the floor. His throat was clamped, his head torn back. A green-silk elbow was under his jaw, the arm crushing his neck, choking him. His gun-wrist was locked in a powerful hand and 'You liar, liar,' Wei whispered in his ear, 'what a pleasure to kill you.'

He pulled at the arm, punched it with his free left hand; it was marble, a statue's arm in silk. He tried to back his feet into a stance for throwing Wei off him, but Wei moved backwards too, keeping him arched and helpless, dragging him beneath the turning glowing ceiling; and his hand was bent around and smashed, smashed, smashed against hard railing, and the gun was gone, clanging into the pit. He reached back and grabbed Wei's head, found his ear and wrenched at it. His throat was crushed tighter by the hard-muscled arm and the ceiling was pink and pulsing. He thrust

275

his hand down into Wei's collar, squeezed his fingers under a band of cloth. He wound his hand in it, driving his knuckles as hard as he could into tough ridged flesh. His right hand was freed, his left seized and pulled at. With his right he caught the wrist at his neck, pulled the arm open. He gasped air down his throat.

He was flung away, thrown flat against red-lit equipment, the torn band wound around his hand. He grabbed two handles and pulled out a panel, turned and flung it at Wei coming at him. Wei struck it aside with an arm and kept coming, both hands raised to chop. Chip crouched, his left arm up. ('Keep *low*, Green-eye!' Captain Gold shouted.) Blows hit his arm; he punched at Wei's heart. Wei backed off, kicking at him. He got away from the wall, circled outward, stuffed his numbed hand down into his pocket and found the knife handle. Wei rushed at him and chopped at his neck and shoulders. With his left arm raised, he cut the knife up out of his pocket and stuck it into Wei's middle – partway in, then hard, all the way, hilt into silk. Blows kept hitting him. He pulled the knife out and backed away.

Wei stayed where he was. He looked at Chip, at the knife in his hand, looked down at himself. He touched his waist and looked at his fingers. He looked at Chip.

Chip circled, watching him, holding the knife.

Wei lunged. Chip knifed, slashed Wei's sleeve, but Wei caught his arm in both hands and drove him back against the railing, kneeing at him. Chip caught Wei's neck and squeezed, squeezed as hard as he could inside the torn green-and-gold collar. He forced Wei off him, turned from the railing, and squeezed, kept squeezing while Wei held his knife-arm. He forced Wei back around the pit. Wei struck with one hand at his wrist, knocked it downward; he pulled his arm free and knifed at Wei's side. Wei dodged and spilled over the railing, fell into the pit and fell flat on his back on a cylindrical steel housing. He slid off it and sat leaning against blue pipe, looking up at Chip with his mouth open, gasping, a black-red stain in his lap.

Chip ran to the kit. He picked it up and walked back quickly down the side of the room, holding the kit on his arm. He put the knife in his pocket – it fell through but he let it – ripped the kit open and tucked its cover back under it.

He turned and walked backwards towards the end of the equipment wall, stopped and stood facing the pits and the pillars between them.

He backhanded sweat from his mouth and forehead, saw blood on his hand and wiped it on his side.

He took one of the bombs from the kit, held it back behind his shoulder, aimed, and threw it. It arched into the centre pit. He put his hand on another bomb. A *thunk* sounded from the pit, but no explosion came. He took out the second bomb and threw it harder into the pit.

The sound it made was flatter and softer than the first bomb's.

The railed pit stayed as it was, blue arms reaching up from it.

Chip looked at it, and looked at the rows of white straw-stuck bombs in the kit.

He took out another one and hurled it as hard as he could into the nearer pit.

A *thunk* again.

He waited, and went cautiously towards the pit; went closer, and saw the bomb on the cylindrical steel housing, a blob of white, a white clay breast.

A high-pitched gasping sound came sifting from the farthest pit. Wei. He was laughing.

These three were her bombs, the shepherd's, Chip thought. *Maybe she did something to them.* He went to the middle of the equipment wall and stood squarely facing the centre pit. He hurled a bomb. It hit a blue arm and stuck to it, round and white.

Wei laughed and gasped. Scrapings, sounds of movement, came from the pit he was in.

Chip hurled more bombs. *One of them may work, one of them will work!* ('Throw and boom,' she had said. 'Glad to get them into the can.' She wouldn't have lied to him. What had gone wrong with them?) He hurled bombs at the blue arms and the pillars, plastered the square steel pillars with flat white overlapping discs. He hurled all the 'bombs', hurled the last one clean across the room; it splattered wide on the opposite equipment wall.

He stood with the empty kit in his hand.

Wei laughed loud.

He was sitting astride pit railing, holding the gun in both hands, pointing it at Chip. Black-red smears ran down his clinging coverall legs; red leaked over his sandal straps. He laughed more. 'What do you think?' he asked. 'Too cold? Too damp? Too dry? Too old? Too what?' He took one hand from the gun, reached back behind him, and eased down off the railing. Lifting his leg over it, he winced and drew in breath hissingly. 'Ooh Jesus Christ,' he said, 'you really hurt this body. Ssss! You really did it damage.' He stood and held the gun with both hands again, facing Chip. He smiled. 'Idea,' he said. 'You give me yours, right? You hurt a body, you give me another one. Fair? And – neat, *economical!* What we have to do now is shoot you in the head, very carefully, and then between us we'll give the doctors a long night's work.' He smiled more broadly. 'I promise to keep you "in condition", Chip,' he said, and walked forward with slow stiff steps, his elbows tight to his sides, the gun clasped before him chest-high, aimed at Chip's face.

Chip backed to the wall.

'I'll have to change my speech to newcomers,' Wei said. ' "From here down I'm Chip, a programmer who almost fooled me with his talk and his new eye and his smiles in the mirror." I don't think we'll have any more newcomers though; the risk has begun to outweigh the amusement.'

Chip threw the kit at him and lunged, leaped at Wei and threw him backwards to the floor. Wei cried out, and Chip, lying on him, wrestled for the gun in his hand. Red beams shot from it. Chip forced the gun to the floor. An explosion roared. He tore the gun from Wei's hand and got off him, got up to his feet and backed away and turned and looked.

Across the room, a cave, crumbling and smoking, hollowed the middle of the wall equipment – where the bomb he had thrown had been splattered. Dust shimmered in the air and a wide arc of black fragments lay on the floor.

Chip looked at the gun and at Wei. Wei, on an elbow, looked across the room and up at Chip.

Chip backed away, towards the end of the room, towards its corner, looking at the white-plastered pillars, the white-hung blue arms over the centre pit. He raised the gun.

'Chip!' Wei cried. 'It's *yours!* It'll be *yours* some day!

278

We *both* can live! Chip, listen to me,' he said, leaning forward, 'there's *joy* in having it, in controlling, in being the only one. That's the absolute truth, Chip. You'll see for yourself. There's *joy* in having it.'

Chip fired the gun at the farther pillar. A red thread hit above the white discs; another hit directly on one. An explosion flashed and roared, thundered and smoked. It subsided and the pillar was bent slightly towards the other side of the room.

Wei moaned grievingly. A door beside Chip started to open; he pushed it closed and stood back against it. He fired the gun at the bombs on the blue arms. Explosion roared, flame erupted, and a louder explosion blasted from the pit, mashing him against the door, breaking glass, flinging Wei to the swaying wall of equipment, slamming doors that had opened at the other side of the room. Flame filled the pit, a huge shuddering cylinder of yellow-orange, railed around and drumming at the ceiling. Chip raised his arm against the heat of it.

Wei climbed to all fours and on to his feet. He swayed and started stumblingly forward. Chip shot a red thread to his chest, and another, and he turned away and stumbled towards the pit. Flames feathered his coveralls, and he dropped to his knees, fell forward on the floor. His hair caught fire, his coveralls burned.

Blows shook the door and cries came from behind it. The other doors opened and members came in. 'Stay back!' Chip shouted, and aimed the gun at the nearer pillar and fired. Explosion roared, and the pillar was bent.

The fire in the pit lowered, and the bent pillars slowly turned, screeching.

Members came into the room. 'Get back!' Chip shouted, and they retreated to the doors. He moved into the corner, watching the pillars, the ceiling. The door beside him opened. 'Stay back!' he shouted, pressing against it.

The steel of the pillars split and rolled open; a chunk of concrete slid from the nearer one.

The blackened ceiling cracked, groaned, sagged, dropped fragments.

The pillars broke and the ceiling fell. Memory banks crashed into the pits; mammoth steel blocks smashed down on one another and slid thunderously, butted into the walls of equipment. Explosions roared in the nearest and farthest pits, lifting blocks and cushioning them in flames.

Chip raised his arm against the heat. He looked where Wei had been. A block was there, its edge above the cracked floor.

More groaning and cracking sounded – from the blackness above, framed by the ceiling's broken fire-lit borders. And more banks fell, pounded down on the ones below, crushing and bursting them. Memory banks filled the opening, sliding, rumbling.

And the room, despite the fires, cooled.

Chip lowered his arm and looked – at the dark shapes of fire-gleaming steel blocks piled through the broken border of ceiling. He looked and kept looking, and then he moved around the door and pushed his way out through the members staring in.

He walked with the gun at his side through members and programmers running towards him down white-tiled corridors, and through more programmers running down carpeted corridors hung with paintings. 'What is it?' Karl shouted, stopping and grabbing his arm.

Chip looked at him and said, 'Go see.'

Karl let go of him, glanced at the gun and at his face, and turned and ran.

Chip turned and kept walking.

SIX

He washed, sprayed the bruises on his hand and some cuts on his face, and put on paplon coveralls. Closing them, he looked around at the room. He had planned to take the bed-cover, for Lilac to use for dressmaking, and a small painting or something for Julia; now, though, he didn't want to. He put cigarettes and the gun in his pockets. The door opened and he pulled the gun out again. Deirdre stared at him, looking frantic.

He put the gun back in his pocket.

She came in and closed the door behind her. 'It *was* you,' she said.

He nodded.

'Do you *realize* what you've *done*?'

'What you didn't do,' he said. 'What you came here to do and talked yourself out of.'

'I came here to stop it so it could be reprogrammed,' she said, 'not to destroy it completely!'

'It was *being* reprogrammed, remember?' he said. 'And if I'd stopped it and forced a *real* reprogramming – I don't know how, but if I had – it would still have wound up the same way sooner or later. The same *Wei*. Or a new one – me. "There's joy in having it;" those were his last words. Everything else was rationalization. And self-deception.'

She looked away, angrily, and back at him. 'The whole place is going to cave in,' she said.

'I don't feel any tremors,' he said.

'Well everyone's going. The ventilation may stop. There's danger of radiation.'

'I wasn't planning to stay,' he said.

She opened the door and looked at him and went out.

He went out after her. Programmers hurried along the corridor in both directions, carrying paintings, pillowcase bundles, dictypes, lamps. ('Wei was in it! He's dead!' 'Stay away from the kitchen, it's a madhouse!') He walked among them. The walls were bare except for large frames hanging empty. ('Sirri says it was Chip, not the new ones!' '– twenty-five years ago, Unify the islands, we've got *enough* programmers, but he gave me a quote about *selfishness*.')

The escalators were working. He rode up to the top level and went around through the steel door, half open, to the bathroom where the boy and the woman were. They were gone.

He went down one level. Programmers and members holding paintings and bundles were pushing into the room that led to the tunnel. He went into the merging crowd. The door ahead was down but must have been partway up because everyone kept moving forward slowly. ('Quickly!' 'Move, will you?' 'Oh Christ and Wei!')

His arm was grabbed and Madhir glared at him, hugging a filled tablecloth to his chest. 'Was it *you*?' he asked.

'Yes,' Chip said.

Madhir glared, trembled, flushed. 'Madman!' he shouted. 'Maniac! *Maniac!*'

Chip pulled his arm free and turned and moved forward.

'Here he is!' Madhir shouted. 'Chip! He's the one! He's the one who did it! Here he is! Here! *He's the one who did it!*'

Chip moved forward with the crowd, looking at the steel door ahead, holding the gun in his pocket. ('You *brother-fighter*, are you crazy?' 'He's mad, he's mad!')

They walked up the tunnel, quickly at first, then slowly, an endless straggle of dark laden figures. Lamps shone here and there along the line, each lamp drawing with it a section of shining plastic roundness.

Chip saw Deirdre sitting at the side of the tunnel. She looked at him stonily. He kept walking, the gun at his side.

Outside the tunnel they sat and lay in the clearing, smoked and ate and talked in huddles, rummaged in their bundles, traded forks for cigarettes.

Chip saw stretchers on the ground, four or five of them, a member holding a lamp beside them, other members kneeling.

He put the gun in his pocket and went over. The boy and the woman lay on two of the stretchers, their heads bandaged, their eyes closed, their sheeted chests moving. Members were on two other stretchers, and Barlow, the head of the Nutritional Council, was on another, dead-looking, his eyes closed. Rosen kneeled beside him, taping something to his chest through cut-open coveralls.

'Are they all right?' Chip asked.

'The others are,' Rosen said. 'Barlow's had a heart attack.' He looked up at Chip. 'They're saying that Wei was in there,' he said.

'He was,' Chip said.

'You're sure?'

'Yes,' Chip said. 'He's dead.'

'It's hard to believe,' Rosen said. He shook his head and took a small something from a member's hand and screwed it on to what he had taped to Barlow's chest.

Chip watched for a moment, then went over to the

entrance of the clearing and sat down against stone and lit a cigarette. He toed his sandals off and smoked, watching members and programmers come out of the tunnel and walk around and find places to sit. Karl came out with a painting and a bundle.

A member came towards him. Chip took the gun out of his pocket and held it in his lap.

'Are you Chip?' the member asked. He was the older of the two men who had come in that evening.

'Yes,' Chip said.

The man sat down next to him. He was about fifty, very dark, with a jutting chin. 'Some of them are talking about rushing you,' he said.

'I figured they would be,' Chip said. 'I'm leaving in a second.'

'My name's Luis,' the man said.

'Hello,' Chip said.

They shook hands.

'Where are you going?' Luis asked.

'Back to the island I came from,' Chip said. 'Liberty. Majorca. Myorca. You don't know how to fly a copter by any chance, do you?'

'No,' Luis said, 'but it shouldn't be too hard to figure out.'

'It's the landing that worries me,' Chip said.

'Land in the water.'

'I wouldn't want to lose the copter, though. Assuming I can find one. You want a cigarette?'

'No, thanks,' Luis said.

They sat silently for a moment. Chip drew on his cigarette and looked up. 'Christ and Wei, real stars,' he said. 'They had fake ones down there.'

'Really?' Luis said.

'Really.'

Luis looked over at the programmers. He shook his head. 'They're talking as if the Family's going to die in the morning,' he said. 'It isn't. It's going to be born.'

'Born to a lot of trouble, though,' Chip said. 'It's started already. Planes have crashed ...'

Luis looked at him and said, 'Members haven't died who were supposed to die ...'

After a moment Chip said, 'Yes. Thanks for reminding me.'

Luis said. 'Sure, there's going to be trouble. But there are members in every city – the undertreated, the ones who write "Fight Uni" – who'll keep things going in the beginning. And in the end it's going to be better. Living people !'

'It's going to be more interesting, that's for sure,' Chip said, putting his sandals on.

'You aren't going to stay on your island, are you?' Luis asked.

'I don't know,' Chip said. 'I haven't thought beyond getting there.'

'You come back,' Luis said. 'The Family needs members like you.'

'Does it?' Chip said. 'I had an eye changed down there, and I'm not sure I only did it to fool Wei.' He crushed his cigarette out and stood up. Programmers were looking around at him; he pointed the gun at them and they turned quickly away.

Luis stood up too. 'I'm glad the bombs worked,' he said, smiling. 'I'm the one who made them.'

'They worked beautifully,' Chip said. 'Throw and boom.'

'Good,' Luis said. 'Listen, I don't know about any eye; you land on land and come back in a few weeks.'

'I'll see,' Chip said. 'Goodbye.'

'Goodbye, brother,' Luis said.

Chip turned and went out of the clearing and started down rocky slope towards parkland.

He flew over roadways where occasional moving cars zig-zagged slowly past series of stopped ones; along the River of Freedom, where barges bumped blindly against the banks; past cities where monorail cars clung motionless to the rail, copters hovering over some of them.

As he grew more sure of his handling of the copter he flew lower; looked into plazas where members milled and gathered; skimmed over factories with stopped feed-in and feed-out lines; over construction sites where nothing moved except a member or two; and over the river again, passing a group of members tying a barge to the shore, climbing on to it, looking up at him.

He followed the river to the sea and started across it, flying low. He thought of Lilac and Jan, Lilac turning startled from the sink (he *should* have taken the bedcover, why hadn't he?). But would they still be in the room? Could Lilac, thinking him caught and treated and never coming back, have – married someone else? No, never. (Why not? Almost nine months he'd been gone.) No, she wouldn't. She—

Drops of clear liquid hit the copter's plastic front and streaked back along its sides. Something was leaking from above, he thought, but then he saw that the sky had gone grey, grey on both sides and darker grey ahead, like the skies in some pre-U paintings. It was *rain* that was hitting the copter.

Rain! In the daytime! He flew with one hand, and with a fingertip of the other, followed on the inside of the plastic the paths of the streaking raindrops outside it.

Rain in the daytime! Christ and Wei, how strange! And how inconvenient!

But there was something pleasing about it too. Something natural.

He brought his hand back to its lever – *Let's not get over-confident, brother* – and smiling, flew ahead.

·COMPLETED IN JUNE, 1969
IN NEW YORK CITY
AND DEDICATED TO ADAM LEVIN,
JED LEVIN, AND NICHOLAS LEVIN

Robin Cook
Coma £2.95

Charles Martel is a doctor turned researcher: his wife died of cancer and he wanted to know why. His world is shattered a second time when his daughter is sick with fever. Suddenly he's a man against odds: against doctors who want to treat his daughter's leukemia the wrong way; against a research institute that puts profits before ethics, against a recycling plant that's dumping cancer-inducing benzene in the rivers. For a man whose daughter's life is on the line, these are odds enough to turn a responsible citizen into a criminal.

'Scalpel-edged tension' DAILY EXPRESS

Colin Dexter
The Dead of Jericho £2.50

A shapely divorcee is found hanged by the neck. A seedy odd-job man is murdered amongst his home porn library. Both of them are neighbours in the rundown Jericho district of Oxford. Inspector Morse takes a more than professional interest in this case, after all he had been about to embark on a somewhat intimate relationship with the lady in question.

'The triumph of the book is the lustful, irascible character of Morse'
THE TIMES LITERARY SUPPLEMENT

Ira Levin
The Boys from Brazil £2.95

A phone call to Vienna in the dark hours of the morning. A message from thousands of miles away cut short by a killer put Yakov Liebermann on the trail of a nightmare.

For three decades he had hounded those who had escaped justice at Nuremburg. Now he must confront a conspiracy of fiendish imagining and a man whom history has branded The Angel of Death.

'Horribly credible, chilling, disturbing . . . a stunner'
SUNDAY EXPRESS

'There's no way to stop once you've started' NEWSWEEK

'You won't stop reading . . . his best since *Rosemary's Baby*'
PUBLISHERS WEEKLY

The Stepford Wives £2.99

Irrational changes of personality occur almost overnight among wives after they move to the suburbs of Stepford.

What is the sinister menace that overshadows this strange community? Why does the secretive Men's Association meet every night in the old house with its shuttered windows? Was Joanna doomed to become like all the other wives?

She had to know before the implications of a second honeymoon became terrifying reality . . .

'Taut, rapid, frightening, quite ferociously readable'
TIMES LITERARY SUPPLEMENT

'Clever and chilling . . . one of the most hair-raising endings I've read in an age' WOMAN'S JOURNAL

All Pan books are available at your local bookshop or newsagent, or can be ordered direct from the publisher. Indicate the number of copies required and fill in the form below.

Send to: **CS Department, Pan Books Ltd., P.O. Box 40,
              Basingstoke, Hants.   RG21 2YT.**

or phone: 0256 469551 (Ansaphone), quoting title, author
              and Credit Card number.

Please enclose a remittance* to the value of the cover price plus: 60p for the first book plus 30p per copy for each additional book ordered to a maximum charge of £2.40 to cover postage and packing.

*Payment may be made in sterling by UK personal cheque, postal order, sterling draft or international money order, made payable to Pan Books Ltd.

Alternatively by Barclaycard/Access:

Card No. | | | | | | | | | | | | | | | | | | |

Signature:

Applicable only in the UK and Republic of Ireland.

While every effort is made to keep prices low, it is sometimes necessary to increase prices at short notice. Pan Books reserve the right to show on covers and charge new retail prices which may differ from those advertised in the text or elsewhere.

NAME AND ADDRESS IN BLOCK LETTERS PLEASE:

....

Name ————————————————————————

Address ————————————————————————

————————————————————————————

————————————————————————————

————————————————————————————

3/87